THE MURDERER'S APE

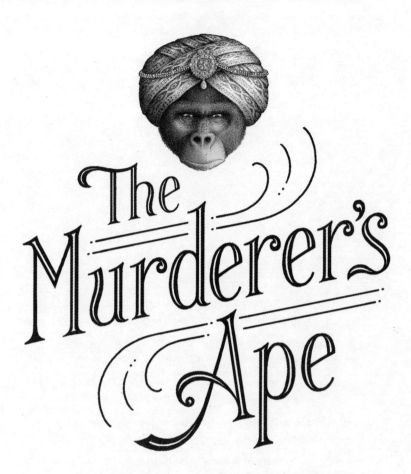

The Murderer's Ape

JAKOB WEGELIUS

Translated from the Swedish by
PETER GRAVES

PUSHKIN CHILDREN'S BOOKS

Pushkin Press
71–75 Shelton Street
London, WC2H 9JQ

Published by arrangement with Random House Children's Books, division
of Penguin Random House LLC. New York, NY, USA. All rights reserved.

The Murderer's Ape was first published in Swedish as *Mördarens Apa*
by Bonnier Carlsen, Stockholm, Sweden, in 2014

First published in English by Delacorte Press, an imprint of Random House
Children's Books, a division of Penguin Random House LLC. New York

First published by Pushkin Press in 2017

1 3 5 7 9 8 6 4 2

Hardback ISBN 13: 978-1-78269-161-7
Trade Paperback ISBN 13: 978-1-78269-202-7

Printed and bound in the UK by CPI Group (UK), Croydon, CRO 4YY

www.pushkinpress.com

CONTENTS

CHARACTERS i

THE TYPEWRITER xxi

PART ONE

———— ✦ ————

PART TWO

PART THREE

CHARACTERS

LUIGI · FIDARDO

Ana Molina

ELISA·GOMES

ALPHONSE MORRO

COMPANHIA · CARRIS · DE · FERRO · DE · LISBOA

CARRIS

Jorge Amadéo Tomás da Costa

RAUL·GARRETTA

João

AYESHA·NARAYANAN

C.A.THURSGOOD · B.WILKINS

GEOFF GERRARD

captain Anderson

maji sahiba

H.R.H. MAHARAJA · of · BHAPUR

Doctor Rosa Domingues

THE TYPEWRITER

The other day the Chief gave me an old typewriter, a 1908 Underwood No. 5. He'd bought it from a scrap merchant down by the harbor, here in Lisbon. Several of the keys were broken and the release lever was missing, but the Chief knows I like fixing broken things.

It's taken me a couple of evenings to mend my Underwood No. 5, and this is the first time I've written anything on it. Several of the keys still stick, but a pair of pliers and a few drops of oil will soon put them right.

That will have to wait until tomorrow. It's already dark outside my cabin window. The lights from the vessels lying at anchor on the river are reflecting in the black water. I've strung my hammock and I'm about to climb into it.

I hope I don't have those horrible dreams again tonight.

~

It's evening again.

The Chief and I were lucky today. Early every morning we go to a harbor café where unemployed sailors wait round hoping to get work for the day. There is not usually anything much, but today we struck lucky and so we have been heaving sacks of coal from dawn to dusk. The pay was poor, but we need every penny we can earn. My back aches, my arms ache and my fur is itchy with coal dust.

More than anything else, though, I'm tired. I didn't sleep well again last night. It must be at least a month since I had a full night's sleep undisturbed by nightmares.

The same dreams return time after time.

Some nights I'm back in the engine room of the *Song of Limerick*. I'm being held from behind by strong arms while the engine is racing and the ship is sinking.

Other nights I dream of Chief Inspector Garretta. It's dark and I don't know where I am. Among the tombs in Prazeres Cemetery, perhaps. The only things I can see are Garretta's small eyes, which shine with a cold gleam under the brim of his hat. And I can smell the acrid gunpowder from his revolver—the shot is still ringing in my ears.

The most horrible dream is the one about the Chief. I am standing in the rain waiting for him outside an iron gate in a high wall. Time passes and I'm chilled to the bone. I try to convince myself that the gate will open at any moment, but I know in my heart that I'm fooling myself. It's never going to open and the Chief is caught behind that wall forever.

There are times when I scream in my sleep. One night not long ago I was woken by the Chief rushing into my cabin waving a big pipe wrench. Hearing my screams, he'd thought someone had crept aboard and was going to hurt me. That was a distinct possibility, for we've made dangerous enemies in Lisbon.

I'm too tired to write any more at present. I'll probably write again tomorrow. I'm really pleased with my Underwood No. 5!

~

It's foggy tonight. It came rolling in from the Atlantic during the afternoon. I went up on deck just now and couldn't see beyond the cranes a short way along the quay. Every so often the gruff noise of foghorns and the ringing of ships' bells can be heard from the river. It sounds a bit ghostly.

The Chief and I have been carrying sacks of coal again today. I was thinking about my Underwood No. 5 while doing it, and now I've decided what I'm going to use it for.

I am going to use it to tell the truth.

The truth about the murder of Alphonse Morro.

So that everyone knows what really happened.

And maybe the writing will help to rid me of my nightmares.

PART ONE

CHAPTER 1
Me, the Chief and the *Hudson Queen*

For those of you who don't know me, the first thing I need to say is that I'm not a human being, I'm an anthropoid ape. I've learned from scientists that I belong to the subspecies *Gorilla gorilla graueri*. Most of my kind live in Africa, in the thick jungle along the banks of the Congo River, and that's probably where I originally came from.

I don't know how I ended up among people, and I probably never shall know. I must have been very small when it

3

happened. Maybe I was caught by hunters or by natives and they then sold me on. My very first memory is of sitting on a cold stone floor with a chain round my neck. It may have been in the city of Istanbul, though I can't be completely certain.

Since then I've lived in the human world. I've learned how you human beings think and how to understand what you say. I've learned to read and to write. I've learned how people steal and deceive. I've learned what greed is. And cruelty. I have had many owners and I would prefer to forget most of them. I don't know which of them gave me my name. Or why.

But I'm called Sally Jones anyway.

⌣

Many people think the Chief is my present owner, but the Chief isn't the sort to want to own others. He and I are comrades. And friends.

The Chief's real name is Henry Koskela.

We first met many years ago when I stowed away on a freighter called the *Otago*. The crew found me, and the captain ordered them to throw me overboard. But the ship's chief engineer stepped in and saved my life. That was the Chief, that was.

We chanced to meet again a couple of years later in the

4

harbor district of Singapore. I was seriously ill and standing chained to a post outside a sleazy bar. The Chief recognized me and bought me from the bar owner. He took me with him to the ship he was working on and gave me food and medicine. That was the second time he saved my life.

When I eventually recovered I was allowed to help the Chief with various little jobs round the engine room. I liked the work, and thanks to the Chief I became good at it too. Everything I know about seamanship and ships' engines I've learned from him.

We've stuck together ever since, the Chief and I. From Southeast Asia we worked our way to Australia. We bought our own steamer, the *Hudson Queen,* in New York and ran her along the coasts of the Americas, Africa and Europe with various cargoes. We were our own masters and made enough money to keep the ship in good condition.

It was a good life, impossible to imagine a better one.

I hope it can be like that again.

~

Just under four years ago everything changed. That's when our misfortunes began. The Chief and I had been sailing in British waters the whole of that summer, and when autumn arrived we decided to head for warmer latitudes to avoid the winter storms in the North Sea. In London we took on a cargo of tin cans bound for the Azores, a group of islands in the middle of the Atlantic.

The journey went well at the start. We had good weather and gentle winds, but our luck ran out early one morning when we collided with a whale. The whale survived, but the *Hudson Queen* took such a thump that her rudder was bent. While we were trying to mend the damage, the weather changed and a violent storm blew up. The *Hudson Queen* drifted helplessly, and if it hadn't been for the drag anchor we'd have been lost. It was only once the wind had eased that we managed to rig emergency steering, set a course for the Portuguese coast and seek refuge in Lisbon.

Once we had unloaded our cargo, the *Hudson Queen* had to go into dry dock for rudder repairs. That took a fortnight and cost all the money we had saved. The Chief went round all the shipping agents in the port, trying to arrange a new cargo, but he found nothing. The quayside was already lined with freighters with empty holds waiting for better days.

The weeks passed. It's never much fun to be stuck ashore, but there are worse ports than Lisbon to be stuck in. We used to spend our Saturdays riding round the city by tram. You won't find smarter trams than Lisbon trams anywhere in the world, not even in San Francisco.

Our mooring in the harbor was below the Alfama district, a poor quarter of the city, sleepy by day and full of danger by night. No one batted an eye at the Siamese twins who sold shoelaces on Rua de São Pedro, nor at the Devil Dancers from the Pepper Coast who were to be found in the darkest alleyways when the moon was waning. In Alfama they didn't even bat an eye at an ape in a boiler suit, and that was good for me.

Most evenings we went to O Pelicano, an inn used by many seamen when they are in Lisbon. It's on Rua do Salvador, a dark and narrow lane rarely reached by the rays of the sun. The owner was called Senhor Baptista. He used to be a cook on the ships of the Transbrazil line and he always offered his guests a glass of aguardiente before they ate. Aguardiente is a sort of brandy, so I usually took a glass of milk instead.

I have many good memories of our evenings in O Pelicano, but I have a bad one too. Because it was in O Pelicano that we first met Alphonse Morro.

CHAPTER 2
Morro

The Chief and I had been working late in the engine
room of the *Hudson Queen*. I remember it was rain-
ing hard when we went ashore to have supper. The light
from the gas lamps round the harbor was glinting off the
wet paving stones of the quay, and dirty water was gurgling
in the gutters and street fountains in the narrow streets of
Alfama.

It was warm and smoky in O Pelicano. The regulars

were squeezed in round the circular tables and several of them greeted the Chief and me with a wave or a nod. There were seamen and stevedores from the harbor, hollow-eyed streetwalkers and sleepless musicians. A big woman in black called Rosa was singing a fado about unlucky love. Fado singers are typical of the poor districts of Lisbon.

One of the guests was a man I hadn't seen before. He was sitting on his own at the table nearest the door, and he looked up from his coffee as we entered. He had a narrow, very pale face, and his eyes shone black under the brim of his hat. I sensed that his eyes followed the Chief and me as Senhor Baptista showed us to an empty table in the inner-most corner of the inn.

Senhora Maria, Senhor Baptista's wife, served each of us a bowl of tomato soup and bread. We had just started to eat when the solitary man by the door stood up and came over to our table. I thought he must have been waiting for us.

"My name is Morro," he said in a low voice. "I hear that you have a ship. And that you need work."

At first the Chief looked surprised, then he looked pleased.

"You've hit the nail on the head," he said. "Take a seat."

The man called Morro threw an anxious look over his shoulder and sat down.

"There are some crates," he said in a voice so low the

Chief had to lean forward slightly to hear him. "They need to be picked up in Agiere, a small port on the River Zêzere. I have a map here."

From his inside pocket Morro produced a folded map and spread it on the table. The Chief studied the map carefully. I realized that what interested him was the depth of the river.

"It's rained a lot in recent weeks," Morro said. "The water level of the rivers is high. You don't need to worry about running aground."

"That will depend on how heavily laden we are," the Chief said. "How many crates are we talking about? And what's in them?"

"Azulejos," Morro said. "You know, ceramic tiles. There are six crates, and each crate weighs about six hundred fifty pounds."

The Chief looked surprised.

"Is that all? Why don't you bring the crates to Lisbon by horse and cart instead?"

"These are valuable and delicate tiles," Morro said quickly, as if he had the answer prepared. "The roads are bad and I don't want the tiles shaken about so that they break. Are you willing to take the job?"

"That may depend on how much you are offering," the Chief said with a smile.

Morro produced an envelope and gave it to the Chief, who opened it and quickly thumbed through the banknotes it contained. I could tell from his expression that there was more money than he'd expected.

"The crates are to be brought here to Lisbon. To Cais do Sodré," Morro said. "If you can finish the job in four days, I'll pay you the same amount again."

The Chief's face lit up.

"You've got a deal," he said, holding out his hand.

Morro shook it briefly and then got to his feet. Without saying another word he pushed his way between the tables and disappeared out through the door and into the night.

~

A couple of hours later the Chief and I strolled back down to the harbor to the *Hudson Queen*. The rain had stopped and a hazy moon was peeping through the broken clouds that were sweeping across the sky. The Chief was in a splendid mood. He had stood a round of drinks for everyone in O Pelicano to celebrate that we had a job at last. And a well-paid job at that.

"Our luck has turned!" he said when we reached the quayside. "With this much money we can fill our bunkers with enough coal to reach the Mediterranean! And there are always cargoes there for a vessel like the *Hudson Queen*."

11

I wanted to feel as happy as he did, but something was holding me back. The man called Morro had made me feel uneasy. His eyes, perhaps? There had been a strange, feverish gleam in them, and I could tell from his scent that he was afraid.

CHAPTER 3
Agiere

The following morning I rose before dawn to light the fire under the boiler. By the time we'd finished breakfast the engine was steamed and the *Hudson Queen* ready for departure. We cast off and steered out into the River Tagus. We set a course northeast, up the wide river.

It was a wonderful autumn day. The sun was shining, and in the wheelhouse the Chief was singing at the top of his voice. It's always the same song that he sings when he is setting out to sea after too many days in harbor.

Farewell, you cruel maiden,
Farewell, goodbye, I say,
For I'm weary now of waiting,
So I'm off to sea again.

My ship is weighing anchor
And we're sailing for Marseille,
My love evoked no answer
So I'm off to sea again.

The first day's voyage went without a hitch. The shipping traffic on the Tagus was busy and we met broad-beamed sailing barges with cargoes of wine, vegetables and fruit, as well as small steamers whose passengers waved to us.

We reached Constância at dusk. It's a small town with whitewashed houses up on a high headland. We moored at the quayside for the night and early the following morning continued our voyage, now up the smaller River Zêzere. The current was stronger here and the Chief had his work cut out to find the channel between sandbanks and reefs. We did not meet any other boats, and we saw very few houses and farms along the banks of the river.

Late in the afternoon we came to a small waterfall. That was as far as we could go. On the south bank there was a stone quay and a solitary house. This—according to the map Morro had given us—was Agiere.

Down in the crystal-clear water we could see many sharp rocks projecting from the sandy riverbed. I stood in the bow and kept a lookout while the Chief brought us carefully alongside the quay.

Once we had tied up we went ashore and looked round. The solitary house proved to be deserted. There was no glass in the windows, and most of the roof at the back had collapsed. A narrow road with brushwood and ferns sprouting down the middle led through trees into the woods. There was nothing to suggest that anyone had been there for a very long time.

Nor was there any sign of crates of tiles.

"What do you think?" the Chief said, scratching his head. "Have we been tricked?"

I shrugged. It certainly looked like that. On the other hand the man who said his name was Morro had paid us a large sum of money in advance. The whole business was very strange. And worrying. This deserted spot felt more than a little creepy.

Back on board the *Hudson Queen* the Chief prepared our supper in the galley while I cleaned the engine for the night.

We were going to stay until morning anyway: it would have been too dangerous to turn round and sail down the narrow river in the hours of darkness with the current behind us.

We ate in the cabin as usual. Then we took out a deck of cards, and the Chief smoked a cigar while we played a hand of rummy. I won, so the Chief had to do the washing up.

It was a fine, still evening. The sun went slowly down, and midges danced in the hazy evening light over the river. I strung my hammock between the mast and one of the shrouds and lay in it looking up at the swallows that were swooping about high above. The Chief sat on deck and spliced new mooring ropes for the lifeboat. When the light became too poor he put aside the work and fetched his hammock.

The noise of the waterfall made us sleepy, and before I fell asleep I could hear that the Chief was already snoring in his hammock.

~

I didn't know what time it was when I woke but the stars were still twinkling in the black sky. It took me a few seconds to recognize what had woken me.

A noise, a kind of squealing noise, was coming from the woods behind the derelict house. A few moments later I saw a light moving in the distance among the trees.

I slid down from my hammock and crept over to the

Chief. He woke with a jerk when I shook his shoulder gently. Seamen on board ship rarely sleep very deeply.

I pointed toward the woods and he followed my finger. The light between the trees was growing stronger, and we guessed it was coming from a swaying lantern.

Hardly a minute later a horse-drawn cart came trundling past the house and emerged on the rough patch of grass by the quay. There were three men sitting on the coach box, and a fourth man was following them on horseback. All four were dressed like farmers—torn jackets, sheepskin waistcoats and slouch hats.

The man on the horse dismounted, stretched and then strode out onto the quay. He had a short black beard that shone in the moonlight as if it had silver glitter in it. The Chief climbed over the rail and stepped down onto the quay to meet him.

"Lord be praised!" the bearded man said, and roared with laughter. "You got here! Saint Nicholas must have been watching over you. Monforte's the name. You can call me Papa Monforte—all my friends do!"

He held out an enormous fist to the Chief and they shook hands.

"My men are keen to get back to their village," Papa Monforte said. "So it would be good if we could get the load aboard straightaway. Would that be possible?"

The three men on the cart had already stepped down and started to untie the ropes holding the wooden crates.

"Yes, of course. That will be no trouble," the Chief said.

"Excellent!" Papa Monforte said with a laugh, and gave the Chief a friendly pat on the shoulder. "Let's get started!"

The Chief came back on board. We lit a couple of paraffin lamps and set about opening the hatches to the hold and starting the steam winch. The Chief worked silently and doggedly. He seemed thoughtful.

"I don't like this," he whispered to me when we were ready to swing out the loading crane. "Who on earth loads tiles in the middle of the night? And out in the wilderness?"

I nodded to show agreement. Everything about it felt wrong.

Papa Monforte and his men stood waiting by the cart. In the light of the lantern I could see them watching the Chief with hard, guarded eyes. The kind of eyes that make you think of soldiers or bandits but not of farmers.

The Chief scratched his chin, which is what he usually does when trying to reach a decision. Then he picked up a lantern and went ashore. I reached out a hand to stop him, but it was too late.

"Everything ready?" I heard Papa Monforte ask.

"Everything's ready," the Chief said. "But before we load the crates I'd like to have a look inside them."

Papa Monforte's face was in shadow. He laughed again, just as loudly as before, but rather less heartily this time.

"Why's that?" he said.

"I want to see what's in them."

"You already know what's in them, my good fellow. The crates are full of azulejos."

I could tell from the Chief's back that he was tense.

"Tiles are delicate things," he said. "I need to check whether any are broken. Otherwise there's always the chance that I'll be blamed if they turn out to be damaged when we arrive at the other end."

"I guarantee that everything is in order," Papa Monforte said in a quiet but harsh tone. "Now let's start loading."

The Chief put his lantern down on the ground and shoved his hands into his trouser pockets.

"No," he said. "We won't. Not before I know what is in the cargo I'm taking on board my ship."

Papa Monforte and the Chief looked at one another in silence for a moment. Then Papa Monforte sighed and raised his hand as a signal.

The next moment his three companions all drew revolvers from the waistbands of their trousers.

CHAPTER 4
A Cargo of Weapons

We loaded the cargo with their pistols pointed at us. The Chief was so angry that his hands shook as we unhitched the crates and stowed them down in the hold. My hands were shaking too, but that was fear. I was terrified the Chief would start arguing with the bandits, or do something silly that would give them an excuse to shoot him.

Papa Monforte and one of his gang had gone up to the wheelhouse and lit the paraffin lamp above the navigation table. They were studying something that I assumed to be the chart of the river. Since the windows were open I could hear them discussing things: Papa Monforte wanted to cast off immediately, whereas the other man thought it would be wiser to wait until dawn. Finally Papa Monforte said, "I'm more worried about the soldiers of the Republican Guard than I am about sandbanks in the river. We have to travel by night. Now let's see about getting away from this place."

They ordered the Chief to prepare things for departure. He refused.

"In that case," Papa Monforte said to the Chief calmly, "I've no more use for you, my friend. You can go ashore, and I'll steer the boat down the river myself. But I'll take this gorilla with me, of course, since she's the one who looks after the engine. If we run aground, she'll be the one I blame—and that will be the end of her!"

The Chief and Papa Monforte stared at one another, after which the Chief went up to the wheelhouse, his face black with rage. This business was not going to end well, that much I knew.

One of the bandits accompanied me down to the engine room to see that I fired up the boiler. He watched in amazement as I shoveled fresh coal into the firebox.

"Strange sort of gorilla you are," he said, spinning his pistol on his finger. "Given the things you can do."

I didn't listen to him. To keep my terror at bay I forced myself to concentrate on what needed to be done. I did my rounds with the oilcan, and I had just finished when the engine room telegraph bell rang. The Chief was giving the order "Slow ahead." I opened the steam regulator, and the pistons and connecting rods began working. The *Hudson Queen* moved out from the quay. I kept thinking of the sharp rocks on the riverbed, and every muscle in my body tensed in expectation of running aground.

Maneuvering a boat running downstream demands speed; otherwise the boat drifts out of control. I guessed the Chief would order "Half speed ahead" as soon as we came out into the current, and that is exactly what he did.

I tried to work out in my head how far we had traveled. Just when I thought we must have reached clear water, I heard a short, dull thud beneath us. I held my breath. For one moment it felt as though time was standing still; then a violent shudder ran through the hull of the vessel. Even above the noise of the engine I heard the dreadful ripping sound of metal being cut open by rock. The bandit and I both fell over. He was back on his feet before me, and he rushed to the ladder to get up on deck.

I shut off steam and lifted one of the floor panels to shine a light down on the keel. But there was no need of light to see what had happened. There are few things more frightening to a sailor than the sound of rushing water down below. Panic-stricken, I began scouring the engine room for blocks of wood and rags to plug the hole. But I needed help; I needed the Chief.

There was chaos on deck. Papa Monforte's men realized we were taking in water and were yelling and arguing about how to save their crates from the sinking ship. One of the bandits was still holding his pistol to the Chief's side. And that was probably all for the best, since the Chief's face looked completely wild.

"Where have we been holed?" he said as soon as he saw me.

I pointed to the starboard side, just in front of the boiler.

"Any chance of reaching the hole from the engine room?"

I nodded.

"Right, then," the Chief said, "let's get to work."

Paying no attention to the pistol, the Chief turned on his heel and walked quickly to the door leading to the engine room ladder.

"Stop or I'll shoot!" the bandit yelled.

The Chief very rarely swears, but what he said over his shoulder to the bandit with the pistol is not fit to be written down here.

The Chief and I did our best to plug the hole, but we

didn't succeed. After no more than a quarter of an hour the water had risen to the engine room floor, and it was no longer possible to reach the hole in the hull. The Chief hurried up on deck to plumb the depth. He wanted to find out how far the *Hudson Queen* would sink before she settled on the riverbed. I followed him.

Papa Monforte and his gang had lowered the lifeboat into the water and were filling it with rifles. Rifles from the wooden crates in the hold!

So it was weapons, not tiles, that we were supposed to have shipped to Lisbon!

Just as the Chief was heaving the lead over the rail, a roar like thunder came from below. The glass in the starboard porthole of the engine room shattered, and a hissing plume of steam rushed out into the cool night air. The Chief and I both knew what had happened: cold river water had risen to the level of the boiler fire tubes and would soon find its way into the glowing-hot furnace. We could expect further explosions—and more powerful ones—very soon.

Papa Monforte and his men were in the grip of panic. They almost threw themselves into the lifeboat. The last of them, the one who had been down in the hold passing up the rifles, had to leap into the water to catch up with them.

The Chief and I also had to leave the ship. There was nothing else for it. The Chief tried to go down to the cabin to fetch the cashbox, but he couldn't make it. Belowdecks the ship was already full of scalding steam.

I can't swim. The Chief put one of the *Hudson Queen*'s two life belts over my head and put the other on himself. Then we jumped into the water. We had only gone about thirty yards from the vessel when we heard another dull explosion behind us. Steam poured from the *Hudson Queen*'s funnel and a white cloud rose toward the night sky.

CHAPTER 5
A Sorry Spectacle

Sodden and frozen, we sat under a willow tree on the riverbank as the *Hudson Queen* went to the bottom. The whole sorry spectacle was lit up by the lanterns and the lamp in the wheelhouse. The Chief hid his face in his hands.

Above all, though, I was happy we were both still alive. A dense mist filled the river valley as the sun rose. As the mist dispersed we could see that our ship was sitting on the bottom. The mast, half the wheelhouse and the funnel were above the surface, and a heron was sitting on top of the mast surveying its hunting grounds. Flotsam and jetsam of all sorts were floating round or had been washed up on the riverbank.

Papa Monforte and his gang had disappeared. We could see that they had moored the lifeboat to a tree close to the quay and the tumbledown house. We walked through the woods in that direction, creeping along for the last bit in case the bandits had sheltered in the house for the night.

Silently and cautiously we pushed the lifeboat out, and the Chief rowed us to the *Hudson Queen* with quick but quiet strokes. We tied the boat to the wheelhouse and climbed up on the roof to survey the damage. The explosions of steam in the engine room did not seem to have blown holes in the deck or in the hull. But what it looked like inside the ship was harder to tell.

There wasn't much more we could do at that stage, and it would have been stupid to hang round longer than necessary. If the bandits were in the house they might emerge and start shooting at any moment.

We left the *Hudson Queen* and began rowing south. The current was with us, so we made good time. The Chief said very little, but he was thinking hard. There were times when a black look came to his face and he pulled on the oars so violently that they looked as if they would snap. I assumed he was thinking about Papa Monforte and his bandits. Or, perhaps, about the man called Morro.

We did not reach Constância until long after midnight. The reflections of the few lights in the little town sparkled on the river. The outline of the church tower showed up against the dark sky. We pulled the lifeboat up on a sand-bank and found a path that led in among the silent houses with their closed shutters.

The town square was not far from the river, and we could see a warm glow coming from an open doorway. As we approached we could smell newly baked bread. The Chief knocked on the door and the baker almost jumped out of his skin when he saw me. Once he had finished staring he sold each of us a warm loaf, and the Chief asked if there was a police station in the town.

"Yes, there is," the baker said. "But our police inspector is attending a wedding in Santarém. It's his constable who is getting married, and neither of them is likely to be back for a couple of days."

The Chief thanked him and we returned to the boat. Without waiting for daylight, we cast off and headed for the River Tagus.

During the morning we were given a lift by a timber

barge that took us on tow. The bargee was a nice man who gave us soup and biscuits even though we had no money to pay him. The Chief had used the last of our money to pay for the bread in Constância, and now we were completely broke. Everything we owned apart from the lifeboat was at the bottom of the River Zêzere.

When we reached Lisbon the bargee cast off the lifeboat; we rowed in to the *Hudson Queen*'s old mooring place and made fast on a beam under the high quayside. Then we went straight to Rua da Alfândega, where the office of the Lisbon harbor police is located.

The harbor police had just closed for the day, and no one was prepared to open up again however much the Chief pounded on the door. He sank to the ground, leaning against the wall of the building, and rested his head on his knees. I sat down beside him, and we stayed like that for a long time until the Chief rose to his feet with a deep sigh. He was gray-faced and his eyes were rimmed red with exhaustion.

"Food and sleep," he said. "That's what we need. Then everything will look a bit brighter. Let's go to O Pelicano."

When we arrived at his inn, Senhor Baptista noticed at once that something was seriously wrong. He and Senhora Maria served us fried fish and rice. The Chief explained that we didn't have a penny to pay, and it looked as if Senhor Baptista hadn't heard him. Instead he fetched a bottle of brandy and poured a glass for the Chief.

"Drink that first," Senhor Baptista said. "And then you can tell me what's happened."

The Chief told him our story and Senhor Baptista listened, his mouth hanging open in astonishment.

"I've never heard anything like it!" he said several times. "Is it really true?"

It was obvious that Senhor Baptista was finding it hard to believe what we were telling him. And I could under stand that. The story sounded unbelievable, even to me, and I had been present throughout.

"That's what really happened," the Chief said. "I swear to it."

Senhor Baptista sat in silence for a while and then said, "They must have been anarchists. They let off bombs and cause riots every so often. Who else would be trying to smuggle arms into Lisbon?"

The Chief shrugged in a tired gesture.

"They were bandits for sure, but I've no idea what kind of bandits. I just know that they forced me to scuttle my own vessel. Their leader called himself Papa Monforte. The one who tricked us into going there was called Morro—and we met him in here!"

"Yes, yes, I haven't forgotten that," Senhor Baptista said. "A frail-looking fellow with a mustache and smart clothes. I'd never seen him here before, but if he comes again I'll ring the police immediately. Have you been to the police yet?"

The Chief told him that we had tried, both in Constância and on Rua da Alfândega.

"In that case I think you should go to the police station at Baixa," Senhor Baptista said firmly. "It's a couple of blocks above Comércio Square and they are open twenty-four hours. The sooner you report this business the better. There's no sense in waiting until tomorrow. I'll give you the money for tram tickets."

The Chief didn't want to take money for the tram. It wasn't that far to walk, he thought. In retrospect, however, I wonder whether we wouldn't have been better taking the tram. If we had done so, everything might have been different, although it's impossible to be sure. You just can't tell, can you?

CHAPTER 6
A Nocturnal Drama

It was dark outside when we left O Pelicano. Arguments and laughter and the mournful tones of out-of-tune guitars reached us from bars and open windows as we walked down toward the harbor; we intended to follow the quay-side to Comércio Square.

The food and drink had done the Chief good. When we arrived by the river he stopped, drew the mild breeze from the Atlantic into his lungs and said, "This is all going to turn out all right, you'll see. Once the police have arrested the bandits, the insurance company will be forced to salvage our ship. They'll have to pay for a new boiler and for new fittings for the cabin. Meanwhile we shall have to live in a hotel and eat at Senhor Baptista's place every day. That doesn't sound too bad, does it?"

That's typical of the Chief. He loses his temper and gets depressed very easily, but it doesn't usually last very long. On this occasion, though, I did wonder whether he really believed what he was saying. It sounded too good to be true.

We were still standing on the quay when I heard quick, quiet footsteps coming up behind us. I turned round.

I didn't recognize the man at first, as his face was shaded by a broad-brimmed hat. He came a few steps closer and said, "Koskela?"

The Chief turned round and we both found ourselves looking at the man who called himself Morro.

The gas lamp outside one of the harbor shops cast a yellowish light on his narrow face. His eyes seemed to be protruding, as if he was afraid. His jacket was unbuttoned, his tie was loose and the light glinted on a silver chain round his neck. In his outstretched and trembling hand he was holding a very small pistol, and it was aimed straight at the Chief's chest.

My heart skipped a couple of beats. Out of the corner of

my eye I could see the Chief start with amazement. Then his mouth snapped shut and he went white in the face.

The seconds ticked past slowly, very slowly. I tried to stay completely still and not show my teeth. Morro's hand was shaking more and more. A drop of sweat trickled down from under his hat and ran slowly down his forehead.

It seemed to take several minutes for the drop of sweat to reach the tip of his nose, where it came to a stop, trembled a little and then dripped off.

And then Morro took a step back, followed by another step, after which he lowered the gun, muttered something inaudible and began running.

The Chief stood rooted to the spot, his jaw clenched, as he watched Morro. Then his cheeks flushed bright red and his eyes flashed.

"Oh no you don't, blast you!" he roared, and took up the chase.

Morro ran in the direction of Comércio Square. It was a mild night and there were plenty of people on the quaysides. I couldn't keep pace with the Chief, but I could see that he was closing in on Morro.

Later, during the course of the trial, there were many people who said that the Chief had thrown Morro into the river. Some went so far as to claim that he had struck Morro on the head before throwing him in. But it simply isn't true!

I saw what happened. The Chief caught hold of Morro's collar to stop him, but Morro lost his balance, tripped over a mooring rope and fell over the edge of the quay. It was an accident, and anyone who says anything different is lying!

When I caught up with the Chief he was standing there panting and looking down into the river. A small locket with a broken chain lay on the quay: I recognized it as the chain Morro had been wearing round his neck. The chain must have been broken in the rumpus just before he fell into the water. I picked it up and put it in my pocket so that it wouldn't get stolen.

People began gathering round us. They were all talking and shouting at the same time. The Chief lay down and looked under the edge of the quay, but there was no sign of Morro there, so he took off his jacket and jumped in.

I should have tried to stop him. The tide was going out, and the current flowing toward the open Atlantic was running at seven or eight knots at least. There was no chance of the Chief finding Morro in the water and, in fact, he could only just keep himself afloat. When his head broke the surface he was already a good twenty yards downstream.

It was lucky there was a barge tied up close by, and the Chief managed to catch hold of one of its mooring chains and hang on it while he gasped for breath. I ran toward him, but a couple of dockworkers got out to the barge before me and pulled him up. I have never, neither before nor since, seen the Chief so miserable and despairing.

"O my Lord," he sniffed. "What have I done?"

The police must already have been close, because two black cars came skidding to a halt on the quay less than a minute later. A broad-shouldered man in a gray woolen overcoat climbed out of the passenger seat of the first car, and a number of constables in blue uniforms emerged from the second. The man in the overcoat made inquiries among the crowd as to what had happened and then ordered the constables to organize a search for the man who had fallen into the water.

People began arriving from all directions, and the constables made a lot of noise trying to get all these inquisitive people to spread out and search for the missing man.

The Chief had recovered somewhat by this point and was running anxiously back and forth along the edge of the quay trying to find any sign of Morro in the black waters.

"We need to move farther downstream," he said with panic in his voice. "Lord Above, if the current takes him out from the shore he won't have a chance. We need a boat."

But then two constables approached us. One of them took the Chief by the shoulder; the other stood with his hand resting on the pistol that was sticking out of an open holster on his uniform belt.

"You, come with us!"

The Chief looked at them in surprise.

"But there's a man in the water. We need to—"

"Other people will have to see about that. Chief Inspector Garretta wants to talk to you."

The two constables led the Chief over to the police cars. I followed them, overwrought and full of uneasy premonitions.

The man in the woolen overcoat was leaning against one of the police cars and flipping through a notebook.

"Name?" he said, without even looking up when the constables brought the Chief to him.

"Koskela," the Chief said.

"Full name, please," the man said, still without looking up.

"Henry Koskela," the Chief said impatiently. "Listen to me now, we must get hold of a boat and lights. . . ."

The man in the overcoat held up his hand to silence the Chief. Only then did he slowly raise his eyes from the notebook. His eyes were expressionless.

"Henry Koskela, you are under arrest," he said.

The Chief stared openmouthed. Before he had time to say a word, the constable pushed him into the backseat of the police car. I took a step forward to go with them, but the man in the overcoat blocked my way.

"No animals in my car," he said in a low voice. "Just shove off, you!"

He climbed into the passenger seat and the car set off. I caught a glimpse of the Chief's frightened face through the rear window as the car disappeared at high speed toward Comércio Square.

There was quite a crowd of people on the quay by now, and the atmosphere was one of excitement. I didn't know what I should do, and while I was standing there in a state of confusion I noticed that the people round me were eyeing me threateningly. Several rough-looking men who didn't seem completely sober were beginning to form a circle round me.

"Now it's that gorilla's turn!" I heard one of them yell.

An older, stern-looking policeman was standing just a few yards away.

"You lot!" he roared. "There's been quite enough trouble here for one evening. Leave the beast alone!"

I ran off without looking back. An empty bottle came sailing through the air and smashed just in front of me, and I heard the policeman shout again. Not until I'd run fifty yards or more did I dare look back. I could see them shaking their fists, but no one was actually following me.

I was soon climbing down one of the rickety ladders that went down the side of the quay to the river. Our lifeboat

38

was still there, bobbing on the water. I untied it quickly and shifted it as far in under the quay as I could. My heart was pounding and fear was making it impossible to think clearly, but I knew that I should be safe there, at least as long as it was dark.

CHAPTER 7
The Murderer's Gorilla

I stayed hidden in the lifeboat for two days and two nights. At first I was terrified that the angry crowd up on the quay would find me. I lay there listening for voices and ready to untie the mooring rope and push the boat out without a moment's delay. The river was my escape route. But if I deserted our usual place at the quayside, how was the Chief ever to find me when the police released him?

At some point late at night I must have fallen asleep from sheer exhaustion. The cold woke me and I curled up under a piece of sailcloth to keep out the raw gray chill of the morning mist rising from the river.

The day that followed seemed the longest day of my life. The waters of the Tagus rushed past, and the sun moved slowly, so slowly, across the sky. And the whole time I was expecting to hear the Chief's voice or to see his face peering under the quay. Why was it taking him so long? Surely the police would let him go once they realized that what had happened to Morro was an accident?

When darkness fell again I was beside myself with anxiety. Where was the Chief? Were the police still holding him? And if so, why? The man in the woolen overcoat frightened me: what if he had harmed the Chief?

Terror and cold kept me awake all night. The more tired I became, the more awful the thoughts that ran through my head. It was a bad dream. The *Hudson Queen* had gone down and the Chief had disappeared. I had no idea what to do.

But with the sun came warmth, and I fell asleep. I must have slept quite a long time, because it seemed to be afternoon when I woke. Fear and anxiety immediately dug their claws into me, and my stomach was aching with hunger.

As dusk began to fall, I realized I would never survive another night in the lifeboat. I had to do something to stop my imagination running riot, and I had to find something to eat.

There was only one place I could think of and that was O Pelicano. Senhor Baptista would give me food, and he would wonder why I was on my own. He would help me find the Chief.

I waited until I had the cover of darkness, then I climbed up onto the quay and dived into the lanes and alleys of Alfama. I pulled my cap down over my face and kept to the shadows between the streetlamps. In spite of that, however, I was seen when I was crossing the tramlines on the bend in Rua das Escolas Gerais. Some old men were sitting playing cards outside a tobacconist's that was still open, and one of them caught sight of me and shouted: "Look! There's the gorilla! The murderer's gorilla!"

Everyone turned round to look, and some pointed their fingers my way. I sped up and tried to stop myself looking back. I could see the sign over the door of O Pelicano just a little farther along Rua do Salvador. Not far now. I could hear loud voices behind me. Inquisitive faces peered out of windows and doorways. I began to run. Some men in front of me turned round.

"Stop the gorilla!" the voices behind me shouted. "It's the murderer's gorilla! Catch her!"

The men in front of me held out their arms to block my way. My heart was beating wildly in my chest.

I leapt through an open gateway that led into a dark yard. There was a drainpipe in one corner, and I began to climb it. Excited voices echoed between the walls of the houses as my pursuers stormed into the small yard. I carried on climbing upward without looking down.

A few minutes later I was sitting crouched on a roof several blocks away. I was shaking all over, and my heart was still pounding fast and hard.

The trembling gradually subsided, and I rocked myself gently back and forth to calm my heart. I had to keep moving, I thought, and I needed food. My mind was in such a spin that those were my only sensible thoughts.

After a little while I worked out where I was. The city looked quite different from the rooftops. My legs were shaky and weak, and I went on all fours so as not to slide down the tiles. Once or twice I was forced to jump from one house to another to make progress. It was horrible.

Eventually I reached a projecting roof opposite O Pelicano. I looked over the edge and saw that Senhor Baptista seemed to have a full house that evening. There were some guests standing outside smoking. Their laughter and general hubbub echoed along the street. How would I dare go down there?

Hunger was making me light-headed, and my stomach was knotted with cramp. I climbed back over the ridge of the roof and at the rear of the house found an inner yard with dustbins. I carefully shinned down a drainpipe and began rummaging through the bins. I struck lucky—someone had thrown away a sack of old bread.

With the sack over my shoulder, I climbed back up the drainpipe and moved across the rooftops until I found a safe hiding place behind a chimney stack. I sat there and ate all the bread in the sack. The crusts were so dry that I had to soften them in the rainwater lying in a gutter.

Tiredness came over me once I had eaten. I leaned back against the chimney stack and looked out over the huge city. There were thousands and thousands of points of light twinkling in the black night. It ought to have felt safe and friendly, but not to me. I was on my own now, and there were dangers lurking everywhere.

In my head I could still hear the shrill voices yelling after me:

"Look! It's the gorilla! Stop her! It's the murderer's gorilla!"

The murderer's gorilla! Why were they calling me that?

I felt a chill run down my spine when I realized why.

They believed the Chief was a murderer.

That he had murdered Morro.

What if the police believed that too?

Was that why they hadn't released him?

Was the Chief going to end up in prison?

CHAPTER 8
The Singing

I stayed there all night, barely moving. My mind was in a complete muddle, and it took until dawn for me to bring some order to my thoughts. Everything would be fine. After all, I wasn't the only one who had seen what happened when Morro fell into the water. Everyone who had been on the quay that evening would be able to tell the police it had been an accident. The Chief wasn't a murderer, so he must be set free. What stupid people shouted on the street was utterly irrelevant.

Now I had to try to get some sleep, and after that I was sure I could find a way of getting in touch with Senhor Baptista.

I found a hole in the roof and climbed down into a filthy loft that stank of pigeon droppings, but at least it was somewhere I'd be able to rest for a while.

My stomach was grumbling again. I fished round in my pocket for some of the pieces of bread I'd saved and I suddenly realized I could feel something else in there too. I drew out a thin silver chain that I didn't recognize at first. Then I remembered. It was the chain Morro had dropped on the quay.

Attached to the chain was a locket, which I opened carefully. It contained a lock of hair, tied with thin red ribbon, and there was a portrait painted on the inside of the locket. Beneath the portrait were three short lines:

My heart is yours.
My life is yours.
To my beloved Alphonse from Elisa.

I felt a stab of pain. The girl in the picture must be Morro's beloved, and she was the one who had written those lines.

But Alphonse Morro was now dead.

Drowned and gone forever.

Poor, poor girl.

And poor Chief. The accident wasn't his fault, but he would never forgive himself; I knew that.

I put my arms under my head and lay down in the dirt on the hard wooden floor.

~

I slept all day. In my dream I heard someone singing in the distance. It sounded beautiful and sorrowful and I believe I cried in my sleep.

By the time I opened my eyes it was already late evening. The pigeons were cooing and flying in and out of a big hole low in the roof. The smell of pigeon droppings stung my nostrils.

After a while I noticed I could still hear the same singing I'd heard in my dream. It was very faint, and sometimes the noise from the street drowned it out.

But it was there.

I climbed out on the roof. The stars were just coming out. There was a gentle breeze blowing from the north, and the singing was coming with it. I listened.

Suddenly—and I couldn't understand why—I felt a strong and warm feeling inside. A feeling that perhaps things were not as dreadful as they seemed.

Without thinking, I slid down the roof tiles, which still retained the heat of the sun, and jumped across a narrow alley to the next house. I climbed up to the ridge of the roof and looked down the other side. The singing was clearer now, and I could see where it was coming from.

There was a woman sitting by the open dormer window of an attic room. She was working on something she had on her knee, and she was singing. She was wearing a shawl over her shoulders, and her dark hair was gathered up in a loose knot.

I still had the warm feeling inside. I sat down with my back to a chimney and listened. After a while I closed my eyes, and a feeling of utter calm came over me.

I think I went to sleep again. I didn't notice the moon rise above the hills inland and spread a cold light over the city. When I opened my eyes the singing had stopped.

The light in the attic room was off.

But the woman was still sitting in the window, and she was looking straight at me. Her face was pale and her eyes wide.

I fled the same way as I had come and didn't stop until I was back in my hiding place with the pigeons.

What on earth had got into me? How could I have been so stupid as to let the woman in the window see me? What if she phoned the police? Or told her neighbors what she had seen? The people of the area might already be gathering to search the roofs for me.

I did not dare leave the loft again until late at night, and by then O Pelicano was already closed. The windows of the inn were dark, and Senhor Baptista and Senhora Maria had gone home. I had no idea at all where they lived.

On the way back to my hiding place I picked some shriveled apples out of a rubbish bin in a backyard. When I'd eaten them I fell into a troubled sleep that lasted until the following afternoon.

Once again I waited for darkness before making my way to the rooftop opposite O Pelicano for the third time. And once again I attempted to summon up sufficient courage to climb down and enter the inn. But there were people coming and going the whole time. If I were simply to stride in through the door the whole of Alfama would soon know I was there. How on earth would Senhor Baptista be able to protect me then?

After some time I noticed that there was a wide wooden gate ajar about ten yards from the door of O Pelicano. From my viewpoint I could see that the gate probably led to an inner yard between the buildings. Maybe O Pelicano had a back door that opened onto that yard?

I decided to take a chance. As soon as the lane was empty of people, I climbed down to the ground. With my heart in my mouth I ran the few steps to the gate, opened it quietly and slipped in. No one had seen me.

I had guessed right. The gateway led into a small dark inner yard. There were two doors leading into the building on the O Pelicano side. The first of them was locked; the second opened on stiff hinges. The noise from the inn could now be heard clearly. I had made the right choice.

I moved cautiously through a short narrow corridor, at the end of which were two more doors. One went into the inn—I could tell from the noise—the other down to the cellar steps. I didn't know what to do. Perhaps I should hide in the cellar and wait there until all the customers had gone home?

I didn't have time to reach a decision before the door that led to the inn opened. Senhor Baptista came through carrying a tray full of empty bottles and pushed the door shut behind him with his foot. When he caught sight of me he jumped and almost dropped the tray to the floor.

"Sally Jones!" he said, and gasped. "Lord Above, you frightened the life out of me!"

He put down the tray and took a deep breath to settle himself. Then he said, "What are you doing here? I mean, shouldn't someone be looking after you?"

I didn't really understand what he meant.

"The Chief has been arrested for murder, you know!"

Senhor Baptista continued. "Were you there when it happened?"

I felt my legs go heavy and my stomach go cold.

The Chief had been arrested! For murder!

"Is it really true, what the newspapers are saying?" Senhor Baptista asked. "That he killed that Morro fellow and threw him in the river?"

I stared at him and shook my head.

"No, I didn't think so," Senhor Baptista said. "I can't say I know Koskela that well, but a murderer? No, he's not that sort."

Senhor Baptista suddenly looked troubled. He looked over his shoulder at the door behind him.

"It's extremely busy here tonight," he said. "Loads to do . . ."

He fell silent and seemed to be thinking. Then he cleared his throat nervously and said, "I don't know why you're here, but perhaps we ought to ring the police so that they can take care of you? You can't manage all on your own."

I shook my head again.

"People have been looking for you," Senhor Baptista said. "There are plenty who think you are dangerous, you know. If you fall into their hands they might hurt you. Really hurt you. And you can't stay here. That could cause trouble for me—and for Maria. I can't risk that. You do understand, don't you?"

I stood quite still. I was having difficulty breathing. Senhor Baptista was my only hope, the only one who could help me.

"This isn't easy," Senhor Baptista said in a sad voice. "I've got no choice, you see. I'm really sorry."

Suddenly he brightened up.

"Maybe we could phone the zoo?"

I shuddered and backed quickly toward the door.

"Wait a minute now," Senhor Baptista said, following me. "Lisbon Zoo is a very fine zoo! I'm sure they would take care of you there. You'd be quite safe. . . ."

I fled. Behind me I could hear Senhor Baptista calling my name.

The alleyway was empty. I grabbed hold of a drainpipe and climbed up as quickly as I could. I didn't look down until I was up on the roof. Senhor Baptista was standing outside the big wooden gate looking up and down the alley. After a little while he shrugged wearily and went back in.

I stayed there for a long time. I knew I ought to hurry away in case Senhor Baptista rang for the police. But I just didn't have the energy.

Eventually I started climbing slowly back across the

roofs. Dawn was beginning to color the sky metallic gray. By the time the sun rose I was already asleep back among the pigeons in the loft.

~

Hunger woke me, but I didn't want to get up. I had no idea what the time was. I lay there half asleep, slipping in and out of incoherent and unpleasant dreams.

Then all of a sudden I heard it again.

The singing.

I struggled up onto my elbows. The pigeons were fluttering nervously round me, and the dust they stirred up made me sneeze. At last I was awake.

When I went out on the roof it was dark. The wind had dropped for the night, and the pure sounds of the singing could be heard clearly. I climbed the same way I had the night before, and the woman in the window almost seemed to be expecting me. She looked at me as I sat down with my back to the chimney.

And I stayed sitting there for perhaps an hour, perhaps two. I didn't want the singing to end. Not until it was completely dark did the woman stop singing and leave the window. A few minutes later she returned, carefully hung something on a hook outside below the window and then closed it.

I remained where I was. After a little while I noticed a lovely smell of freshly baked bread and realized immediately where it was coming from. Half an hour later the light went off in the woman's window. I waited for another half an hour before standing up on stiff legs, jumping across to the next roof and climbing over to her dormer window. It could, of course, have been a trap, but I no longer cared.

There was a cloth bag hanging on the hook. I unhooked it quietly and crept away. Once I was back on the other side of the narrow street I sat down and opened the bag. It contained a whole loaf of bread, some cheese, a bottle of milk and four big apples.

I ate where I was. Then I just about managed to make my way back to the loft, where I fell asleep at once.

~

I stayed in my hiding place for the whole of the next day, and it wasn't until I heard the church bells ringing for vespers that I set off across the roofs and took up my position by the chimney across from the woman's window. The window was closed, and the room inside lay in darkness.

Shortly after sunset the light in the room came on. I caught a glimpse of the woman inside several times, and a little later the window opened. She immediately looked in my direction. I did not move. We looked at one another. Then she sat down with her needlework and began to sing.

Just before midnight she hung out another bag of food for me and shut the window.

~

On the third evening a storm from the Atlantic had moved in over Lisbon. The rain was pouring down and squalls of wind were rattling the tiles on the roofs. I got soaked waiting for the woman to open her window.

Eventually she did look out, peered through the downpour to see if I was there and then shouted over the wind: "If you want me to sing to you tonight you'll have to come in here. Otherwise both of us will catch a cold."

CHAPTER 9
The Woman in the Window

Her name was Ana. Ana Molina.

I didn't know that, of course, when I climbed in through her window that rainy night. She was standing at the other end of the dark room, and although her manner was calm I could see she was keeping one hand on the door handle. She was obviously ready to throw open the door and run if necessary, which was hardly strange given that I must have looked dreadful. My fur was matted and filthy, my overalls had long tears at the knee and at the elbow, and my hands and feet were cut and cracked from all the climbing over rusty metal roofs and rough walls.

I sank to the floor and stayed there.

"My name is Ana," she said quietly after a while. "And I know who you are. People say you are dangerous. Is that true?"

I shook my head.

The pupils in Ana's eyes widened when she realized I understood what she was saying. She studied me closely. Finally she seemed to decide that I really wasn't dangerous. She let go of the door handle and cautiously approached. The acrid smell of pigeon droppings caused her to hold her nose.

"Holy Mother of God, what a stink!" she exclaimed. "There's a bathroom down in the stairwell. Do you want me to fill a bath for you?"

I nodded. Wild gorillas don't really go in for baths, but I have learned to use soap and water to keep myself clean. You have to when you work in an engine room.

While I bathed, Ana scrubbed my overalls and cap in the washbasin. It must have been well after midnight before she set out bread, milk and fruit on the only table in the room. My clothes were hanging by the stove to dry, and I was sitting on the sofa in the kitchen wrapped in a blanket. Ana was sitting opposite, watching me as I ate. Once I'd finished she cleared the table and said, "I'm going to bed now. You can sleep on the sofa in here. I have to go to work early tomorrow morning, but I shan't wake you. When you wake up you must decide for yourself whether to stay. There's more bread and fruit in the larder. If you decide to go you can take as much as you want. I'll be home in the evening, and I'll get dinner for the two of us if you're still here."

Ana put out the oil lamp above the table, said goodnight and went behind a curtain beside the chimney breast. There was a small bed alcove in there with a washbasin. I lay down on the sofa and covered myself with the blanket.

The rain was pattering on the window, and there was the soft crackle of burning wood from the stove. Before going to sleep I thought there was little doubt I'd be there when Ana came home from work the next day. And perhaps she would sing for me, which she had forgotten to do tonight.

~

That's how I ended up moving in with Ana Molina. Once she'd let me in I suppose she didn't have the heart to throw me out. Rumors about the murderer's gorilla had been doing the rounds in Alfama. Ana knew that I had nowhere else to go to. Neither before nor since have I ever met any-one as kind as Ana Molina. Nor anyone who can sing more beautifully.

Ana worked in a shoe factory out in Alcântara. The manager was called Santos and, as I came to realize, he was a real slave driver. Ana got up with the sun every morning but Sunday and bought bread from the Graça bakery, across the street on Rua de São Tomé. After her breakfast coffee she hurried away to be in time for the tram. She didn't come home until nine at night, and she brought the food for the evening meal with her. It was usually sardines with beans or rice. After eating she would sit at the window and sing while darning socks for local people. Darning was her eve-ning job, which she did to eke out the pay she received from the shoe factory. When the small clock on the wall struck eleven she put aside her darning needle and went to bed so that she would have enough energy for work the following morning.

That was Ana's life. And it didn't change much because I had moved in. Not at first, anyway.

I slept right through my first days at Ana's place. I was bone-weary and only woke now and again for a drink of milk or a bite of bread. It wasn't until the third day that I stopped going straight back to sleep. I sat up and looked out of the dormer window. There were gray clouds moving quickly above the rooftops of Alfama. On the other side of the inner yard I could see the chimney I had rested against while listening to Ana sing.

There was a pile of old newspapers on one of the chairs by the table. I immediately thought of Senhor Baptista and what he had said. Hadn't he said that he'd read in the paper that the Chief killed Morro and threw him into the river? But it just wasn't true! Senhor Baptista must have misunderstood.

I lifted the papers onto the table and after flipping through almost all of them my eye was caught by a short notice. It was only two days old.

DIÁRIO DE NOTÍCIAS, Outubro 12

MURDERER ARRESTED

As we reported earlier, the quayside below the Alfama district was the scene of a fatal drama on Thursday past. Alphonse Morro, twenty-six, a clerk employed by the Lisbon Harbor Authority and a resident of Bairro Alto, died after a violent confrontation with a Finnish seaman by the name of Koskela. The body has not been recovered and is believed to have been washed out by the current, which as a result of a combination of an ebb tide and high water levels in the Tagus was unusually strong at the time of the incident. Koskela was arrested at the scene of the crime and taken to Baixa police station. In view of the fact that numerous witnesses unanimously testified that Koskela first assaulted Morro and then threw his lifeless body into the river, Koskela has been charged with murder and transferred to the Lisbon central prison at Campolide.

I read the notice twice, perhaps hoping I had misread it the first time. But I had not. All of a sudden I found it difficult to breathe, as if something was stuck in my throat. I lay down on the sofa again and crept under the blanket, pulling it tight round my head.

That was how Ana found me when she came home from Santo's factory in the evening.

I heard the rustle of the newspaper I'd left on the table. Then she sat down on the edge of the sofa, and her hand cautiously stroked my shoulder.

"That seaman, Koskela, the one they are writing about," she said. "He's your friend, isn't he?"

I gathered my strength a little and then nodded, my head still under the blanket.

"There's always a lot of talk when something like that happens," Ana continued. "Somebody said you worked on Koskela's ship. That you are a ship's engineer. Is that really true?"

I nodded again.

Ana sat there quietly and continued to stroke my shoulder.

"You can obviously read, then," she said after a while. "I mean, you've been looking at the newspaper. Can you write too? Because if you can, I'd like to know what you are called."

I heard her going over to her small desk and opening a drawer. When she came back she said, "I've brought you a pen and paper."

I let go of the blanket and forced myself to sit up. The light from the oil lamp dazzled me at first, but after a few moments I was used to it. I took the pen and wrote my name. My handwriting is awful, but it's legible.

"Sally Jones," Ana said. "Would it be all right if I call you Sally?"

I shook my head. No one I know calls me just Sally.

Ana looked a little confused. Then she said, "Sally Jones, then?"

I nodded. Human beings have two names, a first name and a surname, but I'm a gorilla and I just have the one name—Sally Jones.

"Right then, Sally Jones," Ana said with a little smile. "Will you help me lay the table? I've bought rice and a corn on the cob for each of us for dinner."

After we had eaten Ana sang to me while she sat by the window darning socks. I felt warm and at peace, and afterward I slept all night.

I woke up with an idea. While Ana was at the bakery

buying bread I took the pen and paper and wrote a message. I put the paper by Ana's coffee cup, and she saw it as soon as she came back.

"'I was there. It was an accident,'" she read aloud.

She gave me a serious look, thought for a moment and said, "If that's true, your friend will be found not guilty. At the trial, I mean. No one is found guilty of murder unless there is proof that he or she is the guilty party."

She hesitated a moment before adding: "But the newspaper did say that there are witnesses. . . ."

I shook my head and picked up the pen. I wrote: *They are lying.*

Ana gave me a worried look.

"Why would they do that?"

I thought for a while and then shrugged. I didn't have an answer to that question.

We sat in silence and then Ana stroked my hand.

"It will all come right, you'll see. I can't believe that they will send an innocent man to prison."

In my heart of hearts I suspected she was saying that to comfort me. But I tried not to think so, because I wanted so much for it to be true.

CHAPTER 10
The House by the Nameless Park

When Ana had gone to work I sat at the table wondering what I should do for the rest of the day. I couldn't just lie on the sofa brooding—I'd go mad if I did. After walking round the only room a couple of times, I opened the door to the stairs. It was all quiet. I crept halfway down the staircase and peeped out of a window. Two trams were passing one another at that moment and a truck had to mount the pavement to get past. There was much yelling and tooting. Some old fellows at a pavement café waved their hands to stop the truck from knocking their table over.

The house in which Ana lived was by a small park that had no name but lay just where the dark and narrow Rua do Salvador met the busier Rua de São Tomé. The park didn't have room for more than a couple of benches and a few tall trees squashed in between the houses. An elderly man in a white suit was sitting smoking on one of the benches, and a couple of children in worn school uniforms were playing ball against a tree.

It seemed so unreal that life was going on as usual. Was I the only one in the world who cared about the Chief and what might happen to him?

I stayed for a long time looking out of the dusty window on the staircase. And it suddenly occurred to me that the Chief too must be worried, not only about what might happen to him but also what had happened to me. He wouldn't even know if I was alive or dead, would he? He would certainly never dream I was being taken care of by someone who wanted the best for me. For all he knew I might well have been sent to the zoo and locked in a cage. Or the police might simply have had me put down. I knew the very thought of that would be enough to break the Chief's heart.

The feeling of calm I had worked so hard to achieve was crumbling to dust. I hurried back to Ana's room before the sense of hopelessness overwhelmed me again. I had to find something to do, something that would drive away these terrible thoughts.

My eyes lit on the basket of socks waiting to be darned. I had seen—more or less, anyway—how Ana had done it the night before. I found a darning needle, some wool and a pair of woolen socks with big holes in the heels. Two hours later I had worked out the technique, and I spent the rest of the day darning socks without a break.

Ana had a surprise after supper that evening when she sat down at the window to get on with her evening work. All the socks in her basket were already mended. She patted me on the cheek and proceeded to take a closer look at my handiwork.

"The darns could have been just a little tighter. But apart from that I couldn't have done better myself," she said.

She then opened the cupboard under her kitchen counter and there was a large sack full of bags, each of which had a small label sewn on it. On each label was the name of the family whose socks were in the bag waiting to be darned.

I realized then that I was going to have plenty to keep me busy all day.

~

Every morning after Ana had left for Santos's factory, I took the bag of socks and a chair down to the window on the stairs and stayed there working until I felt hungry. Then I would go back up and have something to eat before returning to the window and darning socks until Ana came home.

The view from the window kept me company and helped me suppress the awful thoughts that constantly lay in ambush in my head. There was plenty to look at out in the street, and after a couple of weeks I could recognize most of the people in the area. I learned which of the local women had no time for one another and which of the schoolchildren pinched apples from the greengrocer's. I knew how often the fishmonger went to the barber and which days the barber bought fish.

One of the people I saw every day was the man in the white suit who had been sitting on a bench in the park the first time I looked out of the window on the stairs. It took me a while to work out that he probably lived in our building.

Every day, just after the church bells had rung for noon, he would appear on the street immediately below my window. He would walk north along Rua de São Tomé and eventually out of sight. Three-quarters of an hour later I would see him walking back the same way. He would stop in the park, smoke a slim cigar and then walk on toward our house. Somewhere down below I could just hear the faint sound of a door closing.

I wondered who this man was. With his well-pressed suit and his beautifully carved walking cane he looked distinguished. His hair and well-trimmed goatee were as white as his suit. His expression was both haughty and morose.

I also noticed that there didn't seem to be anyone but Ana living in the house. The apartment below was always silent, and I heard no one going in and out the door. I sometimes thought I heard the sound of accordion music, but it was impossible to tell whether it was coming from the ground floor of our house or from one of the neighboring houses.

~

When Ana came home from the shoe factory one evening she brought that day's newspaper with her. She turned to a particular page and handed the paper to me.

"It isn't good news," she said with a serious look.

I sat down on the kitchen sofa to read it.

DIÁRIO DE NOTÍCIAS, Novembro 5

A POLITICAL MURDER?

In recent days there have been persistent rumors in circulation suggesting that political motives may lie behind the murder of the clerk Alphonse Morro. According to our sources, Alphonse Morro had decidedly monarchist sympathies. On a number of occasions he is said to have campaigned openly against the republic and for the restoration of King Manuel as head of state. Should these unconfirmed rumors prove true, it would not be beyond the bounds of possibility that the Finnish seaman Koskela was contracted to commit the murder by a leftist revolutionary group. As we know from past experience, the Anarchists do not hesitate to use lethal violence against their political enemies.

Rumors that the crime may have a political motivation are rejected by Raul Garretta, the police officer in charge of the Morro case.

"There is nothing to suggest that the murder has anything to do with politics. It seems rather to be a matter of a chance meeting, which led to a dispute of some sort that then culminated in fatal violence. Events of this kind are unfortunately by no means unusual in and round the Alfama district. I am not, however, precluding the possibility that Koskela may be an anarchist: I would not be at all surprised if he was. Anarchist doctrines, as we know only too well, are particularly attractive to morally underdeveloped individuals."

The date for the trial of Koskela has not yet been set, but it is likely to be within the next two months.

I read this article several times over the following days without becoming any the wiser. I didn't understand politics, and I knew that the Chief had no real interest. The idea of him being an anarchist was a piece of nonsense. I wondered whether the Chief would even know what the word really meant.

There may, however, have been some sort of connection after all. I remembered that anarchists had been Senhor Baptista's first thought when the Chief told him about the shipment of weapons. What could it all mean?

My thoughts did not go farther than that. I decided the most important part of the article was the last bit, where it said that the Chief's trial would be held within two months. That was when the truth would come out and the Chief would be released from prison!

The more I thought about it, the more hopeful I became. The police would be getting to know the Chief better by the day, and no one who knew the Chief would seriously believe he was a murderer!

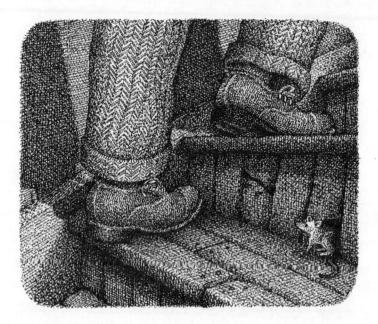

CHAPTER 11
The Tram Inspector

Ana did her best to make me feel safe at her place. But for all that, I was on my guard all the time, ready to make my escape should anyone suddenly come to catch me. I slept lightly at night and woke at every sound in the street. I felt it difficult to get back to sleep once I was awake.

One night just a couple of weeks after I had moved in I dreamt I was hearing heavy footsteps in the distance. I sat up on the edge of the sofa and listened hard. It was no dream. There was someone coming up the stairs. I quickly slipped into the bed alcove and shook Ana gently until she woke.

Half-awake, she needed a few moments to understand what was at issue. Then she too heard the steps approaching.

"Oh my Lord and Creator," she said. "It's Jorge."

Ana swung her legs over the side of the bed, put on her dressing gown and took me by the arm.

"There's no danger," she whispered in hurried tones. "Jorge is my fiancé. He's kind, believe me, but I don't want him to know that you are living here. I'll explain why later. Climb out the window and stay on the roof until I give you a signal. He usually leaves before it gets light. Hurry now!"

No sooner was I out into the cool night air than I heard someone knocking on Ana's door. She quickly closed the window behind me, and I tiptoed silently across the roof until I reached a well-concealed corner behind a chimney a short distance away. I didn't want to eavesdrop when Ana's fiancé was visiting.

Jorge stayed until dawn, exactly as Ana had said. Just as the sun was touching the cross on the church of Santa Cruz do Castelo, Ana opened her window again.

When I climbed back into the dark room, Ana was standing by the sink washing out an ashtray. She was only wearing her nightdress and her hair was all untidy. The room had a stale smell of wine and tobacco, and there was an empty bottle and a knocked-over glass on the table.

Ana turned round and reached for her shawl, which was hanging on a chair.

"Now I need to get tidied up to go to work," she said, quickly wrapping the shawl round her shoulders.

But I saw what she was trying to hide: she had a big blue bruise at the top of her right arm.

~

Jorge's full name was Jorge Amadéo Tomás da Costa. It was written under a photograph of him that hung on the wall in Ana's bed alcove. He had a self-confident smile and was wearing some sort of uniform.

"My Jorge is an inspector on the trams," Ana told me proudly when she showed me the portrait a few days later.

I wondered what an inspector does. I am still not really sure.

The bruise on Ana's arm had started to fade. She sounded full of love when she told me how efficient Jorge was and how important his job was. Ana and Jorge had been engaged for five years, and they intended to get married as soon as Jorge could leave his old mother.

"He is so kind to his mother," Ana said. "And at the moment she needs him more than I do. I can wait."

I knew at that point exactly what I thought of Jorge. He was a swine. And he never gave me any reason to change that view. He would visit Ana about once a week while I was living with her. He usually came in the middle of the night, and I could tell from his footsteps on the stairs that he was drunk. Every time he came I had to rush head over heels out of the window.

"It's both for his sake and for your sake that I don't want him to know you live here," Ana explained on one occasion. "Jorge doesn't like animals, you see. Not everyone does, you know. But they can be good-hearted people for all that."

But Jorge did not have a good heart. On Saturdays he would sometimes come to have dinner at Ana's. Ana would have bought wine from Alentejo, put out her best crockery and cooked *leitão à bairrada,* roast suckling pig. That was Jorge's favorite dish, she told me. As usual I had to climb up on the roof before he came and stay there until he had gone home. But I always stayed close by now, just in case Ana called for me.

It hurt me to hear how he grumbled at her. He thought the wine she was offering was too cheap. The skin on the roast pig wasn't crisp enough. And her new dress looked like a charlady's smock. Jorge always found something to moan about.

Sometimes when Jorge stayed overnight she would have bruises on one or both arms, but I never heard her shout or call out for help. Sometimes, though, after Jorge had gone home, she would weep. And once she said, "My poor Jorge, I feel so sorry for him. He is so full of anger."

CHAPTER 12
Signor Fidardo

Sunday was Ana's day off. That was when she cleaned the house, went to church and wrote a letter to her sister, who was a missionary in Africa. In the evening she cooked something especially nice for dinner.

On the second Sunday after I'd moved in, Ana told me there was a guest coming to dinner. Fortunately it wasn't Jorge.

"Signor Fidardo is coming tonight," she said. "He's my neighbor. And a good friend."

Ana had gone shopping down by the harbor and was intending to make fish soup. While I was helping her chop the vegetables, she told me a bit about Signor Fidardo. He owned the house, and Ana rented her attic room from him. He himself lived on the first floor, and he had his workshop on the ground floor. Signor Fidardo made musical instruments, mainly accordions: he had learned his trade as a boy in Italy. When he was young he had intended to emigrate to America but never got beyond Lisbon, which was where the boat to New York sailed from. Ana did not know for sure, but she believed Signor Fidardo had met someone in Lisbon and fallen in love while he was waiting for the ship. One way or the other he had stayed. He had been living in this house by the nameless little park for almost forty years.

I was nervous before his visit, and Ana noticed it.

"I've already told Signor Fidardo about you," she said to calm me down. "He won't gossip about it to anyone, I promise you."

At precisely seven o'clock there was a light tap on the door. Ana opened and an elderly man in a gleaming white linen suit entered. I had already guessed that Signor Fidardo and the man in the white suit were one and the same. He was carrying a bottle of wine and a large bunch of roses in one hand, and in the other a guitar and a bag from the Graça bakery.

The small room was filled with the scent of a musky aftershave. My nose is very sensitive to strong scents, so I sneezed.

Signor Fidardo looked at me with disapproval. Then he turned to Ana: "Does the gorilla have a cold?" he asked. "In which case it might be better if you and I ate downstairs in my place. I don't want to catch gorilla flu."

"Don't be silly, Luigi," Ana said. "This is Sally Jones, and she will be eating with us."

Before Signor Fidardo sat down he wiped his chair with his handkerchief. I assume he was afraid of getting gorilla hairs on his elegant white trousers.

As soon as the food and wine were served, Signor Fidardo seemed to forget I was there. He and Ana talked about one thing or another, mostly about music and about people they both knew. After he had drunk his coffee Signor Fidardo picked up his guitar and began to play a melancholy tune. Ana leaned back in her chair and sang.

They played and sang until the moon was shining in through the attic window. I was sitting curled up in the corner of the kitchen sofa, and I wanted them to carry on forever. Signor Fidardo played with his eyes closed, and all the sullen furrows in his morose face became smooth.

Signor Fidardo ate dinner with us almost every Sunday. It was usually Ana who cooked the meal, but Signor Fidardo always brought wine and pastries for the dessert. Sometimes he also provided the main course, in which case it was usually lobster from the Mercado da Ribeira market hall down by the harbor.

After we had eaten, Ana would sing while Signor Fidardo accompanied her on the guitar or accordion. He was very talented on both instruments. Ana almost always sang fado: I had heard Dora at O Pelicano sing the same sad songs, but she did not sing them with anything like the feeling and passion Ana brought to them. When Ana sang you forgot the whole world and all your sorrows for a while.

Signor Fidardo wanted Ana to start performing in public.

"You are the most talented fado singer in all Alfama, Ana. In the whole of Lisbon! No, in all Portugal! It's a sin not to allow the world to share your singing!"

That made Ana happy—you could tell from the way her cheeks blushed—but her answer was always the same:

"I'm quite happy singing at home. Appearing on the stage is not for me."

"*Chiacchiere!* Rubbish!" Signor Fidardo would exclaim.

"It's that fellow Jorge who won't let you! Do you think I don't know?"

And then Ana would refuse to talk about it anymore.

I came to see that Signor Fidardo was Ana's best friend, and so I decided I would like him. A little bit, anyway. After all, he didn't like me, did he?

"Heaven only knows what sort of filth is lurking in the fur of a beast like that," he muttered once, looking at me disapprovingly.

"Be careful what you say, now," Ana said. "She understands more than you think."

Then Signor Fidardo looked me straight in the eye for the first time and said, "I doubt that!"

CHAPTER 13
An Evil Premonition

The weeks passed. The day for the Chief's trial was approaching. I was both hopeful and terrified and couldn't think of anything else.

There were nights when I didn't sleep at all. I used to open the window and climb out onto the roof. If the wind was from the west I could smell the salty tang of the Atlantic, and that calmed me down. I thought how lucky I'd been in spite of everything that had happened. I was healthy and well fed, and I could still smell the sea sometimes. I wished the Chief knew that.

That's what gave me the idea of writing to him.

One day after Ana had left for work I fetched a red tin box from the bottom drawer of her bureau. It was the box she used to take out when she was writing to her sister in Africa. It contained a pen, paper, envelopes and a roll of stamps.

There was so much that I wanted to tell the Chief and so much I wanted to ask him. I wrote page after page in my head, but when I tried to get the words down on paper, things didn't turn out as I'd imagined. In the end I decided just to write the most important things:

I'm fine. Hope you will soon be free.

On the envelope I wrote:

To the Seaman Henry Koskela
Campolide Prison, Lisbon
From Ana Molina, Rua de São Tomé 28
Alfama, Lisbon

When Ana was asleep the following night I crept out and put the letter in a postbox a couple of streets away. Four days later the postman brought a small gray envelope addressed to Ana. She did not receive letters very often, so she was surprised. She was even more surprised when she opened it and read the letter.

Dear Ana Molina,

My name is Koskela and I am in jail. They say I have murdered a man, but it is not true.

I have had a letter from you, though I think it was really my engineer Sally Jones who wrote it. I was as happy as any man can possibly be because she is a very good and fine person, and it would make me more unhappy than anything else in the world if she was having to suffer just because I have ended up in prison.

Please, Mrs. Molina, please look after her if I don't get out of this place. Give her some good work to do. She can manage most things.

Please, for the sake of God and all His angels, don't let them put her in a cage.

With respectful greetings,
H. Koskela
Seaman (Victim of Misfortune)

Ana read out the Chief's letter to me. When she had finished reading I went all cold inside. The Chief did not sound like himself at all. There was no joy or hope in his words, and he didn't seem to believe that he would be found not guilty at the trial.

I almost regretted having written to him. I could no longer fool myself that he was strong and happy and just waiting to be released. Instead I had an evil premonition that left me with no peace.

~

Just nine days later, on Thursday, February 3, the Chief was brought before the court. When Ana came home that evening she was carrying a newspaper. She gave me a worried look.

"I have bad news for you," she said hesitantly. "Your friend Koskela has been found guilty of murder. I'm afraid he's been given a long prison sentence. Twenty-five years . . ."

I put my hands over my face and curled up on the kitchen sofa.

CHAPTER 14
Days and Nights

I don't know how long I stayed on the sofa.

Days and nights went by.

Long and dreadful days and nights.

I had neither energy nor will. The only thing I wanted was for the Chief to come back. But it wasn't going to happen. Not for twenty-five years.

And I would probably be dead and buried by then.

Sometimes Signor Fidardo popped in to see us. He looked at me without saying anything, but I could hear him whispering with Ana out in the hall.

"She won't eat anything," Ana said in a tearful voice one evening. "And she scarcely moves. I think she's going to die. I'll have to call a vet soon."

"Do that," Signor Fidardo said, "and they'll take her to the zoo and put her in a cage. Or they'll have her put down. It should have been done long ago."

That made Ana angry. She told Signor Fidardo to go, and she slammed the door behind him.

~

Ana became more and more worried about me. She didn't dare leave me at home alone anymore, so she stayed home from work.

Signor Fidardo came up with a letter for Ana one afternoon. A messenger had brought it to the door, and I heard her open the envelope.

"Well, what's it about?" Signor Fidardo asked.

"It's from Santos. I'll lose my job if I don't go to work this week."

"That's that decided, then!" Signor Fidardo said,

sounding almost relieved. "I'm off to the telephone box to ring the zoo immediately. If you're lucky they'll fetch that gorilla today."

"No, Luigi. Sally Jones is going to stay with me. I have no intention of leaving her on her own until I'm sure she can manage."

Signor Fidardo snorted impatiently.

"Don't be silly, Ana. You surely can't intend to choose a gorilla rather than your job, can you? Let me help you! The gorilla has to go!"

They were silent for a short while, and then I heard Ana's voice: "Will you really help me?"

"Ana, dear, of course I will."

"Then you could have Sally Jones down with you in the workshop. During the day, I mean, when I'm at work. She's no trouble. . . ."

"In my workshop!" Signor Fidardo snapped. "That is absolutely, totally and utterly out of the question! I can't have a gorilla charging round among all my tools and instruments! What kind of impression would that make?"

"I understand," Ana said. "You don't have to explain yourself."

The sound of the door closing stirred me out of my dull state.

88

I thought about what I'd just heard. Signor Fidardo was right. I mustn't let Ana lose her job because of me.

It was time to pull myself together.

~

It took all my willpower to rise from the sofa, but I didn't get much farther than that and ended up sitting at the table. Ana was pleased at first. She believed that I was at last recovering. After a short time, however, she began to have her doubts, since I sat there staring vacantly in front of me just as I had on the sofa. I still didn't touch the milk and fruit she put out for me.

Signor Fidardo came back that evening. He looked tired and anxious.

"Tell me that you will be going to work tomorrow," he said, pleading with Ana.

Ana shook her head.

"But it's absolute madness, Ana! What are you going to live on if you lose your job?"

"I'll find some way," she answered.

Then Signor Fidardo gave a deep sigh. His shoulders slumped.

"*Va bene,* have it your own way," he said, giving up. "The gorilla can come down with me while you're at work. But for two weeks only, and not a day more! After that, if you can't look after her yourself you'll have to hand her over to the zoo!"

Ana beamed and gave Signor Fidardo a hug.

"Thank you, Luigi, thank you. You'll be kind to her, won't you?"

"Not particularly," he said morosely.

Ana gave him a weak smile. Then she turned to me.

"That's all right, isn't it? Being downstairs with Signor Fidardo while I'm at work?"

I had no desire to be a nuisance to Signor Fidardo, no more than he wanted me in his workshop. But both of us wanted Ana to go back to work, so I nodded.

~

Signor Fidardo's workshop was on the ground floor of the house and had two windows looking out onto the street. There was a simple enamel sign over the door. It read:

SR FIDARDO

FABRICANTE DE ACORDEÃO

LUTHIER

It was not a large workshop, but it was very well organized. Along one wall there was a long workbench and a carpenter's bench, above which were tool boards and rows of sash clamps and G clamps. Chisels and turning chisels

90

were arranged in order of size, and there were many tools I'd never seen before. I assumed they were only used by instrument makers.

The other wall was completely taken up by cupboards with hundreds of small drawers and shelves full of glass bottles and paint tins. In one corner was a pillar drill, which looked completely new. There were electric lights on the ceiling to provide good lighting for working, and the light was reflected back off the gleaming varnish on the guitars and violins hanging on a rope stretched across the room. One shelf held a range of accordions of different sizes, all of them decorated with colorful motifs and patterns cut out in brass.

In the workshop there was a poky and untidy little store-room that could be closed off with a door. That was where Signor Fidardo was planning to keep me.

"So that you don't disturb me and frighten away my customers," he explained.

I made space for myself in one corner and there I stayed for the whole day until Ana came to fetch me in the evening.

By the following morning Signor Fidardo had placed a large wooden box in the storeroom. The box was full of buttons: mother-of-pearl buttons, ivory buttons and black ebony buttons.

"They're accordion buttons," he explained. "I bought

the box in a sale of bankrupt stock in Milan, and they need to be sorted according to size, color and material. So get on with it! Ana says you can darn socks, so you should be able to sort buttons. If you're going to spend your days with me, you'll have to make yourself useful. Otherwise I'll pack you off back to Ana, and that means she'll lose her job."

I was reluctant, and for some time I sat motionless glaring at the box and listening to the sounds of Signor Fidardo at work through the door. I could smell wood shavings, varnish and well-oiled metal tools, smells that reminded me of the little workshop the Chief and I had on the *Hudson Queen*.

It made me wonder whether they had workshops in the prison. The prisoners must surely have something to do all day, mustn't they? As long as the Chief was given a good job to do, I thought, he'd be able to put up with being behind bars. For a while, anyway.

Without noticing what I was doing, I had spread a handful of buttons out on the floor and started sorting them.

~

The box contained at least a thousand buttons, and I worked slowly. I was thinking of the Chief all the time, and that was painful. I often found myself drifting off into despairing thoughts and would sit for hours in a state of paralysis.

But, for all that, the work did me good, and after a couple of days my appetite began to return. Ana almost wept with joy when, after a long gap, I tasted some of my supper for the first time.

It took me a week to sort the buttons.

"You took your time over that," Signor Fidardo said.

He tried to sound annoyed, but I could tell that he was surprised that I'd managed the job. He took a piece of rag out of the pocket in his apron, handed it to me and said, "Now the buttons need to be polished. One by one. So that they really shine!"

CHAPTER 15
A Little Red Accordion

Signor Fidardo kept his workshop clean and tidy, but the storeroom was a complete mess. The floor and shelves were cluttered with broken instruments, spare parts, empty paint tins, discarded tools and offcuts of wood of every conceivable variety.

A little red accordion on one of the top shelves had caught my eye on the very first day I spent in there. It was worn and battered and looked as if it had been dropped from a great

94

height. There was a tangle of small bent metal arms poking out through a hole in one side of the accordion.

For some reason my eyes kept going back to the broken accordion, and I had a strange feeling it was trying to tell me something.

I ate with Ana every evening, and after supper she would sing to me while we both darned socks. I noticed that she tried to choose happy songs, presumably to stop me from feeling unhappy. It was kind of her, but happy songs made me feel more sad than sad songs. I don't know why.

When Ana was singing I did my best not to think about the Chief in prison. I thought about the red accordion instead. In my mind's eye I could see its broken mechanism, and I wondered how an accordion actually worked.

The days passed. Polishing accordion buttons is a boring job. I sometimes fell asleep, rag in hand and with a lap full of buttons. One afternoon I fell asleep while Signor Fidardo was testing an accordion that had been brought in for tuning. I heard the music in my sleep, and I imagined it was the Chief who was playing. I could picture him there in front of me, happy and concentrated, the way he always was when he was trying to solve a really difficult mechanical problem.

I woke with a jerk and the dream faded away.

But I knew now what the red accordion had been trying to tell me all along.

I found a set of steps in the corner, climbed up and brought the accordion down from the shelf. Signor Fidardo saw me sitting there examining the instrument.

"It's just scrap," he said. "Used to be a fine instrument to play, but now it's only good for spare parts. You're welcome to it if you want to play with it—but only when you've finished polishing all the buttons!"

That evening I took the bags of buttons with me when I went up to Ana's, and I polished them all night by moonlight. The very last button was clean and shining by the time the sun rose.

The red accordion was mine.

Signor Fidardo went away for the day the following day. He was going to take the ferry across the river to Barreiro to buy beeswax and resin. The moment I was alone I cleared a space below the window ledge in the storeroom and built a table out of a couple of empty packing cases and some wide planks.

Then I picked out all the broken and discarded tools that were lying round on the shelves. There were bent screwdrivers and a blunt saw, worn pliers, hammers, files with the handles missing, bent scrapers and knives with nasty hacks out of the blades. And an old vise with a crooked screw.

I started by taking the handle off a broken screwdriver

and fixing it onto a file instead. Then, using the file, I was able to sharpen the saw and one of the knives. With the saw, the knife, the file and an offcut of oak, I made a handle for the hammer, which I then used to hammer the vise straight. I straightened out the screwdrivers in the vise and used them to fix the loose pliers. Then I lined up all the tools on the short end of the table.

I had my own workshop again.

I had already started to take the red accordion to pieces by the time Signor Fidardo returned from Barreiro. He came to a halt in the doorway and just stood there. I carried on taking the screws out to remove the bellows. After a little while he came over to the table.

"These tools . . . did *you* mend them?"

I turned round and nodded. Signor Fidardo looked confused. Then he said, "And . . . er . . . are you going to try to mend the accordion too?"

I nodded again. Signor Fidardo stroked his mustache absentmindedly. He went back to his own workshop, and I could hear him muttering to himself in Italian.

Signor Fidardo left me to work in peace for the rest of the day. He didn't even say goodbye when it was time for me to go up to Ana's. Before I fell asleep on the sofa that night it occurred to me that I had been with Signor Fidardo for two weeks. I wasn't supposed to stay with him any longer than that, so now I'd have to use Ana's kitchen table for my work on the accordion.

Once Ana had gone to work the following morning, I went down to Signor Fidardo's to fetch my accordion. I was praying he would allow me to take some tools too.

But to my amazement Signor Fidardo seemed to have forgotten that I was no longer welcome. He had hung an electric light over my workbench in the storeroom, and there was a thick book lying on the table.

It was a handbook for accordion makers.

CHAPTER 16
Organs for the Dead

B efore I could repair the red accordion I had to understand how it worked. As an engineer I knew that the
best way of learning how an engine functions is to take it
to pieces and then put it back together. I thought that was
probably also true when it came to accordions.

Taking it to pieces took me a couple of days. Putting it
back together took another four. In the meantime I also
managed to read the handbook from cover to cover.

I took a mental note of all the parts that needed mending or replacing to put the red accordion back in good working order. It was a long list and an expensive one. Every screw and every piece of brasswork would cost. Not to mention varnish, new reed tongues and leather for new bellows. How was I to get the money for all this?

While thinking about it I gently began to remove all the reed plates from the reed block. I carefully cleaned off the rust and old wax from the parts while ensuring that the delicate reed tongues were not damaged in the process.

Then, using a knife, I cut away the leather that had dried on the keys. I also tried to polish up the thin brass grill with its beautiful fretwork decorations, but I discovered that the old brass was split in a number of places. I added "sheet of thin brass" to the list of materials I needed to acquire one way or another.

Next I tried scraping the faded paint and flaking varnish off the walnut cabinet of the instrument. It did not go well. My scrapers and knives made marks on the beautiful wood, and I worked up the courage to take my blunt tools into Signor Fidardo's workshop.

"What do you want?" he asked me in an irritated voice. "Want me to sharpen your knives, do you? What time do you think I've got to do that?"

I shook my head and looked in the direction of the back

corner of the room where Signor Fidardo kept his whet-stone and grindstone. He understood what I meant.

"Sharpening is a job for an expert," he said. "But you're welcome to try if you want to."

When we were on the *Hudson Queen* I was the one who made sure the ship's knives and scrapers were kept sharp. The Chief had taught me the technique. It's mainly a matter of a steady hand and being careful about angles.

Signor Fidardo stood alongside me and watched in amazement as I used his grindstone. I moved on to the whetstone and finished the job by stropping the knives on a leather belt. When I'd finished he inspected the blade on one of the newly sharpened knives. Then he plucked a long white strand of hair from his head and pulled it across the edge of the blade.

The hair immediately fell into two pieces.

He looked at me over the rim of his glasses and said, "Not bad. Not bad at all. For a gorilla, anyway."

As I was on my way back into the storeroom with my tools, I heard Signor Fidardo muttering to himself behind my back: "Not bad for a craftsman, either. I'll be damned. . . ."

~

As soon as I went down to the workshop the following morning Signor Fidardo wanted to talk to me.

"I've been thinking," he said. "And I've a proposal to make to you."

The proposal was that I should start helping him in his workshop. I was to sweep the floor twice a day, dust all the shelves and tables every evening and take rubbish out to the yard whenever necessary. I would also be responsible for ensuring that his knives, scrapers and chisels were kept as sharp as razor blades. That last point was a matter of honor, he added.

"In return for all that," Signor Fidardo said, "you may take whatever you need to renovate your accordion from my workshop. There are a great many things needed, everything from nails to Circassian walnut—I think you've already worked that out. Well now, are we agreed?"

I was just about to offer him my hand when I remembered how afraid Signor Fidardo was of getting dirty, so I nodded instead.

~

The working day in Signor Fidardo's workshop followed a strict routine. That suited me. That's the way it is at sea too.

Six days a week at precisely half past six, Signor Fidardo stepped out onto the street in his white suit and walked round the corner to the Café Nova Goa on Rua do Salvador to take his morning coffee. Half an hour later he had changed into his working clothes and was in his work-shop. By that time I was usually already hard at work in the storeroom.

We worked until nine o'clock, when Signor Fidardo made porridge for us in the pantry behind the workshop. Our breakfast break lasted twenty minutes, after which we worked until one o'clock. Then Signor Fidardo changed into his suit again and walked to one of the small inns in the neighborhood for lunch. I stayed behind and ate sandwiches I had made up in Ana's room before coming to work.

On his way back from lunch Signor Fidardo would smoke a Partagas Aristocrats cigar in the park. Then it was time for his siesta on a bunk in the pantry. I soon discovered that he actually changed into pajamas for his lunchtime nap: his pajamas were light blue, and the trousers were ironed so there was a crease in them.

I tidied up the workshop and sharpened his knives and chisels while he was asleep. He woke up at three o'clock and put on his working clothes again.

Five hours later Signor Fidardo laid down his tools and took a bottle labeled CAMPARI off one of the shelves. He poured himself a small drink and drank it slowly and silently while sitting at his workbench. I had a glass of milk.

By this time it was past eight and we turned out the lights and shut up the workshop for the night. Signor Fidardo went out into the city to have dinner, and I went upstairs to Ana's and waited for her to return from the shoe factory. That was the end of the working day.

~

I enjoyed working in Signor Fidardo's workshop, and the days flashed past.

But the nights were endless. I lay awake and missed the Chief so much that my eyes stung. If the night was dark and cloudy I would often slip out of the window and try to exhaust myself climbing across the roofs of Alfama. Sometimes it worked and I would fall asleep on the sofa when I went back in. For the most part, however, I was still awake when Ana's alarm clock went off at dawn.

I think it was my work on the red accordion that saved me from being driven mad by grief, though my main hope was still to find a way to save the Chief.

~

Sunday was our only day off. For a long time I had no idea what Signor Fidardo did with his free day, but Ana told me one day.

"On Sundays, Luigi plays the organ for the dead," she said. Then she explained: "He puts on his black suit—he actually does have one!—at ten o'clock every Sunday, and he takes the tram out to the cemetery in Prazeres. There he plays the harmonium for the funeral masses in the cemetery chapel. He's been doing it for many, many years. It's the only place he performs publicly. He likes to say that when a really talented musician plays, the audience weeps. His audience always weeps."

We had dinner with Signor Fidardo every Sunday night, and after dinner he and Ana played and sang together. That was the high point of my week.

It finished badly one Sunday, though. Jorge had spent the night at Ana's place the night before, and Ana had an ugly bruise under one eye. She usually managed to hide any mark left by Jorge's fists, but this time there was no way of hiding it. It was there on her face for all to see.

Ana was nervous when it was time for Signor Fidardo to arrive. She kept looking in the mirror and powdering her cheeks until they were almost white. It didn't help. I saw how Signor Fidardo tensed as he entered the room and the lamp shone on Ana's cheek. He put down the flowers, the wine and the pastries he had brought. Ana tried to behave as if nothing was the matter and said how beautiful the bouquet was as she looked for a vase to put the flowers in.

"Was it Jorge who did that?" Signor Fidardo asked. His voice was different somehow. He sounded as if he was choking something back.

"It was an accident," she said. "He didn't mean to. Sit down now; we're having risotto and sausages tonight."

Signor Fidardo sat down. I could see that his hands were trembling.

"What sort of accident?" he said.

"Dear Luigi, it's nothing for you to worry about. Can't we talk about something else?"

I could tell from her voice that she was close to tears.

"You have to leave him, Ana," Signor Fidardo said in a dull voice. "He hits you. People don't hit those they love. *Jorge è un maiale. He is a swine.*"

Tears began to trickle down Ana's cheeks, and she asked Signor Fidardo to leave.

Signor Fidardo gave me a quick look before he left. I don't know whether I imagined it, but I think it was a look of disappointment. Perhaps he thought that I ought to be protecting Ana from Jorge. After all, I did live with her.

And there was a sense in which I agreed with him. There were times when I wanted to give Jorge a thrashing and send him away for good. But I never fight. I don't dare to, because I know how strong I am.

CHAPTER 17
The Werewolf on Rua de São Tomé

The weeks passed. The arrival of spring could be felt in the Lisbon air. Looking out of the window on the stairs I could see the delicate little leaves on the chestnut trees in the small park.

By then the work of mending the red accordion was progressing well. I had the materials and I had the tools. I also had the time, because it didn't take me very long to deal with my daily tasks in Signor Fidardo's workshop.

When I went down to the workshop in the morning I often noticed that the things on my workbench were not lying exactly as I had left them. I realized that Signor Fidardo was following my work even though he did not say anything. Not until he noticed that I was stuck, or that I was about to make a serious mistake.

Then he might exclaim: "*Mio Dio!* The bone glue must be allowed to harden for at least three weeks before you start brushing linseed oil on the cabinet. Even a gorilla should be able to understand that!"

The more I learned about making instruments, the more I admired Signor Fidardo's professional skill. He was not just a very talented craftsman, he also invented and constructed new tools. His collection contained dozens of specially sharpened planes and chisels, vises that could hold pieces of work firmly in place at every possible angle and a tool that drilled, countersank and screwed simultaneously. He seemed to enjoy explaining to me how each of these inventions worked, and I was allowed to borrow them whenever I needed them. The only one of his tools I was forbidden to use was the electric pillar drill.

"I paid a fortune for that," he said. "What would the insurance company say if I let a gorilla borrow it?"

One morning Signor Fidardo's fine pillar drill began to give off a smell of burning and to shower sparks in all directions. Signor Fidardo may have been a master instrument maker, but he had no idea at all about electric motors. He telephoned an electrician's shop in the neighborhood, and they could not send out an electrician until the afternoon.

"Don't touch my things while I'm away," Signor Fidardo said before he set off for the harbor to inspect a consignment of Honduras mahogany which had just arrived by ship from New Orleans.

The moment he was out the door I couldn't resist the temptation to take a closer look at the broken drill.

He came back in a bad mood a couple of hours later. The wood had not been up to standard, and it had also been too expensive. His mood became even worse when the electrician failed to turn up at the agreed time. In fact, Senhor Rosso, as the repairer was called, did not arrive until just after five o'clock, by which time Signor Fidardo had been unable to use his drill all day and was extremely annoyed.

"I would imagine the motor overheated," Senhor Rosso said when Signor Fidardo told him about the smell and the sparks. "There may be something wrong with the ventilation, or it may be something to do with the bearings. Let's take a look."

Senhor Rosso examined the machine and then switched it on. Everything was in order.

"Now, that really is strange!" Signor Fidardo exclaimed.

"Not really," Senhor Rosso said. "Someone has already fixed the problem. The bearings have recently been greased, and the ventilation holes have been cleaned out. You didn't need to send for me, Signor Fidardo."

Once the electrician had left, Signor Fidardo stood staring at the pillar drill and then, all of a sudden, it dawned on him. He turned in my direction and his ears suddenly flushed as red as portside lanterns on a ship. He gave me a severe dressing-down, mainly because I'd made him look ridiculous in the eyes of Senhor Rosso. Eventually he calmed down.

"But as a punishment," he said, "from now on it will be your job to make sure that the drill is always in perfect working order. And if you behave yourself I may even allow you to use it now and again."

~

I can remember being in a good mood when I went up to Ana's that evening. Tinkering with the electric drill had been good fun, in addition to which I had also put the eighth and final coat of varnish on my accordion. It shone like a mirror now, and the next day I was going to get started on making new bellows. I was looking forward to that!

Ana was not home from work yet, so I laid the table for supper and sat down under the blanket on the sofa to wait for her. I must have been tired, because I fell asleep immediately.

When I opened my eyes the full moon was shining in through the window and the clock on the wall said it was a quarter past ten. Ana was over an hour late. That didn't worry me, because they worked in shifts at the shoe factory and the woman who was due to take over from Ana sometimes arrived late. Ana would arrive home any time now.

I fell asleep again, and when I next woke it was with a start. I could hear footsteps on the stairs outside the door.

It took me a few seconds to realize that it wasn't Ana. The footsteps were slow and heavy, and the moment the door handle began turning I remembered I had forgotten to lock myself in. I was at the point of rushing out of the window, but it was too late. The door flew open, and I was still sitting on the sofa with the blanket pulled up to my chin.

It was Jorge. He slammed the door behind him and staggered into the room, exhaling a sharp, stale odor of wine. He opened his eyes wide, trying to see in the darkness.

"G'evening, Ana," he slurred when he caught sight of me. "You been waiting for me? An' you got the table laid. But where the food? Where the wine?"

The moonlight meant that Jorge could only see me as a black silhouette against the window. I remained motionless.

My thoughts stood still too, and I had no idea at all what to do.

"Say somefing, then, woman!" Jorge roared. "Don't jist sit there. Give us some light and get a move on!"

When he didn't receive an answer, Jorge took a step forward and raised his fist threateningly. Then he suddenly froze.

"Ana . . . ?" he said hesitantly, leaning toward me.

And now he saw my face, and our eyes met. I drew back my lips and showed my teeth.

Jorge did not scream he didn't seem to have enough breath to do so. Making a whining noise he stumbled backward, turned round and rushed out the door. I heard him crashing into the walls as he ran down the stairs.

It took me a little while to collect my thoughts. When I realized what had just happened, I hurried to open the attic window. The draft from the window and open door quickly cleared away the unpleasant smell of Jorge's breath.

When Ana arrived home half an hour later the light over the table was on and the water for the rice was just coming to the boil on the stove. I was sitting on the sofa playing a game of solitaire.

"Sorry I'm so late," Ana said, putting down her shopping bag on the worktop. "You haven't been worried, I hope?"

I shook my head.

～

Jorge never came to visit Ana again after that night. She could not understand why. If she tried ringing him from the call box, he would just put down the receiver. When she went to see him to find out what was happening, he wouldn't open the door. She heard from his workplace that he was on sick leave—something to do with his nerves. He did not answer a single one of the possibly hundreds of letters she sent him. Without any explanation he disappeared completely and permanently from her life.

Grief over her lost love made Ana ill, and it was my turn to look after her now, just as she had looked after me when I was unhappy. I had to wake her every morning and bring her breakfast on a tray to make her rise and get ready for work.

It was dreadful to watch her suffering, and my conscience troubled me. On many occasions I was on the point of writing down what had happened that night so she would know. But I didn't.

～

The only one to learn what had actually happened was Signor Fidardo. He bumped into Jorge on the tram by chance. Jorge had lost a lot of weight and was pale; his eyes, which had once been harsh and self-confident, were now anxious and evasive.

"I must warn you, Signor Fidardo," he said in a whisper, "that you may be in great danger. You live in the same house as Ana Molina, don't you? Beware of her! Particularly when there is a full moon. She changes into . . . into a *werewolf*! I've seen it with my own eyes. *Terrifying! Terrifying!* You mustn't tell anyone about it or people will think I've gone mad. But I haven't . . . I haven't . . . !"

Jorge got off the tram and disappeared into the crowd at the Rossio Square tram stop.

Signor Fidardo had a broad smile on his face when he told me about meeting Jorge. In fact, he actually laughed out loud.

"I'm not so stupid that I can't work out more or less what happened. You did well there, really well! Thank you, I'm grateful, Sally Jones!"

It was the first time I had ever heard Signor Fidardo use my name.

CHAPTER 18
The Present

Once upon a time I was in love with an orangutan called Baba. He deserted me, so I know what it's like to be lovelorn. I know that it feels like it will never end. But it does usually. And it did even in Ana's case.

It took some months, though. She worked all day and wept all night. And she did not sing a note the whole time.

Signor Fidardo wasn't particularly concerned about

115

Ana being lovelorn, but he was very anxious about her not singing.

"It's so typical," he said gloomily. "She's finally got rid of that music hater Jorge and now she's stopped singing!"

But Signor Fidardo need not have worried. Once her grief at losing Jorge passed, Ana began singing again, and if anything she sang more beautifully than before. Her voice had become stronger and lighter at the same time.

Signor Fidardo immediately began nagging her to perform in public, and she continued to say no. But it was a different sort of no now—a no that did not sound quite so definite.

~

My red accordion was almost finished. I had made completely new bellows from kidskin. I had built a new cabinet on the bass side, and almost all of the base and the descant mechanism was new. I had rubbed down, painted and varnished all the wooden parts, and the instrument sparkled like a red ruby when the sun shone on the hard lacquer.

The only thing left to do was to cut a new grill from a sheet of thin brass. Signor Fidardo took a big, heavy book down from one of the shelves in his workshop and placed it on my workbench.

"I was given this book many years ago by my uncle. I had

it with me in my knapsack when I came from Italy almost fifty years ago. It is still the best collection of patterns for accordion grills that has ever been gathered together. Choose whichever pattern you think is most beautiful, and then use carbon paper to transfer it to the sheet of brass."

Three days later I had chosen my pattern and copied it onto the brass. It took me another week to saw out the pattern using Signor Fidardo's jeweler's saw. Late one evening I drilled nail holes and, using the smallest size of brass nail, attached the grill to the cabinet of the accordion.

The accordion was finished.

Not completely, however. Something was still missing, and I knew what it was.

Signor Fidardo's book contained several pages of elegant lettering. I copied the letters I needed and cut them out of a piece of brass that was leftover. Once the letters had been filed and polished, I used a chisel of razor sharpness to carefully inlay them on the front of the cabinet.

Now my accordion bore the name KOSKELA in gleaming yellow brass.

~

Signor Fidardo tuned the accordion that evening. He carefully filed each of the reed tongues until it was perfectly in tune. There are many reeds in an accordion, and he didn't finish until Ana came home from work. He invited her in and produced a bottle of Campari.

"We must celebrate," he said. "That's what we always do when an apprentice finishes his first piece of work."

Ana and Signor Fidardo stood there admiring my accordion for a long time. I felt very proud.

"I hadn't realized that it was Koskela who was going to get the accordion," Ana said, and smiled at me.

"Nor did I," Signor Fidardo said. "But we should have known. It's impossible to think of a better present for a man who is locked up."

Then Signor Fidardo played the accordion to test it, and Ana sang fado along with him. It sounded wonderful.

~

The following day Signor Fidardo took me up to the second floor, which was where he had his store. There were sheets of expensive veneers leaning against one wall and, on the shelves above, timber was arranged according to variety and quality. The shelves on the opposite wall were full of musical instruments, some of them in cases with handles and reinforced corners, others wrapped in soft cloth. There were also two harmoniums and a shining bass tuba.

Signor Fidardo took down one of the empty cases. It looked brand-new and had chrome-plated latches and a leather handle. The inside was lined with soft blue velvet to protect the instrument from scratches and dust.

"This case will be perfect for Koskela's accordion!" Signor Fidardo said. "We can't send off such a fine instrument in an ordinary cardboard box!"

That evening Ana wrote a long letter to the Chief. She explained that the accordion was from me, and she told him about my work in Signor Fidardo's workshop. We put the letter in the case along with the accordion, and the next morning we dispatched it all to the Campolide prison. I would, of course, have preferred to visit the Chief and give him the present myself, but that wasn't possible. Prisoners who had been found guilty of murder were only permitted to have visits from their lawyers and from close relatives.

Two weeks went by and I was beginning to worry whether the accordion had reached the Chief or whether it had been confiscated by the prison warders. But then a small gray envelope arrived in the post for Ana. We knew immediately who it was from. Ana opened it and read:

Dear Mrs. Ana Molina,

I have received the beautiful accordion and your kind letter, which I have read many times. You have a heart of pure gold. I know now that my engineer Sally Jones is being well looked-after while I am in

jail. Let me tell you how much easier that makes it
for me to endure my own misfortune.

Give Sally Jones my love. The accordion is very
fine indeed. I have never seen a better one, and I
shall make sure I learn to play, even though there
are heaven knows how many little buttons to learn. I
shall practice every day until I am released from this
godforsaken place.

Yours respectfully,
H. Koskela

The Chief's letter made me happier than I'd been for a
long time. He sounded more like himself than in his previ-
ous letter, and Ana too noticed the difference.

"Your friend doesn't seem to have lost hope," she said.

~

Life was rather empty now that I'd finished the Chief's
accordion. I suddenly had nothing to do during the day.

Signor Fidardo came up with a solution: "Two accordions have just come in for repair. One of them needs the bellows patched and the other needs new straps. Which would
you prefer to do?"

I chose the straps. Working with leather is enjoyable.

The following day Signor Fidardo ordered a new work-bench for me. It was identical to his own, with drawers and pigeonholes, a vise mounted on the side, a tool rack and a leather-padded seat that could be adjusted for height. He rearranged the furniture to make space for the new bench in front of one of the tall light windows.

"There we are," he said when he had finished. "We can't have an instrument maker's apprentice working in a cupboard!"

I was a little hesitant at first. Up until that point no one outside the house—except the Chief, that is—had known I was living there. If I moved out of the cupboard and occupied a place by the window, our secret would be revealed. What would all those horrible people who had called me the murderer's gorilla think about me working for Signor Fidardo? What if they set the police on me? What if they turned on Signor Fidardo?

Signor Fidardo understood my concerns.

"Alfama is the kind of place that considers a seagull doing its business on the bishop's hat to be a real scandal. The people here just love a fuss. They'll talk and gossip about it for a couple of days when they hear that you are working with me. But they'll soon get tired of it and start gossiping about something else instead. Wait and see, believe me."

So I relied on Signor Fidardo, and it turned out exactly as he had said it would. The rumor that he had taken a gorilla as his apprentice spread through Alfama like wildfire. Lots of people found an excuse to visit the workshop to see if the rumor was true. There was often a crowd on the pavement outside my window. But after a couple of weeks people stopped standing out there staring in to watch me working.

Signor Fidardo also started sending me out on small errands round the neighborhood. I collected parcels from the post office and bought cigars at Widow Pereira's tobacconist shop. Sometimes Signor Fidardo even took me to lunch at a restaurant. People said hello to me just as they did to anyone else. No one seemed to remember all that business about *the murderer's gorilla* any longer.

CHAPTER 19
The Grave of Elisa Gomes

Summer had arrived, and the heat was oppressive. During the hours round noon Alfama came to a virtual standstill. The scorching, bright white light of the sun shone down from an unchanging blue sky, and people sought shelter indoors, shutters closed to keep out the heat. Not until evening did the city come to life again. Then the shops reopened and the stallholders on the streets began selling again. Cars, horse-drawn carts and trams pushed their way through the crowded narrow streets.

Bars and taverns began filling up a couple of hours before midnight. Fado music drifted out into the night through open doors. In even the smallest and pokiest little places, the sounds of guitars could be heard, accompanying the singing of melancholy songs about love and sorrow and bittersweet longing. Signor Fidardo was trying to coax Ana to start performing, and consequently he invited her out whenever he knew a talented fado singer was appearing in the neighborhood. I was allowed to accompany them. We heard many fine singers, but none of them had a voice with the spirit and emotional depth of Ana's. That, of course, was what Signor Fidardo was hoping Ana would come to understand.

And eventually she gave in. She promised to accompany Signor Fidardo to Prazeres one Sunday and to sing when he played the organ at the funeral mass. She was nervous for several days beforehand, but there was no reason why she should have been. All those present were entranced by her singing, and even the gravediggers outside the chapel shed a tear.

The following Sunday Ana went again and sang at another funeral.

And the Sunday after that.

Reports of her voice spread round Lisbon. People went out to Prazeres and attended the funerals of total strangers just to hear Ana sing. There were some who said it would be worth being buried themselves just to hear Ana Molina sing.

I used to go with them to Prazeres on Sundays, though I stayed away from the funerals. A gorilla in overalls is hardly proper at occasions of that kind. Instead, I would wander round the cemetery on my own, and strangely enough, I enjoyed it there even though it was a rather creepy place. The raked gravel paths were lined with rows of white mausoleums that resembled small palaces or churches. They had wrought-iron gates in front of the doors and stone crosses on top of the gable ends. It was a whole city for the dead, an enormous labyrinth of one street after another.

I often got lost on my walks round Prazeres Cemetery, and that is how I first came upon the grave of Elisa Gomes. I ended up in a secluded corner I'd never visited before. The people buried here had obviously been unable to afford great monuments and marble edifices. The graves were marked with iron crosses or simple granite stones. I came to a stop at an ill-kept grave covered with weeds and dead leaves. It had a painted enamel portrait of a young woman set into the mossy gravestone and I immediately had a feeling I had seen her before, though I couldn't remember where.

Since I was already late and knew that Ana and Signor Fidardo would be waiting for me at the chapel, I didn't have time to think about it then, but late that evening, before going to sleep, the memory suddenly came to me. I rose quietly, tiptoed over to my overalls and fished in the pocket. There was the silver locket that Alphonse Morro had worn on a chain round his neck and dropped on the quayside before falling into the river. I took out the locket, opened it and studied the miniature portrait of Morro's fiancée. She was very like the girl on the gravestone.

The following Sunday I went back to the mossy gravestone with its enamel portrait. I took out the locket and compared the pictures.

There could be no doubt about it. They were two pictures of the same girl.

According to the inscription on the gravestone she was called Elisa Gomes and she had died four years earlier at the very young age of twenty-three. Why had she died so young? The gravestone offered no clue, but I shuddered— perhaps Alphonse Morro had murdered her? He had certainly been a rogue, no doubt of that. I still had nightmares when I remembered the time he pointed his pistol at the Chief's chest.

I thought I'd made an important discovery, although

even to myself I couldn't explain why it was important. It was just a feeling.

I brushed away the leaves from the grave and stood for a while looking at the portrait of the dead girl. No one seemed to be mourning her anymore.

~

It became a habit for me to visit Elisa Gomes's grave every Sunday. I kept it clean, clearing away leaves and twigs and scraping off the moss and lichen that grew on the gravestone. And gradually I got to know the cemetery caretaker. His name was João, and he was a strange fellow. Not in a bad way, though—quite the opposite.

When I meet people for the first time, almost everyone treats me as a gorilla. That's only to be expected: after all, I am a gorilla. People usually assume that someone must have trained me to wear human clothes, in the same way bears in circuses have been trained to walk on their hind legs and parrots can be trained to swear. There are not many people who realize that I can think thoughts of my own and understand what people are saying. Not until they get to know me, that is.

But with João it was different. He came up to me one day when I was pulling out thistles in front of Elisa Gomes's grave. When I turned round so that he could see my face he didn't even blink. He simply asked in a friendly way whether I'd like to borrow a hoe and a spade.

I nodded and he fetched the tools. Then he carried on chatting to me as if I were an old acquaintance. He didn't appear to find anything strange or unusual about a gorilla tending a grave.

"It's nice that someone is tidying up this grave," he said. "I've often thought about doing it myself. For Elisa's sake— she was murdered, you know, poor girl. In one sense it was an accident, I suppose. You know the story, I expect?"

I shook my head.

"You don't?" João said. "I'll tell you, then. It was like this: Elisa Gomes used to work as a housemaid for a rich banker in Chiado. His name was Carvalho, if I remember rightly. Well, a parcel for the banker came in the post one day, and Elisa took it in. Just as she was about to put the parcel in the banker's study, it blew up. Sky-high! It was a bomb sent by anarchists who wanted to kill the banker. The banker . . . well, he survived, of course. The only one killed was poor Elisa. And she was little more than a child."

João looked really sad. He sighed deeply before continuing.

"Elisa had no family or, put it this way, I've never seen anyone visiting her grave. Apart from her fiancé, a fellow called Morro. He was the one who paid for the grave, though he was just as young and just as poor as she was. He was beside himself with grief. It broke my heart to see him, just broke my heart."

João blew his nose hard and wiped a tear from the corner of his eye.

"He came here almost every day for three years, Morro did. He wasn't one for talking, so I didn't get to know him. But he made sure that Elisa's grave was the nicest and best tended in the whole cemetery. Sometimes he brought flowers—always yellow carnations. One day he just suddenly stopped coming. That must have been about a year ago, and no one has seen a sign of him since. Someone said he'd been murdered too, that a drunken seaman had killed him. Apparently there was something about it in the papers. I don't know if it's true. But he must be dead, Morro must, otherwise he wouldn't have left Elisa's grave to go like that."

A large tear ran down João's cheek.

"Sorry about this," he said with a slight sob. "It's all so sad."

We stood together in silence for a while. Then João went off about his business after telling me where to put the hoe and the spade when I'd finished with them.

I felt downcast and regretful. Up until now I'd thought of Alphonse Morro as a rogue, but now I suddenly remembered how troubled he'd looked that evening at O Pelicano when he came over to the Chief and me. Was it sadness and longing for Elisa I had seen in his eyes?

My thoughts then jumped to what João had just told me about the bomb that killed Elisa Gomes, that it was anarchists who were behind her murder. The newspaper had said that Chief Inspector Garretta believed the Chief was one of those anarchists.

Was it just a coincidence?

Or was it all linked in some way?

And if so, how?

CHAPTER 20
Nights at the Tamarind

The heat continued right through until the middle of October, when the first real rains of autumn arrived and washed away the dust of summer. The drains over-flowed, and the gutters were full of mud. The river turned a grayish brown.

One day I realized that exactly a year had passed since the sinking of the *Hudson Queen* and the arrest of the Chief.

It all seemed so long ago, so dreadfully long ago. But it was just one year. What was twenty-five years going to feel like?

The thought of that made me so sad that for weeks I lost all desire to work. Signor Fidardo noticed it, of course, which is why he gave me the job of renovating a musette accordion the French ambassador in Lisbon had brought in. The ambassador was very attached to his instrument, and Signor Fidardo had to promise to do the work himself.

"Don't let me down now, Sally Jones," Signor Fidardo said. "I'm relying on you to do a first-class job on the ambassador's accordion; otherwise I shall be in trouble."

Signor Fidardo knew what he was doing. I was forced to pull myself together and after just a couple of days I was back in the swing of working in the workshop. Depression gradually eased its hold on me.

~

At about this time Ana started performing one night a week at the Tamarind, a fado restaurant on Rua de São Miguel. The owner of the restaurant hired Ana after hearing her sing at his aunt's funeral at the cemetery in Prazeres.

Saturday nights were Ana's nights at the Tamarind. Signor Fidardo and I always went to listen to her: Ana had made that a condition before agreeing to perform on the stage. If we were there it felt like an ordinary Sunday round the kitchen table at home—that's what she said, anyway.

As time passed Ana became more and more sure of herself and of her audiences too. Quite soon she no longer needed me and Signor Fidardo to be there for her to feel safe. We kept going, however, because no one gets tired of hearing Ana sing.

Signor Fidardo and I had our regular table in a corner close to the stage. Ana had arranged it, and it was lucky she had done so because the little place was always full when Ana was performing. All the tables were booked weeks in advance, which is why the owner of the Tamarind began opening the windows and putting chairs out on the pavement so that people could sit outside and listen. Very soon there weren't enough chairs, and someone came up with the bright idea of bringing his own chair. After that more and more people brought their own chairs every Saturday and found space for themselves on the street. The people in the immediate neighborhood dragged sofas and armchairs into the street, and eventually Rua de São Miguel became so overcrowded that the police thought it advisable to ban cars from the street on Saturday nights. That meant that the constables themselves had a chance to stay and listen, which they did.

Santos, the director of the shoe factory, was very fond of fado. He had once heard Ana singing as she worked and he wanted to hear more. He tried several Saturdays in succession to get a table at the Tamarind, but they were always fully booked. Eventually he got tired of trying and called Ana to his office:

"Miss Molina," he said. "From now on you can have a paid day off on Saturdays, but only on the condition that you sing at the Tamarind on Friday nights as well. That way I might have a chance to get a table now and again!"

Ana's name spread all over Lisbon, not just Alfama. When she was out in the city, strangers would come up to her to shake her hand and make appreciative comments. She even had a secret admirer, who wrote several times a week to tell her how much her singing meant to him. Ana called her secret admirer Canson because that was the brand of writing paper he used. She had no idea who he actually was.

Signor Fidardo was very happy about Ana's success. More than once I heard him say proudly, "What was it I said!" Ana herself took her success in stride. She carried on living as before, working during the day and darning socks in the evening.

But things weren't exactly as they had been before. Thanks to Santos she now had Saturdays free, and she took me on little trips round Lisbon. We sometimes caught the train to Cascais or Estoril and walked along the beach. At other times we took the boat over the river to Barreiro, but most often we went by tram to Jardim Botânico, the Lisbon botanical garden, where we walked on the sandy paths beneath the tall trees.

Ana was quite quiet during our excursions. It didn't matter to me, because it wasn't a sad silence. I think she just needed to have a rest from her own voice.

CHAPTER 21
The Hill Behind the Prison

The days were becoming shorter and shorter. The leaves on the chestnut trees in the park by our house were turning yellow, and soon they were whirling along the tramlines, driven by the biting winds blowing along Rua de São Tomé. One area of low pressure after another rolled in from the Atlantic, bringing cold mists and weeks of rain. I had to light Signor Fidardo's stove several times a day to prevent his precious store of veneers being affected by damp. Winter had come again to Lisbon.

My life with Ana and Signor Fidardo had become everyday life. A good everyday life. I was beginning to get used to the idea that my home was now with them. But I missed the Chief every single day and wished so much that there was some way for me to visit him in prison.

I wrote to him sometimes and he wrote back. Neither of us was a great letter writer, so they were pretty brief notes.

One day we received a letter from the Chief that was different from anything he had written earlier.

Dear Mrs. Ana Molina,

I would like to ask you to do something for me, even though I know I am already in great debt to you. From the window of my cell I can see a hill with two small trees by a vacant lot. If you were to take Sally Jones to that hill I could show her something that I think would please her.

The hill is by the northwest corner of the prison. I shall watch out for you every evening after seven o'clock.

Yours respectfully,
H. Koskela

I read the letter several times, feeling stranger each time I did so. The chance to see the Chief ought to have made me unbelievably happy, and, of course, I was happy, but at the same time I was nervous, perhaps even a little afraid. What would the Chief look like after a whole year in prison? What if he was ill or troubled? What if I didn't recognize him?

Ana noticed how anxious I was.

"Of course we'll go," she said. "It will have to be Sunday evening. I'm busy all the other evenings. I'll find out the train times."

She put her hand on mine and added, "Everything will be fine. I'm sure of that."

This was on a Wednesday and the days that followed were very long. Not to mention the nights—I hardly slept a wink, and by the time Sunday came I was so nervous I couldn't even eat.

On Sunday morning Ana and Signor Fidardo played and sang as usual in the chapel at Prazeres Cemetery. While they were doing so, I tidied Elisa Gomes's grave and helped João rake paths and pull up weeds. I gave him a hand whenever I was there. It helped to pass the time, and João seemed to appreciate my company. He would tell me how the people buried there had died, and there were some horrific tales of murders and strange accidents. He would often frighten himself so much that his voice trembled. But he couldn't tell me any more about Elisa Gomes.

When we arrived back at home it was time for Ana and me to set off for Campolide. Ana was a bit annoyed because I had made my overalls dirty when I was doing the weeding with João. She had washed and ironed the overalls the day before.

"I want your friend Koskela to see that I'm looking after you properly," she explained.

We took the tram to Rossio Station and then got a train for Sintra. I had never been to Rossio Station before. It was big—eight tracks under a high vaulted roof of glass and steel. Messengers, porters and travelers were bustling round the platforms. I breathed in the smell of coal and smoke and listened to the hiss of steam from the great black locomotives. It made me feel at home and calmed my worries for a while.

We found seats in a compartment and watched the platform slide past as the train drew out of the station. Then it entered a tunnel, and for a good ten minutes we saw nothing but our own reflections in the window, lit by the weak light of the electric lamp on the ceiling.

When we came out of the tunnel the conductor

announced that the next station was Campolide. We got off there. Ana asked the stationmaster the way to the prison and we set off on foot.

We were outside the city, but we weren't really out in the country. The people here were poor people who lived in small low houses by the side of the dusty sand roads. Children with sunken eyes stared at us out of dark windows, and scraggy goats were grazing here and there.

We did not have to walk long before the prison loomed a little farther down the road. I had imagined it to be an ugly and depressing brick building surrounded by a high wall topped with barbed wire. And that is more or less exactly what it was like.

We had no trouble finding the small hill the Chief had described, although it took us a while to get there, since we had to walk all the way round the prison. We arrived just before seven o'clock. The clouds were low and blustery, and there was a light drizzle. The prison seemed to be almost deserted, and only a few windows on the ground floor had lights in them. As far as we could see, the prisoners' cells occupied the two upper floors—they had no windows, only small black apertures with bars.

A quarter of an hour went by, and the rain was growing heavier. Then suddenly I caught a glimpse of a face behind the bars of one of the slits on the top floor. A hand poked out and waved to us. My heart leapt and I waved back with both arms above my head. Ana waved too.

The hand disappeared inside, and there was a short delay. Something moved in the darkness behind the bars.

Then we heard sounds—the tentative sounds of a small accordion.

It was playing a favorite little tune I had often heard the Chief humming. It was a Finnish tune and a very sad one. The Chief played several verses of it. At first there were a few mistakes, and I thought it sounded as if he was swearing behind the bars, but then it just grew better and better, and he played the final verses loud and clear and full of spirit. It sounded wonderful. I saw the glint of a tear on Ana's cheek.

After the accordion fell silent we could hear some shouts of approval from the adjoining cells, and Ana and I clapped our hands. We heard the desolate echo of our claps bounce back from the high wall of the prison.

Then Ana began to sing.

She sang a Portuguese melody very similar to the tune the Chief had played. It was sad but still filled with tranquil joy. One by one pale faces began to appear in the small windows of the cells, and rough hands gripped the bars.

The windows on the ground floor opened, and the warders looked out. The whole prison was listening. Even the massive brick building seemed to be listening in wonder.

When the last notes of Ana's song died away, there was absolute silence for a few moments. Then the applause broke out, and it seemed it would never stop.

The Chief and I waved to one another again and carried on waving until Ana gently laid a hand on my shoulder. It was time for us to go or we would miss the last train back to the city.

~

During the year that followed Ana and I would go to the hill behind the prison a few Sunday evenings a month. Every time we went there the Chief had learned a new tune on the accordion, and every time Ana would sing a song to him and the other prisoners.

Our visits meant a great deal to the Chief. More than I understood at the time. Life in the prison was harsh and dangerous. The warders were brutal men, and most of the prisoners were dreadful criminals. But however hard and dreadful they were, all of them wanted to hear Ana Molina sing, which is why they made sure that the Chief stayed alive and was allowed to keep his accordion.

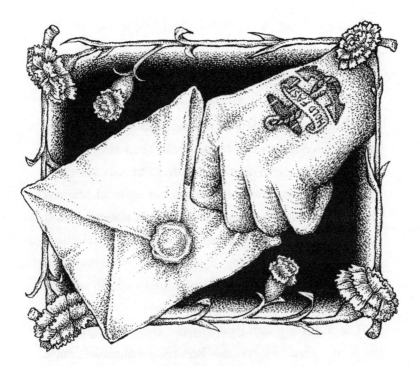

CHAPTER 22
A Greeting from the Other Side

Spring came, bringing with it high pressure and dry winds. At the end of March I finished the French ambassador's musette accordion. The ambassador was more than pleased, and he praised Signor Fidardo's unique craftsmanship.

"Don't let it go to your head," Signor Fidardo said to me in a rather sour tone after the French ambassador had left. "The French are hardly renowned for their knowledge of accordions. We'd have never pulled the wool over an Italian's eyes that easily."

The ambassador paid us handsomely for renovating his accordion. Signor Fidardo thought for a while and then gave some of the money to me. I did not usually receive any wages—Signor Fidardo gave them to Ana instead. I thought that was a good arrangement, since I did, after all, live with her. I didn't want to take the ambassador's money, but Signor Fidardo was stubborn.

"You have earned every cent," he said. "More than that, in fact. I'm sure you can find something nice to do with the money."

The following day I bought the two most expensive boxes of cigars from Widow Pereira's tobacconist's shop. One of them was for Signor Fidardo, and I wrapped the other one in a parcel and sent it by post to the Chief. For Ana I bought a very fine fountain pen for her to use when she wrote to her sister in Africa.

A little while later I gained pleasure from the money that was left. João suggested I should plant something pretty beside Elisa Gomes's grave. It was a good idea because even though the grave was now well cared for, it still looked rather bare and gloomy. Ana helped me choose a beautiful plant from the flower market held on Figueira Square every Saturday. It was a hibiscus with yellow flowers: João had told me that Alphonse Morro always brought yellow carnations for her grave, so I guessed that yellow had been Elisa's favorite color.

The next day I took the hibiscus with me on the tram when we went out to Prazeres Cemetery. When we arrived I went to the office to find João. He was sitting at his small desk drinking a cup of coffee. He gave me a glass of milk and then talked about this and that. We were just about to go to the toolshed to fetch a spade and some potting compost for the hibiscus when there was a knock on the door.

"Ahoy in there! Anyone at home?"

I saw at once that the man who entered was a seaman. He must have just returned from a long voyage in warm climes because he was suntanned and weather-beaten and his shore clothes still had a slight smell of mold. They had probably been stored away in a damp seaman's chest for months.

He did not introduce himself but simply pulled a folded envelope from his pocket and handed it to João.

"Here you are! I promised to deliver this envelope. I've had it with me all the way from the Far East, which is why it's got pretty crumpled."

João took the envelope from him and asked what was in it.

"No idea at all!" the seaman said. "I was given it by some fellow down in the south. He must have known my ship was on its way to Lisbon, and he asked me to bring the envelope and give it to the caretaker of this cemetery. He also gave me a bottle of gin for my trouble. Now I've carried out my side of the bargain, and I'm intending to catch the first tram back into the city, so goodbye to both of you!"

The seaman saluted us with his fingers to his forehead and marched off briskly.

João held the envelope in his hand for a while before looking for a paper knife on his untidy desk. He carefully opened the envelope and took out the contents.

There were two five-pound notes and a folded letter. João whistled—ten pounds was a great deal of money. He adjusted his glasses on his nose and opened the letter.

At first João furrowed his brow as if having difficulty reading something in a foreign language. Then I saw his face go pale, and he stared at the letter openmouthed. The rattle of the departing tram and the tinkling of its bell could be heard through the window.

When João did eventually look up there was fear in his eyes. His hand was shaking slightly as he passed the letter to me. I read it:

The enclosed money, while it lasts, should be used for the care of the last resting place of Elisa Gomes. Let yellow carnations flower upon her grave forever.

João believed in ghosts and was afraid of them. That, in fact, was why he had started working as caretaker of a cemetery. He had hoped that working among graves every day would cure him of his fear of ghosts. But it hadn't worked.

Cold sweat broke out on his forehead, and his lips lost their color.

"That," he said, pointing to the letter in my hand, "that is a message from *the other side*. From a ghost! He has no rest. . . ."

I didn't understand what João was talking about. Who had no rest? My head was spinning, but then, all of a sudden, I understood. It was like an electric shock running through my body.

Alphonse Morro! The letter must have been written by Alphonse Morro!

My heart pounded hard and fast.

Morro was alive!

The letter was proof!

My thoughts were tripping over one another. There was no time to waste . . . no time to waste! I rushed out of the office and ran toward the cemetery chapel.

I had to find Ana and Signor Fidardo.

The funeral service had just started in the chapel. Completely out of breath, I pressed my ear to the door: they had reached the confession of sins. I put my hand on the door handle intending to go in and interrupt the service, but I came to my senses in time and sat down to wait on the bench outside.

An hour later the mass was over. Once the priest and the mourners had accompanied the coffin to the newly dug grave, I took Ana and Signor Fidardo to the cemetery office.

It was a confused meeting. João was still shaken by the letter and wouldn't talk about anything but ghosts. Ana and Signor Fidardo had met João before, but they hardly knew him. Now, of course, they were wondering what on earth it was all about.

Once João had calmed down, all four of us went to Elisa Gomes's grave, where I took out Morro's silver locket and showed it to Ana and Signor Fidardo. Then João patiently told them the whole story, from Elisa Gomes's tragic death to the arrival of the letter containing the money the seaman had brought all the way from the Far East. Ana and Signor Fidardo had many questions, all of which João answered to the best of his ability.

Meanwhile it was getting late in the afternoon and the tall cypresses in the cemetery were throwing long shadows across the rows of gravestones and crosses. We said good-bye to João and walked toward the tram stop.

Ana was just as happy and eager as I was.

"The police never found Alphonse Morro's body," she said. "I remember that—it was in the paper. So Morro must have survived, in which case Koskela is innocent! We must show the letter to the police."

Signor Fidardo sighed.

"'We can certainly do that," he said. "But I'm afraid we shall be disappointed. The police are not likely to take us seriously."

Ana and I both looked at him.

"Why not?" she asked.

"In the first place," Signor Fidardo said, "the police are not going to want to hear that they've sent an innocent man to jail. In the second place, we cannot actually prove it was Alphonse Morro who wrote the letter and sent the money. Even we can't really be sure of that."

I wanted to protest. *I knew* it was Morro who had written the letter!

Signor Fidardo understood what I was thinking. He stopped and looked at me.

"I know how much you want Morro to be alive," he said. "And I'm not saying you are wrong. I am just saying that we must be prepared to find that the police will not be of any help at all. The opposite is more likely."

We walked on in silence.

"The sailor, then?" Ana said when we reached the tram

stop. "He should certainly be able to describe the man who gave him the letter. And be able to say where they met."

Signor Fidardo nodded.

"Yes, of course, you're quite right. But first of all we have to find him. How are we to do that?"

"Can't the police make inquiries?"

"We don't know his name, and we don't know which ship he works on," Signor Fidardo said. "There must be ten thousand seamen in Lisbon and most of them look more or less like the man João described to us. Even if the police agreed to put out a description, it would still be pointless."

The tram came round the corner and drew up at the stop. We climbed aboard, and Signor Fidardo paid for the tickets. On the journey back into the city I recognized what would have to be done.

I wished night would hurry up and come.

CHAPTER 23
The Far East

As soon as Ana had gone to sleep that night I carefully opened the dormer window and climbed out. I spent the next three nights and days searching for the sailor from the Prazeres Cemetery. I looked in every bar, every bordello and every low dive round Lisbon Harbor, all the way from Alcântara to Cais do Sodré and even farther eastward to Santa Apolónia. I visited every seaman's hostel in the city and every seaman's church. I walked the quays until my legs felt numb.

When I got back to Rua de São Tomé, Ana's eyes were red with weeping. She had been beside herself with worry about me. Signor Fidardo was angry and told me off very severely, but he understood why I had been away.

"Well now," he said once he had calmed down. "Did you find the sailor?"

I shook my head.

Then I lay down on the sofa and fell asleep.

The following day Ana took the morning off and went to the police station at Largo da Graça with the letter from Morro. She was very upset when she came home.

"They just laughed at me," she told us. "One of them lost his temper and told me the police don't have time for that sort of nonsense."

Signor Fidardo shook his head despondently and said, "It's just as I thought."

~

I lost all desire to work and lay on Ana's sofa brooding. Was Alphonse Morro really still alive, or was it just wishful thinking on my part? And if he was alive, how could I possibly find him? I swung back and forth between hope and despair without becoming any the wiser.

Signor Fidardo eventually came and fetched me down to the workshop.

"More jobs have come in for us. You'll have to brood and work at the same time! That's what I've been doing for fifty years, and it's worked perfectly well!"

Down in the workshop there was an accordion waiting for me. It had a rattle that needed fixing—it turned out to be caused by loose reed plates. I started mixing beeswax and resin to glue them firm.

Several weeks passed. I worked during the day and spent my nights roaming round the harbor in the hope of coming across the seaman from the cemetery.

There was no trace of him, and as time went by I gave up looking. Instead I began planning how I could stow away on a boat that would take me to the Far East so that I could track down Alphonse Morro myself. But the Far East is a big place, and it would be like trying to find a black peppercorn in a coal bunker. Traveling as a stowaway is always danger- ous, and the last time I did so very nearly led to disaster. I was prepared to risk it again, however, if I couldn't come up with a better solution.

Which I couldn't. But Ana could!

~

She woke me one morning before the alarm clock went off. Outside our window the only light was the gray light of dawn and the only sound the distant clatter of a milk cart bumping over the cobblestones of a narrow street. Ana had put on her dressing gown and her hair was sticking up on end. Her eyes were still bleary with sleep.

"I had a dream," she said, stifling a yawn. "About Alphonse Morro and Elisa Gomes. I think I have an idea."

She asked me to give her Morro's locket.

"It may be a bit of a long shot, but you never can tell," she said as she opened the locket.

She read the short poem that was written under the portrait of Elisa Gomes. Then she nodded to herself.

"This locket," she said, "may well have been the only thing Morro had to remember his Elisa by, and if he is alive he will certainly want it back. What if we could find a way of getting him to come fetch it?"

She looked at me and noticed I was looking disappointed.

"I'm sorry," she said. "I know it's not much of an idea. It seemed much better in my dream."

Every now and again during the course of the working day I thought about Ana's idea. It seemed pointless, but I couldn't help thinking about it. We had absolutely no idea where Alphonse Morro was, so how on earth were we to use the locket to bring him home?

Ana arrived home from the shoe factory a little earlier than usual that evening. I hadn't even had time to heat the water for the rice.

"I came as fast as I could," Ana said as she put down a paper bag smelling of sardines on the table. "I've had another idea!"

And instead of starting to cook the fish, Ana eagerly told me about her new idea.

"We'll send out small notices," she said. "We'll keep the writing short—just the little verse from the locket and our address. We'll have them nailed up in every port in the Far East, and if Alphonse Morro sees one of them he will realize that the message is for him. He'll also know that it means we have his locket here with us!"

Ana looked at me expectantly. I thought through what she had said. Notices. At harbor offices. And at seamen's hostels and bars. In every major port in the Far East.

Yes, it might work. Perhaps. But how were we to send out the notices?

The answer came to me immediately: Senhor Baptista!

Twenty minutes later Ana and I entered O Pelicano. As usual most of the occupants were seamen, sitting leaning on the tables with pipes in their mouths and small glasses of aguardiente before them. Senhor Baptista threw his arms wide in welcome when he caught sight of us. Since we lived in the same district, he and I had frequently met since that evening a year and a half before when I came to ask for his help. It was clear he was still a little ashamed of the way he had driven me away on that occasion. I hoped that would mean he was more helpful this time.

Senhor Baptista gave me a cup of milk and Ana a glass of wine while she explained our business. It took some time to tell the story of Elisa Gomes, the locket, the letter from the Far East and our idea about sending out notices. Senhor Baptista listened with an earnest air, and when Ana came to the reason for our visit he positively beamed.

"Of course I'll help you!" he said. "It will be my pleasure! Every sailor who passes through O Pelicano will take away a bundle of notices. And I'll tell them to stick up at least ten in every port they put into, from Djibouti in the west to Yokohama in the east. I guarantee it will be done! Sailors always come to the aid of a fellow seaman in need. Your message will be spread all over the Orient, you have my word!"

～

The light was still on in the workshop when we arrived back at our house. Signor Fidardo was busy with a complicated glue job that he had to complete before he could finish for the day.

Ana told him our plans and he listened skeptically, his brow furrowed. When Ana asked him what he thought he simply said, "It sounds very romantic."

Ana gave him a look of disappointment.

"So you don't think it stands much chance of succeeding?"

Signor Fidardo hesitated a little before answering. He gave me a worried look and then said, "No, to tell the truth I don't. If Alphonse Morro has moved to the other end of the world he is hardly going to move back just to get hold of a lost locket. And the chance of him seeing one of your notices seems pretty small anyway. That's always assuming he is still alive."

We stood there silently. With some reluctance I recognized that Signor Fidardo was probably right. Ana appeared to feel the same. It seemed to have knocked the spirit out of her. She said, "But we do have to try to do something, don't we? And we have nothing to lose."

Signor Fidardo nodded.

"I agree. And I know someone who might be able to help us with the notices. I'll talk to him tomorrow."

Then he turned to me.

"Just promise me you won't raise your hopes too high and assume that this is going to rescue your friend Koskela from prison. False hopes are worse than no hopes at all."

~

The following week a small printing firm in Bairro Alto delivered two thousand small notices packed in boxes.

The printer gave us an advantageous price because Signor Fidardo had tuned his rickety square piano every autumn for twenty years.

The lines of poetry from the locket were printed right in the middle of every sheet, and under the poem, in smaller letters, was the address of our house on Rua de São Tomé. That was all.

I carried the boxes down to O Pelicano, and Senhor Baptista immediately set about distributing the notices to any of his customers who would shortly be sailing for the East.

Then it was just a matter of waiting, and I knew that the wait would be a long one. It might take a whole year—indeed, it might take several years—for our message to reach Alphonse Morro. If it ever did.

~

Life in the house on Rua de São Tomé soon returned to its workaday routine. Our days were filled with everyday concerns and everyday joys.

Of course I often thought of Alphonse Morro and what else I could do to prove he wasn't dead. But however much I worried and pondered, I couldn't come up with anything new. In the end I was forced to accept I had done all I could, and that helped to put my mind at peace. I thought less and less about Morro and more about what was going on round me. But in the back of my mind I was still counting the days until we could assume that the first of the notices had reached the Far East.

CHAPTER 24
Fabulous Forzini

At the end of May, Lisbon was honored with a visit from a great star. His name was Giuseppe Forzini, and he came all the way from California in America, where he was called Fabulous Forzini.

Fabulous Forzini was an accordion virtuoso. It was said there was no one who could play ragtime and polkas faster than him. People all over the world wanted to see and hear him perform. The papers said he earned an unbelievable six hundred dollars a week when he was on tour, and he spent the money on fast cars, beautiful women, roulette and hand-stitched suits. That's what the papers said, anyway.

Fabulous Forzini was both an American and an Italian. In fact, he and Signor Fidardo came from the same part of the country—Calabria, in southern Italy. That was not a source of pride to Signor Fidardo—rather the opposite. The mere news that tickets for Fabulous Forzini's concert at the Teatro Maria Vitória sold out in less than an hour made him angry.

"People have no taste these days," he snorted. "Fabulous Forzini isn't a real musician, he's a poser! All technique and no real feeling. And he plays a *piano accordion*!"

Signor Fidardo virtually spat out those last two words. Accordions with piano keys instead of buttons were new-fangled devices that he scorned. Signor Fidardo rarely had time for anything modern.

Fabulous Forzini was due to give a concert in Lisbon on Saturday, and late on Friday afternoon a red Chevrolet Superior drew up on the street outside Signor Fidardo's workshop. I noticed it immediately because luxury cars are a rare sight in our district. A broad-shouldered man wearing a three-piece, chalk-stripe suit with a fur-lined cape over his shoulders stepped from the back of the car. He had a broad-brimmed Stetson hat on his head and was wearing pointed black shoes with off-white spats. I realized who it was even before the doorbell rang and the man entered our workshop.

Even Signor Fidardo recognized Fabulous Forzini from his pictures in the paper, but he pretended not to. Of course!

"Well, sir, how can I be of service?"

Fabulous Forzini gave a broad smile and flung out his arms. A precious stone of some kind set in a gold ring shone on the ring finger of his right hand.

"Signor Fidardo!" he exclaimed. "It is I, your fellow countryman, Fabulous Forzini! We meet at last! I am a great admirer of your instruments!"

"Kind of you to say so," Signor Fidardo said with a very slight inclination of his head.

Fabulous Forzini surveyed the small workshop. When he saw me sitting working at my bench, he raised his well-plucked coal-black eyebrows.

"A gorilla mending musical instruments! What a novelty!" he said in a jovial voice. "I thought I'd seen most things during my years as a vaudeville artiste."

"Her name is Sally Jones, and she is not a circus attraction," Signor Fidardo muttered. "And what is it that brings you here, Mr. Forzini?"

"I've come to make you an offer, Signor Fidardo! An offer you can't refuse, as we say in America. I am thinking of having a new accordion made for me. It will be the most beautiful and most mellifluous piano accordion ever made! Nothing but the best is good enough for me! Which is why, Signor Fidardo, you are the only instrument maker worthy of consideration! Well, what do you say?"

Signor Fidardo did not need any time to think it over.

"I am flattered, Mr. Forzini," he said. "But unfortunately I must decline."

Fabulous Forzini's beaming smile died away. He gave Signor Fidardo a look of confusion. Then his smile returned, even broader than before. He narrowed his eyes.

"Aha, I see you are a businessman, Signor Fidardo! I like that! There is no reason for you to be concerned about the money. I shall be more than generous! And I shall pay in advance!"

"It is not a question of money, Mr. Forzini," Signor Fidardo said in an icy tone. "I simply do not build piano accordions! Not for you, and not for anyone else!"

A deep furrow suddenly appeared between Fabulous Forzini's dark eyebrows, and his smile disappeared again.

"*Ma perché?* Why not?"

Signor Fidardo drew himself up to his full height and stroked his mustache before answering.

"The piano accordion is a vulgar instrument only suitable for simple popular music. It's not for me! I am afraid you will have to turn to someone else, Mr. Forzini."

163

A blank look spread across Fabulous Forzini's face, as if he could not really comprehend what he had just heard. Then his cheeks flushed and his eyes became as black as coal.

"*Lei mi insulta!* You insult me!" he growled.

"*Mi scusi,*" Signor Fidardo said. "I had no intention of being rude, but I am quite simply not interested in your offer."

They looked each other up and down for a few moments.

"You will come to regret this, Signor Fidardo!" Fabulous Forzini hissed. "You don't know who you are dealing with! You haven't heard the last of it!"

He turned on his heel and marched out of the workshop, his cape billowing behind him.

~

Signor Fidardo seemed slightly off-balance during the hours that followed. The threat in Fabulous Forzini's departing words hung in the air, and as darkness approached, Signor Fidardo peered anxiously out of the window several times.

It was just before seven o'clock when the red Chevrolet screeched to a halt with two wheels up on the pavement outside our door. A few moments later the door was hurled open.

It was Fabulous Forzini!

There was a hard, dark glint in his eyes beneath the brim of his hat. He stepped into the workshop, carrying a large bag in one hand.

Without saying a word he threw off his cape, his hat and his jacket and rolled up his shirtsleeves, all the time glaring at Signor Fidardo with wild eyes. The latter retreated several paces out of sheer terror. Then Fabulous Forzini grabbed a chair and placed it in the middle of the floor before taking a cream-colored piano accordion from his bag. He put his arms through the shoulder straps, sat down on the chair, his legs apart, and began to play.

He played a tarantella, a sort of Calabrian folk dance I had heard Signor Fidardo play many times before. But not like this. Fabulous Forzini attacked his accordion with frenetic energy, his pomaded fringe falling over his face and the notes of the accordion rattling between the walls of the workshop. Signor Fidardo clung to his workbench as if a gale was roaring through the room. All of a sudden Fabulous Forzini changed tempo; the expression on his face became one of suffering and the notes came slowly, vibrating with pain and longing.

Fabulous Forzini played for half an hour without a break. At first Signor Fidardo seemed taken aback, but toward the end he was listening with closed eyes and a happy smile.

As the last note faded away Fabulous Forzini remained

sitting with his cheek against the accordion. His shirt was sodden with sweat, and his once-so-elegant hair was now a disheveled mess.

"Well, Signor Fidardo," he said, hoarse and out of breath. "Do you still think the piano accordion is only suitable for simple popular music?"

"No," Signor Fidardo answered with a slight quaver in his voice. "I find it necessary to change my mind on that matter."

Fabulous Forzini beamed.

"And you'll build an instrument for me?"

"*Con piacere*. With pleasure," Signor Fidardo said with a slight bow. "If your offer still stands."

~

Fabulous Forzini was still with us when Ana came home from work at around nine o'clock. Signor Fidardo had taken out his guitar and was playing Calabrian songs, drinking wine and talking of his old home. I was sitting in my chair with my legs tucked up, listening.

Ana was wide-eyed with amazement when she recognized our world-famous visitor. Signor Fidardo introduced them. Fabulous Forzini leapt to his feet, kissed Ana's hand with a deep bow and gave her a dazzling smile through lowered eyelids.

Signor Fidardo intervened quickly: "I think you should join us for a glass of wine, Ana. And then sing fado for us."

Ana hesitated a moment, but then she drew up a chair and sat down. Signor Fidardo played the opening notes of one of Ana's favorite songs, and when she began singing, Fabulous Forzini's self-confident seducer's smile disappeared at once. Instead a rather earnest and dreamy expression came to his face, and he carefully wove a gentle web of notes round the melody with his accordion.

As the last note died away Fabulous Forzini exclaimed forcefully: "I will play this song as an extra number at tomorrow's concert. And you, Signorina Molina, shall be my guest artiste!"

~

Fabulous Forzini was a phenomenal accordionist, and he was equally adept at the art of persuasion. First of all he had convinced Signor Fidardo to build him a piano accordion: that was an achievement. Then he persuaded Ana to appear as guest artiste at his concert: that was probably an even greater achievement.

The Teatro Maria Vitória was one of the big theaters in the Parque Mayer amusement park. Ana went there the following day to rehearse with Fabulous Forzini, and when she came home she was pale. She regretted having agreed to do it. The theater had seats for hundreds of people and appearing there would be very different from singing to her loyal audience at the Tamarind.

Signor Fidardo and I were given tickets for the concert. I was at least as nervous as Ana. Signor Fidardo's greatest concern, on the other hand, was which of his suits to wear that evening—the ivory or the cream!

The Fabulous Forzini concert was a great success. As always. But on this particular evening he was not the one who received the biggest and longest applause. That went to Ana. She looked so terribly small standing there beside Fabulous Forzini in the spotlight on the huge stage. But her voice had reached every corner of the theater and every heart in her audience.

Even though Ana had only sung one song she was mentioned in all the reviews in the main newspapers the following day. The director of the Teatro Maria Vitória offered her a small part in a future musical show, but Ana declined.

"Quite right too," Signor Fidardo said seriously. "Your voice is worthy of a much more elevated venue."

Ana laughed at him, as she always did when he was being pompous and highfalutin.

CHAPTER 25
Farol do Bugio

Summer arrived, bringing such heat that it became
almost impossible to work in the workshop. The air
hung hot and motionless in the narrow alleys of Alfama,
and the rotting contents of the rubbish bins and sewers
stank.

Signor Fidardo drew the plans for Fabulous Forzini's
new accordion, and Fabulous Forzini approved them without comment. He wrote that Signor Fidardo should go ahead

and design the instrument in his own way and said, "Then I can be quite sure that my accordion will be a masterpiece." The letter also contained a check for a very large sum of money—though it was only the first part payment.

Signor Fidardo immediately used some of the money to rent a house in the small fishing village of Oeiras, about ten miles west of the city.

"We're going to take a holiday!" he said to Ana. "We've earned one!"

Signor Fidardo, Ana and I went out to the house for a week. Ana swam in the sea and took long walks along the coast. Signor Fidardo sat on the veranda in the shade, smoking cigars and drinking wine.

As for me, I spent my time trying to resurrect the engine of a dilapidated little steam launch that belonged to the house and was moored to a jetty below it. It was a single-cylinder Mumford engine, a type I'd never worked on before, so it was fun.

I had the boat ready for a trip by the morning of our last day but one. I lit the fire under the boiler and we set off after lunch. The weather was splendid—sunny, with a fresh breeze from the sea. I steered a course south and rounded the Farol do Bugio, the lighthouse out in the middle of the wide mouth of the Tagus. Ana sat in the bow, her face turned to the sun and the wind blowing through her hair.

Signor Fidardo was quiet and rather pale. I assumed the motion of the sea was getting to him.

And I couldn't really enjoy the trip either: being at sea again, but without the Chief, felt strange.

~

The summer heat slowly eased its hold on Lisbon. At night, the big, round September moon hung in the sky above the city. Four months had passed since Senhor Baptista started distributing our notices at O Pelicano, and there were only a hundred sheets left. The rest of them were scattered across all the harbors in the Far East.

At night, when Ana had fallen asleep, I crept out onto the stairs and looked down on Rua de São Tomé. I had been doing this for a couple of months. I imagined that one night I would catch sight of Alphonse Morro standing in the shadows between the streetlamps, looking up at our house.

It felt more and more like a dream rather than something that might really happen.

CHAPTER 26
The Viscount

The Viscount de Oliveira is one of Lisbon's richest noblemen. He is also a prominent connoisseur of music and the director of the biggest and finest theater in Portugal, the São Carlos opera house in Lisbon.

The viscount is probably most famous, however, for possessing the largest set of side whiskers in the whole of the Iberian Peninsula. That is why many people recognized him the moment he made an unexpected appearance at the Tamarind one Saturday evening in October. What had brought him there, of course, were the rumors about Ana's voice. People as grand as the viscount are not usually seen in the shabby fado cafés of Alfama.

The viscount was so entranced by Ana's singing that he immediately offered her a solo concert at the São Carlos. Ana thought he was joking—she found it impossible to imagine otherwise.

"Yes, please!" she answered with a laugh. "That sounds nice."

But the Viscount de Oliveira was not joking, as Ana realized a few days later when she received an invitation to come to the São Carlos and rehearse on the big stage.

All the color drained from her face when she read the letter.

"How in heaven's name am I going to get out of this?" she said in an unhappy voice.

Signor Fidardo gave her a serious look.

"The São Carlos acoustics are world-class," he said. "Not many people get the chance to sing there. I think you should take it. You can always say no to a concert at a later stage if you still don't want to do one."

The viscount himself came in his car to collect Ana

from our door the following afternoon. She was pale and tense as they drove away. She returned many hours later with rosy cheeks and shining eyes.

"You should have been there. The acoustics were really quite unbelievable," she said to me. "Every note hung in the air as if it had the wings of an angel! Thank heavens I agreed to do that concert in the first place. . . ."

~

The Viscount de Oliveira's plan was that Ana would be accompanied by musicians selected from the orchestra of the opera house. She, however, wanted the three house guitarists from the Tamarind, and since that was her only demand as far as the concert was concerned the viscount gave way without a murmur.

The concert was to be held at the end of November, and the papers began writing about it several weeks in advance. Never before had a fado singer been invited to sing at the grandest venue in Portugal. Everyone in Alfama was proud of Ana. Whenever she came home from work in the evening, some of the local children would be waiting outside our house. They would beg her to sing just the tiniest bit for them—and, of course, she always did.

Even Santos, director of the shoe factory, was proud of her. One of his employees was about to appear at the São

Carlos! Imagine that! He offered to allow Ana every morning off until the concert to give her time to rehearse. But Ana went to work in the morning as usual. She knew her songs, and she didn't need any more practice. And staying at home with nothing to do made her nervous.

But Signor Fidardo was the one who was proudest of Ana. Proudest by far, though he didn't show it much! He was just a little calmer and a little happier than usual.

"I have always known that this was bound to happen sooner or later," he explained to me. "It's nothing to get excited about."

The tickets for Ana's concert at the São Carlos sold out in two days. Many people from Alfama would have liked to attend, but the cheapest tickets were up in the highest balcony, and there weren't many of them—they sold out almost at once. Ordinary people couldn't afford tickets in the stalls or the lower circles. Fortunately for us, the viscount gave Ana a bundle of free tickets, and she saved the best seats for Signor Fidardo and me.

~

Signor Fidardo managed to stay calm until a week before the concert, when he suddenly took it into his head that his evening suit was old-fashioned and rushed to order a new tailcoat and trousers from the local tailor. Tails are the only permissible dress for gentlemen attending São Carlos. Signor Fidardo went to the tailor's every day to see how his suit was coming along and to check that the tailor was doing his job properly.

It wasn't at all obvious what I should wear to the concert. My blue dungarees were obviously not suitable, and I didn't own any other clothes. Ana solved the problem for me. A few days before the concert she was allowed to choose a dress from the opera house costume department. She brought home a beautiful turquoise dress for herself and a strange costume of cloths of many colors for me.

"It was used in Mozart's opera *The Abduction from the Seraglio*," Ana told us in a delighted voice. "If we just take up the legs a little, I'm sure it will fit you."

I felt really stupid in this bright and colorful costume with puffy sleeves and glass beads sewn into the collar. But I didn't have much choice, so I put on a brave face.

The great day came at last. A car came for Ana in the afternoon and drove her to São Carlos. She and her guitarists were to have one last rehearsal before the concert. A couple of hours later Signor Fidardo and I took the tram down to Baixa and then went up the Santa Justa Lift to the upper-class neighborhood of Chiado. It was a warm and cloudless dusk, and we arrived at São Carlos just as the gas lamps were coming on along the street. The street outside the theater was crowded, and streams of taxicabs were coming and going.

Concertgoers by the hundred were climbing the wide steps leading to the theater, men in black tails and women in evening dresses that shimmered in every color imaginable. Attendants in red uniforms held open the doors and bowed low. It was all more splendid and elegant than I could ever have imagined. Signor Fidardo must have seen how anxious I was becoming, and he took me by the hand before we ascended the steps.

Champagne was being served in the foyer. The scent of expensive perfume hung heavy round the tall marble pillars, and cigar smoke curled up toward the chandeliers and gilded stuccowork on the ceiling. Signor Fidardo stood there straight-backed, a champagne glass balanced elegantly between his thumb and his forefinger. He seemed to be enjoying himself. Unlike me! My peculiar costume was rubbing, and there was something threatening about all this splendor. I wondered how Ana was feeling at the moment.

I suddenly heard a thunderous peal of laughter above the general hubbub of voices. It sounded familiar. For a moment I was confused—who could I possibly know here? I stood on tiptoe to see where the laughter was coming from.

I saw the man almost immediately. He was dressed like

a priest, in a black cassock and white collar with a purple sash round his waist and a skullcap of the same color on his head. That is not how he had been dressed the last time we met, but I recognized him anyway. My heart missed a beat and I could scarcely breathe.

It was the man from Agiere.

The man who had said his name was Papa Monforte.

And here he was now, standing just a couple of yards away from me, in conversation with a man whose face I can no longer remember. The latter said something and Papa Monforte laughed again, the same loud roar. He turned his head just a little at the same time and suddenly caught sight of me. Our eyes met, and the smile on his face froze. I saw a hint of fear in his eyes. I turned away quickly, my heart pounding.

The liveried attendants began ringing small handbells to signal it was time for us to take our seats. The performance was about to start. Signor Fidardo took my hand, and we joined the queue at one of the doors into the auditorium.

CHAPTER 27
Purple

Ana's concert at the São Carlos opera house was a success. She had to sing no fewer than seven encores before the audience would permit her to leave the stage.

For my part, I have only the vaguest memories of the concert. I was utterly sunk in my own thoughts and concerns after the unexpected encounter with Papa Monforte. But I do remember, of course, how immense the auditorium was and how, after every song, the sound of applause rolled round it like thunder. But most of all I remember the searing pain in my stomach when I heard Papa Monforte's laughter ring in my ears time after time. The terrors of that dreadful night on the river washed over me again.

After her performance a car collected Ana from the stage door and drove her to the Viscount de Oliveira's private palace for a gala supper. Signor Fidardo was unable to present her with the flowers he had brought.

When we got home to Rua de São Tomé, Signor Fidardo was still far too overwhelmed by the concert to want to go to bed. He opened a bottle of wine for himself instead and fetched a glass of milk for me. We sat in the workshop waiting for Ana to come home. She arrived by taxi just after midnight, and then she simply had to tell us about the gala supper and all the important and elegant people who had attended in her honor. The director of a large gramophone record company had promised that she would make a record.

"This, Ana, is just the beginning," Signor Fidardo said, a tremor of emotion in his voice. "Believe me!"

It was well into the small hours before we bade one another good night. Before I crept under the covers on the sofa I slipped out onto the stairs as usual and looked down at the street.

There was no Alphonse Morro standing under the streetlight that night either, but there was a car parked just a little farther along the street. The window on the driver's side was down, and I could just make out the silhouette of a man sitting smoking inside. I glimpsed two cold eyes gleaming in the darkness, and I sensed that they were looking at me.

A few minutes later the headlights came on, and the car moved slowly out from the curb and drove past our house. The street became silent and empty once more.

I went back inside and went to bed on the sofa. But I did not fall asleep until dawn, many hours later.

~

The following day was hectic in the house on Rua de São Tomé. One messenger boy after another arrived bringing bunches of flowers and telegrams of congratulations. One of the bouquets was from Ana's secret admirer, the mysterious Canson.

Workmates from the shoe factory and musicians from Alfama and Mouraria came to offer their congratulations and to drink coffee helped down by a glass of aguardiente. Viscount de Oliveira brought champagne, and Director Santos brought chocolate. Guitars were played and songs were sung. Ana was overwhelmed, and Signor Fidardo was happier than I had ever seen him. He took out his accordion and played Italian songs in honor of Ana.

I was there the whole time, of course, but however much I tried I couldn't really join in the celebrations. Seeing Papa Monforte again had not only reminded me of the accident on the river, it had also given me a creepy premonition of future misfortune. It's hard to describe exactly how it felt: it was like a chill wind inside me.

~

The celebrations lasted the whole weekend. Before we went to bed on Sunday evening, Ana made a cup of tea for herself and a glass of warm milk for me. She was happy but weary.

"It's Monday tomorrow," she said. "It will be nice to have an ordinary day after all this fuss."

But Monday did not turn out to be an ordinary day either. Signor Fidardo and I had no sooner started work than there was a messenger boy knocking at the workshop door. Signor Fidardo was busy with something on his workbench, so I went to the door. The messenger handed me a letter addressed to Signor Fidardo. The envelope was made of the very best linen paper, and it was sealed with a big seal of purple wax in the form of a crucifix.

I stared at the seal.

Purple.

There was something familiar about that color. But what?

I gave the letter to Signor Fidardo. He too looked at the seal with some curiosity before he broke it and opened the envelope.

"Purple is the bishop's color, isn't it?" he said, sounding bewildered. "What in heaven's name can this be all about?"

Signor Fidardo opened the letter and read it. At first his expression was one of puzzlement, which turned to one of astonishment and finally to happiness. The letter proved to be from no less a figure than Rodrigo de Sousa, the assistant bishop of Lisbon, and he had written it himself, not left it to a secretary. It concerned the great organ in the church of São Vicente de Fora. The organ was in need of renovation, and the bishop had chosen Signor Fidardo to carry out the work.

Signor Fidardo read the letter to me. Then he gave me a look of satisfaction over the top of his reading glasses.

"It's impossible for any instrument maker in Lisbon to be entrusted with a more important task!" he said proudly.

Bishop de Sousa wanted Signor Fidardo to visit him that very afternoon to discuss the job. Signor Fidardo changed his clothes and tidied himself up before setting off, his back straight and his mustache freshly waxed. He was looking eager and expectant.

I watched him through the window as he climbed into the tram at the stop just down the street. There was a cold lump in my stomach. I had worked out where I had seen the purple color of the seal before.

It was the color of the sash and skullcap Papa Monforte had been wearing at the opera house.

CHAPTER 28
The Bishop's Conditions

I didn't get much done that afternoon. Instead I found myself walking restlessly round the workshop, circuit after circuit, trying to bring order to my thoughts. As the hours passed I became more and more worried.

Signor Fidardo had said that purple was "the bishop's color"—did that mean that Bishop de Sousa and Papa Monforte were one and the same person? It seemed likely. Two days earlier Papa Monforte and I had recognized one another at the São Carlos opera house. And now the bishop wanted to see Signor Fidardo. It could hardly be a coincidence.

Evil premonitions tied my stomach in knots. Something dreadful was about to happen.

Or perhaps it had already happened? Why was Signor Fidardo taking so long?

When Ana came home she saw at once that something was wrong. Signor Fidardo was not in the workshop, and I was so anxious that I couldn't keep still. She took me up to her room and tried to question me about what had happened. Using nods and shakes of my head I answered as well as I could, but she wasn't much wiser by the end of it. Everything was so complicated that I wasn't even sure myself how it all fitted together.

At last, just before nine o'clock, we heard Signor Fidardo's footsteps on the stairs. They sounded heavier than usual. When he came through the door he looked as if he had grown many years older in the few hours he had been away.

"Luigi . . . what on earth is going on?" Ana exclaimed.

Signor Fidardo remained in the doorway. He gave her a brief account of what had happened in the course of the day—first he told of the letter and then of his meeting with the bishop.

"Bishop de Sousa offered me the opportunity to renovate the organ in the church of São Vicente de Fora," he said. "But I was forced to turn it down. The fee was useless. We negotiated for some hours, but it was impossible to come to an agreement. That is why I'm so late coming home."

I could hear that Signor Fidardo was lying—or not telling the whole truth, anyway. Ana knew too. I could tell from the way she looked.

"So that's that," Signor Fidardo finished. "Now I'm going downstairs. It's after bedtime."

With his hand on the door handle he gave Ana a look that was easy to interpret. He wanted her to come out on the stairs with him. They stayed out there a good while, talking to one another in whispers. I could hear every word: human beings seem to have no idea how good a gorilla's hearing is.

"What actually happened?" Ana asked the moment they had closed the door behind them.

"The bishop was very pleasant at first," Signor Fidardo said in a dull voice. "He praised all the work I've done in the past and offered me very generous remuneration for renovating the organ. But after a while it emerged that there was a condition. In order to get the work . . ."

Signor Fidardo made a little pause at this point, as if gathering his breath to continue. I could hear he was upset.

"In order to be given the job I would have to hand Sally Jones over to the police. Or to the zoo."

Ana uttered a strangled cry.

"What are you saying? Why?"

"The bishop said it was unnatural and against God's holy order to allow an animal to live and work as though it was a human being."

Ana seemed to be struck speechless. At least, she said nothing.

"I lost my temper, of course," Signor Fidardo continued. "I told the bishop he could renovate his old organ himself. I expect that was silly of me. It's not sensible to quarrel with a bishop, but I couldn't stop myself. When I left him I was in such a bad mood that I was forced to have a glass or two in a bar to calm me down. It didn't occur to me you would be worried about me."

Ana and Signor Fidardo carried on talking for a while, but I could no longer hear what they were saying: the terrified thoughts running through my mind drowned out their whispers.

~

I didn't sleep at all that night. As soon as Ana had gone to sleep I slipped out to the window on the stairs to keep watch. I stayed there until morning, ready to flee should Papa Monforte come to take me.

I now knew that Papa Monforte and Bishop de Sousa were the same person. The bishop was a powerful man and he was after me. My time in this house on Rua de São Tomé would soon be over. The very thought made my heart ache and my eyes sting with tears.

I also knew that I really ought to leave immediately so that Ana and Signor Fidardo would not suffer because of me.

But where was I to go?

~

The following morning Ana went to the shoe factory as usual. I went down to Signor Fidardo's, and after we had drunk a cup of coffee I carried on with the work I had left on my bench the day before.

Everything was as usual in the workshop, calm and congenial. What had happened the day before seemed very distant, like a bad dream. Perhaps I had allowed my anxiety and bad thoughts to stampede me? That can easily happen when you are tired and overwrought.

But the calm did not last long. An hour or so later a black car drew up outside Signor Fidardo's workshop. It was the same car I had seen from the window on the stairs a couple of nights earlier. Four men stepped out into the street, and I watched them through the window from my workbench.

The workshop door opened and the men pushed their way in. I recognized the first of them immediately, though I had only seen him once before. He was the man in the woolen overcoat who had arrested the Chief on the quayside after Morro had fallen into the river two years before.

"I am Chief Inspector Garretta," he said to Signor Fidardo, at the same time taking a sheet of paper from his inside pocket. "This is a statement from the health and safety office of the city of Lisbon. Your gorilla is a health hazard, and we are here to . . ."

That is all I heard. I ran out of the workshop and up the stairs to Ana's apartment. Hurrying footsteps and angry voices were hot on my heels. I shut the door and locked it; then I opened the window and swung myself up onto the roof.

CHAPTER 29
Cochin

I made my way to my old hiding place in the attic with the pigeons. I hadn't been there for a long time, but very little had changed. Just as before, the pigeons flew in and out through a hole down by the eaves. They were quite unconcerned, whereas I was now as tormented and afraid as I had been then.

I remained there all day and all evening. With the

passing of the hours my pounding heart returned to normal, and I began to feel strangely calm.

There is nothing worse than waiting for something dreadful to happen. Not even when the dreadful thing actually happens. Ever since meeting Papa Monforte's eyes across the foyer of the opera house I had known in my heart of hearts that he would come for me. Now that it had happened, there was no need for me to wait any longer.

I would have to force myself to look to the future. After thinking about it for a while I came up with a plan. I couldn't stay in Lisbon—Bishop de Sousa would have me caged in the zoo. And he had that obnoxious policeman, Chief Inspector Garretta, to help him. Signor Fidardo and Ana couldn't protect me against enemies like that.

So I would have to go. But where? There was only one answer: to the Far East, to try to locate Alphonse Morro. My chances of finding him were small, but that was of no great importance. After all, what else was I to do?

But I couldn't leave Lisbon without first saying goodbye to Ana and Signor Fidardo. When the clock had passed midnight I left the attic and crept across the roofs until I was in sight of Ana's window. The light in the kitchen was on, but the window was closed. I wondered for a moment whether to climb across and knock, but I resisted. If the coast was clear Ana would undoubtedly have left the window open, so perhaps the police were there.

I returned to the attic and tried to get some sleep.

Ana's window was open the following evening. She was sitting there singing quietly in the darkness and watching out for me. When I reached her window I could see that she had been crying. She threw her arms round my neck and hugged me tight.

"Signor Fidardo has an acquaintance who works at the health and safety office," she said into my ear. "He has helped us appeal the decision to have you put in the zoo. We will hear the result within a few weeks, but you will have to stay away from here until then. We've talked to Senhor Baptista, and he has promised to hide you at O Pelicano. The police won't search there. Hurry now before any of the neighbors see you."

Ana let go of me and I left her.

So my plans had suddenly changed again. Perhaps Ana and Signor Fidardo could protect me after all? I would have to let them try, anyway.

I climbed across roofs, crept through backyards and hugged the walls in the darkest alleyways until I reached O Pelicano. On the way there I saw several "wanted" posters with my face drawn on them. They did not look anything like me: all gorillas look the same to human beings.

Senhor Baptista let me into the yard through the kitchen entrance. I could see at once that he wasn't happy to have me there. That was hardly surprising—hiding a fugitive is a criminal offense and can lead to several years in prison.

The door down to the cellar was open. Senhor Baptista lit a lantern and showed me down the steep, narrow staircase. It smelled of damp and rats. Broken furniture, dusty wine jars, packing cases and other junk were stacked untidily round the crumbling brick walls. We moved on into the dark passageways under the building and continued into the farthest reaches, where it looked as if no one had been for decades. There was a little storeroom behind a wooden partition that had been erected between two brick walls. The door was fastened with a padlock, which Senhor Baptista unlocked before gesturing that I should go in.

"It's not very pleasant, I'm afraid," he said apologetically. "But at least you will be safe. I'm the only one with a key. No one will know that you are here. Not even Senhora Maria."

Senhor Baptista cleared away some of the rubbish from the middle of the floor and laid out a mattress. I sat down on the mattress and he locked the door behind him as he left. A sliver of gray light from a flickering gas lamp out on the street filtered in through a dirty cellar window. Otherwise it was dark.

I hoped I would not need to be there too long.

I was locked in the O Pelicano cellar for five days. Senhor Baptista gave me food and let me out to the toilet twice a day, once at dawn before anyone else had arrived at the tavern and then again after midnight when everyone had gone home.

In between those times I was left alone with my thoughts. I sometimes felt I would go mad. Senhor Baptista must have noticed that I wasn't doing too well, because he began giving me books and newspapers for company.

Ana and Signor Fidardo did not come to visit me, and I knew why. If they started frequenting O Pelicano at unusual times the police might easily become suspicious. The newspapers Senhor Baptista gave me told me I was wanted, and a reward had been offered to anyone who tipped off the police about where I was hiding.

Eventually, on the evening of the fifth day, Signor Fidardo came to O Pelicano. He had taken a long and circuitous route to ensure he wasn't being followed by the police. When he saw the condition I was in he was horrified. After a week of darkness and loneliness I wasn't a pretty sight.

"We haven't received a response to our appeal yet," he said. "But it looks promising. You won't have to stay here much longer."

I could tell from his voice that he was trying to sound

more hopeful than he really was. My heart sank. Signor Fidardo looked at me anxiously. Then he said, "Something else has happened too."

He produced an envelope from his jacket pocket and passed it to me.

"This came in the mail to Prazeres Cemetery last week," he said. "João let me have it to show to you."

The envelope had already been slit open, and inside was a folded sheet of paper and a five-pound note. I unfolded the paper and read:

This money is to be used for the upkeep of the grave of Elisa Gomes. I hope the money I sent before has been sufficient until now. Further funds should be made available to you within a couple of months.

My hands trembled as I held the cheap yellowing envelope. The address was printed in the same neat, even handwriting as the letter. The sender's address was not given. The postmark was slightly smudged but I could read it:

COCHIN

PRINCELY STATE OF COCHIN

INDIA

I handed the letter back to Signor Fidardo. Then I hugged him. He didn't back away, even though he would obviously get gorilla hairs on his white suit. Instead he rested his cheek on my head.

"Don't worry, my friend," he said. "We'll see each other again soon."

But I knew that we would not be doing that.

Because at that moment I had come to a decision.

~

My plan was a simple one, and I knew that Senhor Baptista could help me carry it out. The moment Signor Fidardo had left, I explained to Senhor Baptista what I wanted to do. It wasn't that difficult. I simply borrowed the pen he had in his top pocket and wrote the word *Cochin* on a piece of paper. Then I pointed first at the paper and then at myself.

"Cochin?" Senhor Baptista said. "It's a port in southern India . . . and that's where you want to go?"

I nodded.

~

Senhor Baptista worked fast. It helped, no doubt, that he saw a chance of getting rid of me. By the following evening everything was organized.

"We struck lucky," he said. "I went down to the harbor office this morning and talked to an old shipmate who works there. A freighter is due to leave the harbor in a couple of hours. It's an Irish vessel by the name of *Song of Limerick* and she is on her way to Bombay with a cargo of machine parts. I've talked to the skipper, and he's prepared to sign you on as a grease monkey. There's no pay, but you'll have free board and passage. We won't find anything better, I'm sure. Bombay is a big port, and you'll easily be able to find another berth to Cochin."

I wish I'd been able to tell Ana and Signor Fidardo that I was leaving, but there was no time. Senhor Baptista would let them know where I was off to, and Ana would certainly find some way of explaining to the Chief why I was no longer able to come to the hill outside the prison and listen to him playing the accordion on Sundays. All three of them would be worried, but there was nothing I could do about that. I had a chance now to find Alphonse Morro, and I would probably never get another one.

CHAPTER 30
Song of Limerick

I left O Pelicano a couple of hours before dawn and walked quickly through the empty streets down to the river. The few nocturnal walkers I met were either too tired or too drunk to notice me.

The harbor was completely deserted. A gull was screaming in the darkness, and muffled sounds could be heard from the auxiliary engines of vessels along the quay. There was a smell of bilge water and coal.

The *Song of Limerick* was a vessel that looked to have been worked long and hard. Now she was ready to depart, and black smoke was already billowing from her funnel.

There was not a soul to be seen. I had just started walking up the gangway when a man wearing a white peaked cap looked down from the bridge.

"Sally Jones?" he shouted, and I raised my hand in response.

The man came down and met me by the ladder to the bridge. He was an unusually ugly man with a matted beard and a far-from-pretty smile. His teeth, yellow with snuff, seemed to be leaning against each other in an effort not to fall over.

"Anderson's the name," he said. "Captain Anderson. Welcome aboard. Let's go up to the bridge and I'll enter you on the crew list. And there is someone who wants to meet you."

Captain Anderson went ahead and I followed him. Who could it be who wanted to meet me? Did I know any of the crew? Had Ana and Signor Fidardo come to say goodbye? Had Senhor Baptista perhaps told them I was about to set off?

The moment I stepped through the door into the badly lit bridge two policemen stepped forward, one on each side of me, grabbed me by the arms and kicked away my feet so that I fell forward. One of them pinned me firmly to the floor while the other put handcuffs on my wrists and tied my feet with thick wire. It all happened very quickly.

I twisted my head round and saw that there was someone standing leaning on the map table at the other side of the bridge.

It was Chief Inspector Garretta.

"Good!" he said with a satisfied smile on his thin lips. "The chase is over. You nearly got away, I have to admit. Lucky for me there was someone on board who wanted a slice of the reward I'd just posted."

Peering up, I could see the sneer on Captain Anderson's face as he took a large pinch of snuff from his snuffbox. He sat down on the captain's chair, poked the snuff under his lip and casually began scraping the ash out of a corncob pipe that had seen better days.

"We'll be off, then," Garretta said, signaling to the constables to carry me out to the bridge wing. "We still have plenty to do before we can enjoy the good sleep of the just. First we must find a veterinarian and get a certificate to confirm the gorilla is sick, and then we can put her down and dispose of the body. No time to waste! Good night, Captain, and thanks for your help."

Anderson raised two fingers to the peak of his cap in a lazy salute.

I don't remember in detail what happened next. I panicked and began hurling myself this way and that. The two constables had to hang on with all their strength to hold me. I think I managed to bite one of them on the leg. Whatever happened, he gave a loud scream and dropped me headfirst onto the deck.

"Looks to me as if you've got trouble there," I heard Captain Anderson say in a sly voice. "Maybe you can give yourself an easier life, Chief Inspector."

Garretta looked at him without much sign of interest.

"If you are going to kill the gorilla anyway, you might as well leave her here," Anderson said, greed glinting in his eyes. "For fifty escudos I'll throw her overboard once we are out on the open sea."

Garretta looked at the ugly captain with some distaste as he considered his suggestion.

"Okay, then," Garretta said. "Fifty escudos, eh? Cheap at the price if it saves us half a night's work. But what guarantee do I have that you'll really drown the beast?"

Captain Anderson gave a broad grin. The snuff juice trickled down over his teeth.

"What would I gain by not doing it?"

Garretta grinned back.

"You've got a point there," he said, and produced a banknote from his wallet. "It's your responsibility, then, to make the gorilla disappear. But wait until you've put a good distance between you and the coast. We don't want a corpse floating in among the bathers at Cascais. That wouldn't look too good."

A couple of sailors were summoned to help the policemen carry me belowdecks. Someone pulled a bag over my head to stop me from biting anyone else. Then I felt myself being lifted up by many pairs of rough hands. I tried to resist, but it was pointless. My arms and legs were locked as if they were in a vise. Through the sackcloth I could hear the tramp of footsteps on steel decking and voices panting with exertion.

I was eventually dropped with a thump onto something hard and cold. A door slammed and there was the screech of a bolt being pushed across. I lay still and listened. Once I knew I was alone I tried to wriggle my hands out of the handcuffs. It didn't work. In desperation I took to wriggling my way round the floor without having any real idea of what I was hoping to achieve. In the end I gave up and just lay there exhausted. That was when I heard the shouts from up on deck as the mooring ropes were cast off, and then the old steel hull shuddered as the engine began turning the propeller shaft.

I don't know how long I lay there before I heard the sound of approaching footsteps. I heard the mumble of voices; the bolt slid and the door to the room opened. A couple of seconds later I became aware that someone was very close to me. Something slid very quickly between my neck and the cord that tied the bag on my head. It felt like the blade of a knife.

A quick jerk and the cord was cut, and the bag was pulled off my head. I blinked in the light of a paraffin lantern. Captain Anderson was looking down at me. Alongside him stood a man in a filthy set of mechanic's overalls. I pushed myself back with my feet and bared my teeth, ready to fight for my life.

"Calm down, now, calm down!" Anderson said, turning a wooden box upside down to have something to sit on. "The police have gone ashore. We have pulled away from the quay, and the danger is over."

I was in such a state that I had difficulty understanding what he was saying.

Captain Anderson nodded toward the man in the overalls.

"This is Geoff Gerrard," he said. "The two of you will be working together for the next month. So try not to get off to a bad start."

The man called Geoff Gerrard nodded in a friendly way. He had laugh lines round his eyes. Then he took a hacksaw from his belt and went down on his knees beside me.

"Just keep still, now, old friend," he said, "so that I don't hurt you."

And he began sawing through the handcuffs on one of my wrists.

~

A short while later I was standing in the lee of the portside bridge wing taking deep breaths of the cool sea breeze. The stress was still making me feel a little sick, but it was easing slowly. The door to the bridge opened and Captain Anderson stepped out with a cup of warm milk.

"Would you like a dash of rum in it? To calm your nerves, I mean."

I shook my head.

"All right, I won't press you," Captain Anderson said in a good-natured voice as he handed me the cup.

He leaned against the rail of the bridge wing and began filling his corncob pipe with black tobacco. I looked at him. He really didn't look very nice, but appearances can be deceptive. Captain Anderson had fooled Chief Inspector Garretta, and he had saved my life.

"Good to have you on board, Sally Jones," he said. "You've sailed with Henry Koskela, the man known as the Chief, haven't you? And so have I, though it was a long time ago. Nice fellow, that Koskela. And a good seaman. I hear that you are too. They say that you are one hell of an engineer."

Anderson struck a match and winked in a knowing sort of way before adding: "And we don't toss good engineers overboard just like that, do we? He should have thought of that, that idiot of an inspector. What have you done to get someone like that hunting you?"

He didn't seem to be expecting an answer. Instead he put the match to his pipe, took a couple of puffs and went back to the bridge, leaving an acrid smell of cheap tobacco behind him. It was quickly dispersed by the wind, but the smell still lodged in my nostrils.

I drank the warm milk in small sips. I had to concentrate not to spill it, since my hands wouldn't stop shaking. Behind me I could see the million spots of light of Lisbon glittering in the darkness.

Before me lay the Atlantic.

And the long voyage to India.

PART TWO

CHAPTER 31
A Notch in the Blade

I stayed on the wing of the bridge watching the lights onshore disappear behind us one by one. Eventually the coast of Portugal was completely out of sight. Every so often the foam of a breaking wave would make a white flash in the darkness, but otherwise the sea lay black all round us.

I was on my way. There was no turning back.

The door from the bridge opened and Captain Anderson looked out, his stinking pipe in his mouth.

"Ten to midnight," he said. "Time for a change of watch. Are you ready to take your turn in the engine room?"

I still hadn't got over the distress caused by my encounter with Chief Inspector Garretta, but my hands were no longer shaking, so I nodded.

"Look in on the stokers' mess on your way down," Anderson said before closing the door. "I think the cook has put out some supper for you."

The crew on large vessels is usually divided into two watches, one working while the other rests. The watch changes every four hours. That's the way the *Song of Limerick* worked too. I had been told there would be four men in the engine room during my watch: the second engineer Geoff Gerrard, two stokers and me—the grease monkey.

The engineer is boss in the engine room, and the grease monkey is his helpmate, so to speak. The stokers' job is to shovel coal into the fireboxes to keep up steam pressure in the boilers. It's heavy, filthy work. The heat in the boiler room is insufferable and the air thick with coal dust. The grease monkey's work is easier, but it calls for more knowledge of engines and machinery.

I was glad that Captain Anderson had enlisted me as a grease monkey, not as a stoker. I now had to demonstrate that I could live up to it.

I found my three workmates in the stokers' mess, a narrow cabin with a dirty, stained table in the middle and wooden benches fixed along the sides. This was where the engine room personnel ate their meals and played cards when they weren't on watch. A paraffin lantern hung above the table and swung back and forth in time with the movements of the ship. Its glass was yellowed, and the light it cast in that narrow space was gloomy. I took a seat, and Geoff ladled a portion of potato soup into a tin bowl and gave it to me.

The two stokers looked at me without any sign of interest. One of them was big and broad-shouldered with a fair-haired forelock and freckles under the soot on his face. He was cleaning his nails with an unusually large clasp knife. The other stoker was older and of a more sinewy build. He had a black Mexican mustache and a clay pipe in the corner of his mouth. Geoff introduced them to me: the fair-haired fellow was called Paddy O'Connor, and the sinewy one Johnny Doyle. Both were Irishmen, both from Dublin.

"And this is Sally Jones," Geoff said in a cheerful voice, patting me on the shoulder. "The famous Sally Jones! Engineer on the *Hudson Queen*! You must have heard of her, haven't you? And now she's going to join our watch. What an honor, eh?"

Paddy O'Connor greeted me with a brief nod. Johnny Doyle took the pipe out of his mouth and gave a friendly smile behind his mustache.

"Good to have you on board," he said. "Tell me, are you a chimpanzee or a gorilla?"

Paddy rolled his eyes, closed his knife with a loud click and stood up.

"You're a real idiot, you are, Johnny," he said. "Gorillas can't answer questions. They can't talk! See you down below."

And Paddy opened the door and disappeared out into the darkness. When the door closed behind him, Johnny leaned forward a little and looked me in the eye.

"I reckon you can talk. You can, can't you?"

I shook my head.

Johnny smiled again. There were big gaps between the brown teeth in his mouth.

"Makes no difference, mate," he said with a wink. "Geoff will do enough talking for both of you."

Johnny Doyle was right. Throughout the whole of my first watch in the engine room of the *Song of Limerick*, Geoff talked and joked without a break. I have never met anyone so chatty and cheerful. But he also kept a watchful eye on me. He obviously wanted to be sure I was doing my job properly. Nothing strange about that—after all, I was a new member of the crew.

The engine of the *Song of Limerick* was a triple-expansion steam engine made by Wigham Richardson & Co. of England. It was a common enough model, and I knew it well. I knew where to locate all the grease cups and grease nipples, and I knew where to put my hand to check that the bearings were not running too hot.

Geoff was pleased with me. That's what he said, anyway, to the various nosy crewmen who came down to the engine room to take a look at me before the watch changed at four o'clock. Several of them gave me a friendly pat on the head or shoulder and said, "Welcome aboard." Some of them even shook me by the hand.

It felt really good to be on my way at last, and suddenly I no longer felt so bad.

~

That morning we rounded Cabo de São Vicente and sailed into the Bay of Cádiz. The sea was calm and the sun was shining. Not that I saw much of the fine weather: Mr. Bullworth, the engineer on the other watch, set me to work.

"Can you do blacksmith work?" he asked.

I nodded.

"We're short of spanners. Have you made ever made them?"

I had. Spanners are used for tightening and loosening nuts, and they are an engineer's most important tool. The Chief and I had made all the spanners on the *Hudson Queen* ourselves.

"In that case," Mr. Bullworth said, "you'll find an anvil, hammers and fire in the boiler room. There's some iron in the store. On you go!"

By evening I was worn out. Blacksmith work is fun, but hard and heavy. And I hadn't had any sleep for forty-eight hours. Since all the bunks in the stokers' quarters were occupied, I had to live in the engineers' store—a room off the engine room with a workbench in one corner. There was just about enough room to sling a hammock.

Immediately after the evening watch I climbed into my hammock and fell asleep. I don't know how long I'd been asleep when it happened. I just remember that I dreamt I was falling, and then a hard bang on the head woke me.

For a few moments I had no idea where I was or what had happened. The door was slightly ajar and a thin streak of light entered from the engine room. I was lying on the rough steel plates that formed the floor, and my hammock was under me. It had fallen down, taking me with it. But how?

I stood up carefully. The back of my head was bleeding,

and my back hurt. The hammock had been tied to a hook just inside the door. When I looked I could see that the knot was still in place, but the rope itself had given way.

I held the rope ends up to the light and a shudder ran down my spine. There was a neat cut through the rope. It had been sliced with a knife. A very sharp knife, at that.

I tied the rope ends together, put up the hammock and climbed in. But I couldn't get back to sleep. My head was aching and my thoughts were churning.

Besides which, I was on tenterhooks that whoever had cut the rope might came back.

~

There is nothing more important at sea than being able to rely on your shipmates. Every sailor knows that. I knew now that someone aboard the *Song of Limerick* was out to do me harm, but I had no idea who. It wasn't a nice feeling.

I suppose it shouldn't really have come as a great surprise. I already knew that someone in the crew had reported me to the Lisbon police. Chief Inspector Garretta himself had said that much: *Lucky for me there was someone on board who wanted a slice of the reward I'd just posted.* That's what Garretta had said, wasn't it?

Was the person who had sold me to Garretta the same person who had cut my hammock down? Or did I have more than one enemy on the *Song of Limerick*? Those questions worried me more than the cut on the back of my head.

I was going to have to keep my eyes open and be careful. Above all, I didn't want my hammock cut down again. My first thought was to lock the door of the store, but then I remembered that it's forbidden to lock doors from the inside aboard ship. This is a matter of fire safety. So instead I replaced the rope on the hammock with a piece of rusty wire I found in a drawer of scraps under the workbench. It would take a hacksaw or a set of wire cutters to cut the wire. Anyone who tried it with a knife would ruin the blade.

~

We passed through the Strait of Gibraltar later that day. Geoff and I were leaning on the rail taking in the fresh air before going on watch. Through the sun haze we could pick out the high fortified cliff that guarded the northern side of the strait.

"I've heard there are apes living up on that cliff," Geoff said.

I had heard that too. I think they are actually a sort of monkey.

"Perhaps they're relations of yours? Do you want us to put in so you can visit them?"

I looked at Geoff. His face was a mass of laugh lines. He

nudged me in the ribs to show he was joking, but I already knew that—Geoff was always joking. With everyone and about everything. He teased the captain and the mate, ribbed the stokers and the deckhands, needled the cook and the first mate, Mr. Bullworth, who was a sullen fellow. No one took offense. Quite the opposite, everyone on board liked Geoff. And I did too: I was lucky to have him as the engineer on the same watch.

I wondered whether to show Geoff what had happened to my hammock. He would probably be able to work out who was guilty. Geoff knew most of what was happening on board.

I decided not to, though. Seamen who tell tales on shipmates are not popular. The sensible thing to do was to solve my problems for myself.

~

I was off duty between twelve and four that night, and I slept soundly until Mr. Bullworth stuck his head in and shouted that it would be time for me to go on watch in ten minutes. When I took down my hammock I remembered to take a close look at the wire.

I saw it immediately. The rusty wire had been scraped clean at a point close to the eyelet, and a couple of the metal strands were cut.

Someone had attempted to cut down my hammock again while I was asleep. Whoever it was hadn't noticed in the darkness that I'd replaced the rope with wire. Presumably he had just opened the door slightly, shoved his hand through and sliced with the knife where he knew the hammock was attached.

I stowed my hammock away behind the workbench and hurried to the stokers' mess to try to get some breakfast before going on watch. I wasn't especially happy that I'd managed to trick my unknown enemy: I was, in fact, quite worried that he had tried to hurt me again.

Who could it be?

I found the answer to that question sooner than I could have imagined.

Geoff was sitting in the mess eating a plate of porridge. Still half-asleep, he served up a plate for me. It was luke-warm oatmeal porridge, burnt to the pan. The cook found it very hard to wake up in the morning, and breakfasts on board were often pretty hit-and-miss.

Johnny Doyle and Paddy O'Connor had already finished eating. Johnny was puffing away on his clay pipe and Paddy, as usual, was cleaning his nails with his big clasp knife. The blade shone when it caught the light of the paraffin lantern swaying above the table. I stopped suddenly with the spoon halfway to my mouth and stared at Paddy's knife.

There was a notch in the sharpened edge, and the blade was discolored round the notch with what looked like rust.

"What are you staring at, gorilla?" Paddy said.

Our eyes met. His were small and pale blue. And full of rage. At that moment Paddy O'Connor and I both knew where we stood.

Johnny took the pipe from his mouth with a little laugh.

"That was a pretty stupid question, Paddy. Gorillas can't answer. They can't talk. Surely you know that?"

"Shut your mouth!" Paddy snarled. He stood up and left the mess.

Geoff looked up from his porridge in surprise at Paddy's disappearing back.

"What was all that about?"

"No idea," Johnny said with a shrug. "He must have got up on the wrong side of the bed or something."

CHAPTER 32
Storm Winds from the Sahara

I actually felt relieved. Known enemies are preferable to unknown enemies and, moreover, I could guess why Paddy O'Connor had a grudge against me. Many stokers hope to be promoted to grease monkeys so they can escape the heavy work in the coal bunkers and feeding the fire. I've no doubt that Paddy O'Connor was furious that I— a gorilla—had been given the job he wanted.

For the next two nights I slept in my hammock undisturbed. When I met Paddy in the stokers' mess he pretended nothing had happened. I wondered whether I should show some goodwill by giving him and Johnny a hand with the stoking now and again, but I decided not to. It might be misunderstood in some way and simply make things worse. Better to do what Paddy was doing and behave as if nothing was amiss.

The days passed, one watch following another. In order to avoid Paddy I stayed away from the stokers' mess when I was off duty. Sometimes I just stayed in the engine room, making tools or working on something else. Sometimes, if the weather was fine, I would sit up on deck in the lee of the after-deckhouse.

Geoff found me there one day and produced a small folding chessboard from his pocket.

"Do you know what this is?" he asked.

A conjurer called Silvio had taught me to play chess years before. Silvio had also taught me various other skills, such as reading and writing. It was all a long time ago, but I hadn't forgotten. So I nodded to Geoff.

"I thought as much!" he laughed. "I've not had anyone to play against on board the *Limerick*. Come on, let's have a game and you can show me how good you are."

From that day on, Geoff and I played chess almost every time we weren't on watch. In the beginning he used to win easily, but I soon learned his strategies and tactics, and after that I hardly ever lost a game.

~

We hit bad weather south of Sardinia. A storm from the Sahara was passing across the Mediterranean and bringing strong dry winds with it. Fine desert sand gathered in every crack and crevice on deck and my fur began itching the moment I went outside. We sailed a southeasterly course at half speed for several days, holding the bow to the waves.

My job was to control the throttle valve that regulated how much steam reached the engine. The more steam, the higher the speed. It was up to me to cut off the steam to the engine every time the stern of the ship rose out of the water. This was an important task. When a stern rises, the propeller may come above the surface, which means there is no water resistance and consequently the propeller races. Unless the steam pressure is reduced very quickly, the engine races out of control. That can be very frightening; the noise alone is enough to make your guts churn. But it can also cause serious damage to the engine and to the hull—if worse comes to worst, the ship may be lost.

Mr. Bullworth was not too happy that Geoff had put me in charge of the throttle valve.

"Was it wise to put all our lives in the hands of a gorilla?" he muttered.

"Dealing with the throttle valve is always part of the grease monkey's job," Geoff said, managing to be serious for once. "And Sally Jones is no worse than any other grease monkey I've sailed with."

As for me, I wasn't at all worried. It's an important function, but not a difficult one.

Early in the morning of the second day of the storm, however, something happened that shouldn't have.

We had been on the dogwatch that night, and just before the change of watch at four o'clock Geoff went up to the bridge to lubricate the steering mechanism. I remained alone down in the engine room, concentrating on looking after the throttle valve.

Suddenly, just as the vessel was going down into a trough between waves, two powerful arms took hold of me from behind. For one moment I assumed it was Geoff teasing me as usual. But it wasn't. The arms that were gripping me were strong and black with soot.

The stern of the ship slowly began rising out of the water. That was the moment when I ought to have been ready to shut off steam. But my arms and chest were held in a grip of iron, and I couldn't move—indeed, I could scarcely breathe.

"Now then, you!" Paddy O'Connor hissed in my ear. "Now we'll show them what happens when a gorilla is put in charge of machinery!"

I tried to get a grip with my legs and twist out of Paddy's arms, but I could already feel that the angle of the ship was changing. At any minute now the propeller was going to break the surface. But Paddy's grip remained firm. In panic I threw my head back, and as I did so his shoulder came in contact with my cheek. I realized that if I stretched my neck and twisted my head as far as I could, I could sink my teeth into Paddy's upper arm.

Paddy roared in pain and released his grip. The engine was just beginning to race, so I hurled myself at the throttle valve and cut off the steam. At the very last moment!

When I turned round Paddy was standing clutching his arm. The whites of his eyes gleamed in his soot-stained face.

"Damn you, you animal, you! You bit me!" he snarled.

Then he hurried out of the boiler room and disappeared.

A few minutes later Geoff returned. He was smiling as usual, but there was a questioning look in his eyes.

"I heard the engine beginning to race just now," he said. "You didn't fall asleep on duty, did you?"

I shook my head, my heart still pounding.

After that I watched my back and made sure I was never left alone with Paddy O'Connor. And I always bolted the door of the storeroom when I was going to sleep, even though it was forbidden.

CHAPTER 33
Rue des Soeurs

The storm abated after three days. We were steering
east and were now within a couple of days of the Suez
Canal.

But there was a sudden change of plan. The shipping
office telegraphed new orders to Captain Anderson, telling
him to head at once for the Egyptian port of Alexandria,
where an urgent and important cargo was waiting for us.

The following morning Geoff and I were leaning on the

rail as the *Song of Limerick* steamed in between the break-waters that protect the harbor at Alexandria. There were at least fifty vessels lying at anchor in the roads and tug-boats and barges were moving among them. Feluccas, those small Egyptian sailing boats with lateen sails, completed the scene. The breeze coming off the shore was a heavy mix of all the wonderful scents and foul smells of a great city.

We continued to a quay in the inner basin, and no sooner had we moored than the landing stage was surrounded by eager street vendors. Captain Anderson gave orders that none of them were to be allowed on board. Thieves are the scourge of a vessel in port.

Captain Anderson himself took a horse-drawn cab to the harbor office to find out about the cargo we were to take on. On his return he told us that the cargo would not be ready for three days and meanwhile we would take the opportunity to fill our bunkers with coal.

A couple of hours later a fully laden coal barge lay to alongside us, and the dirty and exhausting job of filling the *Song of Limerick*'s bunkers began. The whole crew—apart from the captain, the first mate and the cook—helped out with shovels, sacks and the loading crane, but it still took three days. It didn't bother me: as long as we were all work-ing together Paddy O'Connor couldn't do me any harm.

Once the bunkers were full the first mate told us we

still had a few more days to wait because the cargo we were expecting had been delayed. He didn't tell us what it was, nor did Captain Anderson. Clearly, for some reason, it was a secret.

The crew was given shore leave. All the seamen, except those needed to guard the ship, crowded round the water hose on deck, anxious to wash away the coal dust. A little while later a jolly gang of men, clean-shaven with wet-combed hair and dressed in their very best shirts, went down the gangplank. Jolliest and loudest of all was Paddy O'Connor, who was shouting and carrying on as if he owned the whole of Alexandria.

"Better hold on to their hats, these Arabs! Or their turbans, rather! Tonight I'm going to show them how a real northerner lets his hair down!"

There was a line of horse-drawn cabs down on the quayside, waiting to take the seamen into the city. In order to save a couple of coppers, as many men as possible squeezed into each cab. All except Paddy O'Connor, who looked for and found a taxi and sat alone in the backseat with a broad grin on his face.

"Take me to a really posh bar! And make it snappy!" he yelled at the driver so loudly that everyone on the quay could hear him.

"How can Paddy afford to take a taxi, do you reckon?" I

heard one of the sailors mutter in a surly voice. "When we were in Lisbon I had to pay his bill at O Pelicano because he'd drunk away his last cent, and more."

~

I stayed on board, although I didn't have to. It was nice to have some time to myself. In order to give the people left to guard the ship a chance to buy cigarettes and postcards, a couple of the street vendors were allowed to come aboard. I didn't have any money, of course, but the first mate was kind enough to give me five Egyptian piastres, which was enough for a picture postcard, a stamp and a bag of oranges.

The postcard had a picture of a large square in Alexandria. On the plain side I wrote Ana and Signor Fidardo's address on Rua de São Tomé in Lisbon and a short message:

Journey going well. Don't worry about me.
Sally Jones.

Now that I had a moment to myself and the time to think about it, I realized how much I was missing Ana and Signor Fidardo. They must be really worried about me, which gave me a bad conscience. I hoped the postcard would calm their fears.

After dropping the card into the box for outgoing mail

in the telegraph operator's cabin, I sat down in the sun and for the rest of the afternoon, ate oranges and watched the ships at anchor.

After supper I went down to the engineers' storeroom and immediately fell asleep in my hammock. It was over a week since I had last had a full night's rest.

~

I was wakened the next morning by the noise of the returning sailors who'd been out on the town the whole night. They were coming back on board in time for the change of watch.

Last to arrive was Paddy O'Connor, who had to be carried aboard by Johnny Doyle and a deckhand. They'd found him in a bordello on Rue des Soeurs, where he was sitting in the bar singing indecent Irish songs and arm-wrestling with the madame of the place. Rue des Soeurs means "Sisters' Street" and is the main thoroughfare in Alexandria's notorious red-light district. Every well-traveled sailor knows it.

Paddy was now sound asleep with his mouth open. He had a bundle of Cuban cigars sticking out of his breast pocket, and his hand was clamped round the neck of a bottle of five-star gin. When his shipmates laid him down on the deck, coins and notes tumbled out of his pockets.

Captain Anderson came down from the bridge to view

the scene. His face grew dark when he caught sight of the money, the cigars and the brand of the gin.

"Since when has Paddy O'Connor been a wealthy man?" he asked.

No one answered. They were all wondering the same thing.

Captain Anderson pulled the hose off the reel, turned on the tap and aimed the jet straight in the face of the sleeping drunk. Paddy woke with a jerk, spluttering and spitting.

"Report to the bridge in ten minutes, O'Connor," Captain Anderson said, turning on his heel.

Johnny Doyle helped Paddy to get into dry clothes, and the cook brewed a pot of coffee as strong and black as tar. Paddy drank several mugs, but it didn't appear to be of much use. His forehead was as pale as a corpse, and the cold sweat pouring from him stank of pure spirits.

The conversation that took place on the bridge between Captain Anderson and Paddy O'Connor did not last more than half an hour. When Paddy emerged he looked even more miserable than he had earlier. A little more sober, though. He went to the stokers' quarters without saying a word, and there he packed his few possessions. Not even Johnny Doyle could get him to divulge what had been said.

Pale-faced and weak at the knees, Paddy O'Connor left the *Song of Limerick*. With his seaman's kit bag on his shoulder and his seaman's book in his back pocket, he plodded along the quay and disappeared between two warehouses.

That was the last we saw of him.

~

What was it that had happened?

We all wondered.

Geoff, of course, was the one who managed to dig out the truth. Geoff, who was everyone's friend, coaxed the second mate into telling him all he knew.

Captain Anderson had no time for informers, and ever since we left Lisbon he had been wondering who tipped off the police that I would be aboard the *Song of Limerick*. The informer had been given a ten-pound reward by Garretta— a very large sum of money for an ordinary seaman. Captain Anderson had guessed that the informer would give himself away the moment there was an opportunity to go ashore and start splashing the money round.

And that was precisely what Paddy O'Connor had done.

But Paddy would not confess to the captain. Instead he said he had found ten one-pound notes in a tin hidden behind the pipework in the engine room. There was no way that Captain Anderson believed him, but since he could not prove he was lying he allowed Paddy to sign off rather than sacking him. That would look better in Paddy's seaman's book.

Paddy and his money were the talk of the *Song of Limerick* for a long time. In the end everyone agreed that Captain Anderson had done the right thing. Squealing on a shipmate for money is a serious crime, even if that shipmate happens to be a gorilla. And Paddy, unfortunately, was the type to do that sort of thing. Even Johnny Doyle had to go along with that.

CHAPTER 34
A Strange Beast

We remained in Alexandria for a few more days. The deckhands spent their time scraping old paint off the funnel, chipping rust off the ship's sides and touching up the paint. Down in the engine room we cleaned out the boilers, adjusted bearings and repacked the seals of any valves that were leaking. We were beginning to get tired of life in port and looking forward to casting off and getting under way again.

Late one evening the cargo we had been waiting for arrived. At last! A small caravan of vehicles drove along the quay where the *Song of Limerick* was moored. First of all there was an open car carrying two uniformed customs men. That was followed by two trucks, one of which was loaded with bales of hay; the other was carrying a big metal cage. We couldn't see what was in the cage because the sides were covered with sheets of plywood.

The fourth vehicle was a gleaming black Daimler with velvet curtains over the rear windows. The chauffeur leaped out of the car and opened the doors for his passengers. A tall thin man in a double-breasted suit and Panama hat was the first to step out. It was obvious he was a company director, and he looked up at the *Song of Limerick* with a severe expression on his face. A younger, shorter man wearing a pith helmet and crumpled khaki shirt emerged behind him.

"I see you've chosen a rust bucket that's just about ready for the scrap heap," the tall man in the suit said. "Couldn't you have found something better, Mr. Wilkins?"

The younger man, whose name was obviously Wilkins, dried his forehead with a handkerchief and pushed his small spectacles back up his nose.

"Not at such short notice, unfortunately, Mr. Thursgood, sir. But the shipping company guaranteed—"

"Yes, yes, yes!" the man in the suit interrupted him

impatiently. "Tell someone to fetch the captain. We don't have all night."

A little later the deck was a hive of activity. A couple of the crew opened the cargo hatches and turned the boom of the deck crane out over the quay. The second mate and two deckhands reorganized the hold so there was space for the bales of hay and the large cage.

Mr. Thursgood—the man in the suit—together with Mr. Wilkins and the customs officers accompanied the captain up to the bridge to deal with the paperwork. Once that was done the first mate signaled for the cargo to be loaded, and the cage was slowly lifted from the quay. Mr. Thursgood and Mr. Wilkins watched from the bridge. They looked nervous, especially Mr. Wilkins, who was mopping his brow with a handkerchief almost the whole time.

Every now and again strange, mournful bellows and dull, threatening snorts could be heard from the cage, and some of the sailors on deck looked at one another anxiously. What kind of beast was concealed behind those plywood sheets?

As soon as the load had been lowered into the hold, the crew gathered round the open hatch and peered down. On the bottom of the cage was a layer of hay, and on the hay lay a camel, chewing cud. After every second chew it produced a raucous roar.

The moment I saw the camel I thought there was something strange about it, although I couldn't put my finger on what it was. Not, that is, until Geoff laughed and exclaimed: "Take a look at that! It's got one hump too many!"

So that's what it was. This camel did not just have one hump or two humps, it had *three* humps! I had no idea that there were such animals as three-humped camels!

The cage was securely fastened for the voyage ahead, and the plywood sheets were removed. An electric light was connected so the camel would not have to live in darkness. When Mr. Thursgood, obviously the owner of the camel, had satisfied himself that the animal was safe and well, he went ashore and was whisked away in his black Daimler. Mr. Wilkins remained on board: it was his job to look after the camel on the voyage to India.

Before Mr. Thursgood left I heard him say to Mr. Wilkins: "It's up to you now to make sure my camel reaches Bombay in good condition. There is a great deal at stake, Wilkins, don't forget that!"

"Of course not, Mr. Thursgood, sir," Wilkins answered.

~

The *Song of Limerick* sailed from Alexandria on December 18 and steered an easterly course across waters that had an oily sheen. There was a long, slow, rolling ground swell.

The following morning, off Port Said, we took on a pilot and were given clearance to start our passage through the Suez Canal. We were part of a convoy consisting of some dozen vessels. On both sides of us the banks of the canal were lifeless and sun-scorched. The only features to break the tedious monotony were the occasional Bedouin camps.

Twenty-four hours later we dropped off our pilot in Port Tewfik and headed out into the Red Sea. The water sparkled green, and the sky was a radiant blue from horizon to horizon. The weather was so splendid that our first and second mates left the cargo hatch open to give the camel more light and fresh air. The animal lay in its cage, contentedly chewing hay. Every now and again it would stand up, stretch its legs a little, turn its muzzle up to the sun and with total unconcern deposit a heap of dung on the floor of the cage.

Our other passenger, Mr. Wilkins, was far less happy with life at sea, and every time I saw him he had a deep furrow of worry in his brow. He got on the crew's nerves with his anxious questions and endless complaints. One moment he was worrying whether the camel's cage had been properly secured, the next he was concerned that the beast's drinking water was tainted. He even inquired whether we had a camel-sized life jacket on board. And so it went on.

After a couple of days, however, Mr. Wilkins calmed down. That was Geoff's doing. He took the time to answer all his questions and to explain to him calmly how things functioned on board ship. Only then did Mr. Wilkins feel confident that the camel was safe down in the hold.

That was Geoff all over. He made sure he was on good terms with everyone he met.

Mr. Wilkins started joining Geoff and me when we were playing chess. He was quite a reasonable chess player himself, and he played against us in turn. He also told us how he had ended up accompanying a three-humped camel to India.

"It's more than a little strange when I think about it," Mr. Wilkins said. "A year ago I couldn't have imagined in my wildest dreams that I'd be involved in an adventure of this sort. I was living in London and working as a zoologist for the Royal Society. My job was to catalog rare and extinct species of animals, a quiet and peaceful occupation I'd been doing for years. Then one day I received a letter from a mining company, Thursgood & Thursgood Co. Ltd. The company director, a certain Charles Allen Thursgood, wanted me to call on him at his office."

"Thursgood?" Geoff wondered. "Do you mean the fellow who was with us when we loaded the camel?"

Mr. Wilkins nodded and then continued his tale.

"I wondered if there had been some sort of misunderstanding. Why would the director of a mining company want to meet me, a zoologist? But I decided to go and meet him anyway, purely out of curiosity. When I went to his office Mr. Thursgood was very friendly and gave me a glass of whisky. He asked how much I was paid at the Royal Society, and when I told him what I earned he gave me a sympathetic look. He thought I ought to be paid much more than that, since I was the top expert in the country when it came to rare and extinct animals. I agreed with him, of course. Mr. Thursgood eventually came to the point—he offered me a new job. It was all about finding a living *rare* animal, and by rare Mr. Thursgood meant *unique*. He wanted to become the owner of an animal of which there was only one specimen. If I could find such a beast for him he would pay me an absolutely enormous sum of money."

Mr. Wilkins told us that he hadn't immediately agreed to the proposal. Nor, however, had he said no; he had asked for time to think about it. Three days later he had made up his mind: the thought of *the absolutely enormous sum of money* had suddenly made his ordinary cataloging job seem trivial.

"So I said yes," Mr. Wilkins said.

"I'd have done the same," Geoff laughed. "But what did the company director want a rare animal for? Did you ever discover that?"

"I did indeed. He was intending to give it away. To an Indian maharaja."

"To a maharaja? But why?"

"I asked him that too," Mr. Wilkins said. "And he told me his company was involved in diamond mining and the company geologists had recently discovered a source of diamonds in a small Indian state called Bhapur. The discovery seemed to be a truly promising one, but before they could start test-drilling they had to be given the go-ahead by the maharaja, who was the absolute ruler of Bhapur."

Mr. Thursgood had explained to Mr. Wilkins that the Maharaja of Bhapur was famous for his unbelievable wealth and for the life of luxurious dissipation he led. Also for his changeable moods and his capricious temperament. It made Mr. Thursgood uneasy to think that the future of the diamond mining project was in the hands of such an unpredictable individual. Consequently he intended to go to India himself and put the company plans to the maharaja, but in advance of this meeting nothing was to be left to chance. The diamond project was to be unveiled in the grand manner, which would include persuasive presentations by renowned geologists as well as tempting estimates of the amount of money the maharaja would make out of the business.

In addition to all that, there needed to be a gift, and that was perhaps the most important thing of all. Mr. Thursgood had to have something truly outstanding to give to the maharaja before he broached the question of diamond mining.

But what can you give to a maharaja who already owns a palace, luxury cars and jewelry worth many millions of pounds?

Thursgood had employed a firm of private detectives whose task it was—with the utmost discretion—to gather all the known and unknown facts about the maharaja's life and interests. Among the many things the detectives uncovered was the fact that the maharaja had his own zoo tucked away in the huge garden of his palace. It was no ordinary zoo: it was a collection of the most unusual and valuable animals. It contained, for instance, the last living example of the Tasmanian marsupial wolf and many, many other strange creatures.

Mr. Thursgood knew at once that what he needed to present to the maharaja was a new, unique addition to his zoo. A present of such magnificence would guarantee that the maharaja gave his approval to the diamond mining.

"And that is why Mr. Thursgood employed me," Mr. Wilkins continued. "So for the past few years I have been traveling the globe in search of an animal sufficiently unusual to be a suitable addition to the maharaja's zoo. I have corresponded with zoologists in every corner of the globe, and I have visited hundreds of national parks. I have hunted the Abominable Snowman in the Himalayas and fished for the Storsjön Monster in the lake near Östersund in northern Sweden. And with every passing week Mr. Thursgood became more and more impatient. About a month ago he was on the point of firing me, but then, in the nick of time, I received a letter from Egypt."

"Aha!" Geoff exclaimed. "And would that letter have been about a camel, by any chance?"

Mr. Wilkins nodded.

"That's right," he said. "A colleague of mine in Cairo had heard rumors of a camel with three humps in a small village on the edge of the Sahara Desert. Camels with three humps are extremely rare. I set off for Egypt at once, located the camel and bought it for Mr. Thursgood. The seller was a powerful Bedouin sheikh who knew the value of his unique possession. The price was very high."

"How high?" Geoff asked, being nosy.

"Higher than you could ever imagine," Mr. Wilkins answered in a rather superior tone.

"Crikey, now I see!" Geoff laughed. "So that's why you were so worried that something might happen to the camel."

Mr. Wilkins nodded earnestly.

"It would be dreadful. Especially now that we are so close to our destination. As long as the camel stays healthy until we reach Bhapur, my job will be done."

"And Mr. Thursgood will give you an absolutely enormous sum of money!" Geoff said.

"Precisely!" Mr. Wilkins smiled, and a dreamy expression spread across his face.

"We'll drink to that!" Geoff said, raising his coffee mug.

As for me, well, I thought Mr. Wilkins seemed altogether too much in love with money. And that's not a very pleasant trait.

CHAPTER 35
The SS *Minsk* Goes Down

The fine weather held until we came out into the Gulf of Aden, where we met a strong headwind. The ship began pitching violently in the choppy sea, and the wind was increasing by the hour. By the time we were passing the point of the Horn of Africa a full storm was raging. We were exposed to the open Arabian Sea and mountainous waves as high as two-story buildings. Keeping her head to the wind, the *Song of Limerick* steamed along at no more than five knots, her bow disappearing from time to time in a maelstrom of roaring, foaming water.

Mr. Wilkins became seasick when he had to muck out the camel down in the dark hold. Being seasick is no fun, I know that. There was a time when the movement of a ship often made me feel ill, but things have improved with the years. These days I merely feel a little lethargic and listless.

In Mr. Wilkins's case seasickness made him lose the will to live. He shut himself in his cabin and wasn't seen for several days. During that time we took it in turns to tend the camel, and we quickly noticed that something was the matter. The animal had stopped eating and stopped drinking. It just lay there staring vacantly into the darkness of the hold. When the vessel heeled to the side, it slid across the floor of the cage and smashed into the bars. Now and again it roared unhappily, but for the most part it showed few signs of life.

After a while we realized what was affecting the camel: it too was feeling seasick. If you looked carefully you could see that it was pale and green round the muzzle.

Geoff and I lashed bales of hay to the bars inside the cage so that the camel would not get injured when the ship rolled. We made sure it always had fresh water and that there was hay in the manger. There wasn't much more we could do and, in fact, there was no real cause for concern.

Camels can go for ages without food and water, because the humps on their backs are reserves of fat that can last for months.

"And after all, this fellow even has an extra hump to rely on," Geoff said with a laugh.

~

The storm showed no sign of easing off, and to spare both the crew and our supply of coal Captain Anderson set a course for Socotra, an isolated rocky island 120 nautical miles east of the coast of Africa. Twelve hours later we were dropping anchor in a sheltered bay, protected from wind and waves.

After a storm there is always a great deal to be put right on board ship. Everyone's clothes and kit are sodden. Storerooms and workshops are in a shambles. Wherever you look there are things, both large and small, that are broken and in need of repair. But before we settled down to all this, Captain Anderson made sure that everyone had a chance to rest. He was a good captain was Captain Anderson.

Mr. Wilkins improved once the swell subsided. He looked utterly miserable when he first emerged from his cabin. His skin was pale as a corpse, and exhaustion and lack of sleep had left him with blue-black rings round his eyes. A little color returned to his unshaven cheeks after he'd had a bite to eat, but it disappeared as quickly as it had come when Geoff told him the state of the camel.

"Oh, Lord Above, please don't let it be true! Don't let it be true!" Mr. Wilkins exclaimed before hurrying down to the hold.

During the days that we lay at anchor Mr. Wilkins did everything in his power to help the camel recover. He tried feeding it with sugar water and with gruel, but the camel immediately threw up what little it had eaten. Mr. Wilkins was beside himself with worry. It was beginning to be obvious that the camel was using up the fat reserves in its humps, and the middle hump seemed to have shrunk a little.

The wind at last began to abate somewhat, and the mercury in the barometer began to rise. We weighed anchor and resumed our voyage east. The wind was still strong and the seas still running high, but we could now sail at eight knots. Always assuming that nothing unforeseen occurred, we should be in Bombay within ten days. Mr. Wilkins was counting the hours.

Scarcely had the island of Socotra dropped below the horizon before the unforeseen did occur. Late in the afternoon Sparks, our telegraph operator, picked up a Mayday call from a Russian ship by the name of the *Minsk*. Her position was no more than fifty nautical miles south of us, and Captain Anderson immediately set a new course to take us to the vessel in distress.

Mr. Wilkins must have realized that something was happening, since the *Song of Limerick* was now taking waves abeam and beginning to roll heavily. He went up to the bridge to find out what was going on. I wasn't there, of course, but Geoff told me later what had passed between Mr. Wilkins and Captain Anderson. Geoff, in turn, had heard it from a seaman who happened to be on the bridge at that point.

Captain Anderson had explained to Mr. Wilkins that we had received a Mayday call and were heading south to come to the aid of the *Minsk*. Mr. Wilkins had then completely lost control of himself.

"But that's absolutely out of the question!" he exclaimed. "As captain your responsibility is to bring your cargo safely into harbor. Mr. Thursgood's camel is seriously ill and needs to be got ashore as rapidly as possible. I insist that you sail us straight to Bombay!"

"Mr. Wilkins," Captain Anderson answered. "Think about what you are saying for a moment. Human lives are in danger!"

"And the camel's life might also be at risk!" Mr. Wilkins continued without noticing how angry Captain Anderson's face had grown. "Do you have any idea what the camel is worth? We don't have time for missions of mercy!"

Captain Anderson was so enraged that he bit through the stem of the old corncob pipe that lived permanently in the corner of his mouth.

"Get out of here!" he roared, flakes of snuff and tobacco flying in all directions. "And if you have any sense in that thick skull of yours, Mr. Wilkins, keep out of my sight!"

After that scene Mr. Wilkins didn't dare show his face on the bridge or in the officers' wardroom for the rest of the voyage. He must have realized he had disgraced himself, for nothing is more sacred to seamen than the duty to help those in distress at sea. The next time it could very easily be their own lives that were dependent on someone coming to the rescue.

~

Dusk was falling when we arrived at the position from which the *Minsk* had sent her distress call. We sailed in circles round the area all night and all the following day. Even the off-duty sailors joined in, and everyone who could be spared kept a lookout for any traces of the *Minsk*. Since I'm a good climber I was hoisted up the foremast with a pair of binoculars round my neck, and I hung there in a boat-swain's chair for two days and nights, scanning the tossing sea. Apart from a whale and a couple of schools of dolphins, all I saw was a mass of big gray waves topped with angry foam. They winched me down every other hour and gave me a cup of tea to keep me warm.

The search was called off on the morning of the third day. Another vessel in the area had discovered an oil slick and wreckage. A little while later they rescued a lifeboat with seven Russian sailors in it. The men were sodden and frozen, but they were alive. And then a capsized lifeboat was also found. It had probably been overturned by the swell caused by the sinking vessel. The captain of the *Minsk* and five of his crew had perished. Their bodies were never found—there are many sharks in the waters off East Africa.

Before continuing our voyage to Bombay, Captain Anderson gathered all the crew of the *Song of Limerick* on deck to listen to a reading from the Bible. Then he produced a bottle of whisky and poured every man a dram so we could drink to the memory of the men who had drowned.

~

The *Song of Limerick* was now both late and well off course. We had at least twelve days' sailing between us and Bombay. The camel was lying in the hold, sliding listlessly from one side of its cage to the other. There was no sign of it regaining its appetite, but apart from that it did not appear to be particularly ill. Perhaps it was quite simply bored. And that wouldn't have been so strange.

Mr. Wilkins, however, did not take the matter lightly, and he tried everything to persuade the camel to eat. When Geoff pointed out that the camel actually had all the nourishment it needed in its humps, Mr. Wilkins threw his hands up in despair: "And that is exactly the problem! Take a look for yourself!"

He pointed at the camel's humps, and it was quite obvious that the camel really was drawing nourishment from one of its three, the middle one to be precise. Twelve days at sea had turned the beast from a three-humped camel into a two-and-a-half-humped camel.

The weather improved as we approached India. In a gentle northeasterly monsoon wind the *Song of Limerick* steamed toward Bombay at a steady fourteen knots with dolphins playing in her bow wave.

The mood on board rose, as it always does after a testing storm. Mr. Wilkins was the only one not made happier by the fine weather. The camel was still refusing to eat even though the motion of the waves was now very modest. The crew opened the hatch above the cage and that seemed to cheer the animal up a little. It stretched its muzzle toward the sunlight and even tried to stand on its legs for a while.

But it still would not eat, not even when Mr. Wilkins

offered it cooked vegetables he had bribed the cook to give him.

~

We sighted land on the evening of January 5, and by the following morning we were dropping anchor in the roadstead off Bombay. In a couple of days we would be alongside the quay unloading our cargo.

A ship is a little world all of its own. It has its own laws and it operates according to its own time scheme. When you go on watch after watch, day after day, it is easy to forget the other, wider world beyond the ship. Since leaving Lisbon I had scarcely given a thought to what would happen when we reached Bombay. But that moment was now approaching.

I felt a knot of fear in my stomach when I saw the huge and populous city, which in the heat haze seemed to be hovering somewhere between sea and sky. How on earth was I to find Alphonse Morro all on my own among these millions and millions of people in this strange country? How was I even going to manage to continue my journey from Bombay to Cochin? Without someone to help and protect me I was no more than a gorilla without a master.

I suddenly felt that my voyage to India may have been a terrible mistake.

CHAPTER 36
Bombay

I wasn't the only one worried by our arrival in Bombay. Mr. Wilkins was on the verge of a nervous breakdown. The camel had eventually begun eating its hay again, but the middle hump of the three had all but disappeared.

In his desperation Mr. Wilkins was trying to force-feed the poor beast with pork crackling and large pieces of pure lard. This made the camel angry, and it bit his hand.

Geoff was the only one on board who seemed to feel

254

sorry for Mr. Wilkins. Several times I saw them standing together by the rail, deep in earnest conversation. I don't know what they were talking about, but Mr. Wilkins began to be a little calmer after their first conversation.

Customs and immigration officers wearing smart uniforms came out from the harbor in streamlined steam launches to clear us for entry to British India. Then came the harbor pilot. We weighed anchor and made our way into our mooring in the Queen Victoria Dock.

Mr. Charles Allen Thursgood, company director, was waiting for us on the quayside. He was dressed in a three-piece linen suit and wearing a tropical helmet. He must have taken the passenger liner from Alexandria to get to Bombay before us. Presumably he had left his Daimler in Egypt, since he was now leaning on a cream-colored Cadillac instead. Two uniformed Indians were shading and cooling him with huge fans.

As soon as the gangway was put out Mr. Wilkins went ashore with his baggage. His lips were almost white, and it looked as if his legs were having difficulty supporting him. The sweat was dripping from his forehead. Many of us in the crew stood on deck and hung over the rail, curious to see how Mr. Thursgood would take the gloomy news about his camel.

Mr. Wilkins had scarcely managed to utter more than a few words before Mr. Thursgood grabbed him by the shirt collar and roared loudly enough to be heard along the whole quayside, "What are you telling me, man? Only two humps left? What do you mean two humps? For God's sake, I can't give the maharaja a perfectly ordinary camel, you raving idiot!"

I couldn't hear Mr. Wilkins's answer. He was talking quickly and quietly and was cowering as if afraid of being hit. Mr. Thursgood actually did look as if he was tempted to give the zoologist a thrashing. But he didn't. And, strangely enough, the company director's anger appeared to be cooling, and he began to listen to what Mr. Wilkins was saying with an expression that became more and more interested. In the end he even patted Mr. Wilkins on the shoulder and gestured to him to get into the car. Mr. Wilkins had an air of manifest relief.

How had Mr. Wilkins managed to placate the director? We had no answer to that question. Mr. Thursgood got into the car and sat beside Mr. Wilkins in the backseat, and then, with spinning tires, they set off. And that was that. I certainly wouldn't miss Mr. Wilkins, and I didn't believe anyone else in the crew would either.

A couple of hours later two Indian camel drivers arrived with a receipt to prove they had bought the camel from Mr. Thursgood for a small sum of money. The cage was hoisted ashore and the camel taken out. Swaying happily, it was led away along the quay by its new owners and bade the *Song of Limerick* farewell with a mighty bellow.

I was glad things had turned out well for the camel. It would undoubtedly have a better life with the camel drivers than in a cage in a zoo. Camels like to work, and they enjoy company. Just like people.

~

My voyage on the *Song of Limerick* ended well for me too. Later that day I was called up to the bridge, where Captain Anderson wanted to talk to me. He took me out to the wing of the bridge, and we surveyed the noisy hustle and bustle on the quayside. There were the usual foul gurgling noises as Captain Anderson sucked on his smelly pipe to try to get it going.

"So then, Sally Jones," he said. "I would have liked to keep you with us aboard the *Limerick*—it's a nuisance to be losing a good grease monkey. But I know you want to sign off in Bombay, don't you? Senhor Baptista told me you are on your way to Cochin."

I nodded.

"Cochin is seven hundred miles south of here," Captain Anderson continued. "There is a connection by rail, but it would be better if we could come up with a place for you on a ship. Cochin is India's most important harbor for the export of pepper, so it shouldn't be a great problem to find a vessel going that way. Geoff has already offered to take a turn round the harbor and see what's available."

Captain Anderson puffed thoughtfully on his pipe. Then he looked at me.

"Senhor Baptista told me why you want to go to Cochin. He said you are looking for a man who can prove that Koskela is innocent of murder. Is that right?"

I nodded again.

"Koskela is a good fellow," Captain Anderson said. "And so are you. Apart from the fact that you are a she, of course. And a gorilla."

He produced an envelope and a worn purse from his jacket pocket and gave them to me.

"I wish I had been able to do more to help you," he said. "This is the best I can manage."

I opened the purse. It contained fifteen pound notes.

"I took it from the ship's cash box," he said. "It's what the shipping company ought to have paid you in wages for the voyage. Don't go and spend it all on bananas the moment you go ashore. You'll only end up with a sore tummy!"

Captain Anderson winked and smiled at his own joke. Then he told me to open the envelope and said, "If you run into any trouble it may be helpful to have this document to show people."

The document in the envelope was a certificate of discharge, written on the official paper of the shipping company. It stated that I had served the company as grease monkey on the *Song of Limerick,* that I had signed off at my own request and with a first-class testimonial. The letter concluded with the following lines: *Sally Jones is a seaman in the British merchant marine. Anyone who mistreats her in any way will be severely punished in accordance with British maritime law.*

"That last bit is not completely true, of course," Captain Anderson said. "But there is no way landlubbers will know that."

The letter was signed by Captain Anderson himself and decorated with a dozen official stamps. It looked very formal and important.

"People take official stamps extremely seriously in this country," he explained. "A well-stamped document will take you a long way in India!"

I would have liked to give Captain Anderson a hug, ugly as he was, but, of course, I didn't. We shook hands and I went down to the hold to help with the preparations for unloading the machine parts. The uneasiness I had been feeling for the past few days was suddenly gone. I was pleased both about the money and about the letter, but the best thing of all was that Captain Anderson knew where I was going and why. That meant that I no longer felt I had to face my difficult task completely alone.

~

The following morning Geoff went ashore early and returned at midday with good news. He had found a British-registered coaster, the *Malabar Star,* which was sailing for Cochin the next day to pick up a cargo of spices.

"A fine vessel," he said. "Moored in the north basin, just a mile or so from here. Their second engineer has broken his arm, and you'll be taking his place. They all seem to be decent people."

~

Saying goodbye to my shipmates on the *Song of Limerick* was not a particularly sad business: seamen are used to goodbyes and don't make much fuss about it. Everyone patted me on the back and wished me luck.

Then Geoff accompanied me to the *Malabar Star.* We walked through the morning rush in the port of Bombay. Sailors, beggars, British soldiers, Arab merchants, pickpockets, market women and hordes of dirty children all fought for space between cars, cows, rickshaws, cyclists, birdcages and market stalls.

My nose stung from all the smells and my eyes were dazzled by the colors. The noise echoing between the buildings that lined the streets and alleyways would have drowned out an Atlantic storm. I was grateful to have Geoff to show me the way and wished he had been able to come all the way to Cochin with me.

It took us about an hour to get there. The *Malabar Star* was already under steam and on the point of departure, but there was no one on deck apart from an Indian sailor who was chipping rust off the rails. Geoff ignored him and hurried straight up to the bridge deck.

"Let me show you something," he said cheerfully. "You'll be getting your own cabin on this voyage."

Geoff opened a cabin door, on which there was a brass plate with the words SECOND ENGINEER.

"Here we are. This is it," Geoff laughed.

I should have suspected that something was afoot. Geoff seemed too much at home—how could he simply march aboard a strange ship and open any old cabin door?

It's easy to be wise after the event, but at that moment I had no idea what was about to happen.

No sooner had I stepped over the threshold than the cabin door slammed behind me and the key turned in the lock. From the outside!

"Sorry about this, old friend," I heard Geoff say on the other side of the door. "I was made an offer that was too good to decline. Enormous sums of money are difficult to resist! And I've no doubt you'll do all right anyway! So long!"

At first I thought Geoff was just joking and was sure he would open the door again. Then I heard his footsteps fading away.

I was still locked in the second engineer's cabin when the *Malabar Star* cast off half an hour later. It didn't matter how hard I pounded on the door, no one came to open it.

Through the air vent I saw that we were sailing slowly past steamers at anchor and Arab dhows with tall masts, and then we finally rounded the last pier and headed out into the Indian Ocean.

I noticed immediately that the *Malabar Star* was steaming north.

And Cochin lies south of Bombay.

We were sailing in diametrically the wrong direction!

I kicked, thumped and hurled myself at the cabin door until I was exhausted. In the end I just crouched down in a corner of the small cabin. It was like a horrible dream. I simply did not understand.

A little while later a key turned in the lock and the door opened. I hadn't even managed to stand up before I saw a revolver pointing at me.

"Stay calm now," Mr. Wilkins said. "Mr. Thursgood won't be too pleased if I have to shoot you."

CHAPTER 37
The *Malabar Star*

G eoff had sold me!

In exchange for payment, he had helped Mr. Wilkins lure me into a trap.

Mr. Wilkins told me this while keeping his revolver pointed steadily at my chest. Then he started laughing. "You don't understand, do you? When the camel's third hump disappeared, the animal became worthless. That was a disaster. *But you were there instead!* A gorilla who can play chess! Almost too good to be true! You will make the perfect present for the Maharaja of Bhapur!"

Mr. Wilkins's sweaty, flushed face grinned with self-satisfaction. He continued talking, laughter still in his voice, but I was no longer listening. I put my head in my arms and sank down on the floor. That made Mr. Wilkins stop laughing and his voice became severe.

"You'll get some food in a couple of hours. But only if you stay calm and behave yourself."

He backed out of the cabin door and locked it behind him.

~

The voyage of the *Malabar Star* took just under three days. I remained lying on the hard floor of the cabin the whole of the first day. There was a bunk fixed to the wall beside me but it didn't occur to me to climb up and lie on it. It was as though I'd fallen into a deep, dark hole in which nothing mattered any longer. My mind was in a complete spin.

Mr. Wilkins came in several times to check on me. He was annoyed that I wasn't eating any of the food he brought me.

"I think you are ungrateful," he said, sounding a little hurt. "The maharaja's zoo only houses the rarest and most valuable animals. You ought to feel honored and proud instead of lying there sulking."

When afternoon came and I had still not moved, Mr. Wilkins became uneasy. He didn't dare approach too closely to see how I was; he stayed over by the door talking to himself.

"This simply can't be true! First of all I have problems with the camel and now with the gorilla. It's as if there's a curse on me. How can I be so unlucky? What's Mr. Thursgood going to say?"

By the evening my head had stopped spinning. I sat up and tried to pull myself together. First of all, I thought about Geoff and what he had done to me. I found it incomprehensible. Then I thought about the Chief. I knew how worried he would have been when Ana told him that I had set off for India on my own. He would be writing to her every week asking if I had shown any signs of still being alive. And every week she would have to answer that she had heard nothing, that I had disappeared without trace. As time passed all my friends would begin to assume I was dead. They couldn't possibly guess that I was locked up in a maharaja's zoo, could they? The Chief would be sick with worry.

A sense of hopelessness overwhelmed me again and I sank back to the floor.

Mr. Wilkins returned late in the evening, his patience beginning to wear thin.

"Pull yourself together, gorilla!" he yelled in a voice that shook with rage. "If you are going to be a suitable gift for the maharaja you need to be healthy and happy and cooperative. Or else"—he looked at me, his eyes cloudy behind his spectacles—"it will be the worse for you. Much, much worse."

He cocked his revolver and aimed at me. He looked as if he really wanted to pull the trigger, but he didn't. Instead he shoved the pistol into the waistband of his trousers and left the cabin, slamming the door behind him.

～

I must have fallen asleep at some point during the night, and by the time I woke it was starting to get light. The ship was rolling gently in the waves, and there was a safe feeling about the familiar muffled thud of the steam engine. I had dreamt I was back in my cabin on the *Hudson Queen* and the Chief was at the wheel up in the wheelhouse. It was a wonderful dream and I closed my eyes and tried to go back to sleep.

It didn't work, though, and I lay there staring into the gloom light of dawn. My body ached from lying for so long on the hard floor. After a while I stood up and moved up to the bunk.

It occurred to me that Ana and Signor Fidardo would certainly be trying to discover what had happened to me. They knew I had sailed for India on the *Song of Limerick* and sooner or later they would get in contact with Captain Anderson. He would tell them I had traveled on from Bombay aboard a ship going to Cochin. And at that point the trail would disappear.

I sat up with a start. The thought of Captain Anderson had suddenly made me wide-awake.

From the inside pocket of my overalls I took the envelope containing the discharge certificate and the fifteen pound notes Captain Anderson had given me. What a stroke of luck that Mr. Wilkins had not thought to go through my pockets! The certificate might perhaps prove to be my salvation. It stated who I was and also that no one should do me any harm.

But who was I to show the certificate to?

Mr. Wilkins?

He would just throw it into the sea and laugh at me. Nor would Mr. Thursgood be in the least worried by what Captain Anderson had written.

My hope spluttered out as quickly as it had flared up.

But within just a few moments a new idea had come to me. The certificate might be of some use after all. I took a short pencil from my back pocket—I always had one with me, along with an oily rag and a small spanner.

On the reverse side of the certificate I printed a message in big letters:

> *I arrived in Bombay on the* Song of Limerick. *Was tricked by one of the crew called Geoff Gerrard. He sold me to an Englishman, the director of a mining company. His name is Thursgood. He intends to give me as a present to the Maharaja of Bhapur and I shall end up in a cage in his zoo. Help! SJ.*

I wrote Ana and Signor Fidardo's name and address in Lisbon on the envelope and put the letter back in it. I then tucked the envelope under the lining of my cap, along with the pound notes.

I was pretty sure that Mr. Wilkins would not allow me a chance to escape on the way to Bhapur, but I might have an opportunity to pass the letter secretly to someone else who could post it for me. Fifteen pounds would be more than enough to pay the postage and to provide a fine reward to anyone prepared to help.

Now that I had a plan I had a little spark of hope in my

heart. And suddenly I felt hungry and reached out for the plate of sandwiches and the bottle of milk Mr. Wilkins had left by the door the night before.

When Mr. Wilkins brought my breakfast a little while later he was over the moon to see that I had eaten and was on my feet again.

"I knew you would come to your senses! Geoff said you were a smart gorilla."

~

The rest of the day passed very slowly. All that could be seen through the small air vent in the cabin door was sea and more sea, all the way to the horizon. We were far from land, but from the position of the sun I managed to calculate that we were holding a northwesterly course and following the Indian coast at a distance.

Apart from eating the food brought by Mr. Wilkins I had nothing to do. It is difficult to keep your spirits up when you are alone with your thoughts. I tried not to think of Geoff, but I couldn't help remembering how he and Mr. Wilkins had stood at the rail deep in earnest conversation a few days before we arrived in Bombay. That must have been when they reached an agreement that Geoff would help Mr. Wilkins lure me into a trap. And now I also understood how Mr. Wilkins had managed to pacify Thursgood on the quayside. He had obviously been telling the company director about me—the chess-playing gorilla.

If only I had known!

It is never nice to be tricked, but to be tricked and deceived by a man you thought was your friend is dreadful. I saw now that I had never really known Geoff. Perhaps no one on the *Song of Limerick* had really known him, even though he was so friendly with everyone on board. That was horrible. And sad at the same time.

Later I also gave some thought to Paddy O'Connor. I was no longer so certain that he was the one who had betrayed me to Chief Inspector Garretta in Lisbon. Paddy swore he was innocent and told Captain Anderson he had found the ten pounds hidden in a tin box in the engine room. Perhaps he was telling the truth. If so, I believed the tin box must have been Geoff's. Geoff sold me in Bombay; he could equally well have been the one who did it in Lisbon.

Whether that's the truth is something I shall never know for certain.

CHAPTER 38
Karachi

In the morning of the third day I saw a low-lying coastline appear to starboard. The color of the seawater changed to brown, as it does off the delta of a river. Where were we heading?

When Mr. Wilkins brought me my breakfast roll he also had a colorful piece of fabric over his arm. He put the dish with the bread down on the floor and threw the fabric on the bunk. He kept his eyes and his revolver on me the whole time.

The fabric turned out to be a sort of smock, and with it went a small cylindrical hat with a tassel.

"Get changed," Mr. Wilkins said. "I'll take your overalls and cap. You've no more use for those rags."

I remained where I was sitting on the bunk and shook my head slowly. I had the envelope and money hidden in my cap and I had no intention of handing it over.

"Don't cause trouble, now," Mr. Wilkins said in an irritated voice. "You are soon going to meet Mr. Thursgood, and I want you to look clean and tidy. So hurry up and change! At once!"

I shook my head again.

An angry red flush colored Mr. Wilkins's pale cheeks. He was under strain, that much was obvious. He was probably worried that Mr. Thursgood wouldn't be satisfied with me.

"What is the matter with you?" he snarled. "Is it that you don't want to change in front of me? Is that what the problem is?"

I thought for a moment, and then I nodded.

Mr. Wilkins gave a hoarse, joyless laugh.

"For God's sake," he said, "I'm a zoologist! I've seen a

naked gorilla before! All right, I'll come back in ten minutes, by which time you'll have changed. Understood?"

As soon as Mr. Wilkins left the cabin I investigated the new clothes. I was lucky: the cylindrical hat was made of two stiffened strips of material with paper between them. By turning the hat inside out I could slip the envelope and the notes in between the paper and the fabric lining. The hat looked a little dented but I managed to straighten it out and to change into the smock before Mr. Wilkins came back.

~

When the *Malabar Star* came alongside a quay that afternoon I still had no idea where we were. I couldn't see any sign of a town, just a flat harbor district with cranes, railway tracks, low warehouses and wide wooden wharves.

Hours passed without anything happening, and it had begun to grow dark by the time Mr. Wilkins came to fetch me. He handcuffed me and led me out to a car waiting on the quayside. We sat in the backseats. Mr. Wilkins stank of sour sweat and was constantly having to slide his glasses back up on his nose.

We drove along a wide country road that followed the railway line. Damp warm air poured in through the open windows. After a little while we passed one or two houses by the roadside, and soon there were more of them, and they were bigger. There were fires burning at the street corners, and we could see street sleepers in the shadows, their eyes glinting in the beam of the car's headlights.

The car stopped at a railway station and two porters immediately leapt out to carry Mr. Wilkins's baggage. On the wall above the entrance to the station I read the words KARACHI CANTONMENT RAILWAY STATION. We were still in India, then, in the city of Karachi.

There was a train standing at the platform, and a young man with a ginger mustache and tropical helmet raised his hand in greeting when he caught sight of us. He shook hands with Mr. Wilkins and studied me with a look of amusement and superiority.

"Ah, so this is the present for the maharaja, is it? This is what the diamond mining project depends on?" he said. "Mr. Thursgood is waiting for you. I do hope this gorilla lives up to what you promised, Wilkins! For your sake, old boy!"

I discovered later that the man with the ginger mustache was called Slycombe and he was Mr. Thursgood's secretary.

"The director has reserved three whole coaches for the company," Mr. Slycombe said in a smug voice. "One for himself and me, one for the rest of the staff, and one where we can all work and hold meetings. You will be in a compartment of your own with the gorilla, Wilkins. That will be nice for you, won't it?"

Mr. Wilkins didn't seem to be listening to him. He was shaking with nervousness and merely muttered something inaudible in reply.

Mr. Slycombe walked ahead of us to one of the coaches, opened the door and beckoned us to get in first.

The coach was furnished with big, shiny leather arm-chairs and oriental carpets. Mr. Thursgood, the company director, was sitting in one of the armchairs. He was dressed in a silk smoking jacket and slippers with small tassels. In one hand he was holding a brandy glass and in the other a cigar, from which smoke spiraled up to the fans that, with a quiet hum, were slowly turning on the ceiling. The director only had eyes for me, and he hardly seemed to notice Mr. Wilkins. We looked at one another, and there was doubt in his eyes.

"I can't say I'm particularly impressed so far, Wilkins," he said. "Looks like an ordinary gorilla to me. Apart from the ridiculous clothes, that is."

"Indeed, forgive me, sir. They were the best I could come up with for her to wear. We were in rather a rush in Bombay as you—"

Thursgood silenced Mr. Wilkins with a gesture.

"Slycombe," he said. "The chessboard."

Mr. Slycombe disappeared out of the door at the end of the coach and immediately returned with a small table that had a chessboard inlaid in its surface. He put the table in front of Mr. Thursgood's armchair and placed all the chess pieces in their starting positions.

"Right then, Wilkins," Mr. Thursgood said. "Now we shall see!"

Mr. Wilkins, his hands sweaty and fumbling, unlocked the handcuffs and led me over to the chessboard. He also whispered in my ear: "Don't you dare let me down now!"

Mr. Thursgood gestured for me to make the first move I was very tempted to pretend that I didn't understand, but it would probably have been the last thing I ever did. So I started with an ordinary pawn opening, and Mr. Thursgood responded by moving his knight.

After each of us had made ten moves or so Mr. Thursgood stood up, gave me a pleased look and took a puff on his cigar. Then he turned to Mr. Wilkins.

"That's quite sufficient. I'm satisfied that the gorilla is a uniquely remarkable beast and the maharaja will be quite overwhelmed. You've done well, Mr. Wilkins! Well done!"

Mr. Wilkins's spectacles had steamed up again with the tension. He looked as if he was about to collapse from relief.

CHAPTER 39
The Station Inspector in Jodhpur

When the train departed from the station an hour or so later I was sitting shackled to the window bars in the small compartment occupied by Mr. Wilkins and me. Mr. Wilkins had gone to the restaurant car to have dinner.

On the wall beside the door of the compartment there was a large framed poster advertising the railway company, the GREAT INDIAN PENINSULA RAILWAY COMPANY. The illustration on the poster showed a very splendid and very detailed map of British India. My eyes searched here and there and eventually found Bhapur. It was a small princedom almost at the top of the map and at the foot of the Himalayas, in the part of India called the Punjab.

I worked out that it must be about eight hundred miles from Karachi to Bhapur, and if the train kept a speed of thirty-five miles an hour we would be there within twenty-four hours.

If that was the case I only had a day and a night to come up with some way of posting my letter to Ana and Signor Fidardo. But how was I to do it? I was both locked in and shackled. The tiny spark of courage I had managed to summon was fading away to next to nothing.

~

In preparation for the night, an attendant dressed in the yellow uniform of the railway company came and pulled down two made-up beds from the wall above the seats in the compartment. Mr. Wilkins shortened the chain that shackled me to the window bars before he climbed into bed. At first I didn't understand why, but then I realized he wanted to make sure I couldn't reach him when he was in bed. He was afraid I'd attack him while he slept. That, presumably, is also why he hid his revolver under his pillow; at least, that's what I assumed.

I didn't sleep a wink that night. I was kept awake by the aching hopelessness in my heart and, as if that wasn't enough, Mr. Wilkins snored worse than a hippopotamus. I have heard sleeping hippopotamuses in the jungle, so I know what I'm talking about.

The train traveled more slowly than I had expected, and it stopped for long periods during the small hours. By morning we were only at the city of Hyderabad, and I understood that the journey to Bhapur would take considerably longer than twenty-four hours. More like a week!

That was good. I needed the time.

The railway station in Hyderabad was packed with people pushing and shoving noisily. No sooner had our train come to a halt than vendors of every kind rushed to the windows to show their wares to the passengers on the train. They offered fabrics, fruits, mugs of hot tea, caged birds, flowers, pictures of gods and goddesses and candies of every variety.

Goods and money passed back and forth through the barred windows. Mr. Wilkins bought five greasy sugar doughnuts with some sort of sticky filling. He ate three of them, one after another. And he looked at me with an expression I couldn't really read—it wasn't so much unfriendly as shamefaced.

After smacking his lips and licking the sugar off his

fingers he said, "I'm off to the restaurant car again. You don't mind, do you?"

I didn't understand what he meant.

"I don't want you to feel lonely," he explained in a mild voice. "Would you be lonely if I went to the restaurant car for a while?"

I shook my head. The less I saw of Mr. Wilkins, the better I liked it.

He forced a smile and pushed the two remaining doughnuts over to my side of the compartment table.

"There you are! I saved them especially for you. I don't want you to think I'm a bad person, because I'm not. You understand? I know things will turn out well for you in Bhapur, otherwise I'd have never let Mr. Thursgood give you to the maharaja. You do understand that, don't you?"

I didn't move.

Mr. Wilkins smiled again.

"I shall be well paid by Mr. Thursgood, I'm not denying that. But I have to live too, don't I? And I'm not doing this just for the money. Not at all! I'm also doing it for you! You will really get on well in Bhapur! The environment there will suit you much, much better than a filthy engine room!"

Mr. Wilkins pushed the doughnuts over to me.

"Have one! They're good! Expensive too! Not every gorilla gets offered delicacies like that."

I still did not move.

Mr. Wilkins narrowed his eyes.

"Don't be ridiculous, now. Take a doughnut. Show me we are friends!"

I should, of course, have taken a doughnut to keep Mr. Wilkins in a good mood. But I just couldn't. I turned away instead and looked out the window. He found that impossible to tolerate and grabbed the doughnuts and threw them out the window.

"I'm altogether too kind," he snarled. "That's my problem. Stupid too. How could I ever have imagined you were capable of understanding why I've done what I've done? You're just a gorilla!"

And he stormed off to the restaurant car.

～

Mr. Wilkins did not return to the compartment for the rest of the day. And that suited me perfectly! I needed time on my own to think. The stop in Hyderabad had given me an idea.

What if I could pass the letter and the money to someone on the platform while the train was standing in a station?

I looked at the map. The next major city on the line was Jodhpur in Rajasthan. Then came Jaipur, Alwar, Delhi and Ambala. And between each of the main stations came a good number of smaller ones. At one of these many stops I ought to be able to find an opportunity to hand my letter out through the window to someone who looked reliable. That depended, of course, on Mr. Wilkins being out of the compartment at the time. It was lucky for me that he was so fond of the restaurant car.

I felt just a crumb of hope returning.

~

The landscape outside the train window was flat and dry, and the farther east we traveled the more desertlike it became. There was nothing but sand and stones and low thorny bushes as far as the eye could see. Every so often I saw camel trains in the distance.

We reached a town called Barmer late in the afternoon. I felt my pulse rate increase as the train slowed down. I took off my hat and laid it on my knee, ready to take out the envelope and the money.

This might be my opportunity!

But just as the train drew into the station, the door of the compartment flew open with a bang. I jumped with fright. Mr. Wilkins was back. I felt I'd been caught and held my breath. Did he suspect something?

No, apparently not. I could breathe again. Mr. Wilkins had only come back to the compartment in order to buy more sweet things from the vendors on the platform. Perhaps he didn't think it right to buy things through the window of the restaurant car.

This time Mr. Wilkins bought a bag of plums and a large jam slice topped with cream and brown sugar. He started eating it as soon as the train was in motion again. It was not a pretty sight. The jam was bright green and trembled like a lump of grease. The cream smelled off, and flies moved in from every direction to get a taste of it. Mr. Wilkins waved them away, tucked in and sighed with pleasure as bits of jam stuck to the sparse whiskers round his mouth. Once that was finished he moved straight on to the plums, disposing of them at great speed. He spat the plum stones straight back into the bag. After a while he was obviously beginning to feel full, and he held the bag out to me, sneered and said, "Why don't you have the last one? You've earned it!"

He stood up and disappeared back to the restaurant car. I looked in the bag. There was a solitary plum, buried in sticky plum stones. I threw the whole lot out of the window.

~

Mr. Wilkins's appetite for the sweet things offered by station vendors was worrying. If he continued to buy things at every station, my plan would never work.

I need not have worried. That night Mr. Wilkins began

suffering from a sore stomach and I heard him moaning and groaning in his bed for some time before he had to hurry to the toilet along the corridor.

We gorillas rarely have stomach trouble—perhaps we are less susceptible to bacteria than human beings. Or perhaps we are not so stupid as to eat the dicey sweet things offered by Indian station vendors. Mr. Wilkins spent the latter part of the night and the morning rushing between his bed and the toilet. The toilet was through the wall from our compartment, and for once I wished that gorillas didn't have such good hearing.

The train stopped in Jodhpur at about nine o'clock. Mr. Wilkins was busy in the toilet, and I had the money and the letter for Ana and Signor Fidardo on my knee. To hide my face so that only my eyes were visible I had wrapped myself in a sheet. I had seen many women dressed in similar fashion during the train journey.

There was the usual pushing and shoving among the vendors on the platform. They yelled and shouted and held up their wares to the barred windows, but none of them looked very reliable and I didn't dare pass out the envelope. Then, all of sudden, an Indian station inspector appeared and stood with his back to me. I tapped him on the shoulder and quickly pulled my hand back in. He turned round.

His face was plump and clean-shaven, and he had friendly eyes.

"Yes, ma'am?" he said, screwing up his eyes to see into the dark compartment.

I poked the envelope out between two bars and, rather hesitantly, he took it.

"Ah, I see . . . you want me to post this for you?" he said, reading the envelope.

I nodded.

"But there's no stamp. And since it's going to Europe it may be quite expensive."

I hastened to hold out the fifteen pound notes, taking care, however, to conceal my hairy fingers.

He looked at the notes in astonishment.

"That's far too much, ma'am," he said. "One should be enough."

At that moment the coach gave a jerk and the train began to move. The station inspector tried to hand me back some of the notes, but I just shook my head. A few moments later we lost sight of one another.

It was done! I was shaking all over as the tension eased and my heart filled with joy. I had succeeded!

A little while later Mr. Wilkins staggered into the compartment, his forehead bathed in a cold sweat and his face whiter than the sheet I had wrapped myself in. He took two steps into the compartment and came to an abrupt halt. His eyes widened. Then he turned on his heel and ran back to the toilet.

~

Now, in retrospect as I write this, I know that my letter never did reach Ana and Signor Fidardo. I have no idea why not. I suppose it's a long way from Rajasthan to Portugal and a lot can happen to a letter on the way.

But even though the letter got lost, it was still my salvation. I was so sure that Ana and Signor Fidardo would receive my letter and do all they could to help me, and it was that conviction that gave me hope.

Without that hope I would never have survived the months that followed.

CHAPTER 40
Delayed Meetings

The moment Mr. Thursgood heard that Mr. Wilkins was unwell he arranged for me to sleep in a compartment of my own. He did not want to take the risk of me being infected. A gorilla with an upset stomach would hardly make a pleasing gift.

In order to keep an eye on me during the day, Mr. Thursgood had me chained to one of the tables in the coach in which he and the staff of Thursgood & Thursgood Co. Ltd.

worked. The staff included specialists in a whole range of different fields, and they all had fine titles, such as engineer or professor or director of finance. They all shared the one aim, which was to persuade the maharaja to agree to Mr. Thursgood's business proposition, and they spent all day every day practicing their presentations. Listening to them quickly became tedious.

The days passed. We left the deserts of Rajasthan behind us and moved on into the Punjab. Here I saw plantations of fruit trees and people harvesting rice on the paddy fields close to the rivers.

During the sixth morning of our journey we crossed the border into Bhapur, and within a couple of hours we were steaming into the capital city of the princedom. It was also called Bhapur and it looked like all the other cities we had passed through in recent days. People and animals were everywhere, and the houses were two stories high and crowded close together along the dusty streets.

Our train journey continued north from the capital toward the next station, Sunahiri Bagh Palace, the royal seat of Bhapur, which was where we were to leave the train. A short time later the train halted at a grand castle built of gleaming pink stone. I wasn't the only one to assume that this was the maharaja's palace, but we were wrong. The pink castle was just his private railway station. The platform was inlaid with a mosaic of oriental patterns, and there was a brass band of at least fifty men in white uniforms and red turbans waiting to greet us. They struck up a noisy welcoming march. Mr. Thursgood looked immensely pleased by our reception.

Six gold-colored Rolls-Royces drove us from the station to the Bhapur Grand Hotel, where we were to stay for the night. I was given a room of my own. It was so grand that I hardly dared enter it. My head was spinning with all the new impressions. The windows looked out over an enormous garden with topiary, rose beds and fountains as far as the eye could see. Hundreds of flamingos were parading on the banks of a large pond, and there were servants down on their knees along the paths and flower beds, trimming the grass with silvery scissors.

In the distance Sunahiri Bagh Palace rose out of the heat haze. It had more towers, cupolas, balconies and windows than I could count.

I sank to the floor—all this luxury was utterly strange. And, in a way, threatening. I felt such longing for the Chief that my eyes filled with tears. And for Ana. And for Signor Fidardo.

I thought of the letter I had posted and that made me feel a little better.

That evening Mr. Thursgood and his staff put on a dress rehearsal in one of the many meeting rooms in the hotel. At the end of it he said, "Tomorrow will see the moment of truth. We have been preparing for this moment for over a year, and if we do everything perfectly we shall succeed! And if so, we can expect riches that others can only dream of!"

Everyone cheered. Everyone except me, that is.

That night I slept in the softest bed I have ever slept in. In the morning I had to catch hold of the bedpost in order to drag myself out of it. A servant wearing silk pajamas and a turban brought a huge bowl of fresh fruit for my breakfast. I couldn't remember when I had last eaten anything so delicious.

Mr. Wilkins fetched me from my room when it was time for us to leave. The six Rolls-Royces were waiting outside the hotel, and they drove us through the park to Sunahiri Bagh Palace. Close-up the palace seemed unbelievably large. The moment the cars drew up they were surrounded by servants, who opened the doors for us. Then a small elderly man with a gray beard and melancholy eyes came down the palace steps. He was wearing an elegant suit, and he had a tall hat on his head. Supporting himself with a gilded walking cane, he went up to Mr. Thursgood.

"My name is Sardar Bahadur," the man said, and bowed.

"I am the maharaja's first minister and most important counselor. My title is diwan. His Highness the maharaja bids you a heartfelt welcome to Bhapur, Mr. Director Thursgood. He looks forward to meeting you."

"And I look forward to meeting His Highness!" Mr. Thursgood said, and held out his hand. "It will be a great honor."

The diwan shook Mr. Thursgood's hand and said, "But unfortunately your meeting cannot take place today. His Highness was playing cricket yesterday, and at present he is feeling extremely stiff and aching. I have scheduled a time for you at quarter past four tomorrow afternoon."

Mr. Thursgood opened and closed his mouth without a sound emerging.

"Until we meet again!" the diwan said, then bowed and walked back into the palace.

Mr. Thursgood stood there looking foolish. Then he pulled himself together and, with forced good humor, said, "That gives us another day to prepare. That's no bad thing!"

The caravan of gold-colored Rolls-Royces turned round and took us back to the Bhapur Grand Hotel.

We had another dress rehearsal that evening. The atmosphere was just a touch flat.

The following day we once again made the short journey to the maharaja's palace, and once again Diwan Sardar

Bahadur met Mr. Thursgood at the steps of the palace. The diwan's forehead was furrowed with deep worry lines.

"Unfortunately the maharaja is unable to receive you again," he said, bowing apologetically. "The court astrologers have advised His Highness to avoid meetings of all kinds today. I have booked a new time for you—tomorrow at twelve o'clock."

Mr. Thursgood was on the point of protesting but managed to restrain himself. Instead he gave a stiff bow and said, "Quite, I understand. In that case we shall enjoy another day of His Highness's unique hospitality"

At half past eleven the following day we were there once more. Mr. Thursgood was unable to hide his irritation any longer when the diwan apologetically explained that the maharaja was occupied and thus could not receive visitors. His Highness had a headache brought on by a small celebration the evening before to mark the birthday of one of his favorite wives.

"His Highness will receive you tomorrow at three o'clock, Mr. Thursgood," the diwan said quietly in response to Mr. Thursgood's testy questions.

~

Two weeks passed and Mr. Thursgood and his band of experts had still not met the maharaja. They had, however, heard every possible excuse as to why that particular day's meeting must be postponed to the following day.

One day the maharaja was about to leave on a tiger hunt; another day he was occupied with a particularly exciting game of bridge with some of his wives; there were days when he was constipated after having eaten too much and others when he felt weak from having eaten too little; there were days when the state of the weather put him in a bad mood, or it might be that some item of clothing refused to sit properly; on other days he was simply unavailable in general and no more detailed explanation was offered.

The mood among the mining company experts remained quite good all the same. The engineers, the professors and the rest had no objection to their extended residence in a smart hotel. As for me, during the daytime I was chained under a sunshade out on the marble terrace with a view over the maharaja's park. Food and drink was available to guests on the terrace all day every day, and Mr. Thursgood's party saw to it that they ate and drank as much as they could manage. The worst glutton was, as we might expect, Mr. Wilkins. What little weight he had lost during his stomach trouble went back on tenfold thanks to the laden buffet table at the Bhapur Grand Hotel. Very occasionally he took a short walk in the park, and when he did he was accompanied by a servant pushing a drinks trolley.

The only person who really suffered from the long delay before meeting the maharaja was Mr. Thursgood himself. He was sick with rage and humiliation.

We drove to the palace twenty-one days in succession only to return to the hotel with our business still unheard. On the twenty-second day—a Tuesday at the end of February—Diwan Sardar Bahadur unexpectedly announced that the maharaja was now ready to receive Mr. Thursgood and his party.

CHAPTER 41
An Audience in the Durbar Room

The diwan walked in front of us, leading the way into the palace. The splendor was almost beyond belief. Wherever our eyes went they were met by gold and silver and white marble. I heard Mr. Thursgood's men whispering about the old paintings and statues in the rooms we passed through: they said that every single object was worth a fortune.

We came to tall double doors guarded by two stern

soldiers with drawn sabers. They swung the doors open, allowing us into an enormous room with a high vaulted ceiling. I later learned that this was the Durbar Room and was where the maharaja received visitors or hosted receptions of various kinds. Eight great crystal chandeliers, each of them twice the size of the wheelhouse on the *Hudson Queen,* flooded the room with light. On the floor lay at least two hundred tiger skins arranged in a circle. The tigers' heads were all facing the middle of the room, where the Maharaja of Bhapur was seated on a golden throne. He was dressed in an ankle-length silk robe with a high collar, and his turban sparkled with precious stones of many colors.

The maharaja studied us apathetically, his eyes shaded by heavy dark eyelids, while at the same time twirling the ends of his well-tended mustache.

"Welcome, Mr. Thursgood," he said in a drawling voice and without standing up. "I apologize for you having to wait for an opportunity to meet me. As you know, I am head of state and have many duties. My days are simply not long enough to deal with everything."

I noticed a quick smile flit across one side of Diwan Sardar Bahadur's mouth, and then he gave us a sign that we were to sit in the chairs set out before the maharaja's throne.

Mr. Thursgood, director of the mining company, remained on his feet.

"You have nothing to apologize for, Your Highness," he said, and bowed so deeply that there was some danger of him tipping over. "I shall be eternally grateful for the quite *fantastic* reception we have received in Bhapur! It is a *tremendous* honor to meet Your Highness! You are, after all, acknowledged to be the *foremost* of all the princes of India."

Thus began Mr. Thursgood's carefully prepared eulogy to the maharaja. The speech as a whole took fully twenty minutes. He concluded with a brief account of the business proposition he had come to offer.

And then finally he said, "In a moment I shall ask my colleagues to present the diamond project in detail, but before doing that I should like to take the opportunity to give Your Highness a modest present."

Thursgood pointed at me.

"This, Your Highness, is Sally Jones, the chess-playing gorilla. I would go so far as to claim that she is unique, one of a kind. With your permission I should like to give a small demonstration of the talent of this remarkable gorilla."

"Please do, Mr. Thursgood," the maharaja said, stifling a yawn.

Everything had been carefully practiced time after time. Mr. Wilkins opened two folding chairs and a small chess table and placed them on the floor in front of the maharaja.

Mr. Thursgood sat in one of the chairs and I sat in the other. We began to play.

The maharaja, who had looked bored to death during Mr. Thursgood's long and fawning speech, suddenly seemed to come to life. He leaned forward to follow the game attentively. After a dozen moves or so Mr. Thursgood stood up with a smile of satisfaction on his face: "As you can see for yourself, Your Highness, this gorilla is truly unique. And now she is yours!"

Thursgood bowed and signaled to Wilkins to remove the chess table so that the geologists could begin their presentations about diamond mining. The maharaja stopped him: "Come, come, Mr. Thursgood! Sit down, please. The game is not over yet!"

Mr. Thursgood remained standing and gave an uncertain laugh.

"I'm not sure I understand what Your Highness means. . . ."

"The game should be played to the end," the maharaja said. "I want to see who wins."

Mr. Thursgood laughed again, but it sounded very strained.

"Your Highness, I merely wanted to give a demonstration of the gorilla's talents. You have seen what she can do.

Would it not now be appropriate for my geologists and engineers to show—"

"Mr. Thursgood," the maharaja interrupted him. "You surely don't wish to put me in a bad mood? Please do as I ask and finish the game."

The small twitches in Mr. Thursgood's face revealed his inner struggles. Finally he forced his face into a grimace that was presumably intended to represent a smile.

"But of course, Your Highness, of course. With great pleasure!"

It was easy to see through Mr. Thursgood's chess tactics. He played hard and he played confidently, aiming for a quick victory. And he didn't play badly at all. I had great difficulty extricating myself from the traps he set for me. But one by one his attacks failed. He began to sweat and to chew his bottom lip nervously. Suddenly I was the one on top. I could hear Mr. Wilkins breathing heavily behind me: he seemed to be finding it difficult to inhale enough air.

Without undue haste I tightened the noose round Mr. Thursgood's white king. Between each move he stared at me with a peculiar mixture of rage and pleading in his eyes. His hands were trembling when I forced him to sacrifice his queen in order to stay in the game.

Apart from Mr. Wilkins's heavy breathing the great

room was completely silent throughout the game. When I eventually checkmated Mr. Thursgood's king, the members of his staff could be heard muttering in fear.

The maharaja stood up, clearly a sign that the audience was over. Mr. Thursgood rose to his feet and said in a confused-sounding voice: "But Your Highness . . . we haven't talked about the diamonds yet! About the mining! You must hear what my geologists have to say. . . ."

"Unnecessary!" the maharaja said. "I am honored by your visit, and I shall accept your generous gift with gratitude. But I wish no part in your mining project."

The maharaja paused for a moment and then said with a gentle smile, "And you must surely understand, don't you, Mr. Thursgood? I simply couldn't do business with a man who can't even beat a gorilla at chess!"

CHAPTER 42
An Oath of Loyalty

It very nearly came to a riot when Diwan Sardar Bahadur was showing Mr. Thursgood and his party out of the palace. The company director completely lost control of himself. He shook his fist at me and at the maharaja, and he shouted and roared so much that he ended up foaming at the mouth. Then he began kicking Mr. Wilkins in the shins so that Wilkins yelled to high heaven. Guards came rushing up from all directions, but the maharaja sat there calmly on his throne and watched the commotion. There was something cruel about the smile that played on his full sensual lips.

When the gates had been closed behind Mr. Thursgood and his staff, the maharaja burst out laughing. He laughed for a long time and he laughed loudly. The diwan seemed both shaken and upset by the fuss, but he still laughed politely along with his master.

"Your Highness," the diwan said when the maharaja had finished laughing. "What do you want me to do with the gorilla? Shall I take her to your zoo?"

The maharaja stood up. He was the same shape as a beer barrel, I thought. Slowly and with his hands behind his back he walked round me.

"A gorilla that plays chess is of course a fine addition to my exclusive collection of animals," he said to himself. "But I wonder . . ."

He stopped and stood in front of me.

"Do you understand what people say to you?" he asked.

I nodded.

He rubbed his chin thoughtfully.

"Is that absolutely certain? Or do you just nod at everything you hear?"

I shook my head.

The maharaja smiled, but he didn't seem completely convinced.

"What does four plus three add up to?" he asked.

"Your Highness," the diwan said. "I don't think the animal can speak. . . ."

The maharaja silenced him with a gesture but kept his eyes on me the whole time.

I held up seven fingers.

The maharaja clapped his hands in delight.

"Excellent! I can make use of this gorilla! She can be my new aide-de-camp."

The diwan's eyebrows shot up in astonishment.

"Aide-de-camp . . . ? But, Your Highness, a gorilla . . . surely hardly suitable?"

The maharaja's face darkened.

"Not suitable? Then I'd better make her diwan instead. Would that be more suitable, do you think?"

The diwan's face went pale.

"Clearly not, Your Highness," he responded. "I beg your forgiveness, Your Highness. I shall organize the practical details at once."

Whistling cheerfully to himself, the maharaja left the Durbar Room.

~

Diwan Sardar Bahadur sat down in a chair with a heavy sigh. He gave me a look of concern and slowly shook his head.

"Ah, the times we live in," he muttered to himself. "The times we live in."

Then he took a little silver bell from his inside pocket. The moment he rang the bell a door opened at one end of the room, and a servant in a blue smock and red turban ran up to us. The diwan rapidly scribbled a few lines on a piece of paper and gave it to the servant. The servant glanced through the message, bowed and gestured me to follow him. My legs were trembling so much that they would barely carry me. Everything was happening so quickly I was in a state of complete confusion.

The servant led me though the palace, a labyrinth of corridors, passages, staircases, balconies, verandas and narrow bridges over pools containing carp and goldfish. We passed through dining rooms, libraries, smoking rooms and open galleries that faced out onto paved inner courtyards with bubbling fountains and colorful flower beds. Wherever we went I saw fine gentlemen with overhanging bellies and bushy beards. Some of them were in uniform, their chests heavy with medals, whereas others were dressed for hunting or for sport. Some of them were playing billiards and drinking; others were simply sleeping in comfortable armchairs.

It occurred to me that all the people in the palace were men and there was no sign of a woman anywhere.

A wide spiral staircase led us downward and finished in a large cellar, where fifty or so men were sitting on the floor, bent over sewing by the light of the electric lamps on the ceiling. The walls were shelved from floor to ceiling, and the shelves were packed tight with fabrics of every color and pattern you could imagine. This was obviously the maharaja's tailoring shop.

The servant passed the slip of paper to one of the tailors, who immediately began taking my measurements. It took a while, and the tailor scratched his head in thought several times. Once he was finished, the servant and I continued our journey through the palace.

Our next stop was also a cellar. We went through a wooden gateway into a marble vault that was shaped like a cupola. The air was thick with steam. The servant showed me into a little booth and gestured to me to take my clothes off. A few minutes later two enormous men wearing loincloths and nothing else came to fetch me. They spoke Turkish to one another and were almost as hairy as me.

I was made to sit in a stone bathtub for two hours while the Turks took turns scrubbing me with boiling-hot water alternating with water that was icy cold. After they had scrubbed me they combed my whole body, dropping perfumed oils on my fur so that I smelled of jasmine and chrysanthemum. It was all very unpleasant, and I wouldn't have gone along with it if I hadn't suspected that my life depended on me being a willing victim.

When I went back to the booth, the smock and hat Mr. Wilkins had given me were gone. In their place was a hanger on which hung a pair of green trousers and a long yellow shirt with a high collar. Both garments were made of shimmering silk and decorated with elegant gold embroidery. On the floor there was a pair of pointed slippers with silver buckles.

Once I had put on these clothes, the servant placed a tight-fitting little cap on my head, and round it he wound and plaited a silk scarf that must have been at least seventeen feet long. When he had finished he held up a mirror and I saw my face crowned by an enormous turban of brilliant blue silk. The servant gave me a quick smile.

~

Diwan Bahadur was sitting waiting for us on a bench in one of the inner courtyards of the palace. He was smoking a hookah, and wreaths of white smoke were rising gently toward the starry sky above. It was late evening by this time.

He gestured with his hand, inviting me to sit beside him.

The servant who had been accompanying me all the afternoon stationed himself in the darkness under a fig tree.

The diwan placed a paper on the bench between us. It was an oath of loyalty to the maharaja and, as the diwan explained, everyone in the palace had to sign it. He had brought along an ink pad so that I could sign it with my thumbprint, but I pointed to the pen in his breast pocket. He gave it to me and I wrote my name on the paper.

"You are undoubtedly a very remarkable gorilla, Sally Jones," the diwan said in an earnest voice. "I wish you all good fortune in the palace here."

He puffed at the mouthpiece of the hookah, and the small piece of charcoal on top of the tobacco glowed in the dark. After very slowly blowing the smoke out through his nostrils, he added, "And you will undoubtedly need it."

The diwan waved the servant over and told him to make sure I was given something to eat and after that was shown to my room.

By this time I was so tired that I didn't even try to remember the directions as we walked through the palace. The servant led me to a dining room, where a table was immediately laid with bread, water and a bowl of fruit.

Once I had eaten he took me to my room. It was huge. The bed alone was bigger than my cabin on the *Hudson*

Queen. As soon as the servant left me I lay on my back on the soft feather mattress. On the ceiling above, hanging upside down, was a lizard that was making small *tuk-tuk-tuk* noises. I closed my eyes and listened. For one moment I felt sure that everything that had happened that day must have been a dream.

Then I fell asleep.

CHAPTER 43
The Lord Chamberlain

My first days in the maharaja's palace were confusing. I had no idea what I was expected to do, and I hardly dared leave my room for fear I would get lost. I lay on the bed most of the time, wondering whether I should run away.

Running away would not have been difficult. I would only need to climb out of my window at night and disappear in the palace park under the cover of darkness. The park was neither guarded by walls nor by sentries.

But what would I do then? Cochin was more than twelve hundred miles to the south, and I stood no chance of getting there without help. And the only help I could hope for would be from Ana and Signor Fidardo. In my letter to them I had written that I was with the Maharaja of Bhapur, so if I ran away from here they would never find me.

So I decided to stay, even though it was not without risk: this was made clear to me a few days later when I was summoned to the Lord Chamberlain's office.

The chamberlain was in charge of all the aides-de-camp. He was sitting behind a large empty desk when he received me. His eyebrows were larger than a normal man's mustache, and his mustache was reminiscent of the tails of two overgrown raccoons.

I had to stand there waiting for a good ten minutes while, in silence, he carefully polished several of the medals hanging on his chest. Eventually he looked up and studied me. He did not like what he saw, and he made no effort to hide it.

"The maharaja has appointed you an aide-de-camp," he said. "That is an elevated and honorable post. The maharaja's aides-de-camp are usually recruited from the most important families in the princedom. There are candidates who have been waiting for many years for their turn to attend for interview. Which is why there are people in the palace who are rather . . . how shall I put it . . . *bewildered* as to why His Highness the maharaja decided to appoint you in particular as an aide-de-camp. That does not, of course, mean that anyone—and certainly not me—questions the maharaja's decision! Absolutely not! The maharaja is a uniquely wise and enlightened ruler!"

The chamberlain's hands had begun to shake, and he clenched them together on the table in front of him.

"Now then," he continued. "It still hasn't been finally decided what your tasks are to be. The maharaja is leaving today for our neighboring state, Kapurthala, where he and his team will play an important cricket match. He will be away for some weeks. While he is away he wants you to take a good look round and to learn to find your way about the palace. You are to take your meals in the aide-de-camps' dining room. Any questions? No, of course not, you are just a gorilla, after all. You can't ask questions. . . ."

He suddenly leaned forward across the table and looked me straight in the eye. He lowered his voice to a threatening hiss, as if afraid someone apart from me would hear him: "Don't go thinking that you can feel secure, gorilla! The maharaja tires of things just as quickly as he takes to them. And once he is tired of you, it is likely you will find yourself in a cage in the zoo. Or you will be used as tiger bait! Personally speaking, I hope it will be the latter! As do many other people! You have no friends here, not a single one!"

I stood quite still and did my best not to look afraid. The chamberlain rang for a servant to show me the way back to my room. Once I was alone I sat on the wide window ledge and looked at the clouds passing across the sky. I tried to think of pleasant things, indeed of anything apart from what the chamberlain had said with such a malevolent light in his small gray eyes.

A short time passed. Then I felt the corners of my eyes beginning to sting and I crept into bed and buried my face in the pillows. My heart ached as if it was about to burst. I longed so much to be with the Chief and Ana and Signor Fidardo.

~

During the two weeks that followed I roamed the palace from early morning to late evening. I came to recognize that Sunahiri Bagh Palace actually consisted of a large number of smaller buildings that seemed to have grown together by means of a confusion of tunnels, bridges, terraces and balconies. It was, in fact, a whole town, with different districts and blocks.

In the middle of the palace was the Durbar Room.

Immediately adjacent to that lay the maharaja's private residence, which was guarded by some of the maharaja's bodyguards. No one was allowed to enter unless the maharaja sent for them.

North of the maharaja's residence was the government quarter where civil servants and clerks worked at long rows of desks in echoing halls. Ministers had offices of their own: they were all fat men with tall hats, bushy beards and worried eyes.

The northern end of the palace, the part that faced the elephant stables and the garages, was occupied by the servants. Cooks, waiters, cleaners, musicians, gardeners, craftsmen, animal attendants, chauffeurs and many others lived there. I felt more at home there than in the superior parts of the palace.

I went there every day until a kind chauffeur told me that I should not be doing so. The chamberlain would punish me if he learned that I spent my time among the servants. I was an aide-de-camp and therefore a courtier, and it was not appropriate for courtiers to mix with the servant class.

All those leisured and indolent gentlemen who populated the dining rooms, bars and billiard rooms of the palace were, as I now discovered, courtiers. They were there to keep the maharaja company when he was in the mood to enjoy himself. Most of them were also responsible for some simple duties. Most of the functions of the aides-de-camp, for instance, were in the maharaja's residence. One of them had the task of checking how many pairs of shoes the maharaja possessed, another had to ensure that his nail scissors were kept sharp, a third had to puff up the maharaja's pillows before he went to bed and a fourth spent his time picking the pips out of the ten grapes the maharaja always ate after his lunch. There were thirty-two aides-de-camp, each as arrogant as the next, and they were constantly quarreling about which of them had the most important function.

The only thing they all seemed to agree about was that I had no right to be in the palace, especially not as one of their number. I avoided them as far as I could.

∿

During my wanderings I came across a whole wing at the eastern end of the palace that was completely closed off. It was called the zenana, and unlike the rest of the palace it was surrounded by a high wall. There was only one gate in this wall, and that was guarded day and night by ten soldiers armed with lances, swords and rifles. No one seemed to be allowed either in or out. At first I thought the word *zenana* meant "treasury," which would have accounted for both the wall and the guards. But *zenana* did not mean that.

I learned the truth about the eastern wing by eaves-dropping. Much of my day was spent sitting still in some hidden corner and listening to what passersby were talking about. That was the only way I had of discovering how things functioned in the palace. After all, I was unable to ask questions, and no one could be bothered to tell me anything.

It turned out that the zenana was the women's section of the palace. That was where the maharaja's wives, mistresses and female relatives lived. The wives were called maharanis, and there were eighteen of them. The mistresses were called concubines, and according to palace rumor there were twice as many of them.

So now I had an explanation for why no women were to be seen round the palace. They were only allowed out of the zenana for certain major festivals. And no man—apart from the maharaja—was permitted to set foot in the zenana. The punishment for anyone who entered the zenana illegally was the harshest in the ancient law code of Bhapur: to have your head crushed under the foot of an elephant.

I shuddered and wondered whether the prohibition on visiting the zenana also applied to me.

I would have an answer to that question sooner than I could have imagined.

CHAPTER 44
Recruited as a Spy

The maharaja returned in triumph from Kapurthala. He and his cricket team had beaten the home team led by the Maharaja of Kapurthala. The two maharajas were cousins, and each of them considered himself to be the best cricket captain in India. There had thus been a great deal at stake in the match.

A three-day national holiday was declared in Bhapur. The inhabitants of the capital city were exhorted to go out on the streets and celebrate. Bread was distributed among the poor, and prisoners were pardoned and released from jail. The festivities in the palace lasted from morning to night.

As for me, I didn't see much of the celebration, I merely heard talk of it later. The reason was that as soon as the maharaja returned from Kapurthala the chamberlain ordered me to go to my room and to stay there.

"I need to know where you are in case the maharaja asks for you" was how he explained it.

I did not leave my room for five days. Late on the fifth evening a servant came and signaled for me to go with him. We went to the Durbar Room and then from there through an archway that was hidden behind one of the room's many marble statues. In the archway was a door guarded by two soldiers. They stepped to the side and held the door open for us. We were now in the maharaja's private residence.

The servant left me when we reached a library lined with beautifully carved bookcases, the shelves of which were filled with thick volumes in antique leather bindings. The maharaja was there, lying on a well-padded sofa, dressed in a dressing gown and with an electric heating pad crowning his very large stomach. He was reading, not one of the beautiful old volumes but a glossy magazine with a motorcycle on the cover.

"Ah, there you are at last," he said, letting the magazine fall to the floor. "Push me to the music room."

For a few moments I didn't understand what he meant, but then I saw that the sofa had wheels and that two sturdy handles were attached to one end.

The music room was next door to the library. The shelves there were filled from floor to ceiling with gramophone records rather than books.

"I am a great lover of music!" the maharaja said proudly. "Every month I send for all the latest records from Europe and America. No one in the whole world owns more gramophone records than I do!"

A gramophone stood on a table in the middle of the room, and alongside it was a substantial stack of records still in unopened envelopes. The maharaja told me to park his sofa alongside the table. He picked up one of the records and put it on the turntable. The sounds of an orchestra and singing immediately began to emerge from the big horn.

"Shut the doors so we can have some privacy and pull up a chair for yourself," the maharaja commanded.

I did as he said. Once I was seated, the maharaja turned up the volume of the gramophone. I was forced to lean toward him to hear what he said. "We have to have music playing while we talk," he whispered in a serious voice. "I have a very powerful enemy! *Maji Sahiba!* She has eyes and ears everywhere!"

~

Maji Sahiba, as I now learned, was the maharaja's mother. She was the oldest of the women in the zenana, and she was the one who ruled the roost in there. She was also the only person in the whole of Bhapur who was neither afraid of the maharaja nor in the least bit interested in what he thought or wanted.

"I have eighteen wonderful maharanis," the maharaja said earnestly, "and forty-six lovely concubines. I love them all. And they all love me, of course! In a pure and elevated way! But every time I go into the zenana to visit any of them, Maji Sahiba is lying in ambush and nabs me instead. There is *always* something she wants to criticize or complain about! And she won't give up until her whining and nagging have driven me out of the zenana. There is no limit to the woman's bossiness!"

The maharaja gave a bitter sigh and then told me to go and fetch him a glass and a crystal carafe of whisky. Once he had fortified himself with a couple of generous measures, he went on to tell me the various ways he had tried to outdo Maji Sahiba. For a while he had—in the greatest

319

secrecy—smuggled his maharanis and concubines out of the zenana when he wanted to meet them. It worked for a couple of weeks, but then Maji Sahiba had discovered what was going on and put a stop to his tricks. She had informers all over the palace.

Then the maharaja had attempted to make his visits to the zenana when Maji Sahiba was asleep or otherwise occupied—walking in the park, for instance, or having her mustache plucked out in the zenana beauty parlor. But she soon saw through this strategy and ceased following a regular schedule. So the maharaja could never be sure whether she was asleep or out for a walk or just sitting there bored and quarrelsome and waiting for him.

"What I need, then," the maharaja said, "is an informer of my own inside the zenana. A spy! Someone who can tell me what Maji Sahiba is doing at any particular time. So that I know when I'm going to have a free run!"

He took a mouthful of whisky.

"The question is *who*?" he continued. "Obviously my informer cannot be a man, since I'm the only man allowed into the zenana. Nor, however, can it be a woman, as a woman is not allowed to leave the zenana. . . ."

The maharaja screwed his eyes up and gave me a cunning glance. He looked very pleased with himself.

"But you are neither a man nor a woman—you are a

gorilla! Apart from me, you are the only one in the whole palace who can move freely both inside and outside the zenana! *You shall be my spy!* My secret weapon against Maji Sahiba!"

During the weeks since I had come to the palace I often wondered why the maharaja appointed me an aide-de-camp instead of incarcerating me in his zoo. Now I had the answer.

∼

I remained in the maharaja's apartment until morning while he eagerly ran through everything he considered it necessary for me to know in order to fulfill my duties as a spy. He explained how to find my way round the zenana and who was who among the many wives and concubines. I did my best to follow him, but it wasn't easy. What made it even more difficult was that the maharaja spoke very quickly, jumping from one topic to another whenever things came into his mind that he considered important.

By the time I left his apartment the shimmering pink light of dawn was entering the palace windows. Servants, cleaners and waiters were rushing silently round the corridors in preparation for the courtiers waking for the day. The scents of newly baked bread and fresh-cut flowers filled the air. My head was in a spin from everything the maharaja had told me, and I worried I was already forgetting much of it.

CHAPTER 45
Maji Sahiba

I was given my first task as spy in the zenana that very afternoon. I was to pass a greeting card from the maharaja to one of his maharanis, who was celebrating her name day. At the same time I was to see if I could discreetly discover where Maji Sahiba was and what she was doing.

There was only one way into the zenana from the men's part of the palace. It was a tunnel, which started behind a secret door in the maharaja's bedroom. Until now it had never been used by anyone apart from the maharaja and the soldiers who guarded it. The narrow tunnel was lit by torches on the walls, and it wound its way underground like the hole left by a gigantic worm. I found it more than a little creepy down there all on my own. After a while I came to a door covered in red leather. I opened it and stepped into the zenana.

It resembled the rest of the palace in its excesses of luxury and wealth. Some of the women gave me long searching looks; others laughed and patted me as if I was a dressed-up pet. I hoped they would soon get used to seeing me there—a spy, after all, needs to be as inconspicuous as possible.

My first task was to locate Sharmistha Devi. That was the name of the maharani who was to be congratulated on her name day. According to the maharaja she shouldn't be difficult to recognize. Most of his wives and concubines were Indian and had beautiful dark skin and shining black hair, but Sharmistha Devi was blond and had blue eyes. Before she married the maharaja and moved into Sunahiri Bagh Palace her name had been Lorraine Thompson and she had starred in musicals on Broadway in New York.

She wasn't the only one of the maharaja's wives to come from abroad. He was in the habit of reading European and American gossip magazines and often fell madly in love with the actresses, dancers and singers he saw in these papers. He invited the most beautiful stars to his palace, showered them with jewels, money and expensive clothes and then courted them during a moonlight walk in the palace park. They usually turned him down but returned home bearing his gifts. Some remained, however, and there were several film actresses from Los Angeles, an operetta singer from Milan and a ballet dancer from Paris living in the zenana.

I found Sharmistha Devi lying on a sun lounger by a turquoise swimming pool. She did not seem particularly pleased with the card. She was probably wondering why the maharaja had sent a gorilla instead of coming himself. I then hurried on to the second and more important of my two missions: to discover what Maji Sahiba would be doing that afternoon.

The maharaja had told me that she was usually to be found either in her private apartment or in one of the zenana gardens. Or she could sometimes be found in the beauty department, and as the latter was very close to the swimming pool, I decided to start my search there.

I walked briskly past rows of salons for manicures, pedicures, hairdressing and skin care, but Maji Sahiba was nowhere to be seen. So I moved on to the rose garden, where I almost immediately caught sight of a large older woman sitting in a deck chair in the shade of a fig tree. She had a book in her lap and was snoring loudly.

The woman was wearing a pink sari, a sort of dress that consists of a single long piece of fabric. Almost all the women in the zenana were wearing saris, but only one of them was allowed to wear a pink sari: Maji Sahiba.

I immediately rushed back through the underground tunnel to the maharaja's apartment, and as soon as I entered his smoking room the maharaja leapt from his chair and came to meet me.

"Well? Did you find Maji Sahiba?"

I nodded.

"Where was she? In one of the beauty salons?"

I shook my head.

"In the garden?"

I nodded.

"What was she doing? Busy with her roses?"

I leaned my head to one side and rested my cheek on the back of my hand.

The maharaja beamed.

"She's asleep! Wonderful! Not a minute to waste!"

Within seconds the maharaja had disappeared into the tunnel to the zenana.

~

During the weeks that followed I spied on Maji Sahiba almost every day. The maharaja was tremendously pleased with me—so pleased, in fact, that he ordered the chamberlain to give me a bigger and better room right next door to the maharaja's own apartment. The other aides-de-camp hated me even more than before. The aim of every courtier was to become the maharaja's favorite, and that position now seemed to be occupied by a gorilla.

No one could understand why he valued me so highly. As far as they could see, all I did was run small errands in the zenana for him. The spying was a secret between the maharaja and me.

But how long could it stay that way?

It seemed likely that sooner or later Maji Sahiba would begin to wonder how the maharaja always managed to evade her. It could only be a matter of time before she put two and two together. Or before someone else did and told her I was the maharaja's spy.

What would happen then, when the maharaja no longer had any use for me? Presumably I would find myself in a cage in his zoo. I tried not to think about it, concentrating instead on making sure my role wasn't uncovered.

But that was not enough. Not enough to deceive Maji Sahiba, anyway.

∼

I was keeping watch from behind a marble pillar outside Maji Sahiba's bedroom window one morning when a balcony door opened suddenly and I heard her deep commanding voice:

"You! You there behind the pillar! Come here at once!"

I froze, paralyzed! Should I run? But if so, where?

While I stood there panic-stricken and at a loss as to what to do, Maji Sahiba stepped out. At close quarters she looked immense and terrifying, with thick black eyebrows and skin that reminded me of an antique leather armchair.

"Right, my dear gorilla!" she said brusquely. "You'd better come with me and we'll have a chat, the two of us. Come on, quickly now before anyone sees us!"

She took a firm hold of my arm and led me into her apartment. The furnishings were simple and old-fashioned, quite unlike the flash and ostentation of everything else in the palace.

"You have been spying on me," she said without beating about the bush once the door was closed behind us. "That is why I never catch that useless lump of a son of mine in the zenana these days. Am I right?"

I realized at once that it would be a mistake to try to lie to this woman. And pretending not to understand wouldn't help, either. So I nodded.

Maji Sahiba looked me straight in the eye. I didn't try to avoid her gaze. Her hard features seemed to soften slightly.

"I have heard that you are a remarkable animal," she said. "And it seems to be true."

She sat down heavily on one of the plain chairs with which the room was furnished. I remained standing, my heart beating hard. How was this going to end?

Maji Sahiba seemed sunk in her own thoughts.

"My son is a tyrant," she said after a while. "He is a stupid bully and an incurable sensualist. Just like his father and his father's father. Instead of thinking of the good of his people, he is only interested in his own dissolute pleasures. The people of Bhapur are poor. Schools and hospitals are falling down. The roads are crumbling. And he does nothing! Instead he spends millions of rupees on expensive sports cars and endless feasting for all the incompetents he fattens up in his palace. It is a disgrace! And I've been trying to tell him so for years."

Maji Sahiba suddenly looked very weary.

"My son has never listened to me," she continued. "And he is not likely to do so in the future, however much I nag him. Which is why I shan't let on that I know you are spying on me. It wouldn't do any good anyway—he would just find some other way of avoiding me. And you would end up in a cage in his zoo. Or as food for his tigers, and I don't want that on my conscience."

Maja Sahiba stood up. Her strength seemed to have

returned. She folded her arms and said, "But you must stop sneaking round and spying outside my bedroom window. I won't tolerate that. In the future I shall tie a red ribbon on the rail of my balcony when I think my son may visit the zenana. I want him to stay away at all other times. This must remain our secret. Are we agreed?"

I nodded.

Then Maji Sahiba stroked my cheek with her hand and told me to go.

That was the only time she ever spoke to me or even recognized my existence. I never had the chance to show her how grateful I was.

But I hope she knew anyway.

~

The weeks went by. Life in the palace became quieter and calmer the closer we came to summer. The heat meant that everything came to a halt for several hours every afternoon.

My days were monotonous and boring. Spying in the zenana had become routine: all I needed to do now was check for the red ribbon tied to the rail of Maji Sahiba's balcony and I knew whether it was safe for the maharaja to enter or not.

The rest of the time I had to remain in my room in case the maharaja needed me. I spent most of my time sitting up in a window that looked over the park. Once a day I made a small scratch on the window ledge. I thought that the day when Ana and Signor Fidardo would come to fetch me came closer with every scratch. Then we would travel to Cochin together, find Alphonse Morro and have the Chief set free.

Deep down inside me there was a voice that whispered that this was just wishful thinking. It was a voice I did my best not to listen to.

CHAPTER 46
Checkmate

The better I came to know the maharaja, the more clearly I saw how right Maji Sahiba was about him. He devoted all his time to pleasure. If it wasn't cricket it was polo, hunting, food and feasting. He was completely uninterested in governing his country—that was taken care of by the ministers in the Bhapur government. The maharaja's only significant contribution was that he met them in his residence once a week and listened to what they had to report.

There was a special room furnished for these meetings, which always took place on a Monday morning. At one end of the room stood a high throne on which the maharaja sat, and at the other end of the room there were ordinary chairs on which the ministers sat. The maharaja was always dressed in a light shift and had a rug over his legs. This covered the fact that the throne was actually a specially constructed luxury toilet. After the excesses of the weekend, the maharaja was always constipated and needed to sit on the toilet for at least two to three hours. And to ensure that his time wasn't wasted, he took the opportunity to meet his ministers at the same time.

His only other contribution to the government of his princedom was to appoint or dismiss ministers. He did this whenever it suited him.

One day he said to me, "I'm bored with my ministers. I want to shake the government up a bit. You can help me—it will be great fun! As much fun as when you beat that company director at chess!"

I prepared for the worst.

The maharaja's idea wasn't fun, it was simply cruel. He was intending to have each of the twelve ministers play chess against me, and only those who managed to win would retain their posts. The results of the chess games would be publicized across the whole country, which meant that anyone who lost against me would lose his honor and his good name as well as his post. Being beaten by a gorilla would, of course, bring shame upon them.

I decided immediately that I would allow all the ministers to win.

A couple of days later the maharaja gathered all his ministers in one of the many rooms in the palace. They had been told what was at stake. A number of them looked calm and self-confident; others looked grimly nervous. A few of them seemed utterly terrified by what was to come.

The first one I was matched against was the Minister of Internal Affairs. He was a skillful player, and I scarcely needed to do anything at all for him to win.

Things were more awkward with the next minister, the Minister of Agriculture, for it quickly became obvious that he was a novice at the chessboard. Trickles of sweat ran down the poor man's plump cheeks, and his hands shook every time he moved a piece. I was forced to make a number of very serious errors to allow him to emerge as the victor.

After I had lost the third match, this time against the Minister of Defense, the maharaja suddenly interrupted this strange chess tournament and threw the ministers out. Then he turned to me, his eyes glowing with black rage.

"You are letting them win," he snarled through his teeth. "Why?"

I had underestimated the maharaja. For some silly reason I hadn't believed he was sufficiently competent at chess to recognize that I was cheating against myself. A cold shiver ran down my spine.

"Now I understand," he said slowly. "They have bribed you!"

I shook my head.

"Don't lie!" he roared. "Why else would you help them? They must have promised you something. What? What have they promised you? Answer me, you treacherous gorilla!"

I lowered my head and stared at the table.

The maharaja stared at me. Then he began to walk round and round the room restlessly.

"It doesn't make sense," he mumbled to himself. "They can't have bribed the gorilla. They would never dare to . . ."

He came to a halt in front of me.

"The matches will continue at nine o'clock tomorrow morning," he said. "If I notice that you are still helping my ministers to win I shall have my bodyguards use you for target practice. Understood?"

I nodded.

"Don't imagine for one moment that you can deceive me," he continued. "Chess is a game that originated in India, and part of every maharaja's education is to achieve mastery in the game. I started to play before I could walk.

334

Emanuel Lasker, the German world champion, lived here in my palace for four years. Just to give me private lessons!"

Having said that, the maharaja left the room with firm and determined steps.

"I don't understand it," I heard him muttering. "Why was the gorilla losing on purpose? Why?"

I was left alone, trembling in every fiber of my body. I remained seated until I was sure my legs would support me, then I rose and went to my room with the maharaja's last words still echoing in my ears.

What Maji Sahiba had told me about her son now came into my mind. She knew her son very well. The maharaja really did think only of himself. Any concern about the misfortunes of others was quite alien to him. That was why he found it impossible to understand why I would allow the ministers to win.

⁓

On the stroke of nine the following morning I met the maharaja's ministers in order to continue our matches. It had become clear to me during the night that I would have to do my very best to win the rest of the games. It was a pity for the ministers, but I had no choice. It was now a life-and-death issue for me.

After we had been waiting for half an hour the diwan

came in and told us that the maharaja had gone tiger hunting. The chess matches were postponed until further notice.

The maharaja returned from his tiger hunt three days later. I was ready for the chess tournament to start again, but it was not to be. The maharaja appeared to have completely forgotten about it. His ministers breathed a sigh of relief, and so did I.

But the maharaja had not forgotten. The following day the chamberlain ordered me to move out of my large room next to the maharaja's apartment and to go back to my old room. The order had come from the maharaja, and the change of room was his way of punishing my disobedience. I was no longer the favorite aide-de-camp. The chamberlain could not conceal his malicious pleasure.

As for me, I was happy I no longer had to play against the ministers, but I did wonder why the maharaja had interrupted the tournament. Was it really as simple as him suddenly being seized by a desire to hunt tigers?

Or was he afraid? Afraid that I would carry on losing to his ministers on purpose? Because then he would have been forced to let his bodyguards use me for target practice even if he did not actually want to see me dead. After all, it would not be proper for a maharaja to be seen to make empty threats.

CHAPTER 47
The Flying Maharaja

By the end of April the heat had become almost unbearable. The temperature in the afternoon often reached over one hundred degrees in the shade. The maharaja decided to take some of his court with him and to retreat to his summer palace in Simla.

Simla, as I learned, is a town in the cool mountain district at the foot of the Himalayas. The rich and powerful of India all gather there during the hottest months of the summer. The maharaja's courtiers talked of Simla as if it were the Kingdom of Heaven: a life of luxury, feasting and exciting gossip from morning to night. To me it sounded like a dreadful place.

The weeks before departure were an anxious time in Sunahiri Bagh Palace. The maharaja was deciding which members of the court he would be taking to Simla and which would be left behind. None of the courtiers wanted to miss the trip. They all became even more obsequious to the maharaja than usual, while taking every opportunity to spread lies and ugly rumors about one another. The atmosphere in the palace was so poisonous that the air was almost too foul to breathe.

Once the removal van had departed, life in the palace calmed down. The maharaja had not chosen me to go to Simla, and I was glad. While he was away I no longer had to stay in my room the whole time, and I started spending my days in the palace garage instead. That's where the maharaja kept his collection of cars. He owned fifty-eight in all, every one of them an exclusive make such as Rolls-Royce, Duesenberg or Lanchester. He also had twice that number of motorcycles, and there was a luxury yacht in Bombay Harbor in constant readiness to sail should the maharaja feel like a boat trip.

I spent hours going round looking at the beautiful cars

and motorcycles in his garage. I would lift the hoods to study the engines. The mechanics paid no attention to me and just left me to it. Day after day I hoped one of them would hand me a tool and ask me to help with something, but it never happened.

~

After just three weeks the maharaja returned unexpectedly from Simla. According to his plans he should have been there for another month. Everyone in the palace wondered what was going on.

What had happened was that the British king, George V, had acquired a private airplane, and news of this had reached Simla. So now the maharaja wanted a plane of his own, and he wanted it immediately. The order for a DH 60G Gipsy Moth had already been sent to the de Havilland Aircraft Company outside London. The plane was the same model as King George V had bought.

An airfield and hangar were to be built in the palace park immediately. The maharaja gave the order for workers to be brought in by bus from all over Bhapur. The airfield and hangar were finished in less than a month.

The whole court was infected by the maharaja's sudden interest in flying and airplanes, and flight became the talk of the palace. Hardly anything else was talked about. The maharaja had an extremely elegant flying suit sewn for him out of the very finest buckskin, and he went round showing off in it for days on end.

The airplane was delivered direct from England by a pilot of the Royal Air Force. He flew the whole way in just over a week, landing at Paris, Rome, Cairo, Baghdad and Karachi on the way. He brought with him a mechanic from the de Havilland Company.

They were given a magnificent reception in Bhapur, with the whole court and all the palace servants lining the landing strip and waving Union Jacks. The new hangar had been decorated with miles and miles of garlands of flowers, the maharaja was wearing his new flying suit—of course!— and the orchestra of the princedom was playing an air force march that the maharaja had had composed for the occasion.

The cheering was deafening as the pretty yellow and red plane came gliding down from the sky and landed. I was standing very close to the landing strip and, like everyone else, waving my flag like mad. There was just one question going through my mind: *How long would it take to fly from Bhapur to Cochin?*

~

No sooner had the plane landed than the maharaja was eager to take a trial flight with himself at the controls.

To his great disappointment he was not allowed to. The pilot explained that according to British law all pilots must have a pilot's license. Until the maharaja had gained his license he would have to be satisfied with flying as a passenger.

The very next morning the Royal Air Force pilot began teaching the maharaja how to fly. The maharaja thought the lessons were taking far too long and, with a mixture of threats and bribes, he persuaded the pilot to skip the boring parts of the instruction. Consequently less than a week later he gained his license.

To celebrate the maharaja's first flight as pilot, everyone in the palace was ordered out to line the airstrip, while the women in the zenana sat on the roof behind screens made of thin fabric and watched through small opera glasses. It was a fine day. The sun was shining, and there was a gentle breeze blowing from the mountains to the east. Pennants of every conceivable color fluttered against the blue sky.

The maharaja took off without any problems and then made a sharp turn, presumably to fly a circuit of honor over the zenana. The plane lost height and crash-landed right into the *pilkhana,* the stable for the palace elephants. The public jubilation quickly became horrified screams.

The fifty elephants escaped unharmed, as did the maharaja. The only one to be injured was the Royal Air Force pilot in the passenger seat. He broke his thumb. He left the palace the following day to return immediately to London. He blamed his broken thumb, but everyone understood that he was terrified of having to fly with the maharaja again.

The de Havilland mechanic was able to repair the plane, and then he too wanted to return to England. The maharaja managed to convince him to stay, but not until a contract had been signed which exempted the mechanic from ever, under any circumstances, having to fly with the maharaja.

The accident did not lead the maharaja to lose his desire to fly. He blamed the incident on the five court astrologers who had failed to warn him against flying on an unlucky day. The astrologers were dismissed and new ones appointed. After a careful study of the stars the new astrologers announced that the coming Saturday would be a good day for the maharaja to make another attempt at flying.

The maharaja was pleased and, as a reward, promised that each of the astrologers in turn would have the honor of accompanying him in the air. The following day the astrologers announced that they had made a slight error when interpreting the stars and there was in fact no day suitable for a flight within the coming year.

The maharaja became angry and dismissed the new astrologers. He then ordered the mechanic to prepare the plane for immediate takeoff and selected one of the officers in his bodyguards as the man to have the honor of accompanying him.

The maharaja's second flight went well. He managed to get up into the air and back down to the ground without destroying the airplane or anything else. He came within a hair's breadth of ending his trip in the flamingo pond rather than on the landing strip, but that was all.

The next day, when it was time for the maharaja to fly his plane, the officer in the bodyguards felt very unwell and was unable to accompany him. This time the maharaja told Diwan Sardar Bahadur to get ready for a flight up into the blue sky. The diwan begged and pleaded to be excused on grounds of his great age, but the maharaja showed no mercy.

For some reason the maharaja never wanted to fly alone, and during the following weeks he compelled one courtier after another to be his companion on his unsteady flights above the palace grounds. Anyone who had flown with him once would do almost anything to avoid a second flight. The palace doctor's consulting room was full of ministers and officers who were suddenly suffering from headaches, high temperatures and stomachaches the moment the maharaja donned his buckskin flying suit.

343

He, meanwhile, became more and more irritated by his cowardly subjects, and one day he called the whole court to a meeting in the Durbar Room.

"Is every man jack of you a coward?" he asked. "Isn't there a single one of you who is both willing and happy to have the honor of flying with me this afternoon?"

There was almost complete silence.

The only sound was the slight mutter that could be heard when I took two firm steps forward and raised my hand.

CHAPTER 48
Emergency Landings and Champagne

The Gipsy Moth is a two-seater biplane with a four-cylinder, air-cooled petrol engine that produces ninety-eight horsepower. I was familiar with the model from before, because the Chief is interested in airplanes. I used to cut out newspaper articles about pilots and airplanes for him, and I used to read them myself when we were in harbor. The Chief is not a great one for reading, but he used to save the articles about flying in a box in his cabin on the

Hudson Queen. They all disappeared, of course, when the ship sank in the Zêzere.

I had never really had any dreams about flying, which is why I was so surprised at how wonderful it was the first time I flew with the maharaja. All my anxiety disappeared from the moment we swung out onto the airstrip for take-off. I liked the regular, safe-sounding pulse of the engine and the solid craftsmanship that showed in all the details of the plane. I felt a pleasant tickle in the pit of my stomach as the plane lifted off.

A few minutes later we were hundreds of feet up in the air and my face was being fanned by a beautifully cool wind. From my seat in the forward cockpit I had a clear view in all directions. The flat landscape below us faded into a haze over on the horizon. The groves of trees looked like clumps of grass and the buildings like lumps of brown sugar. I felt I had left all my troubles on the ground, among all the pettiness down there.

A short while later, however, the fun came to a rapid end. Without warning the engine began to cough and splutter when we were flying at high speed at a low altitude. The maharaja made a wide turn to head for home, and at that moment the engine died.

We were lucky not to make a crash landing, but if I'm honest I have to admit it was because the maharaja gave a skillful performance. He picked up a little height and then began to glide down toward a sandy track that ran across a field. The plane bounced and swerved when we touched the ground, but the maharaja managed to stop without it overturning, ending up on its nose or running into a ditch.

In spite of the successful emergency landing the maharaja was in a vile mood. He called the plane a rubbish machine and kicked the undercarriage. He then produced a flare from the emergency kit and fired the rocket so that it exploded in a blinding flash of light hundreds of feet up. It would easily be visible from the palace.

While waiting for the rescue team the maharaja produced his emergency rations—a cool box of caviar from Georgia and two bottles of Dom Pérignon champagne—and sat down in the shade of a solitary tree out on the field.

All the farmers of the district, along with their families, cows, goats and dogs appeared out of the woods that surrounded the field. They stopped at the edge of the trees and looked in wide-eyed amazement at the maharaja and his strange machine.

While the maharaja was feasting on his rations I found the toolbox and a technical manual under the pilot's seat. I lifted the engine cover and took a look. I had never worked on an airplane before, but engines are engines and it was not difficult to locate what was wrong. A wire to the altitude regulator of the carburetor had got stuck, and that had caused the engine to be fed a fuel mix that was too weak at low altitudes. The fault was easily put right.

The maharaja had fallen asleep under the tree, but he woke up when I swung the propeller and started the engine. He came rushing over with a bottle in his hand and yelled out of breath, "What do you think you are up to with my airplane, gorilla?"

It took a while to make him understand that I had mended the engine and we could fly again. That put him in great high spirits, and he ordered an immediate takeoff.

At the same moment, however, three gleaming gold Rolls-Royces were approaching along the sandy track, and the maharaja missed them by a whisker before clearing the treetops at the far end of the field by no more than ten feet. He shouted with delight.

Down on the ground the courtiers in the rescue party stared up at us with foolish expressions on their faces.

~

Everyone at court believed the maharaja's enthusiasm for flying would soon pass, which was what usually happened with his interests, according to the gossip I heard in the corridors of the palace. There had been a time when his only interest was hunting antelopes with trained cheetahs.

Then he had spent all his time organizing bloody combats between angry bull elephants in an arena outside the pilkhana. After that he had become addicted to playing roulette and decided to open a casino in the palace. But by the time the casino was ready to open, the maharaja had tired of gambling and was spending all his time playing polo. And so it went on.

His interest in flying proved to be very different. It did not fade, and two months later the maharaja was still taking a daily flight in his Gipsy Moth. And I was with him every time.

Initially I accompanied him because everyone else was afraid to. When he was behind the joystick the maharaja was a danger, not only to himself but to anyone else in the vicinity of the plane. But practice brings competence, and the maharaja became more and more skillful at maneuvering the airplane. After a while a flight with the maharaja no longer meant putting your life on the line. The courtiers began hanging round the hangar and hinting to the maharaja that they would willingly take a turn as passengers.

But it was too late.

The maharaja wanted no one but me in the plane with him. I was not only capable of looking after the plane's engine, I was also a good navigator. No one else at court had skills of that sort.

The Chief had taught me how to navigate at sea, and finding your way round in the air is not very different. Apart from a map you need a chronometer, some sort of speed indicator, a compass, a pair of dividers, a protractor and a ruler. The Royal Air Force pilot had left all these things behind in a bag.

Every flight started in the Royal Aviation Lounge, a large room the maharaja had had built as an upper floor in the hangar. The walls were decorated with photographs of himself and his Gipsy Moth. In the middle of the floor stood a large, well-lit table, which was where the maharaja laid out his map of Bhapur and showed me the route he wanted us to take. I then drew the compass bearings on the map, measured distances and estimated flying times. Once we were aloft it was my job to ensure that we stuck to our flight plan, and I would give hand signals to the maharaja when it was time to change course.

Our flights crisscrossed the whole of Bhapur, and we were often away from early morning to late evening. Very soon all the maharaja's subjects had seen his plane more than once. If we landed in a field or meadow to eat lunch we would quickly be surrounded by a small crowd. The maharaja usually behaved as though they didn't exist. Dirty children, thin women and men bowed and worn by toil seemed to affect him badly. Deep down I believe he was rather afraid of them.

In one way or another every flight became an adventure. On one occasion we collided with a vulture and were forced to make an emergency landing on a stretch of level stony ground outside a small village close to the border of Patiala, the neighboring princedom. As we touched down, one of the struts of the undercarriage snapped, and we were too far from the palace to be able to summon help with a flare. The maharaja completely lost control of himself, swearing and yelling about his own bad luck and how useless the airplane was. Then he sat and sulked in the cockpit, drinking champagne.

In the meantime the people of the small village worked up the courage to approach the plane. The men looked at the broken strut and talked quietly among themselves. Eventually, between them, they managed to hoist up the plane enough to inspect the damage properly. Within a couple of hours they had replaced the broken strut with a new one that consisted of a piece of bamboo attached with tough ropes of coconut fiber. It was a great success.

It was late evening by the time the repair was finished, and we had no choice but to spend the night in the village. With considerable reluctance the maharaja allowed himself to be taken to one of the primitive huts, where the women offered him food, but he refused even to look at the bread and watery chicken soup they put in front of him. I wondered whether he realized that the villagers were offering him the very best they had.

Early the following morning, immediately after a breakfast of dry bread and goat's milk, we risked an attempt to take off. The undercarriage held up and we were safely aloft.

As soon as we landed back at Sunahiri Bagh Palace the maharaja sent for his interior minister and ordered him to visit the village where we had spent the night.

"I want them to be helped to dig a well and irrigate their fields so that they can grow something worth eating. And you will have to get rid of those dreadful mud huts and give them proper houses instead! I'll pay all the bills!"

The minister of the interior looked confused. This was the first time the maharaja had ever shown any interest in how the country people lived in his princedom.

"You do understand what I mean, don't you?" the maharaja snapped angrily. "The next time I have to make an emergency landing in that village I want it to be a bit more comfortable!"

CHAPTER 49
A Deceitful Plan

There was a sense in which the maharaja changed during the months we flew together. Or, at least, he changed toward me. It showed in particular when we landed for lunch breaks.

In the early days the maharaja had only taken food for himself, and he always sat on a rug a little way away from the plane while he ate. One day he asked me if I'd like an apple that he was too full to eat, and the following day he arranged for me to be provided with a lunch box of my own. A short while after that he stopped moving away from me to eat and allowed me to sit beside him on the rug.

While we sat there eating, he used to talk about flying, and how the plane behaved in different situations, and about the things we had seen from the air. Most of the time he was happy and cheerful. Not always, though. Sometimes a mood of melancholy came over him, a mood almost of sorrow, and then he would just sit and stare vacantly in front of him.

The maharaja never told me what he was thinking about when he looked so despondent, but nor did he drive me away and ask to be left in peace. I wondered how many of his courtiers he could simply sit in silence with. I was perhaps the only one.

~

The de Havilland mechanic was given the sack. The maharaja didn't like him and gave the job to me instead. That suited me. Between our flights I serviced the engine and saw to it that the rudder cables and levers were properly lubricated. The only times I needed to leave the hangar was when the maharaja wanted me to spy on Maji Sahiba.

The maharaja quite often came out to the hangar for no particular reason. He seemed to like to watch me working on the engine and he asked me various technical questions. I answered as well as I could by pointing and showing. There were even times when, quite without thinking, I would hand him a spanner or a screwdriver to hold, and when he had held any of my oily tools he would always smell his hands afterward and a dreamy distant look would come to his face. I think, perhaps, he would have liked to work on the engine himself, although, of course, that would have been quite improper for a man of his rank.

~

Thanks to the airplane my life with the maharaja had taken a quite unexpected turn. I had to admit to myself that I now had a rather good life. I enjoyed tinkering with the plane, and I always looked forward to the next flight. My days passed quickly.

My nights, on the other hand, were long. I often lay awake unable to sleep for thinking of my friends in Lisbon. I knew how worried about me they must be, and it somehow seemed wrong that I should be enjoying my time with the maharaja and his airplane. After all, the purpose of my trip to India was to find Alphonse Morro and save the Chief, not to have a good time.

There wasn't much else I could do. I was still counting on Ana and Signor Fidardo helping me once they received my letter. All I could do until then was wait. Wait and survive! That was my plan, and I had to stick to it.

But the months were passing without me hearing anything from Ana and Signor Fidardo. The hot summer became the monsoon season with cooler weather and rainy days. By the time the rains were over in September, more than six months had gone by since I handed the letter to the station inspector in Jodhpur. By this stage I ought to have received a reply from Lisbon long ago, and I began to wonder whether my letter had got lost on the way. If that was the case I would be waiting in vain for my friends to come and rescue me.

But in the back of my mind I had begun to develop a fallback plan:

To steal the maharaja's Gipsy Moth and fly myself to Cochin!

The thought had occurred to me the very first time I saw the airplane. At that time I had simply been playing with the idea rather than believing it was something I really could do. Things were different now. As the airplane mechanic, I could come and go in the hangar at will. Even at night. No one would notice if I prepared the plane for departure late one evening when there were celebrations going on in the palace. With a little luck I could start the engine and be out on the airstrip before anyone suspected anything was amiss. And once I was airborne no one could stop me.

As long as I didn't crash-land, that is, but I should be able to avoid that. The maharaja had never allowed me to pilot the plane, but after all the hours in the air I had a pretty good idea how to fly it.

So stealing the airplane would not be a major problem and nor would flying it to Cochin. The *real* problems would start the moment I landed there. Where to go in Cochin? How to avoid being arrested by the police? How to go about finding Alphonse Morro?

I did not have a good answer to any of these questions. In spite of that, I did eventually come to a decision: if I hadn't heard from Ana and Signor Fidardo within the next two months I would steal the plane and fly to Cochin.

Once that decision was made I began to sleep better at night, although sometimes, particularly when the maharaja and I had spent the day flying, I lay awake tossing and turn-ing. I was imagining how the maharaja would react the day he discovered I had disappeared with his airplane. I had no doubt he would be furious and immediately put a price on my head. But he would also be sad—I knew that.

What I was planning was deceitful. But I had no choice.

CHAPTER 50
Sabotage

The maharaja was famous for his parties, and he usually organized at least two or three every week. They were splendid feasts with hundreds of dishes, an abundance of expensive wines, orchestras and entertainment provided by buxom dancing girls from Lahore.

The courtiers loved the maharaja's feasts, and they had been growing uneasy of late because he seemed to have lost some of his party spirit. These days there was rarely more than one decent party a week, and sometimes not even that.

They noticed a number of signs that suggested the maharaja was not the man he had been. He was seen much less frequently in the palace bars and billiard rooms; there were no longer any late-night poker sessions followed by Turkish baths and a whisky buffet. The maharaja was clearly not himself.

The explanation was a simple one: after a long day behind the joystick of his airplane, the maharaja had no energy to spare to party or play billiards even if he still enjoyed those things.

I seemed to be the only one who understood this. Everyone else at court believed that flying was somehow warping the maharaja's mind. I couldn't avoid hearing the gossip that went round. Some people were of the opinion that the vibrations in the plane were causing a softening of the maharaja's brain tissue; others believed that the fumes of the fuel were causing a personality change. Whichever it was, it was thought to be serious.

And, of course, none of this was helped by the amount of time His Highness spent in the company of a gorilla. All of the courtiers were in agreement on that point. The chamberlain and the aides-de-camp hated me more than ever.

At the beginning of October the maharaja invited his cousin, the Maharaja of Kapurthala, to make a state visit. It was actually Diwan Sardar Bahadur's idea, because the atmosphere between the cousins had been rather frosty since the cricket match a few months earlier. The diwan thought it important they should meet and get over their differences.

The Maharaja of Kapurthala was received with great pomp and splendor. While the ministers of the two prince-doms met and discussed various important issues, the two maharajas devoted their time to eating, drinking, hunting peacocks and playing polo, billiards and tennis. They competed with one another the whole time, which was what they appeared to do whenever they met.

The maharaja had kept a surprise in store for the last day of the state visit—it was a surprise he hoped would both impress the Maharaja of Kapurthala and make him jealous. He was going to take him for a flight in his Gipsy Moth.

I always kept the airplane in absolutely tip-top condition, so there was no need for me to make any special preparations for their flight. In spite of that, I went to the hangar early in the morning, undid the covers over the cockpits and gave all the chrome and brass surfaces a quick rub-over with my polishing rag. I polished the varnished propeller with wax until it shone like a mirror. I took a few steps back and thought there was unlikely to be a smarter and better cared-for Gipsy Moth in the whole world. I understood why the maharaja was so keen to show off his beautiful airplane.

Through the crack between the hangar doors I could see the crowd beginning to line up along the airstrip. Nearly time! I climbed into the plane and sat in the pilot's seat to give the levers one last check to ensure they were all functioning smoothly.

That was when I discovered something was wrong.

The elevators did not respond as they should when I pulled the joystick toward me.

In a flash I leapt to the ground and examined the tail wings. The elevator cables were loose!

How was that possible?

I hurried back to the pilot's cockpit and crawled in behind the seat. There, in the rear part of the fuselage, the control cables to the tail wing ran along the sides, and despite the poor light I quickly found the thumbscrews used to adjust the tension on the cables.

They had been loosened almost to the point of becoming detached.

My heart was pounding.

Someone had tried to sabotage the plane.

My hands were shaking as I readjusted the cables, all the

while thinking how I could postpone the flight. The danger was that the saboteur might not have been satisfied with just disabling the elevators: there are many other ways of turning an airplane into a death trap.

How was I to make myself understood? How was I to warn the maharaja of the danger? He certainly wouldn't cancel a flight just because I seemed nervous for no particular reason. Certainly not this flight, anyway.

I climbed down from the plane and quickly removed the engine cowling. There wasn't much time now. I eased open the bottom plug to allow out a little fuel, which I sniffed and then tasted on the tip of my tongue. The fuel seemed all right. I took out the oil filter and checked it. That looked fine too. No iron filings or any foreign matter in it.

I swung the engine into life and let it tick over while I went through all the levers, instruments and cables. Then I checked the undercarriage and tires. When I had finished, the engine was still running gently and smoothly.

As far as I could tell there was no longer anything the matter with the airplane.

The next thirty minutes were among the most nervous half hours I have ever lived through. The doors to the hangar opened and a small squad of soldiers from the bodyguard helped roll the plane out to the airstrip. The orchestra was playing and people were cheering. I went and took my place among the aides-de-camp at the side of the airstrip. In my head I kept running through everything about the plane in case there was anything I had failed to check.

The sounds of cheering and applause greeted the Maharaja of Kapurthala as he climbed into the passenger cockpit. The cheering became even louder when the maharaja swung the propeller to start the engine and took his seat in the pilot's cockpit.

They were ready to take off.

The maharaja released the brake and the plane rolled along the runway. Then a voice hissed in my ear: "In ten seconds it will be all over for you, gorilla. The tigers are waiting!"

I turned round.

It was the chamberlain. Under his mustache his thin, pale, grinning lips revealed two rows of yellow teeth. His eyes flashed.

At that moment the accelerating airplane was reaching the far end of the runway. I looked in that direction in horror. What did the chamberlain mean? What was about to happen?

A second later the plane rose from the ground and climbed skyward in an elegant curve. Everything happened just as it should.

"What . . . what the devil . . . !" the chamberlain panted.

He stared at the plane, his eyes wide and his mouth hanging open.

It took a minute, but then I understood everything. I suddenly realized why the elevator had been sabotaged.

Without a functioning elevator the plane would have been unable to lift off the ground. It would have just trundled on across the grassy ground beyond the runway and careered at full speed straight into the shallow flamingo pond.

There would have been a first-class scandal, and the blame would have been laid at my door. After all, I was the one responsible for keeping the plane airworthy. My punishment would undoubtedly have been a harsh one.

And that, of course, was the point of the sabotage.

I turned round again. The chamberlain was disappearing into the crowd. But many of the aides-de-camp were still there: they were glaring after the airplane with looks of disappointment on their faces.

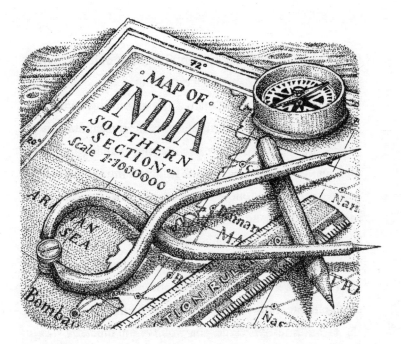

CHAPTER 51
Saudade

The chamberlain had sabotaged the maharaja's airplane simply to get at me. He must really have hated
me; otherwise he would never have taken a risk of that sort.
I now realized that he would not give up until I was locked
up in the zoo or fed to the tigers.

I would have to change my plans. Staying in the palace
had become too dangerous, and I decided to flee as soon as
possible. Most of my preparations had, in fact, already been

made. I had torn out a dozen or more pages of maps of India from a big atlas in the palace reading room. That hadn't been difficult: the courtiers weren't much given to books, so the reading room was almost always empty. I had drawn details of my route on the maps and noted flying times. My plan was to fly southwest until I sighted the Indian Ocean, and then I would follow the coast down to Cochin. I had fuel for thirty-six hours of flying time, which should be sufficient to take me the whole way.

I would leave in ten days, on the fourteenth of October. That was the maharaja's birthday. It was dreadful, I know, to plan to steal his plane on that day of all days, but during the evening festivities no one would notice what I was up to in the hangar. If I was really lucky no one would notice I was missing until the following morning.

The only thing I hadn't managed to arrange was a disguise to put on as soon as I landed in Cochin. I had decided to disguise myself as a little old woman with a shawl over her face. It had worked at the station in Jodhpur. I was intending to steal the clothes from the zenana.

Once the Kapurthala state visit was over, an atmosphere of calm spread over the palace and I saw no sign of the maharaja for several days. He must presumably have been confined to his bed after all the partying. But then one morning he came to the hangar and told me to get ready for a flight: he was still feeling rather weak, so it would have to be no more than a short spin before lunch.

When we arrived back, the maharaja told me to come to his apartment later in the afternoon. He was intending to pay a visit to the zenana and, as usual, he wanted me to make sure the coast was clear before he did.

This would be my chance to steal a disguise. I didn't think it would be too difficult, as the women in the zenana owned more than enough clothes and every day they forgot items and left them scattered round the gardens and the swimming pool.

I arrived at the maharaja's apartment that afternoon and waited in the music room. It seems he was suffering a mild recurrence of bellyache and was otherwise occupied for the present.

In view of my plan to steal clothes I was feeling rather nervous and couldn't keep still. Lying beside the gramophone was the latest stack of new records the maharaja had received from Europe. I flipped through them to give myself something to do. Very few of the envelopes had been opened. The maharaja did not listen to more than a fraction of the records he bought, and the majority would go straight up on the shelves.

My brain did not take it in at first, and I failed to recognize what I was looking at. But then I felt a warm wave surge through my body as, with trembling hands, I picked up one of the records from the heap.

The title of the record was printed in small letters right at the bottom of the sleeve. It was called *Saudade*. I'd heard that word before. In Lisbon. I believe that *saudade* is the Portuguese word for "melancholy."

The artiste's name was printed at the top of the sleeve: Ana Molina.

The picture on the sleeve was a photograph of Ana. She was sitting in the dark, but her face was lit and her gaze was focused somewhere in the far distance. She looked exactly as she had the night I first saw her sitting singing in her attic window.

My head went into a spin. Without thinking I carefully opened the sleeve and took out the record. *I must hear her voice* was the only thought in my mind.

I had often watched the maharaja putting records on the gramophone, and I knew how to do it. First came the sound of a sad guitar playing a simple sequence of notes; then came the song. I recognized the melody immediately. I had heard it so many times before.

At that moment I would have given the world to be back in the house on Rua de São Tomé.

I had to sit down in one of the maharaja's armchairs,

and there I stayed, listening to Ana with my eyes closed. I forgot time and I didn't hear the maharaja enter until his harsh voice drowned the music.

"You're taking a liberty, aren't you?" he said. "I don't remember giving you permission to play records on my gramophone."

I was on my feet in a second. There was something completely unreal about standing there in front of the maharaja at the same time as listening to Ana singing her most beautiful songs. The two things did not go together.

The maharaja must have noticed that something had thrown me off-balance.

"You aren't ill, are you?" he asked, suddenly sounding anxious.

I shook my head.

We stood in silence for a few moments, and during that short time I saw a change come over the maharaja's face. His eyes went blank and seemed to be looking straight through me. Then he looked at the gramophone.

"What kind of music is that?" he asked. "What a wonderful voice. Who in all the world can sing so beautifully?"

I still held the record sleeve and I handed it to him. He took it and looked at the photograph of Ana.

"And so beautiful too," he muttered, ". . . so beautiful."

He sat down in one of the armchairs, and without taking his eyes from the sleeve he listened to the record right to the end. He seemed to have forgotten I was in the room.

After the last song he looked up with a rather dazed expression.

"Put the record on again," he said. "And then you can go. Out to the hangar, that is. I've changed my mind. I've no wish to visit the zenana now."

I did as he asked. When I turned round on my way out of the music room he was still sitting there looking at the photograph of Ana.

And her singing filled the room.

~

My chance to steal a disguise was lost, but I felt happy for all that. Happy to have heard Ana sing. Happy that she had made a record, as she had been promised after the concert at the São Carlos opera house. Now people could listen to her all over the world, even here in distant India.

For the next three days I waited impatiently for the maharaja to summon me to his apartment again. But he did not. I didn't see him at all, which was strange.

Things were beginning to become urgent. The maharaja's birthday was just six days away, and I had to get into the zenana before that or postpone my escape. Or set off for

Cochin without a good disguise to put on when I arrived there.

As things turned out, however, I was not going to need a disguise at all. My escape never happened.

Rumors began spreading round the palace. The maharaja had apparently shut himself away in the music room and was neither eating nor sleeping. He was sitting there night and day listening to the same record.

The record of a Portuguese singer.

Everyone in the palace was certain that this could only mean one thing: the maharaja was in love. This was how he always behaved when he fell in love with a beautiful and talented artiste from Europe.

I didn't know what to believe. Could it really be true?

I learned the answer a few days before the maharaja's birthday. He made an unexpected visit to the hangar one morning and sank into the chair in which he usually sat when watching me working on the plane. He looked dreadful. His skin was a sickly shade of pale yellow and his eyes were bloodshot from lack of sleep.

He sat in silence for a long time, staring in front of him. Now and then he sighed deeply. Then he said in a broken voice, "I've no desire to fly today. I've no desire to do anything at all."

I nodded carefully. The maharaja looked at me.

"It's your fault," he said. "You were the one who put on that record. I ought to find some way of punishing you . . . or perhaps rewarding you . . . it all depends. . . ."

His voice died away and his gaze turned inward.

I didn't really know what to do. It seemed wrong to carry on tinkering with the airplane when the maharaja wasn't feeling well. So I pulled up a stool and sat beside him. We sat together without saying a thing, as we had often done on our trips in his Gipsy Moth.

Before the maharaja stood up and went back to the palace he asked me a question, which was something he very rarely did. Unless it was something about the airplane, that is. But now he said, "Have you ever been in love?"

I nodded.

He seemed to think about my answer for a while.

"In that case you know how it feels," he said with another pained sigh. "I've invited her to come here. Ana Molina, I mean. Pray that she says yes! If she doesn't, I shall die of the sorrows of love!"

CHAPTER 52
An Unexpected Invitation

What if she says no?

That was the first thought that came to my mind when the maharaja told me he had invited Ana Molina to Bhapur. Instead of feeling happy I felt terrified. Terrified that this incredible possibility might come to nothing.

For nights I lay awake, sleepless, trying to imagine how Ana would respond to the invitation, how she would feel about it, how she would ask Signor Fidardo for advice, how she might finally reach a decision about the maharaja's invitation.

I am here, Ana! Don't say no! These were my thoughts— time after time. Don't say no!

~

I was worrying unnecessarily. I know that now. I also know what happened when Ana received the maharaja's letter. I know because she has told me herself.

It began with a card from the British ambassador in Lisbon: Sir Colville Barclay, the ambassador himself, wanted to meet Ana about an important and urgent matter.

Ana immediately ran downstairs to Signor Fidardo's workshop and showed him the card.

"It must have something to do with Sally Jones," she said with a lump in her throat. "It must, mustn't it? Don't you think?"

Signor Fidardo removed his spectacles, and Ana could see that his hand was shaking.

"Probably, probably," he said. "Let us hope it is good news."

The following morning Ana took the tram to the British embassy, where she was immediately taken to Sir Colville's office. They had met before, at the party after Ana's concert at the opera house. The ambassador began by telling her he had bought her new record.

"It's wonderful! Quite lovely!" Sir Colville said. "But that's not why I've asked you to come, Miss Molina. There is a matter that has reached my desk, which I need to discuss with you personally."

"Does it have anything to do with Sally Jones?" Ana asked immediately.

Sir Colville gave her a look of surprise.

"No," he said. "No, I'm not sure I understand. Who is that?"

Ana found it difficult to hide her disappointment.

"A friend," she said. "A friend who has disappeared in India and I had hoped . . . well, I had hoped you had news of her."

"In India," the ambassador said. "That really is a strange coincidence. I don't know about your Sally Jones, but I am very familiar with India. In fact, India is why I have invited you here today. In our diplomatic postbag we have received an invitation for you to visit an Indian maharaja. The Maharaja of Bhapur, to be specific."

From a drawer in his desk the ambassador took a large gold-colored envelope and a small box made of carved ivory. The envelope contained a letter to Ana from the maharaja and a first-class ticket on the liner RMS *Mongolia* from Marseille to Bombay. In the box was a bracelet studded with gleaming red rubies.

Ana was dumbstruck! Understandably! What could a bracelet like that be worth? She read through the maharaja's letter several times. No one had ever written anything like it to her before. Not even Canson, her secret admirer.

Esteemed and Worshipped Miss Ana Molina!

You have changed my life! I am a great connoisseur and lover of music, but not until I listened to your spellbinding voice on my gramophone were my ears opened to the highest spheres of beauty available in this art. And when I saw your photograph on the record sleeve I realized that incomparable talent and the perfection of womanhood have been united in the noble perfection of your person.

My aching and throbbing heart will waste away and wither to a shriveled leaf in my breast unless I am permitted to see you and to hear your lovely voice in live performance. I beg you to do me the infinite honor of being my guest here in my palace in Bhapur. I shall do everything in my power to give you a welcome worthy of a true Goddess of Art and Beauty!

Your humble and eternally faithful servant,
Maharaja of Bhapur

Sir Colville chuckled a little when he saw Ana's expression.

"The Maharaja of Bhapur is a romantic sort of fellow," he said. "Though rumor has it that he has a small squad of poets to help him compose his love letters. But one way or another, it is clear he would like you to visit him. It is, of course, completely up to you whether you say yes. I should just like you to know what you can expect should you agree to go. The maharaja will inundate you with priceless gifts, and then he will ask you to marry him. That is what he always does when he invites famous and beautiful artistes with whom he has fallen in love. He already has five or six in his harem. So think carefully before you decide."

Ana thought for a short while.

"What will happen if he proposes to me and I say no?" she asked.

"You would not be thrown into a dungeon under the palace, if that is what is worrying you, Miss Molina. If you say no, the maharaja will give you a magnificent farewell gift and allow you to travel home. Say what you like about the Maharaja of Bhapur, he does know how to behave like a gentleman when it is necessary."

∿

Ana was utterly confused by the time she left the embassy. Before the meeting she had been quite sure that Sir Colville had summoned her to talk about me. That was not particularly surprising. Ever since I sailed from Lisbon on the *Song of Limerick* a year earlier, Ana and Signor Fidardo had been doing everything they could to find out what had happened to me. And since India is under British rule they had been in frequent contact with the British authorities.

A shipping company in Southampton had helped them make contact with the captain of the *Song of Limerick*, which was unloading a cargo of cotton in a port in South Africa at that point. Captain Anderson sent a telegram informing them I had left his vessel in Bombay a month before and that I had gone on to Cochin in a ship by the name of the *Malabar Star*. Captain Anderson did not know what happened after that, but he promised to try to find out the next time the *Song of Limerick* docked in India.

Ana and Signor Fidardo's next step had been to write to the British consul in Cochin asking whether he knew of a gorilla who had recently arrived there in a ship called the *Malabar Star*. After two long months they received a brief reply from a secretary at the consulate:

Unfortunately it has proved impossible to answer your inquiry. Cochin is a major port through which vast quantities of cargoes—including exotic animals—pass every day. Malabar Star, *moreover, is a not uncommon name for vessels on the west coast of India.*

Ana and Signor Fidardo did not give up. They wrote more letters to numerous shipping companies and to various consulates in British India. Most of them did not respond, and none of those that did answer had heard anything about a gorilla on the loose. Ana and Signor Fidardo began to fear I had disappeared for good somewhere in India.

Ana had passed on these reports to the Chief. It was hard to tell him the truth, but she could not lie to him. The Chief's answering letter arrived a few days later and, after reading it, Ana felt a little more hopeful than before:

Dear Miss Molina,

Thank you for your kind and thoughtful letter and thank you for all you have done to find out about our Sally Jones. Also, please thank your friend Mr. Fidardo from me. You are good and wonderful people!

I would be telling a lie if I didn't say how much of a disappointment your letter was. It must have been very difficult for you to write it. But I want you to know that Sally Jones has disappeared before. There was a time when she disappeared in the jungle of the Congo and I was sure I had lost her forever, but she came back.

I can't really understand why she signed on a vessel sailing for India, and you say nothing about that in your letter. Perhaps she just wanted to smell the sea again. I could understand that because in her heart of hearts she is more of a seaman than most people I have sailed with in my time. Please don't be sad. I believe she will come back this time too. She would do anything rather than bring sorrow on those who are fond of her.

With respectful greetings,
Henry

P.S. In your letter you mention a Captain Anderson. I know him and he is a good man. You can be sure that he will have done his best to help Sally Jones.

Many months had passed since then. Ana had sometimes contemplated traveling to India to search for me, but the journey was more than she could afford. In any case, Signor Fidardo advised her against it.

"It would probably end up with you disappearing too. Then I should have to go to India and look for both you and Sally Jones. And at my age, that is something I would rather be spared!"

Now, however, as Ana realized on the way home from the embassy, everything had changed. In the pocket of her cape she had a ticket to Bombay and the journey would not cost her a cent! What's more, she had been invited there by a maharaja, who in addition to being rich must also be powerful.

I'm sure he'll be able to help me find Sally Jones, Ana thought.

By the time she arrived home at Rua de São Tomé she had already come to a decision. She would say yes to the maharaja and she would travel to Bhapur.

CHAPTER 53
Seven Hundred Pearls from Bahrain

O ne week later Signor Fidardo was waving goodbye to Ana as she took the night train from Rossio Station to Madrid. He knew she would go, whatever he thought. The only thing he had demanded of her was a promise that she would not allow herself to be shut away in the maharaja's harem. She had promised him that.

Ana traveled on from Madrid to Marseille by train, and there she went aboard the liner RMS *Mongolia*. Even this part of the journey had been a great adventure for Ana. She had lived in Lisbon almost all her life and had never been outside Portugal.

The *Mongolia* was an almost-new liner, and everything was elegant and luxurious. Ana did not possess either the clothes or the jewelry necessary to parade on the promenade deck, but the maharaja had foreseen that. He had ordered the shipping company to fill the wardrobes in her cabin to bursting point with elegant clothes and evening dresses.

After twelve days at sea Ana reached Bombay, where a Rolls-Royce was on the quayside ready to take her to the railway station. Two first-class coaches were waiting there, for her and her alone. She was feeling more and more nervous about meeting the maharaja. What could he be like, someone who could afford all this? And how was she to repay him for all his gifts?

～

The reception Ana was given at the maharaja's private station in Bhapur was beyond anything she could have imagined.

Fireworks lit up the sky, the state orchestra played a grand medley of the tunes on Ana's record and thousands of red rose petals drifted down from a hot-air balloon hovering above the platform. The maharaja's bodyguards fired a salute, and thirty elephants in ceremonial apparel blew fanfares with their trunks. The maharaja, sitting on the biggest of the elephants, was dressed in a costume of gold brocade, and there were seven hundred pearls from Bahrain sewn into his turban.

"It was an awful experience," Ana said when she told me later about her arrival in Bhapur. "I felt like the smallest person in the world and yet I was the one everyone was looking at."

I know exactly what she meant, because I was there. The whole court was lined up five deep below the platform. In our hands we had flags to wave and confetti to throw. Ana really did look very small and afraid when she stepped down from the train. She looked as if she thought all the soldiers and drummers and enormous elephants had gathered there to attack her.

I was standing in the back row, struggling to resist the urge to run forward and throw my arms round her. A month had passed since I learned that Ana had accepted the maharaja's invitation, and since then I hadn't stopped thinking about this moment. But I was still unprepared for the feeling of happiness that spread through every part of my body: I had never been so happy to see someone in all my life.

But it was essential that I stay in the background. Ana was the maharaja's guest, and he had been rehearsing the welcoming ceremony for a week to make a truly stunning first impression. If Ana was to catch sight of me she would completely forget the maharaja preening himself up there on his most magnificent elephant. To make himself look even more elegant he had squeezed his big belly into a tight corset, and was I to spoil this moment for him he would not forgive me in a hurry.

~

I did not catch a glimpse of Ana for the next three days. The maharaja was entertaining her from morning to night. He showed her round the place and arranged excursions in the neighborhood. She was taken for a ride on an elephant and out to hunt tigers in the maharaja's game park.

One afternoon he invited her on a boat trip on an artificial lake with bubbling fountains and flowering laburnums along its shores. The lake had been constructed to provide somewhere for the maharaja to be rowed round in his purpose-built royal barge, the oarsmen being twenty young men dressed in uniforms copied from those of the British Royal Navy. The barge and the oarsmen together formed the Royal Bhapur Navy, of which—of course—the maharaja was admiral.

The maharaja was proud of his wealth and he wanted to show Ana everything he owned.

And I knew he was saving the best until last.

That is why I did not leave the hangar and the airplane for one second during those days. It was Ana's fourth day in the palace when a servant brought me the message I had been expecting. I was to prepare the plane at once—the maharaja was going to take his guest for a flight.

~

I was waiting by the airplane when the maharaja and Ana came walking across the grass toward the landing strip. It was one of those moments that is both impossible to forget and difficult to remember in detail. I was anticipating it so eagerly that it flickered before my eyes like a jerky film.

Ana did not catch sight of me until they were quite close. Then she suddenly slowed down, before stopping and staring openmouthed. I think the maharaja was in the process of telling her something because he continued walking and gesticulating with his hands. When he noticed that Ana was no longer at his side he turned round. By then she was running toward me and I toward her.

I ran straight into Ana's arms, and she squeezed me so tight I could hardly breathe. When she finally released me and looked me in the face, tears were running down her cheeks. She had still not managed to get a word out.

The first to speak was the maharaja.

"What . . . er . . . um . . . er . . . what's going on?" he asked, virtually talking to himself.

Ana let go of me and instead gave the maharaja a real hug. "Thank you, Your Highness! This is the best surprise you could have given me!"

This was, of course, a slight misunderstanding on Ana's part. That morning the maharaja had promised her a surprise, by which he meant a flight in his airplane. Ana, however, believed that I was the surprise.

CHAPTER 54
Tears of Joy and Some Light Refreshments

A little while later the three of us were sitting round the big table in the Royal Aviation Lounge. Ana was still so moved that she had to borrow a handkerchief from the maharaja to dry the tears of joy from her eyes. The maharaja ordered up "some light refreshments," which were brought over from the palace on five full serving trolleys. He did not like talking without something tasty to eat and drink.

When Ana had collected herself, she began to explain

to the maharaja how she and I knew one another. She told him how we had met in Lisbon and how I moved in with her after my friend the Chief had been imprisoned for the murder of Alphonse Morro. She went on to tell him about my work in Signor Fidardo's workshop and about our discovery of the grave of Elisa Gomes. Then she described the mysterious letters and money from Cochin and my hasty departure for India on the *Song of Limerick*.

The maharaja seemed to be listening attentively, but I knew him too well to be deceived. He quickly lost interest in the long and tangled story and sat gazing longingly into Ana's brown eyes.

After Ana had finished her story, the maharaja sent his servant for coffee, liqueurs and a trolley bearing a special selection of Belgian chocolates. Then it was his turn to take up the story. Ana now heard for the first time about our dealings with Mr. Thursgood, the company director, and about the chess match that led to me joining the maharaja as his aide-de-camp. The maharaja continued with a description of the many exciting flights he and I had made together. Much of this involved his exploits as a pilot, and he omitted altogether my function as his spy in the zenana. He considered that to be a state secret.

At this point the maharaja neatly and elegantly changed the subject: "Speaking of airplanes," he said, "I do believe, dear Miss Molina, that it's high time I took you for a little trip in the air. I've taken the liberty of having a small present sewn for you."

He gave a sign to one of his servants, who brought over a parcel wrapped in tissue paper. The parcel contained a flying suit identical to the maharaja's, though it was, of course, smaller and cut for a woman.

Ana thanked him for the splendid present, but she clearly did not feel we had finished talking about her and my reunion.

"So, Your Highness, was it pure chance that Sally Jones and I met one another at your palace in Bhapur?" she asked.

The maharaja's face took on a slightly irritated expression for a moment. He was impatient to see Ana in the elegant and snug buckskin flying suit.

"No," he said. "Chance does not rule in Bhapur. I am the one who rules here! And now I want to sweep you up into the clouds, Miss Molina! Are you ready?"

It was only now that Ana seemed to realize what awaited her.

"I have never flown before," she said cautiously. "I'm not sure I dare. . . ."

The maharaja's eyes widened uneasily.

"Surely that doesn't matter? It's not in the least dangerous. Great fun! It really is, isn't it?"

The maharaja turned to me for support.

I nodded.

"Well, in that case, of course I'll come," Ana said bravely. "Where can I change into my fine suit?"

The maharaja beamed and gave me a grateful look.

~

After her trip in the airplane Ana wanted to spend some time alone with me, but there was no chance of that. The maharaja had reserved one of the palace bathhouses just for her, and it was time for her to start getting ready for that evening's dinner party.

It would be almost a week before I met Ana again. The maharaja had planned more or less every minute of her visit. One morning, however, she was permitted to take a short walk alone, and she rushed over to me in the hangar. She was dressed in a beautiful sari and wearing a string of pearls long enough to encircle her neck several times. It looked about the same length as the foresheet of a small boat.

Ana hugged me and told me that she'd had a serious talk with the maharaja the night before. She had explained to him that she would very soon have to travel to Cochin with me. We really had to look for Alphonse Morro.

The maharaja had been rather sullen—initially, anyway.

He'd questioned Ana about this fellow Morro and why she was so interested in him. Ana gave him the whole context, explaining how Morro was the only person who could prove that Koskela was innocent of the murder for which he had been imprisoned. At this point the maharaja's face had grown even darker—now he wanted to know why Ana was so keen to see Koskela free. Ana had to explain to him that it was for my sake, not hers: she scarcely knew Koskela.

"He seems to have a terribly jealous nature, your maharaja," Ana whispered.

I nodded. I had no difficulty in agreeing with that

Ana continued with her report, and now there was a glint in her eye.

"Once the maharaja understood that I'm not in love with either Morro or Koskela his mood immediately improved and he said Cochin is a wonderful place for a trip. He owns a luxury yacht—can you believe it?—in Bombay, and we sail for Cochin in ten days' time. It's already been decided!"

I was uncertain what Ana meant when she said *we,* so I pointed at myself and gave her a questioning look.

"Yes, of course," she said, giving me another hug. "You'll come too. I was careful to ask him that."

It was time for Ana to hurry back to the palace, where the maharaja had invited her to a champagne breakfast in the pleasure pavilion of his rose garden.

Five days after this Ana gave a concert in the palace park. She was accompanied by a famous sitar player, Enayat Khan, whom the maharaja had brought in from Calcutta. Four hundred guests were invited, and they all came. Among the audience were the Maharajas of Patiala, Kapurthala and Ravhajpouthala, as well as the British governor-general of the Punjab. The three maharajas were accompanied by hordes of servants and courtiers, and three large tented encampments had to be erected in the park to provide accommodation for everyone. *Tented encampments* is probably the wrong term, since they were more like towns, the tents themselves resembling real palaces with paintings on the walls and crystal chandeliers hanging from the roofs.

I only managed to hear part of Ana's concert, since I was busy preparing the maharaja's Gipsy Moth for the flying display he was intending to put on before the great banquet in Ana's honor.

Before we took our seats in the plane the maharaja told me that his cousin the Maharaja of Kapurthala had recently acquired a plane. It was, moreover, a more recent model than his own.

"He's trying to outdo me, the fool!" the maharaja said. "I'll have to put on something a bit extra at this display.

Something my cousin can't do. What do you think about looping the loop? It can't be that difficult, surely?"

I gave him a thumbs-up, hoping he was just joking. He wasn't! But flying upside down proved to be not too bad anyway.

~

The celebrations after the concert lasted for seven days of unbroken eating and drinking. Once his noble guests had departed, the maharaja was forced to have three days of ayurvedic massage to relieve his flatulence. Only then was he fit for our journey to Cochin.

CHAPTER 55
The HMS *Rana*

It was a beautifully clear morning when we boarded the maharaja's private train, and five days later we arrived in Bombay. We were then driven in a cortege of cars to the Royal Bombay Yacht Club; from there a steam launch took us out to the HMS *Rana,* the maharaja's yacht, which was at anchor in the roads.

The HMS *Rana* was a very fine vessel, well designed and well constructed down to the smallest detail. The fittings were as costly as anything in the maharaja's palace. Only twenty of the eighty-strong crew were sailors, the rest being there simply to serve the passengers.

I had estimated that we would reach Cochin in four days at the most, but I soon realized the voyage was going to last considerably longer. The maharaja was in no hurry. He wanted to be able to sit under a parasol on the sundeck and drink champagne with Ana without being disturbed by unpleasant headwinds, which meant that we proceeded south along the coast of Malabar at the slowest speed possible. Most of the time we sailed near enough to the coast for the beaches of white sand and the coconut palms swaying in the gentle southwesterly breeze to be visible through binoculars. Every afternoon we dropped anchor for the night to allow the maharaja to take Ana ashore for romantic excursions in the sunset.

I tried to be patient. After all, we were on our way even if we were moving so slowly. But I did find it strange to be at sea and not have anything useful to do. My only meetings with Ana were when the maharaja summoned me, which happened no more than a couple of times during the voyage. Once we had come aboard the HMS *Rana* he no longer needed me either to spy on Maji Sahiba or to look after his airplane. Added to which he obviously wanted Ana all to himself.

We eventually arrived off Cochin late one afternoon when the sun was glowing red on the western horizon. Cochin is situated on a peninsula between the Indian Ocean and Vembanad Lake, a great lagoon of brackish water in which ships are protected from wind and waves. An ancient gunboat guided us in through the sandbanks round the approach to the port, and a seventeen-gun salute was fired from the walls of the fortress. A small crowd had gathered along the wharves that lined the shore, and they were waving their hats and flags to welcome us.

When the HMS *Rana* had dropped anchor I was summoned to one of the maharaja's many private rooms. It was Ana who had sent for me. The maharaja had given her permission to meet me for a short time before dinner.

Ana looked tired, and she seemed rather annoyed.

"I can't stand much more of this luxury life," she whispered. "The maharaja is immensely thoughtful and generous, but it's becoming *too* much. And I get headaches from all the champagne. I don't think he drinks anything else!"

I nodded. I knew what she meant.

"I've tried several times to talk to him about Alphonse Morro," she went on, "asked him how we should go about finding him, but I haven't had a proper answer. He seems completely uninterested. The only thing he wants to talk about is how enjoyable it will be to go duck shooting with the Maharaja of Cochin."

I learned that Ana and the maharaja were leaving the following morning to make a state visit to the Maharaja of Cochin. They would be spending several days at his palace, the Hill Palace, about eight miles inland. I was to remain on board the *Rana*.

Ana could see I was disappointed, and she took my hands in hers.

"Don't worry," she said. "I'll fix this somehow or other. We won't leave Cochin until we are certain whether Morro is here. I promise you."

~

Their visit to the Maharaja of Cochin lasted five days. Ana told me later that what had pleased our maharaja most was that the Hill Palace was so much smaller than Sunahiri Bagh Palace.

"Even my yacht is more luxurious than his palace!" the maharaja had gloated to Ana many times.

More celebrations awaited them when they returned to the *Rana*. There were dinner parties, afternoon teas and garden parties with the British consul and other important dignitaries in Cochin. For every invitation the maharaja received onshore, he organized something twice as grand on the *Rana*. On the few occasions I saw Ana she was looking pale and exhausted.

As for me, restlessness was driving me crazy. Day after day found me doing nothing but wandering back and forth along the deck of the *Rana*. Every now and again I would stop and peer out over the muddy waters of Vembanad Lake. Skiffs and barges and small tugs plied between the vessels anchored in the roadstead. Beyond them, no more than a nautical mile away, lay the city of Cochin. All I could see of it were the warehouses along the water's edge and a church tower that rose above the tops of the palm trees.

My thoughts often flew across the water with the gulls and, hovering low over the city, I would catch sight of Alphonse Morro. Sometimes I would see him sitting drinking coffee at a street café; sometimes he would be carrying sacks in the harbor. On one occasion I looked through a window and saw him lying in bed with a bottle in his hand. Another time he was standing on the quayside with a suitcase, all ready to depart.

My fantasies made me even more impatient; they made my fur prickle and itch.

I was so close now.

On our eighth day at anchor a larger ship pulled alongside the *Rana* and a woman came aboard. She was Indian and dressed in a simple sari. She handed a letter to the officer on watch, and when he had read it the woman was brought to me. She bowed with her hands together in front of her in the Indian manner.

"My name is Ayesha Narayanan," she said in a soft voice. "I am secretary to Diwan Al-Faroud, the Maharaja of Cochin's prime minister. Miss Molina has talked to the diwan about you. She says you are a very unusual gorilla and you can understand what people say to you."

I nodded and bowed in the same way as she had. The woman called Ayesha smiled. She had a nice smile, and behind her small steel-rimmed glasses her eyes were wise. For some reason it was quite impossible to guess her age.

"Miss Molina has also told us why you and she have come to Cochin. You are looking for a man called Alphonse Morro who came here from Lisbon. The diwan has instructed me to help you."

At last! I thought. Bravo, Ana!

I have known for a long time that human beings have no idea how to interpret the noises made by a gorilla, which is why I always try to remain silent. That way there can be no misunderstanding. But now I was so excited that I couldn't help making some happy gorilla sounds. They did not seem to worry Ayesha. She said, "I shall do my best to find this Morro man. There is, of course, a problem. Miss Molina said that Morro is on the run, so it is quite possible that he isn't using his real name. That might make it harder to find him. But if I understood rightly, you have met Alphonse Morro and know what he looks like."

I nodded vigorously.

"In that case it would be useful if you come with me," Ayesha said. "The two of us can make inquiries together. If you are ready we can set off for Cochin straightaway."

CHAPTER 56
Ayesha

We went to Cochin in Ayesha's tender, and on the way she told me we would start looking for Morro in a part of the city called Fort Cochin, which was where all the Europeans lived.

The boatman came alongside a low stone pier and we stepped ashore. In the shade of a large eucalyptus tree there were a number of sleeping rickshaw drivers, and Ayesha woke one of them and gave him an address. Then we set off.

The barefoot rickshaw driver pulled us at a run along empty, dusty streets. We passed neat houses with shaded verandas, well-tended gardens and drawn blinds over the windows. A platoon of Indian soldiers was marching round a large parade ground in the blazing midday sun. Shaded by a parasol, a British officer was shouting orders. There was no one else in sight. Fort Cochin was a sleepy place, and if Alphonse Morro was there it should not be too difficult to find him, I thought. The excitement made me jumpy, and I found it hard to keep still.

The rickshaw drew up outside a tall wrought-iron gate that led into a garden the size of a park. On the far side of the lawns stood a long white bungalow surrounded by raked gravel drives.

"This is the Cochin Club," Ayesha said. "Most British residents are members, and a number of other Europeans as well, I think."

Ayesha went first. We saw no one until we stepped inside the open double doors. There was a large room, furnished in quite a simple style with scattered groups of armchairs and sofas. A billiard table occupied the middle of the floor, and along one of the short walls ran a bar counter made of a dark wood. Flies were buzzing round the motionless fans on the ceiling.

A tall thin man was drying glasses behind the bar. He

was an Indian, and he was dressed in a kind of waiter's uniform. Ayesha said hello, and the bartender answered her greeting, giving me a quick questioning glance as he did so.

"Alphonse Morro," Ayesha said. "Do you know the name?"

The bartender put his head to one side while he thought.

"He's Portuguese," Ayesha added.

The bartender finished drying the glass and put it down on the bar.

"We haven't had anyone from Portugal as a member of the club since the da Gama family moved to Bombay. And that was many years ago. Though I've got a feeling a man from Portugal was here not long ago. He was asking about membership."

"What did he look like?" Ayesha asked.

The bartender thought about it.

"I don't really remember," he said. "Thinning hair, if I remember rightly. Quite slovenly dressed. I took him for a spice merchant. It was the smell, I expect."

Ayesha looked at me and I shrugged. That description did not tell us very much.

"Do you remember what the man was called?" Ayesha asked.

"I'm afraid I don't."

Ayesha thanked the bartender for his help, and we went out into the midday heat. The rickshaw driver was waiting where we had left him. Ayesha thought for a while and then gave him a new address to drive us to.

The next stop was in the direction of the harbor. It was a two-story stone building with a skim of white roughcast. Its windows were shaded by small tiled roofs.

"This is where the Cochin Chamber of Commerce has its office," Ayesha told me. "I'm not sure they'll let you in, but we can always try."

We went up to the first floor and entered a narrow room with a long counter all along one side. Fixed to the wall behind the counter were rows of filing cabinets. A man emerged through a doorway when Ayesha rang the bell on the counter. He looked very English with his reddish hair, linen suit and bow tie. His forehead was covered in freckles, and he was sweating profusely. His first words were "No pets allowed in here! You'll have to leave your gorilla outside. If you please!"

There was no need for Ayesha to make a sign. I turned round at once and went back to the street.

Ayesha came out less than ten minutes later and joined me in the shade of an overhanging roof.

"According to the clerk at the Chamber of Commerce,"

she said, "there is only one Portuguese firm in Cochin. It's a trading company called Albuquerque Trading on Napier Street. Have you heard of them?"

I shook my head.

"I think we should visit them anyway," Ayesha said. "If Alphonse Morro is in the city, the people there should know him. Fellow countrymen tend to stick together."

That sounded right, so we set off. Napier Street turned out to be quite close to the Cochin Club, on the other side of the wide parade ground. We stopped outside number fourteen, a white building with a roof of sunbaked tiles like all the others in Fort Cochin. There was an enamel plate on the gate at the front of the building:

ALBUQUERQUE TRADING CO.
LISBON—GOA—COCHIN

A gravel path led through a small and rather ill-kept garden in which weeds were threading across the ground. The door was open, and we stepped into a cool office furnished with two desks and several tall metal filing cabinets. A yellowing print of Comércio Square in Lisbon hung on the wall.

There was a man sleeping at one of the desks. The fans rotating on the ceiling were making his sparse hair flutter.

The man was an Indian, and assuming the nameplate

on his desk was correct his surname was Gavuyor. He suddenly opened his eyes and, still half-asleep, put on a pair of spectacles and stared at me in confusion. Perhaps he thought he was still dreaming.

"What can I do for you?" he asked, taking a step back. "Who are you?"

Ayesha introduced herself.

"And the gorilla? It looks dangerous. Why do you have a gorilla with you?" Mr. Gavuyor asked uneasily.

Ayesha gave me a quick look of apology. Then she said, "Don't worry about her. She is the diwan's pet, and I brought her with me because she likes riding in rickshaws."

Mr. Gavuyor continued to stare at me for a time, then his eyes moved to Ayesha.

"I see," he said. "And what do you want?"

Ayesha explained.

"Alphonse Morro?" Mr. Gavuyor said when she had finished. "I've never heard the name before. Who's he?"

"He's Portuguese," Ayesha said. "From Lisbon. I know he was in Cochin about a year and a half ago."

Mr. Gavuyor shook his head.

"He must have been traveling through. He certainly doesn't live here now, anyway. There is only one Portuguese resident in Cochin—my boss, Senhor Duarte."

"Can we meet him? Is he here just now?" Ayesha asked.

"No," Mr. Gavuyor answered.

"Where can I find him?" Ayesha asked patiently.

"At our warehouse. Godown Fifty-Eight B on Bazaar Road."

That was all Mr. Gavuyor had to tell us. He began rearranging the papers on his desk to demonstrate he had no more time for us.

Once we were back out on the street, Ayesha gave an order to the rickshaw man; we climbed in and he took us back the way we had come.

"Bazaar Road is in the part of the city called Mattancherry," Ayesha explained. "The simplest way to get there will be by boat."

The boatman and the tender were still waiting for us where we had left them. After casting off we followed the Cochin Peninsula south. The excitement I'd felt a little while earlier had gone and been replaced by a different sort of excitement—more fear than anticipation now. If Mr. Gavuyor was right we should very soon find out whether Alphonse Morro was in Cochin.

And Ayesha understood that too.

"There used to be masses of Portuguese people in Cochin," she told me. "In fact, they were the ones who founded the city many centuries ago. But now the only time you hear Portuguese spoken is among the seamen in the harbor. Senhor Duarte may very well be the only person from Portugal who is still a resident. If that is so, there are only two alternatives as far as Morro is concerned. He has either adopted the name Duarte and become boss of the Albuquerque Trading Company, or he is no longer in Cochin."

I nodded. It was as simple as that.

CHAPTER 57
Mattancherry

Mattancherry was quite different from the British part of the city. From the water, anyway. In Fort Cochin the shoreline had been clean, tidy and empty. Here it was muddy and dirty and there were people everywhere. Fishermen had hung their enormous scoop nets on drying frames close to the harbor mouth. Then came warehouses with wharves built out over the water on piles. Potbellied merchants jostled with bearers passing sacks and barrels from one man to the next. There were loud and argumentative auctions on every wharf. The quarreling and the haggling could be heard far out over the water, where fully laden rowing boats and sailing barges were busily passing to and from the cargo vessels out in the roadstead. The oarsmen sang in time with the rhythm of their oars, and the usual stench of a tropical port was blended with the smell of pepper, vanilla, cardamom and coffee beans.

We drew in alongside one of the rickety wharves and walked between two storehouses. A narrow lane took us through to Bazaar Road, and we soon found Godown 58B. It was a three-story building with thick stone walls and small window apertures covered with grills. It looked as if it had been there for many centuries. Inside it was dark and oppressively stuffy. Coconut-fiber sacks were stacked from floor to ceiling, and the pepper dust irritated our noses.

Two Indians seated on high stools were making entries in enormous ledgers. When Ayesha asked for Senhor Duarte one of the men pointed upstairs.

We climbed a narrow staircase. On the second floor we found a booth with glass walls and a fan on the roof, and in the booth there was a man bent over a desk.

Ayesha gave me a questioning look. I suddenly felt completely empty. All my courage and strength deserted me.

The man at the desk was big and bald. His drooping, morose face glistened with sweat in the light of the desk lamp. He did not look in the least like Alphonse Morro.

～

Ayesha introduced herself and explained our business yet again. Senhor Duarte did not recognize the name Morro either, and he was quite certain that he was the only Portuguese national living in Cochin. Just as Mr. Gavuyor had told us.

"How long have you been stationed here?" Ayesha asked.

"Three months," Senhor Duarte answered. "I was sent here from the company's main office in Goa. The man who was boss here before me caught malaria and had to be replaced. What was his name . . . ? Ah yes, Simão, Alfredo Simão. A dreary fellow. From Lisbon, I think. Vanished as soon as I arrived. I hardly had time to do more than say hello."

"Where did he go?"

"No idea. May have taken the boat to Goa. Or Singapore. Or Australia, for all I know. Or maybe he just lay down under a coconut palm and died. I don't really care. But he certainly isn't still in Cochin."

～

That was all Senhor Duarte had to say. In the tender on the way back to the HMS *Rana,* Ayesha sat in silence. She was thinking. I assumed she was disappointed that we hadn't found Alphonse Morro, but she could not have been more disappointed than I was.

My journey to India had been in vain. All I'd learned was that Morro could be anywhere in the world—apart from Cochin. Before I went aboard the HMS *Rana,* Ayesha put her hand on my shoulder and said, "I'm really upset that I haven't been able to help more. I wish you all good fortune for the future."

I bowed to her with my hands together in front of me, just as I'd seen her do.

~

After two more days the maharaja was tired of Cochin with all its receptions and garden parties. He was suffering from heartburn and a touch of gout. It was time to go home.

Late on the last evening before our departure, Ana and I were standing by the rail looking at the lights on all the vessels riding at anchor in the roadstead. The Chief and I had often done the same on the *Hudson Queen.* Gazing out over a foreign harbor at night was a pleasure the Chief was unlikely to have ever again.

Ana tried to console me after she heard that Ayesha's and my searches had led to nothing, but consoling me was not easy. My whole being ached with disappointment and I could scarcely drag myself out of my bunk in the mornings.

Then we saw the navigation lights of a small boat approaching from the eastern shore of the inlet. Ernakulam, the city where Diwan Al-Faroud had his palace, lay over there. I did not recognize the boat until it was very close.

It was Ayesha's tender.

I met Ayesha by the rope ladder down the side of the *Runa*. She was looking tired but eager, and she waved to me to come down.

"What's happened?" Ana asked.

"Permit me to explain later, Miss Molina," Ayesha said. "I would like to take Sally Jones ashore with me. It may be very important and we only have a few hours before your ship sails."

I jumped down into Ayesha's boat, and her boatman drew away. As we steered out across the dark waters Ayesha explained why she had come to fetch me.

"When we parted," she said, "I felt I had let you and Miss Molina down. And I couldn't stop thinking about Alfredo Simão, the man Senhor Duarte mentioned. Yesterday morning I went to the customs office in Fort Cochin and found out that no one by the name of Simão has left Cochin during the past four months. Nor were there any records of him having died here. That meant that Alfredo Simão must have left Cochin illegally. *Or that he is still here.* But where is he hiding? I asked myself."

The lights of Mattancherry were coming closer as Ayesha went on with her report.

"I spent the rest of the day going round Mattancherry and Fort Cochin asking after Alfredo Simão. No one had heard of him. Just as I was about to give up I remembered that Alfredo Simão had been suffering from malaria. So he must have needed medical treatment. I drew up a list of all the doctors in Cochin and began visiting them one by one. After only five visits I encountered a doctor who knew the man I was looking for. Knew him very well, in fact, having treated him for malaria for over a year. And listen to this! He told me that Simão is still in Cochin. He has a rented room in the Jewish quarter of Mattancherry, and the doctor gave me the address. It's very near the synagogue, and we are on our way there now!"

I took Ayesha's hand and squeezed it hard. She smiled, but it was a cautious smile, as if to say that I shouldn't start celebrating too soon.

CHAPTER 58
Night in Jew Town

The quays and wharves in Mattancherry were lit by lanterns and by the fires fishermen had made along the shore. People were hustling and bustling about in the lanes that cut between the dark warehouses, and there were the sounds of laughter, mournful singing and loud foreign voices.

At this time of day it was almost impossible to push

416

through the crowds on Bazaar Road. Ayesha gave me brief descriptions of the different stalls and small shops we passed. There were Muslim silversmiths, jewelers from Calcutta and Brahman opium dealers. Money changers exchanged rupees for British sovereigns and dealt in gold and smuggled emeralds in the back rooms of shops. Bonfires of rubbish were burning on the street corners, and cows and goats were wandering freely through the streets.

Jew Town, the Jewish quarter, started where Bazaar Road ended. It was noticeable how quiet and calm things were there. Ayesha led me into a narrow, dark cul-de-sac at the end of which stood a synagogue. Standing in the darkness outside the closed entrance was a man wearing a skullcap and a robe long enough to reach the ground. He had a curly, shining black beard.

Ayesha and the man in the skullcap exchanged a silent greeting. Then the man guided us through narrow passages between rough walls, across courtyards and finally through an arched gateway and up a staircase. A woman with an oil lamp was waiting there. She opened a door and showed us into a small room, furnished with a narrow bed and a small rickety desk with two drawers. A pale crescent moon in a hazy night sky was visible through the only window.

"This is where Alfredo Simão lived until two weeks ago," the man in the skullcap said. "He's gone now."

I felt a stab of disappointment.

"Alfredo was very ill toward the end," the woman with the oil lamp said. "I think he had begun to prepare himself for death. There were some days when he felt a little better and on those days we used to help him walk down to the waterside. He liked to look out across the sea."

She wiped a tear from the corner of her eye with the sleeve of her blouse. The man in the skullcap spoke: "It was on one of our walks that he saw a notice that someone had pinned up. It had an effect on him. A strange effect. He no longer seemed to be at peace with himself, and he suddenly decided to go—he left us in the middle of the night. He simply said that he had to go home. I know he had a little money put aside, and presumably he bought a passage on one of the ships in the harbor. I hope to God he gets home alive."

The woman went to the desk and opened one of the warped drawers, from which she took a crumpled piece of paper. She passed it to Ayesha, who looked rather confused.

"It's the notice Alfredo saw at the harbor," the woman said. "It was nailed up on one of the beams on the wharf. I don't know what it means, but Alfredo must have understood it. After all, it was the reason he departed."

Ayesha passed the paper to me.

I didn't need to read it. I had known the few extra lines by heart for a long time:

> *My heart is yours.*
> *My life is yours.*
> *28 Rua de São Tomé, Lisbon*

CHAPTER 59
Disappointments

A new day was dawning. A thick silvery mist hung over the hills inland, and occasional light flurries of wind ruffled the smooth surface of Vembanad Lake. Everything was very still as we left Mattancherry in Ayesha's boat. I was shaking all over. The tension refused to ease its hold on me, and the scene we had just witnessed kept running through my mind. I felt the first shoots of joy growing in my heart.

A pillar of gray smoke was rising from the funnel of the

HMS *Rana*. As we came nearer I could see Ana standing at the stern rail, her eyes searching for us. Ayesha's boatman brought his tender alongside, and Ayesha and I climbed aboard. Ana seemed relieved to see us. I think she had been afraid I would be left behind.

"Where have you been?" she asked, giving me a pat. "I thought I was going to have to ask the captain to delay our departure. What have you been up to?"

First of all Ayesha explained why she had taken me ashore. She went on to report what we had found out in Jew Town. When she had finished I produced the paper that had been in Alfredo Simão's drawer and showed it to Ana. Her hand went to her mouth, and her eyes widened in astonishment. For a few seconds she was dumbstruck.

"But surely that must mean that Alfredo Simão and Alphonse Morro are the same person? It must, mustn't it?" she said quietly. "You found him!"

At that moment we heard the dull, spluttering noise of the steam winch on the foredeck of the *Rana*. The anchor was being raised.

Ayesha knew she had very little time, and she quickly told Ana what the man and woman in Jew Town had told us about Alfredo Simão's departure from Cochin.

"Home?" Ana asked. "Did he really say he was going home?"

Both Ayesha and I nodded.

"He's on his way to Lisbon!" Ana exclaimed.

She put her arms round me and squeezed me tight, and I put my arms round her.

One of the mates came and said that Ayesha would have to leave the ship now—the anchor was up and it was time for us to depart. Ayesha quickly took my hand, and Ana's too, then she climbed down into the tender that was waiting for her.

"I'll check which ships sailed from Cochin Harbor the night Alfredo Simão set out!" were the last words we heard Ayesha shout to us before her boatman pushed off from the side of the *Rana*. "I'll telegraph you a list as soon as I can. Safe journey!"

Ana and I stood at the rail waving to her until her boat had disappeared out of sight behind us. A short while later the HMS *Rana* was steaming out into the Indian Ocean on a northerly course.

~

Ayesha's telegram arrived before noon that same day. It was very brief and contained the names of three vessels. Two of them were sailing from Cochin to Piraeus in Greece, and the third was making for Naples in Italy.

Three ships, all sailing for Europe.

Alphonse Morro could be aboard any of them. It was easy to travel on to Lisbon from Piraeus or from Naples.

Ana sent a telegram back to Ayesha, thanking her sincerely for all the help she had given the two of us.

Once that was done she wanted to tell the maharaja the good news immediately. He would need to know that she and I had to return to Lisbon as quickly as possible— the best way would be to take a liner direct from Bombay.

But there was no sign of the maharaja all day, and just before dinner Ana received a large parcel in her cabin. It was from the maharaja, wrapped in gold paper and tied with embroidered silk ribbon. Inside there was a dress that Ana could never even have dreamed of, and with the dress was a short, beautifully printed message:

Dear and Wonderful Ana,

Join me for a simple supper on the afterdeck. Let us meet just as the orb of the sun is hiding its face behind the infinite line of the horizon.

Your own Maharaja

Ana, of course, knew perfectly well what she could expect when she put on the fantastic dress and joined the maharaja for supper. It can't have been pleasant. Some hours later I received a message delivered by a servant that Ana wished to meet me in her cabin. The supper was obviously over.

Ana was sitting on the edge of the bed and had changed back into a simple, ordinary dress.

"He asked me to marry him," she said in an unhappy voice. "I felt such a wretch when I said no. He was so sad, poor fellow. It was awful."

The maharaja had taken Ana's refusal like a gentleman and tried to hide his disappointment as well as he could. That just made her even more conscience-stricken. I kept her company until she decided to try to sleep.

No sooner had I left Ana than a servant came with a new summons, this time from the maharaja, who wanted to see me. I went to his cabin expecting the worst.

But it was worse than I could have imagined. The maharaja's eyes were red from weeping, and he was sitting slumped on the floor holding a half-empty bottle of champagne.

"She doesn't love me," he sniffed. "My life is over.... I have nothing to live for! I have to talk to someone or I shall throw myself into the sea!"

For two hours I sat listening to the maharaja's inconsolable weeping. Every so often he would indicate that I should fetch another bottle of Dom Pérignon from an enormous ice bucket on the bedside table.

At long last his tears did dry up. Then, with a last sniff, the maharaja told me to fetch a leather-bound folder that lay on the desk in his adjacent study.

"I received this by courier from England when we were in Cochin," he said, opening the folder. "It is the latest de Havilland model. What do you think?"

The folder contained the photographs, plans and technical specifications of an airplane. We studied the drawings until dawn. When I left the maharaja he had just fallen asleep in an armchair with the folder open on his knee. His lips formed a gentle smile. He had already decided to telegraph in his order for the new airplane the following day.

∽

The maharaja slept far into the afternoon, which meant Ana had an opportunity to spend time with me. Since the time for farewells was fast approaching, she wanted help to write a little thank-you speech to the maharaja. It was a fine speech, but when Ana read it out I was seized by an uneasy feeling. I had a premonition that things might not work out in the way Ana and I had thought.

The sun had just gone down when Ana received a message from the maharaja. Dinner was about to be served. I returned to my cabin while she hurried to change into an elegant dress and do her hair.

I walked uneasily back and forth in my cabin during the next few hours. I couldn't get the premonition out of my mind. Something bad was about to happen; I felt that in my bones.

There was a knock on my door just before midnight. It was one of the servants. He said I should go to the afterdeck at once—that was the maharaja's order.

When I arrived Ana and the maharaja were sitting opposite one another at an elegantly laid dining table. There was a crystal chandelier above them, in which there were real candles enclosed in small glass lanterns. They looked as if they were having an enjoyable time, but the look that Ana gave me told a different story altogether.

∼

Later I heard from Ana what had happened during the dinner, before the maharaja sent for me.

At first, she told me, the mood had been rather tense. The maharaja looked pale and was exaggeratedly polite to her. He was, understandably, feeling self-conscious after the rejection of his marriage proposal the night before. He got over it, though, the moment he started talking about the airplane he had ordered. He became his usual self again and entertained Ana by describing in detail the technical sophistication of all aspects of the new de Havilland model.

Over dessert Ana had cleared her throat and tapped her glass for attention. It was time for her little speech, which went something like this: "The kindness and generosity of Your Highness has been beyond description. I shall never forget my time with you in India, but my journey is coming to its end. When we reach Bombay I shall bid you farewell and return to Lisbon. I hope Your Highness will visit Lisbon one day, so that I have an opportunity to repay some of your hospitality."

The maharaja seemed truly pleased by the speech. He raised his glass and they drank a toast.

Then Ana had gone on to say, "And if Your Highness does not object, I shall be taking Sally Jones with me."

At first he did not seem to understand what she meant.

"You want to take Sally Jones with you?" he asked, in some surprise. "To Lisbon? But, my dear, that's just not possible. She is an aide-de-camp. And my airplane mechanic. I'm afraid I simply cannot do without her."

This was followed by a tense and awkward silence while Ana tried to think what to say.

"Your Highness," she said eventually, "Sally Jones has

friends in Lisbon, one of whom has been unjustly sentenced and imprisoned. He needs her help—"

"I need her too," the maharaja interrupted brusquely. "We've just ordered a new airplane! Of course Sally Jones will want to stay here and fly it with me. I'm certain of that."

Ana had not known how to respond, but the maharaja had then suggested they ask me what I wanted. That was when he sent a servant to fetch me.

~

So I had joined them, and from the look on Ana's face I could tell that something had gone terribly wrong.

"Ana tells me that she wants to take you to Lisbon," the maharaja said, smiling at me. "Unfortunately I've had to explain why that's not possible and why you would much rather stay with me in Bhapur. We have many things to prepare before the arrival of the new airplane! We shall have a wonderful time, don't you think?"

We looked at one another. Suddenly the maharaja's face looked worried, though he continued smiling.

"We will, won't we?"

When I failed to nod, his smile faded and disappeared.

"Would you rather go to Lisbon with Ana? Really?"

Now I nodded.

The maharaja tried to arrange his features and look

unconcerned, but his eyes were unable to conceal how hurt he was. It was painful to see.

"I'm afraid," he said in a forced voice and turning to Ana, "I own the gorilla and I have no desire to give it to you. You must travel alone, Miss Molina."

Then he stood up and left the table.

CHAPTER 60
Playing for High Stakes

That same evening I was ordered to leave my cabin and hand back my aide-de-camp's uniform. For the rest of the voyage I shared quarters with the other servants right in the bows of the ship. This was on the maharaja's orders. I was no longer an aide-de-camp, just an ordinary servant, and as such I was immediately put to work. I cleaned, polished brass, washed sheets and scrubbed toilets from early morning to late night. It didn't worry me—I had missed having anything to do ever since we came aboard.

What did concern me, though, was that Ana and I were no longer permitted to meet. The maharaja had expressly forbidden it. I caught a glimpse of Ana every so often. The maharaja no longer kept her company, and she sat alone, even for meals, under a sunshade on the afterdeck. He, from what I heard, did not even leave his cabin.

~

The return voyage from Cochin was faster than our outward journey. We made one brief stop to take on fresh water, but that was all.

My mind was made up. Once we were approaching Bombay I intended to desert the HMS *Rana*. I knew Ana wouldn't leave India without me: she would stay in Bombay and wait until we could meet and travel back to Lisbon together.

But how was I to jump ship? I can't swim, which means that the only possible course was to steal a lifeboat, which could only be done at night when the ship was at anchor.

The HMS *Rana* had two lifeboats. They were located amidships, one on each side of the bridge. It would be completely impossible to launch one of them without being

431

detected. But as luck would have it, there was a third life-boat at the stern, on the upper deck known as the sundeck. I would need to discover whether it was possible to use that boat.

One night, after the servants with whom I was sharing a cabin had fallen asleep, I crept up to the sundeck. The sky was bright and starry, and there was a warm night breeze. The foam of our wash shone white in the gleaming light of the moon. I hurried over to the lifeboat and examined the davits from which it hung. The construction was simple, and it should be possible to launch the boat single-handed.

That was all I needed to know. Just as I was turning to slip back quietly belowdecks, I saw a figure emerge on the sundeck from the other side. It was the maharaja—it was impossible to mistake his outline. As quick as a flash I crouched down and crept into the darkness under the life-boat. The maharaja walked out to the middle of the sundeck and stood there, hands behind his back, gazing at the moon. He hadn't noticed me.

He began strolling back and forth, every now and again sitting down for a while on a deck chair with his head in his hands. Then he would stand up and start walking again. Round and round, muttering to himself the whole time. He sounded both angry and sad, though mainly sad.

After an hour of this both my legs had gone to sleep and my back was aching from sitting bent double under the lifeboat. I was praying the maharaja would go back to bed, but he just carried on walking round and round, and round and round again.

Another hour passed and a weak glimmer of light was beginning to show on the eastern horizon. The new day was chasing away the shadows of night, and I wouldn't be able to stay hidden much longer.

The maharaja came to a sudden stop, his gaze fixed in my direction. I kept utterly still, hardly daring to breathe. For several very long moments I was sure I had been dis-covered, but he turned and looked out over the sea with his back to me.

I took the chance to crawl out of my hiding place and, on stiff legs, tiptoe over to the ladder that went from the sundeck. Then, without looking back, I ran all the way back to the servants' quarters. Quiet snuffles and snores could be heard from all the bunks except mine, so no one had noticed I had gone. I crept under the covers without mak-ing a sound and lay there with a racing heart waiting for the door of the cabin to be hurled open at any moment. But nothing happened. In spite of everything, the maharaja must not have seen me.

~

I now had an escape plan and I knew it could work, though it depended on us anchoring for the night at some point during the voyage. Launching a lifeboat from a moving vessel is both difficult and dangerous, and to do so alone would be impossible.

The closer we came to Bombay, the more nervous I became. What if we didn't stop until we got there? If that happened I would not have a chance to escape, and I did not have a plan B.

On the last night of the voyage, however, the HMS *Ranu* unexpectedly dropped anchor in a beautiful bay with beaches of white sand on which fishermen were cleaning their nets beneath swaying palm trees. I heard we were to remain there until the morning, though no one seemed to know why.

This was my chance.

On the orders of the cook I spent that evening chopping onions in the galley. I waited eagerly for the black tropical night to fall over the bay. Just before ten o'clock the cook told me I could stop work for the night, and shortly after that I was lying in my bunk listening to the steady breathing and gentle snores of the sleeping servants. When I heard two bells ring I knew it was two hours after midnight. Time for me to move. I pushed my blanket aside and put my feet on the floor.

Hazy clouds hid the moon as I crept up to the sundeck. Everything was pitch-black, which was good. The tension made my heart race and my hands shake as I started loosening the ropes that held the lifeboat in place.

I stopped. A sudden feeling of being watched made me turn round, and I saw someone sitting in one of the deck-chairs. The face was in shadow, but I knew at once who it was.

"Come over here and sit down," I heard the maharaja's voice say in the darkness.

I was caught—and I felt more than a little stupid. But strangely enough I didn't feel afraid. I walked over toward him, plodding and defeated, and sat in the deck chair beside his.

"I suppose you thought I didn't see you earlier this evening," the maharaja said, sounding pleased with himself. "But I did. And I knew at once what you had in mind. You are intending to steal my lifeboat, aren't you?"

There was no point in shaking my head and pretending to be innocent. It would just make the situation worse. So I nodded.

The maharaja said nothing for a while. Then he said, "This is the second time you have underestimated my intelligence and my powers of observation. Do you remember the first time?"

He gave me a moment to think before he continued.

"The first time you underestimated me was when I arranged a chess competition between you and my ministers. You surely remember that, don't you? You let my ministers win, and you thought I wouldn't notice. But I did, didn't I?"

I nodded again. I hadn't forgotten that unpleasant occasion. I remember in particular how incomprehensible the maharaja found it that I would rather lose at chess than ruin the lives of his ministers.

The maharaja stretched forward to reach a table that stood by his deck chair. There was a small oil lamp on the table, and he struck a match and lit the wick. A warm, flickering light illuminated the deck round us.

There were two more things on the table: an hourglass and a prettily carved box with gold inlays that glittered in the light of the lamp. I knew what sort of box it was even before he opened it.

It was a folding chess set.

Without a word the maharaja opened out the chessboard and placed the pieces. Then he said, "This time I am going to make absolutely certain that you play as well as you can, Sally Jones. If you lose this game, I shall take you back to Bhapur, and Ana will have to return to Europe alone. But if you win . . ."

The maharaja broke off and took a long, narrow envelope from his pocket and placed it on the table.

"If you win, you may have this envelope. It contains two tickets for the liner *Kaisar-i-Hind,* which departs from Bombay for Lisbon tomorrow. One ticket is for Ana; the other is for you."

I didn't know what to feel or think. Did the maharaja really mean what he said?

As if in answer to my unspoken question he nodded earnestly.

"This is not a trick. If you win I have no intention of forcing you to stay with me. You may go with Ana. You have my word of honor as a maharaja. Right, now choose—do you want to play with the white pieces or the black?"

The maharaja sounded sincere, but I still found it hard to believe him. But what did I have to lose? I reached out and moved one of the white pawns two squares forward.

CHAPTER 61
An Exchange of Turbans

The maharaja proved to be a very good chess player. I recognized at once that it had not been empty boasting when he told me he had received private lessons from a world champion. Using tactical moves I had never seen before he quickly gained an advantage. Every time it was my turn to move, I was forced to think hard until the very last grains of sand were running through the hourglass.

Halfway through the match I thought I was about to

turn the game my way, but the maharaja anticipated my moves and I suddenly found I had lost both my queen and my two bishops. Then, with an elegant encirclement, he rendered my only remaining knight harmless.

I could see that the maharaja could checkmate me in four moves. And he saw it too. The game was over. The maharaja gave a confident grin.

But something unexpected happened. Instead of checking my king, the maharaja took one of my pawns with his queen. It was a very bad move. No less than catastrophic, in fact. All of a sudden I was the one with an advantage, and in two moves I took his queen and a rook. Five moves later I checkmated him. I had won.

I waited for the outburst of rage but, instead, he handed me the envelope with a smile and said calmly: "Congratulations! Well played!"

In some confusion I looked at him, but his smile just grew broader. I took the envelope and opened it carefully, and there were two tickets to Lisbon on the *Kaisar-i-Hind*!

I looked up and met the maharaja's eyes. They were filled with pride and happiness.

And all of a sudden I understood.

The maharaja had let me win. He had lost the game on purpose.

Without stopping to think I held out my hand. That, of

course, was a completely inappropriate thing for a servant to do. But without a moment's hesitation the maharaja took my hand in both of his and shook it long and hard. His round, laughing face shone brighter than the moon.

~

For a long time we sat there watching the stars in silent togetherness. When the anchor watch rang four bells, the maharaja stood up and said, "This fresh sea air gives one a healthy appetite. A little night refreshment would go down well, don't you think? I wonder if Ana is hungry too? Would you mind going to ask her? Meanwhile I shall order up something for us."

Ana was surprised and relieved when I knocked on her cabin door and showed her the envelope with the tickets.

"You can't imagine how angry I was with him," she said. "I was seriously considering going to the police in Bombay and reporting him for kidnapping. Not that it would have been of much use, I suppose."

Once Ana had dressed we went down to the afterdeck, where the maharaja was choosing the wines that would go best with the fifty or so delicacies that were already on the table. He had obviously realized that Ana was angry with him, because he seemed a little nervous. The first thing he said when we sat down was "I know I have behaved badly.

Please forgive me if you can, Miss Molina. I should die of sorrow if you were to think badly of me when you are at home in Lisbon. You won't, I hope? You wouldn't want the life of a poor maharaja on your conscience, would you?"

"No, Your Highness," Ana said calmly but still quite sharply. "I would not. You are forgiven. But I should like an explanation of your strange behavior over the past few days."

The maharaja looked at her in astonishment. He was not used to being spoken to like that. For a moment I thought he might get angry, but then his shoulders bowed and he gave a deep sigh.

"Yes, of course," he said slowly. "I owe you that, I suppose. You will understand, Miss Molina, that I am a maharaja. That is, I am used to getting my own way. So if I wanted ... Let me put it like this. ... I believed that Sally Jones would want ... What I mean is, I thought Sally Jones should stay in India and ..."

The maharaja fell silent, searching for the words. He seemed unable to find them, and he squirmed uncomfortably. It was very unusual to see him like this.

"I think I understand what Your Highness means," Ana said in a friendlier voice. "What made you change your mind?"

The maharaja gave me a quick look before he answered.

"I discovered that Sally Jones was planning to escape. And that made me . . . well, it made angry at first, of course. But then I thought what a shame it would be and how happy it would make you if I let you go back to Lisbon together."

The maharaja stopped and he looked rather puzzled, as if he was finding it difficult to understand what he had just said.

"So Your Highness decided to allow mercy to take precedence over legal rights," Ana said to help him out of his difficulty.

The maharaja's face lit up.

"Precisely," he said. "I let mercy take precedence over legal rights! That is exactly what I did. And now we've talked enough about that, don't you think? Cheers!"

We all raised our glasses, and the crystal made a beautiful ringing sound as they touched. The maharaja looked very relieved.

~

Our last night on the HMS *Rana* was long and happy. The maharaja did his very best to be an entertaining host and told us all about his triumphs as a sportsman and a tiger hunter.

Between dessert and coffee he wanted to show us his skill as a cricketer. He disappeared briefly and returned fully equipped with pads, helmet and bat and wearing the official colors of the Bhapur team. He was followed by a servant carrying a silver bucket full of cricket balls. Ana and I took turns throwing the hard leather balls, which the maharaja then struck with his bat. One by one, the balls flew out into the darkness and we heard the splash as they landed far out in the water.

Before we said good night and went to bed, Ana sang a melancholy fado about departures and farewells. Large tears rolled down the maharaja's cheeks.

~

The following morning the HMS *Rana* weighed anchor and we left the sheltered bay. It was a passage of no more than three hours to Bombay, and immediately after lunch we were dropping anchor again. Ana's baggage was transferred to the *Rana*'s steam launch, and then she and I were taken to the King Albert Dock, where the P&O flagship, the RMS *Kaisar-i-Hind*, was ready to sail for Europe. The maharaja came with us to see us off.

He gave Ana a pearl necklace as a parting gift. At first she did not want to accept it. She said that she had already received so many wonderful presents from the maharaja that she was almost ashamed. But he turned a deaf ear to her protests.

"Every minute of your visit has been worth more than ten pearl necklaces to me," the maharaja said with a slight bow. "I am in your debt, Miss Molina, not the reverse!"

Ana kissed his cheek and promised to think of him every time she wore the necklace.

Then the maharaja turned to me.

"There is no present for you," he said earnestly. "But I want to ask something of you, which is that you will never forget me. Which is why I want us to exchange turbans. Will you do me that honor?"

The question was unexpected, but I nodded in agreement and we removed our turbans. I had never seen the maharaja bareheaded before. His long hair was pulled up into a shining black knot, which was held in place by a broad wooden comb. He passed me his turban and I gave him mine. Then the ship's steam whistle told us it was time for Ana and me to go aboard.

When the *Kaisar-i-Hind* began to move, Ana and I were at the rail waving to the maharaja. Standing there on the quayside with my turban on his head, he waved back.

~

I had never traveled first class on an ocean liner before. Everything was elegant and luxurious, but I didn't let it impress me too much—not after cruising on the HMS *Rana*!

As we might have expected, the maharaja had booked the most expensive cabins on the ship for Ana and me, which meant that we dined at the captain's table. The captain was a Scot by the name of MacAllister, and he had heard of me before. I am, in fact, quite well known among seafaring people.

One of the other guests at the captain's table was a wealthy Indian businessman from Calcutta. On our first evening on board he noticed my very beautiful turban with all its many small glittering jewels. Ana told him how I had received this turban from the maharaja. The Indian businessman looked at me, his eyes wide with admiration, and said, "You may perhaps not know, but exchanging turbans is very important in India. Traditionally you only exchange turbans with your very best friend."

PART THREE

CHAPTER 62
Reunions

The voyage from Bombay to Lisbon took three weeks. At dawn on the eighteenth of February the RMS *Kaisar-i-Hind* steamed into the mouth of the Tagus, and Ana and I stood on deck watching a pale sun rising behind the seven hills of Lisbon.

In many ways it felt like returning home. But there was something else too. I'd worried about this moment a great deal during the voyage because I knew I had powerful and dangerous enemies in Lisbon. With luck they believed me dead, but that could not be relied upon. What if Chief Inspector Garretta had learned that Captain Anderson had tricked him? What if he knew I was on board the *Kaisar-i-Hind*? If that was the case he would be waiting for me at the landing stage and would catch me the moment I stepped off the ship.

While two harbor tugs were helping the great liner to draw alongside the Cais do Sodré, I was nervously scanning the small crowd on the quay for Garretta. Neither he nor any other policemen were visible.

But I did see Signor Fidardo!

He was standing there straight-backed, holding a bouquet of red lilies in front of him, his suit dazzling white in the gray dawn light. He looked very small as he watched the ship, his eyes eagerly searching for Ana and me.

I had a warm feeling in my heart. In a flash I forgot about Garretta and all my worries, and I began jumping and waving for all I was worth.

～

A couple of hours later we were all sitting round the kitchen table in Signor Fidardo's small apartment on the second floor of the house on Rua de São Tomé. He was treating us to sandwiches, cakes and a big welcome-home tart from the Graça bakery.

Signor Fidardo was much the same as before. He took our homecoming calmly, but I saw the hint of a tear in the corner of his eye when he looked at Ana and me. And he had grown thinner. His face had acquired new shadows and wrinkles—the sort of wrinkles caused by worry, I thought, with a pang of conscience.

Ana told him about her journey to Bhapur, her reception at the station and her first meeting with the maharaja. She described the palace and the park and then how, as if by a miracle, she had found me.

Signor Fidardo couldn't believe it was pure chance that had brought us together.

"I wonder whether Sally Jones had a finger in the pie when the maharaja invited you to Bhapur," he said to Ana, at the same time looking searchingly at me over the rims of his glasses.

I could neither nod nor shake my head. It was all too complicated to be answered with a simple yes or no. So I winked with one eye and took another piece of cake. Ana laughed and scratched the bristly hair on my head with her hand.

"I think it's time you started writing all this down," Signor Fidardo said. "Sally Jones's memoirs. They would make interesting reading."

I did not take his suggestion seriously, but the thought must somehow have stuck in the back of my mind.

Signor Fidardo brewed several pots of coffee, and Ana made two trips to Graça for more sandwiches. There was so much to talk about. Signor Fidardo wanted to hear all about the maharaja's incomparable parties and about the great concert in the palace park. He also wanted to hear everything Ana knew about my adventures as the maharaja's airplane mechanic. When I showed him the maharaja's turban he studied it carefully and then said, "It's a unique work of art. And the stones are genuine. I do believe the maharaja has made you a very wealthy gorilla."

I shrugged. It was irrelevant to me. I would never part with the maharaja's turban, however much money I was offered.

Ana concluded by describing our voyage to Cochin and our search for Alphonse Morro with the help of Ayesha Narayanan. Signor Fidardo listened attentively, from time to time giving me a serious and worried look. After listening to it all he said, "Let's hope that Morro and Alfredo Simão really are one and the same individual. And that he really is on his way to Lisbon. And that he survives the journey!"

I could tell from his voice that he had his doubts, but it did not change my mind. I knew what I knew: Alphonse Morro would soon be back in Lisbon.

It was dark outside the windows by the time we broke up, and the gas lamps along the street had been lit for several hours. We all helped carry Ana's travel trunk up to her apartment. It smelled stale and stuffy up there, and there was a great pile of letters behind the door. Most of the letters were in identical cream envelopes of the Canson brand. They were from Ana's secret admirer, who still wrote to her every week—and she still had no idea who he was.

There were several bills, and there was also a small gray envelope with Ana's name and address printed on the front in untidy letters. Ana opened that envelope first, since we both knew who it was from.

Dear Mrs. Ana Molina,

I am so happy that I felt I must write to you even though I know it will be quite a long time before you get back from India. I had a letter today from your friend Signor Fidardo and he told me you had sent him a telegram to say you had found Sally Jones.

I wish I had the words to say how happy I am. Thank you, thank you!

Yours respectfully,
Henry

I read the Chief's letter several times that evening while Ana was unpacking. There was barely enough room in her wardrobe for all the beautiful dresses and saris the maharaja had insisted she keep. By the time her trunk was empty, it was high time we went to bed.

Ana fell asleep almost at once, but I lay awake listening to the sounds of the city outside the attic window. Once my eyes were used to the dark, I took out the Chief's letter and read it through several more times. I felt restless, but in a happy way. We had found Morro and he was alive. And he was on his way to Lisbon. Soon we would be able to show the whole world that the Chief wasn't a murderer.

~

As soon as the shops opened the following morning, Ana went out and bought me a new cap and new overalls. She knew I wouldn't want to go round in my Indian clothes. The overalls were a perfect fit once she had taken them in a little here and let them out a little there.

That afternoon we took the train from Rossio Station out to Campolide. Low clouds covered the sky, and there was a cold wind along the wide sandy streets. As we walked toward the prison Ana told me that she had continued to come here and sing to the Chief and other prisoners two Sundays a month even after I had left for India on the *Song of Limerick.* I was pleased to hear it, but I wasn't surprised. After all, I knew Ana.

Nothing had changed. The prison looked just as grim and deserted, and the little hill was still littered with rubbish and overgrown with thistles and dry weeds. But when Ana began to sing it was as though everything that was gray and dirty brown suddenly became bright with color. The ugly became beautiful, the sad and soulless came to life. Pale faces appeared behind the iron grills that covered the small windows of the building. Hands were pushed out through the bars. A hand came out through the bars of the Chief's cell. It waved and I waved back.

The hand was taken in and immediately afterward the sound of the Chief's accordion could be heard. The tones of the instrument played lightly and freely round the melody of Ana's song. It sounded so wonderful I could scarcely believe that it was actually the Chief playing.

The sun broke through and warmed us. Ana sang and the Chief played for almost an hour. I felt that they already knew one another, even though they had never actually met.

CHAPTER 63
Waiting

Now the waiting began.

Waiting for Alphonse Morro.

I spent the first days sitting by the window on the stairs outside Ana's apartment and watching the street below. I had estimated that Morro's journey from Cochin to Lisbon would take him at least a month, but probably not more than two months. It was now six weeks since he left Cochin, so I had to be ready. Morro might come walking round the corner at any time. Or get off a tram and look up at our house.

After I'd been sitting there for three days Signor Fidardo came and gave me a serious talking-to.

"If Alphonse Morro has come all the way from India to meet you and to get his locket back, he'll come to find you. You must come down to the workshop and make yourself useful! You'll be more use down there than staring out of the window until your eyes glaze over!"

Signor Fidardo had fitted blinds on the big windows in the workshop. That was for my sake. If everyone passing along the street could look in and see I was back, it wouldn't be long before word reached Chief Inspector Garretta.

Two accordions had just come in for repairs. One of them was a Scandinavian melodeon and the other a big, chromatic Hohner with loose keys. I settled for the Hohner.

"You need a real job to be getting on with," Signor Fidardo said. "Something that will keep your mind occupied."

It was nice to be back in the workshop. After a couple of days in the old routine, it felt as if the journey to India had been no more than a dream.

~

One day Signor Fidardo went off into the city without saying where he was going. He left straight after breakfast and was out all day. Ana and I were eating supper when he knocked on the door of her apartment. Ana asked him in and served an extra portion of soup.

We could tell at once that Signor Fidardo had something to say to us, but he saved it until we had finished supper and Ana had made coffee. Then he lit a cigarette and told us.

"Last night I was lying awake thinking. About that mysterious fellow in Cochin. Alfredo Simão. And I had an idea."

He picked some shreds of tobacco from his upper lip before continuing.

"Every Portuguese citizen who goes abroad has to have a passport. Passports are issued and registered by the passport office here in Lisbon, and I know a man who works there. He's an office manager, but in his spare time he plays the lute. I made his instrument for him."

Signor Fidardo took a sip of his coffee.

"I spent today visiting my friend and I asked him to check whether a passport had been issued in the name of Alfredo Simão. It obviously wasn't an easy request, because it took half the day before I received an answer."

Signor Fidardo took another sip of his coffee. Then he

looked at me and said, "The answer was no. No one by the name of Alfredo Simão has a Portuguese passport."

We sat in silence for a few moments and then Ana said, "What does that mean?"

"It means," Signor Fidardo said, "that the man in Cochin who called himself Alfredo Simão was an impostor. He must have traveled to India on a false passport. The most likely explanation is that his real name is something different."

"Yes, Alphonse Morro," Ana said. "But we knew that already."

Signor Fidardo gave her a slightly irritable look.

"No, we did not know. We assumed it was so, and now it looks as though our assumption was correct. On the other hand, we still don't know whether Morro was intending to return to Lisbon when he left Cochin. All we can do is hope. But don't forget that there is a considerable risk we shall be disappointed."

He was looking at me when he said that.

Once Ana had gone to sleep that night, I slipped out to the window on the stairs. After hearing Signor Fidardo's exciting news I had found it impossible to sleep. I felt that Alphonse Morro was closer than ever, and I sat there watching the street until dawn.

~

I sat there again the next night. And the one after that. A week passed, followed by another week. I kept watch every night, expecting to see Alphonse Morro standing out there in the darkness looking up at our house.

And one night it happened.

What I had been waiting for.

CHAPTER 64
Familiar Handwriting

The man came walking up Rua de São Tomé. He was walk-ing slowly and keeping close to the walls of the houses. He stopped under a streetlamp twenty yards or so from our house. I felt a shiver of excitement and studied him closely.

He was thin and his hands were pushed down deep in the pockets of his short, dark coat. His face was obscured by the brim of his hat, but I thought I glimpsed a slim mus-tache on his upper lip.

Just the kind of mustache that Alphonse Morro had.

He was the right height too.

And his shoulders sloped, just as Morro's did.

I held my breath and kept absolutely still. The man under the gas lamp also stood quite still, with his eyes fixed firmly on our house.

How long did it last? I don't know. It felt like a second and it felt like an eternity. The street was deserted. But then a night tram came clanking up the hill from the square at Largo das Portas do Sol, and the man quickly retreated into a side alley. For a moment or two I thought he had gone, but once the tram's headlamp had passed the man emerged from the alleyway.

He looked up at our house again, and I had a strong feeling he was trying to gather the courage to cross the street and knock on the door.

What should I do? My first thought was to wake Ana or Signor Fidardo, but that would mean leaving the window, and the man might disappear while I was away.

I was still trying to make up my mind when the man suddenly started walking. He turned up his coat collar and walked past our house, going north along Rua de São Tomé.

Without stopping to think I rushed down the stairs to the outside door. My hands were shaking so much I had trouble opening the lock. When I eventually did manage

462

to open the door, I was about to rush out and run after the man. But I stopped myself, went back into the hall and put on one of Signor Fidardo's dirty painting smocks and a big blue cap he used to wear to keep the dust out of his hair when he was sanding something down.

The man had not gone far. I caught sight of him fifty yards down the steep street, Calçada de Santo André. Instead of running to catch up, I eased back and tried to think clearly.

Should I try to grab the man? Walk straight up to him and show him who I was? I didn't doubt that Morro would recognize me.

I couldn't decide, so I followed him instead. Bent forward slightly, hands in his pockets, his eyes on the ground in front of him, he seemed completely immersed in his own thoughts. He wasn't in a hurry and didn't turn round.

After some time we were down on the Praça da Figueira. The man crossed the square there and walked on westward, over the deserted Praça do Rossio and up the hills to the Bairro Alto quarter. Then he turned off into a small, dark and narrow street by a park I did not know the name of. I had dropped back slightly, and by the time I came round the corner the man was gone.

I stopped, unsure what to do. Had he seen me following him? What if Morro was hiding in one of the dark doorways along the street, waiting for me to walk past? What if he still had the pistol he had threatened the Chief with?

My racing thoughts were brought to a halt by a light going on in a third-floor window right across the street. I walked quickly over to the doorway beneath the window. It was shut and locked, but behind a piece of yellowed glass there were four names—one for each floor. The name one down from the top was written in an elegant hand: *Pêro Botelho.*

I didn't recognize the name, but there was something familiar about the handwriting. I was almost sure I had seen it before.

Was it from the letter that Morro sent along with the money?

I studied the frontage of the building. There was a drainpipe passing close to the lit window. The street was deserted. It was the middle of the night, and if I was careful there was no reason why anyone should see me.

It didn't take more than a few seconds to climb up to the third floor. The curtains on the window were only half-drawn, and through them I could see into a very small room with overfull bookcases and some drawings pinned up on the walls. A desk stood in one corner, and in another was a narrow, neatly made bed. Beside the bed was a small chest of drawers, on which stood a gramophone. The man

464

I had been following was standing by the gramophone. He had just put on a record and to my amazement, even with the volume turned low, I heard the sound of Ana's voice.

He turned round and went over to the desk, where there was a penholder, an inkwell and a typewriter. Alongside the typewriter lay a pile of writing paper and a stack of envelopes, all of the same cream color.

It suddenly came to me where I had seen the handwriting on the name tag down on the door: it wasn't the letters from Morro, it was the letters sent by Ana's secret admirer.

Before the man sat down at the desk I caught a glimpse of his face. It was narrow and pale and had a slim black mustache, but apart from that the man did not look especially like Alphonse Morro.

Quietly and carefully I slid down the drainpipe and began to make my slow way home, disappointment making my legs feel as heavy as lead.

CHAPTER 65
The Telephone

I wondered whether to write Ana a note telling her the name of her mysterious admirer but decided not to. The man called Pêro Botelho obviously wanted to keep his secret, and he had every right to do so. And Ana found it exciting to have an unknown admirer to fantasize about.

So Ana and Signor Fidardo never did learn what I'd been up to that night, though they undoubtedly noticed that something had happened. I was no longer so sure that Morro was going to turn up, and it was now almost three months since he had left Cochin. He may have died of malaria on his journey, or perhaps he had moved from Cochin to hide somewhere else. Somewhere I would never be able to find him.

I tried to convince myself that Morro had simply been delayed along the way. There were any number of possible reasons: maybe he'd had trouble finding a ship from Piraeus or Naples to Lisbon, or maybe he'd chosen to break his journey somewhere to rest.

With every day that passed, I found it more and more difficult to keep my spirits up.

The same thing happens when a ship's boiler springs a leak. The steam hisses out and there is nothing left to power the engines. I no longer had the energy to keep watch at the window at night and instead lay awake on Ana's sofa, staring up at the ceiling and thinking of the Chief in prison. It seemed likely he would be there for another twenty years. If I'd reached Cochin two weeks earlier than I did, Morro would not have escaped me. And the Chief would perhaps have been free. But I'd arrived two weeks too late. Two miserable weeks!

I was so tired in the morning that I scarcely had the energy to get out of bed, and I had great difficulty concentrating in the workshop. Signor Fidardo knew what the matter was and he started giving me new tasks. Until then I had spent most of my time repairing the mechanism of different varieties of accordion, but now Signor Fidardo made me start work on stringed instruments. To do that I had to learn more about working with wood. He allowed me to use all his expensive special tools and patiently showed me the proper techniques.

My first task was to change the neck on a cello. It was both difficult and urgent, in spite of which Signor Fidardo made me do it all myself. I had to work without a break from morning to night for a whole week. And as soon as the cello was finished, I started repairing a lute that had developed a crack in its curved back. Then it was right back to an accordion. By the end of the working day I was too weary to lie awake worrying, and I would fall asleep the moment I had eaten my supper.

I realized Signor Fidardo was doing this on purpose. He pushed me so hard there was very little left for him to do himself. Fabulous Forzini's piano accordion had been finished long ago, and the great star had come to collect it in person while I was in India. I was sorry I never had an opportunity to see the finished instrument. It must have been a real masterpiece.

Signor Fidardo had been well paid for the job, but most of the money had gone to settle old debts. Some money was left over, however, because he bought a telephone—a modern telephone with the mouthpiece and the earpiece joined. Signor Fidardo was very proud indeed of his new telephone.

It was given a place of honor in the workshop, and alongside the telephone table Signor Fidardo placed his very best armchair—one he'd made himself—so he could sit comfortably while he talked.

The only thing missing was someone to talk to. Signor Fidardo's friends and customers rarely rang. They much preferred to come to the workshop and have a chat over a cup of coffee or a glass of something.

But one Wednesday afternoon, quite unusually, Signor Fidardo's telephone did ring. He hurried over to the telephone table and lifted the receiver expectantly. After listening for a few moments, his mouth turned down at the corners.

"I am very sorry, senhora," he said. "You must have been put through to the wrong number. It does happen sometimes, unfortunately. The woman at the telephone exchange must have a bad memory for numbers. . . . What? . . . Well . . . yes, that's right, I do live at Rua de São Tomé twenty-eight. . . . Yes, of course you can. . . . I'll see you then. Goodbye."

Signor Fidardo put down the receiver and looked at me. He seemed confused.

"That was a doctor," he said. "She didn't seem to know who she was talking to, but she still wanted to come here this afternoon. I've no idea what it's about. Strange."

Signor Fidardo was preoccupied and faraway for the rest of the day. I could see that the doctor's visit was upsetting him. Doctors rarely come as bearers of good news, do they?

~

There was a knock on the street door at half past five. Signor Fidardo did not open up until I'd had time to hide in the storeroom off the workshop. We were in the habit of doing that these days, just in case.

I watched through the keyhole in the storeroom door as Signor Fidardo opened up for his visitor. She was a thin, lanky woman with graying hair tied in a bun under her hat. She looked lost and hesitated at the door before coming in.

"My name is Rosa Domingues," she said, shaking Signor Fidardo's hand. "Dr. Rosa Domingues. I was the one who rang you earlier. I'm sorry to bother you, but it's to do with one of my patients. Can you give me a minute of your time?"

"Of course," Signor Fidardo said, pointing to the big table in the middle of the workshop. Once they were seated, the doctor began explaining her visit.

Dr. Rosa Domingues said she worked in the infectious diseases ward of São José Hospital. A very sick man had been brought into her ward the day before. He'd arrived at the hospital in the backseat of a taxi, the driver having found him lying unconscious in a waterfront street down by Cais do Sodré.

"It took me no time at all to make a diagnosis," the doctor said. "I've worked in Angola, and I'm familiar with the symptoms of malaria. In the present case the disease is very far advanced and I think it unlikely that the patient will survive."

Malaria.

The word hit me like an electric shock. I clenched my hands and held my breath.

"Given that he has malaria, the man must have been in the tropics fairly recently," Dr. Domingues said. "Since the taxi driver found him down by the harbor, it may be that he has just arrived here. But I'm guessing. The man has barely said a word since regaining consciousness. He has no identification papers and refuses to give his name. In fact, he's a bit of a mystery."

"Do please go on," Signor Fidardo said, his voice revealing the stress he was feeling.

"The patient had tremors and a temperature of almost one hundred and four when he was admitted. We've managed to bring his temperature down, and this morning he asked for a pen and paper. This is what he wrote."

The doctor took a slip of paper out of her handbag and gave it to Signor Fidardo, who looked at it.

"Rua de São Tomé twenty-eight," he said. "Your patient wrote down the address of this house?"

My heart began beating faster and faster.

Ship from the tropics . . . this address . . .

I knew that Signor Fidardo must be thinking the same thing. He stroked his chin as he stared at the paper.

"Tell me," he said. "Is it possible that this man contracted the disease in India?"

"Indeed it is, quite possible," Dr. Domingues answered. "Why do you ask?"

I couldn't stay hidden any longer. I opened the door of the storeroom and stepped out into the workshop. The doctor's eyebrows shot up.

"This is Sally Jones," Signor Fidardo said. "Unless I'm very much mistaken, this is who your patient wants to meet."

CHAPTER 66
The Patient

We took the tram to Martim Moniz Square. It couldn't have taken more than a quarter of an hour, but it seemed much longer. On the other side of the tram windows, people, cars and shop windows flickered past like a film as we went along the narrow streets of the Mouraria quarter. My flesh tingled with excitement, and I was finding it hard to think straight.

Signor Fidardo and Dr. Domingues were sitting beside me and conversing in low tones.

"Have you been in contact with the police?" Signor Fidardo asked.

"Of course," Dr. Domingues said. "They checked whether there was any ongoing investigation that might involve my patient, but there was nothing. That's all they do in such cases."

By now the sun was low above the buildings, and the people hurrying across Martim Moniz Square cast long shadows on the paving stones. We continued on foot up a steep side street and came to an archway in a high wall. Through the archway was the hospital, a collection of gloomy four-story buildings. Dr. Domingues led us to a door marked INFECTIOUS DISEASES, STAFF ENTRANCE.

Once inside, I had to put on a white coat and face mask, as well as cloth bags over my feet.

"Hygiene rules," the doctor said apologetically. "It's actually against regulations to bring animals into the hospital."

We walked along long deserted corridors with bare walls and worn, polished floors. The smell of cleaning polish and disinfectant couldn't hide the sweetish, sickly smell of disease. Through the open doors we could see big wards with rows of beds. The air was full of sighs and groans, sometimes even cries of pain and despair.

474

We came at last to a closed door, and Dr. Domingues gave us a serious look before opening it and leading us in.

If I close my eyes I can still see that room as clearly as when I was standing in the doorway looking in. It was a very small room. The plaster on the walls had flaked off in places, and some of the tiles on the floor were cracked. Under the bed there were faint stains that had proved impossible to scrub out. The window, which had a rusting handle and hinges, was slightly open, but the room was still stuffy. Apart from the white-painted iron bed the only furniture was a simple wardrobe, a medicine cupboard and a hospital trolley. There were flies buzzing round inside the globe lampshade.

A man was lying motionless in the narrow bed, his eyes closed. Dr. Domingues went to the bedside and carefully touched his arm. Slowly, as if with enormous effort, the man opened his eyes. First he stared at the ceiling and then turned to the doctor. Only then did he look at me.

My first thought was that he had lost weight. His cheeks were sunken, which made his eyes look bigger than I remembered. He had shaved off his slim mustache.

Apart from that, Alphonse Morro looked just the same as before.

I removed my face mask and we looked at one another.

"Sally Jones . . . ," he said almost inaudibly. "That's your name, isn't it?"

Outside the tall windows of the hospital, twilight was masking Lisbon in a blue haze. The dull yellowish glow of the lamps on the ceiling lit the dark corridor where Signor Fidardo and I waited while Dr. Domingues checked Alphonse Morro's temperature and gave him his medicine for the night.

When we went back into the room, Morro was propped up with a pillow behind him. Dr. Domingues had brought chairs for me, Signor Fidardo and herself.

"Thank you, Doctor," Alphonse Morro said once we had all sat down.

He turned to Signor Fidardo.

"Who are you?" he asked with suspicion in his voice.

"My name is Fidardo," Signor Fidardo answered calmly. "I am an instrument maker, and Sally Jones has been working in my workshop for the past few years. She was made homeless when Captain Koskela was sent to prison."

Alphonse Morro nodded and closed his eyes as if he suddenly didn't have the energy to keep them open.

"I understand," he said in a weak voice.

"Do you understand that you have stolen three years of an innocent man's life?" Signor Fidardo asked him.

Alphonse Morro cowered down a little, and his face

looked pained. The doctor looked at Signor Fidardo and said in a low voice, "He mustn't get upset. . . ."

But Morro raised his hand from the bedcovers and said, "Thank you, Doctor, but don't worry about me. I don't deserve it. My name is Alphonse Morro and I've been on the run for three years. I left Lisbon to save my life, and to stop anyone from searching for me I let everyone believe I was dead. It seemed like a good idea. Only later did I discover that a man had been imprisoned for murdering me. You must believe me when I say it wasn't my intention. My conscience plagued me, but I was afraid to come back. Until now."

We sat in silence for a time. Then, turning to me, Morro asked, "Were you the one who found my locket?"

I nodded.

"That's what I thought," Morro said. "But how did you know I was alive? And that notice with the poem . . . how did that reach Cochin?"

I looked at Signor Fidardo. He cleared his throat and told Alphonse Morro the whole story of how I had come across the grave of Elisa Gomes and how the letters and money he'd sent to the caretaker at the cemetery convinced us he was alive. He went on to tell Morro how Ana came up with the idea of sending out the notices all over Southeast Asia. And lastly he told him about my visit to India.

Morro listened attentively, his feverish eyes switching between Signor Fidardo and me. When Signor Fidardo finished, a look of calm spread across Morro's face.

"Thank you," he said. "I'm glad that there will be an end to—"

Morro suddenly began to heave with loud, dry coughs. His body tensed and he was obviously finding it hard to breathe. When he was able to speak again, his voice was hoarse and dull.

"Dr. Domingues," he said. "Early in the morning I'd like you to ring all the big newspapers and ask every one of them to send a reporter."

At first it looked as if Dr. Domingues was going to object, but then she nodded earnestly.

Morro turned to me once more.

"No one is going to believe me at first, but I can prove who I am. And as soon as my identity is verified, Henry Koskela will be set free. Anything else would be unthinkable."

Morro took several short, rattling breaths before going on: "I realize there are many things you must be wondering about, and I promise you will have all the answers. But not yet. It would be dangerous for you. What I have to tell will cause trouble—a lot of trouble. . . ."

His cough returned. Dr. Domingues stood up and felt Morro's forehead.

"Senhor Morro," she said. "You are burning up. You must rest now."

Morro lifted the doctor's hand from his forehead and held it weakly while his thin body was racked by another fit of coughing. We could hear that his strength was waning.

I put my hand in my pocket and took out the locket I had been carrying for so long. I went over to the bed and put it in Morro's hand. He looked at it and looked at me, and his eyes were as troubled as they had been in O Pelicano three years before. But he no longer smelled of fear. Just of disease.

When we left the room Alphonse Morro was lying there with his eyes closed. He was holding the locket to his heart.

CHAPTER 67
Alarm

I should have been beside myself with happiness.

Everything I had hoped and fought for had fallen into place. Morro was alive. He was back in Lisbon. And the Chief would soon be free.

But somehow I was more sorrowful than happy as Signor Fidardo and I left the hospital in the mild evening air and started walking toward the tram stop. Sorrowful and uneasy at the same time without really knowing why.

Signor Fidardo stole a thoughtful glance at me every now and again. He looked as if he wanted to say something but held back from doing so.

When we got home he came up to Ana's apartment with me. She had just finished work and was cooking rice when we came in.

"Do you have any wine in the house?" Signor Fidardo asked.

Ana looked at him warily.

"If you do, I think we should open a bottle," he said with a smile. "We have cause for celebration. Alphonse Morro is alive. He is in Lisbon, and we have just met him."

Ana put down the saucepan and clapped her hands to her mouth. She stood like that for the whole time it took Signor Fidardo to tell her about Dr. Rosa Domingues and our visit to São José Hospital.

"But that's fantastic!" she said when he'd finished, and tears of joy welled up in her eyes. "We've done it! We've succeeded!"

She put her arms round me and gave me a long, tight hug while Signor Fidardo found a bottle of wine and opened it. He poured me a glass of apple juice. It wasn't until after we'd all drunk a toast that Ana noticed something wasn't right.

"But you don't seem very happy," she said, looking at me in surprise.

Signor Fidardo put his hand on my shoulder.

"Of course Sally Jones is happy," he said. "I think it's just that meeting Alphonse Morro has upset her a little. Morro is very ill, and to tell the truth I doubt if he'll be with us much longer."

~

We stayed up late that night. Ana and Signor Fidardo were so happy for me. Signor Fidardo told Ana several times about our meeting with Morro and what we'd talked about. She was keen to hear every single detail.

"He had a high fever," Signor Fidardo said. "And it's possible his mind was wandering a little. He obviously thought we might be in danger if he told us why he'd fled Lisbon and made everyone believe he was dead. He said something about his story being likely to stir up a great deal of trouble."

"What kind of trouble?" Ana wondered.

Signor Fidardo rubbed his shoulders.

"No idea," he said. "He didn't explain. As I said, I think the fever meant he was imagining things."

Ana gave me a questioning look.

I shrugged too, though I hesitated a little first.

I hadn't understood what Morro meant either, but I was pretty sure he hadn't been hallucinating. That's probably why I was feeling so worried.

By the time we broke up to go to bed I was beyond weariness. It had been a very long day. I slid down under the covers on my sofa, shut my eyes and tried to imagine what it would be like when the huge black iron doors of the prison swung open and the Chief walked out to freedom.

But it was a different picture that kept playing on my inner screen. I saw Morro in his bed in the hospital, and I could hear his voice in my head: *"I left Lisbon to save my life, and to stop anyone searching for me I let everyone believe I was dead. . . ."*

What did Morro mean by that? Had his life really been in danger three years ago? If so, why? Had someone been threatening him? If so, who?

I had no answers to these questions. Not yet, anyway. Not until Morro had told the newspapers everything he knew.

And it didn't really matter to me why Morro had fled Lisbon in the first place. The only thing that mattered was that he was back and the Chief would be set free.

I lay on my side and tried to think of something nice to help me fall asleep. Tomorrow was going to be a great day!

But sleep wouldn't come, and my thoughts continued drifting from one thing to another. Morro's words refused to leave me in peace. Something told me they were important and that I must do my best to understand them. And that it was urgent.

I tossed and turned on the sofa. Eventually I slipped out to drink a glass of water, and instead of going back under the covers I sat on the edge of the sofa.

I tried to think clearly, but it was difficult to know where to begin. My thoughts were pulling in different directions, and I was finding it impossible to impose any order on them. I could come up with questions but not answers.

And then suddenly a picture popped up in my memory

I remembered Bishop de Sousa at the São Carlos Theater. I remembered the exact moment our eyes met across the crowded room and we recognized one another. At first what I saw in his eyes was surprise, but it was quickly followed by a hint of fear.

That was a fact. I wasn't mistaken: the Assistant Bishop of Lisbon had been afraid. But why? The answer came to me immediately. The bishop had been afraid for the simple reason that I had recognized him!

And he had every reason to be afraid. He had tried to smuggle a consignment of weapons into Lisbon. I had no idea what he wanted the weapons for, but it must have been something illegal, something distinctly wrong for a bishop to be involved in. That's why he had been in disguise at

Agiere and calling himself Papa Monforte. And that's why I was a threat to him. I knew too much.

Of course! Initially he had tried to get rid of me by convincing Signor Fidardo to hand me over to the zoo. When that didn't work he sent Chief Inspector Garretta to take me by force and kill me.

Everything was becoming clearer. I concentrated hard to hold on to the chain of thought. It was all about secrets—dangerous secrets that the bishop and Garretta had been prepared to kill for.

Suddenly I began to see how Morro fitted into the picture. He was the one who had employed the Chief and me to fetch the crates from Agiere. Morro must have known it was weapons, not tiles, we were to bring to Lisbon. That must have been what made him so nervous in O Pelicano that I could smell the fear on him.

Morro too had known the bishop's secret, and he must have understood what a dangerous secret it was: *"I left Lisbon to save my life . . ."*

That's what he had said to me and Signor Fidardo earlier that evening, and at last I thought I understood what he meant.

Morro had fled from Lisbon to escape Bishop de Sousa and Chief Inspector Garretta! He had pretended to be dead so that they wouldn't come looking for him!

For one moment I was satisfied with having worked things out. A moment later I felt a knot of anxiety in my gut.

Alphonse Morro was back in Lisbon, and he was intending to spill everything he knew to the newspapers.

What would happen if Bishop de Sousa or Chief Inspector Garretta got to know that?

The knot in my gut became tighter. I wished it was already morning, that the newspapers had already spoken to Morro, that the whole city already knew he was still alive. Only then would I feel at ease. Only then

~

These thoughts went round and round in my head for hours. Finally, from sheer exhaustion, I must have fallen asleep.

The clock said quarter to one when I suddenly opened my eyes.

Someone was banging on the door. That was what had woken me.

Ana came out of her bed alcove in her nightdress with a cardigan over her shoulders.

"Open up! It's only me," we heard Signor Fidardo's voice say from the other side of the door.

He was in his pajamas and nightcap and looked quite

funny. But that was the last thing I was thinking at that moment.

"Morro has disappeared," he said breathlessly.

I was fully awake by now.

Signor Fidardo sat down heavily in a chair while Ana lit the oil lamp over the kitchen table and I put on my overalls.

"I've had Dr. Domingues on the telephone," he said. "A policeman came to the hospital three quarters of an hour ago. He came to arrest Alphonse Morro and said that Morro wasn't the patient's real name. According to him the patient was a mentally disturbed criminal who had escaped from prison and had to be returned there."

Ana put her face in her hands in horror.

"The policeman never stated his name," Signor Fidardo said. "Just that he was there to take Morro. Dr. Domingues refused, of course. She told him the patient was too ill to be moved. Then the policeman became threatening and forced the doctor to show him to Morro's room. When they got there . . ."

Signor Fidardo took a deep breath: "When they got there the room was empty."

"Empty?" Ana repeated.

"Yes, empty. Morro wasn't in the bed, and his clothes were gone from the wardrobe. Without asking the doctor's permission, the policeman started searching all the other wards. Dr. Domingues demanded—without any success— to see his warrant, and after a while he left."

"And Morro?" Ana asked.

Signor Fidardo nervously twirled one end of his mustache. "Gone," he said. "Dr. Domingues searched the whole infectious diseases section and there was no sign of him. Morro must have left the hospital. The doors between the wards are locked at night, so presumably he left through a window."

We sat in silence for a while. I was having trouble ordering my thoughts. Faint sounds could be heard from outside. A dog was barking, and there was the distant clang of the bell of a tram. A car braked to a halt, but the engine was left idling.

"I don't understand," Ana said. "How could that policeman have known . . . ?"

"That's what I asked Dr. Domingues," Signor Fidardo said. "She couldn't understand either. The only other person who knew about Morro was the hospital chaplain. Dr. Domingues wanted him to be ready to give Morro last rites if his condition deteriorated. It must have been the chaplain who tipped off the policeman."

I could still hear a car engine ticking over farther down in the street.

Suddenly I understood.

A policeman. Looking for Morro. Who knew we had been at the hospital . . .

We were in danger.

I stood up quickly to close and lock the door. But I was several seconds too late.

"You are quite right!" a harsh voice said from the darkness of the hall. "That is what happened."

CHAPTER 68
Tram Number Four to Estrela

Ana and Signor Fidardo turned round at the same time. The man's face was in shadow, but the flickering light of the lamp picked out two narrow eyes below the brim of a hat. The man had one hand in the pocket of his heavy overcoat; in his other hand was a revolver.

It was Chief Inspector Garretta.

"Where is he?" Garretta said, stepping quietly into the room.

Neither Ana nor Signor Fidardo answered. All three of us were staring at the gleaming weapon that was pointed at us.

"Well?" Garretta said, cocking his revolver with a loud click.

Signor Fidardo swallowed hard. "You are not here on official duty, Chief Inspector," he said in a surprisingly steady voice. "We are not obliged—"

"Shut up!" Garretta cut him off. "Don't do the legalistic stuff with me. There's no point at all. . . ."

A grin passed quickly across the policeman's square face as he added, "Especially not with that stupid cap on your head."

Signor Fidardo's pale cheeks flushed red with annoyance.

"I'm asking you again," Garretta said. "Where is Morro? Where have you hidden him?"

"He's not here," Ana said.

She spoke very quietly, but the anger in her voice was unmistakable.

"Senhora Molina," Garretta said, unexpectedly polite. "I am a great admirer of your music, so it pains me to have to intrude on your home. But I have no choice. Alphonse Morro has no friends in this city. None, apart from the people in this house, that is. The gorilla and the accordion mender visited him today, which is why it seems likely that this is where he's hiding. Am I right?"

He paused, but not long enough for Ana to have time to protest. Then he continued, "You are protecting a criminal, and I need to arrest him and take him with me. It's as simple as that. So you have a choice. . . ."

He aimed his revolver at me. Both Ana and Signor Fidardo gasped.

"Either you tell me where you are hiding Morro or I shoot the gorilla. Which I should have done long ago anyway. I'll count to three, after which there'll be a bang. You'd better cover your ears, Senhora Molina, because I shouldn't like to damage your fine musical ear!"

"For God's sake, man!" Signor Fidardo exclaimed. "Are you out of your mind? Morro isn't here! And we have no idea where he's gone!"

"One . . . ," Garretta said.

Ana started to stand up, but Garretta quickly pushed the table so she was trapped between it and the cupboard behind her chair.

"Two . . . ," he said.

There was silence. Ana and Signor Fidardo looked at one another wide-eyed.

"Three," Garretta said.

At the very same moment Signor Fidardo almost screamed: "In my workshop! Morro is in my workshop!"

With his revolver still pointing at me, Garretta looked searchingly at Signor Fidardo. Then he lowered his weapon.

"You're a bad liar, old man," he said. "So Morro isn't here after all."

Garretta put his revolver in his overcoat pocket.

"In that case there is only one other place to look," he said, walking toward the door. "But don't think I've finished with you. I've more important things to deal with just now, but your turn will come! Good night!"

~

I had never believed that Garretta would shoot, which is why I hadn't been afraid. It seems strange, but that's the way it was.

The moment he closed the door behind him, I knew what I had to do. I leapt up from the sofa, opened the attic window and climbed out on the roof. Neither Ana nor Signor Fidardo had time to stop me. I reached the ridge of the roof just in time to see the headlights of Chief Inspector Garretta's car light up the buildings farther along Rua de São Tomé.

By the time I had climbed down to the street the car had disappeared. I ran in the direction it had driven. The occasional nocturnal pedestrians I met moved aside when

493

they saw me. My knuckles were connecting hard with the paving stones as I ran, my lungs were bursting and my eyes were full of tears.

When I reached the Largo das Portas do Sol, I had to give up. There was no sign of the car on the square, and I had no idea which direction Garretta had taken from there. Exhausted, I sank to the ground, my back to a lamppost.

It took me several minutes to gather my breath and my thoughts. It was essential I find Morro before Garretta did. But where was he? Where to start looking?

I suddenly heard Garretta's voice in my head.

In that case there is only one other place to look.

That is what Garretta had said, *only one other place to look . . .*

I stood up quickly. Now I knew where he was going! It was so obvious!

A tram with its lights on was idling at the stop on the square. The driver was taking a snooze before setting off. I was lucky—it was a number four, the night tram to Estrela. The tram that stopped outside Prazeres Cemetery.

CHAPTER 69
The Shot

Five minutes later—it felt like a lifetime—the tram moved off. I had boarded it quietly right at the back, without the driver noticing. The journey took us down through the narrow streets of Alfama, the electric lights in the tramcar spreading a weak yellow glow that blinked when the tram rocked and swayed round corners.

I was absolutely certain now.

Alphonse Morro had left the hospital to go to Prazeres Cemetery.

He wanted to make one last visit to Elisa's grave.

That must be it, and Garretta had also come to the same conclusion. He was likely to arrive there before me.

Perhaps not, though! The cemetery was an absolute maze, and Garretta had not visited it as often as I had. And it was night, so he might well get lost, whereas I knew the way like the back of my hand.

What would happen if I did get there too late, though?

In my heart of hearts I knew there was only one answer to that question. *Garretta would kill Morro.* He would kill him to prevent him revealing the truth about what had happened three years earlier.

All of a sudden I was finding it difficult to breathe—I was panting in short, sharp bursts. I put my head between my knees and tried to force myself to take slow, deep breaths.

I will get there in time, I thought. I must get there in time.

After a while I was able to sit up straight again, and looking out of the window I saw that we had just passed through Chiado. The streets were becoming darker and more deserted the farther west we went.

We arrived at last. As soon as the tram stopped, I pushed open the doors and rushed toward the gates of the cemetery. The tram continued on its way and disappeared round the next bend, the hum of the electric cables above the track slowly fading away. The only sound now was the rustle of the damp night breeze through the tall cypress trees in the cemetery.

No, there was another sound too. A barely audible clicking. A noise I knew well. I stopped and looked round. A short distance away, very close to the cemetery wall, there was a parked car. A black Model T. Garretta's car!

It looked empty. I ran over to it. The clicking sound was the noise made by an engine as it cooled down. The hood was still warm, which meant that Garretta couldn't be far in front of me. I hurried into the cemetery.

There were no lights on in the caretaker's cottage. I hesitated for a moment, wondering whether to wake João. But it would take too long and I was in a hurry.

I tried to move quietly so that the crunch of the gravel underfoot wouldn't give me away, but my legs refused to obey. They wanted to run! Quickly! Quickly! The endless rows of family graves and mausoleums flashed past like the walls in a tunnel.

Everything looked different at night, and I was suddenly unsure where I was. Should I turn right or left at the next crossing? Or had I already gone wrong and ought to turn back?

I stood there, of two minds as to what to do. The branches of the cypresses rustled, and the wind carried the faint hum of the city outside the cemetery. Otherwise all was silent.

When the moon peeped through the haze, I recognized where I was and was about to move on, but something made me stop. A sound. A footstep on gravel.

I held my breath and listened. The sound had stopped. Or had it been my imagination in the first place?

There was no time to think about it. I had to move on. I hadn't gone far when I was forced to slow down again: the moon had disappeared behind clouds, and all the shadows had joined together and made the darkness impenetrable. Stepping carefully, I followed the edge of the gravel path. I tried to suppress an uncomfortable sensation that there was someone very close to me. I stopped time after time and listened for footsteps, but I heard nothing.

The moon came out again and I could see a small hill with three tall cypress trees outlined against the night sky. The area with smaller gravestones and simple crosses lay beyond that, and Elisa Gomes's grave was among them. I sped up. My breath was coming in bursts, and the pain in my chest had returned.

I struck the path that led up the small hill and ran as fast as I could. The wet gravel was tearing at my knuckles, but it was no more than a couple of dozen yards to the top of the hill and I'd be there.

Then I heard a sudden crack.

A short, sharp crack.

Instinctively I ducked, losing my balance as I did so. One leg folded under me and I crumpled at the foot of one of the cypress trees.

Everything went quiet again.

Unnaturally quiet.

The seconds ticked slowly by. The crack had sounded like a pistol shot, and it was difficult to determine the direction or the distance. But I had a feeling that the sound had come from the other side of the small hill.

I got to my feet—shakily. My legs would barely support me. Clouds were covering the moon again and I could see nothing but the vague shapes of gravestones. Everything was still.

I was about to take a cautious step forward when a movement in the darkness stopped me.

Between two gravestones the silhouette of a large figure loomed out of the general darkness, and I saw someone walking along the path in my direction.

I froze and held my breath under the lowest branches of the cypress tree.

It was Garretta. He was walking quickly and had his revolver in his hand. I had no more than a brief glimpse of his face as he passed me. We were barely more than a couple of yards from one another, but he was watching where he put his feet and didn't see me. When I cautiously turned to watch him, he had already been swallowed up by the darkness.

The acrid smell of gunpowder was still hanging in the air.

I don't know how long I stayed under the cypress tree. It was as if I'd been struck by some form of paralysis and was no longer able to move or to think.

~

I have only vague memories of what happened after that.

The moon must have peeped out of the clouds, and I remember the cemetery being bathed in a cold, pale light as I slowly walked along the path between the graves on the far side of the small hill.

I was looking for the grave of Elisa Gomes. I found it, but I also found something else. Lying on the ground in front of the gravestone was a black shapeless mound. For a short moment I had no idea what it was, but then I saw an arm lying outstretched, as if reaching for the gravestone. It was a human body.

Alphonse Morro.

I knew at once who it was, and I knew he was dead.

That must have been when I screamed. I have no memory of uttering a sound, but according to João a long, high-pitched wail was heard from the cemetery shortly after the shot was fired.

All I remember is sitting down by Morro and taking his hand. It was very thin, and it was still warm.

I just sat there.

The darkness of night slowly became the gray of dawn.

I held Alphonse Morro's outstretched hand in mine as it slowly grew cold.

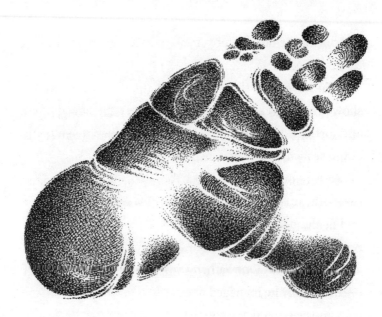

CHAPTER 70
Footprints

The gunshot had wakened João. At first he thought he'd been dreaming and lay awake listening to the silence for some time.

Then came the scream. He told me later that it was simultaneously the most terrible and the most sorrowful sound he'd ever heard.

"I was sure it was the scream of a ghost rising from its grave," he said. "I closed all the shutters on my windows and bolted the door before creeping back to bed and hiding under the covers."

João stayed like that until the clock on his bedside table showed half past six and the sun had risen. Then he dressed and fortified himself with a cup of coffee before venturing out to see what had happened.

Poor, poor João, it was awful for him to be the one to find that scene of horror. He stood for ages, simply staring at me and at the dead body of Alphonse Morro. Then he began repeating the same words time after time: "Our Father, who art in Heaven . . . Our Father, who art in Heaven . . ."

Eventually he managed to get me to my feet and lead me back to the caretaker's cottage, from where he telephoned Signor Fidardo. João was so shaken he was scarcely able to make sense, and it took him some time to explain what had happened. Half an hour later Signor Fidardo arrived in a taxi to fetch me.

João rang the police as soon as we'd gone, just as Signor Fidardo had told him to do. João was still so upset that he found it hard to get the words out, which meant that the police assumed he was drunk. Not until he had called them three times did they promise to send a patrol to the cemetery.

Two hours later the cemetery was closed off and the police began to investigate the murder.

I was asleep on Ana's sofa by that time and I slept through the whole of that day and the night that followed. The morning after that I drank a glass of milk and went straight back to sleep.

Ana stayed at home to take care of me. I slept and slept, waking only when I needed something to drink. I could still feel Alphonse Morro's cold, thin hand in mine. I remembered the look of happiness in his eyes when I gave him the locket in the hospital. And in my head I heard the sharp crack of the revolver over and over again until I fell asleep.

For five days and five nights I lay there on the sofa, barely moving. I was aware of nothing that was happening during that time.

Only later did I learn about it.

~

The police inspector in charge of the investigation of the murder in the cemetery was called Fernão Umbelino, and he was the one who told me how he had solved the case. Inspector Umbelino was an excellent narrator, and every detail of the story he told me is stored in my memory.

He arrived at Prazeres Cemetery at nine o'clock in the morning and began by examining the scene of the crime. The inspector was a very fat man and consequently slow-moving, but his eyes and his brain made up for that. Within half an hour he was in a position to draw his first conclusions.

The murdered man had been killed by a single shot through the heart. Marks in the gravel revealed that the murderer had been concealed behind a gravestone a little over five yards from his victim when he fired. No bullet casing had been left on the ground, which suggested the murder weapon was a revolver rather than a pistol, since the latter usually leaves bullet casings scattered round. Given that it was also dark, the murderer must have been a good shot.

Up to this point Umbelino had been sure of his deductions. He did not, however, know who the victim was, since the dead man was carrying no papers nor anything else that could point to his identity.

The footprints of four people were found in the gravel round the crime scene. Three of them were easily identified: the victim, the murderer and the caretaker, João. The fourth set of prints were more confusing. They had been made by someone who appeared to have walked barefoot while also using their knuckles for support. Umbelino followed the tracks backward and eventually found a very clear set of prints in the soft earth at the foot of a cypress tree. He could see then that the fourth individual was not an ordinary person. The inspector had never seen footprints like them.

Umbelino sent for an artist the police employed to draw pictures of suspected criminals. The artist copied the mysterious footprints, and the drawing was sent express delivery to the Lisbon Zoological Gardens. The answer came back an hour later: one of the experts at the zoo stated that in all probability the prints were those of a large ape, most likely a gorilla.

At that point Fernão Umbelino began to suspect that this was not a routine criminal investigation.

~

After lunch that day Inspector Umbelino interviewed João for the first time. They met over a cup of coffee in the caretaker's cottage, and João was extremely nervous. He had decided not to tell anyone I had been at the scene of the crime. He was afraid I might be suspected of the murder, which was very thoughtful of him.

Umbelino opened the interview by asking João if he knew who the dead man was.

"His name was Alphonse Morro," João answered. "And he is a ghost."

Umbelino's eyebrows went up.

"I mean ... he was already dead when he died," João said, trying to explain himself better.

"I see. Like that, was it?" Umbelino said calmly. "And when did this Alphonse Morro die for the first time?"

"He was murdered three years ago."

"Murdered that time too, was he?"

João nodded earnestly.

"Though he didn't die *properly* that time. He wrote letters afterward. *From the other side.* And sent money. For the grave. For us to take care of it."

"So he sent money for his own grave?"

"No, no, no! For Elisa's grave. She was his fiancée."

Umbelino made a few notes and scratched the back of his neck.

Then he said, "We'll come back to that a little later. Now I want you to tell me about the gorilla."

João blushed bright red, as I suspect he always does when he tries to lie.

"About Sally Jones?" he said. "I don't know anything about her. Who is she?"

Inspector Umbelino smiled a friendly smile. His blue eyes shone in his big ruddy face.

"So the gorilla's called Sally Jones," he said, making a note of it. "And what was she doing at the scene of the murder?"

Poor João did not know what to say. Umbelino put down his pen and his notebook and looked at him.

"I think we'd better take this step by step from the beginning, João," he said. "I've got plenty of time."

João knew he was a useless liar and thought Inspector Umbelino seemed to be a nice man. Just as well, then, he thought, to tell things as they were.

He took a deep breath and started telling the whole story, from the time he and I met by the grave of Elisa Gomes two years earlier right up to Signor Fidardo coming to collect me in a taxi just a couple of hours before.

Umbelino had heard many strange stories in his twenty years as a detective, but few of them came close to being as strange as this one.

CHAPTER 71
Inspector Umbelino and the Truth

After interviewing João, Inspector Umbelino went to the police station at Baixa. He went down to the registry department and asked them to check two names: Alphonse Morro and Elisa Gomes. Both names were listed in police records as murder victims. Elisa Gomes had died as a result of an assassin's bomb seven years before, and Alphonse Morro, her fiancé, had been murdered at the harbor by a seaman three years later.

Now, after another three and a half years, a man had been shot and killed at the grave of Elisa Gomes, and according to the caretaker of the cemetery that man was Alphonse Morro. It was obvious that something wasn't right. Inspector Umbelino, unlike João, did not believe in ghosts. Apart from which, it must be impossible to shoot a ghost, mustn't it?

So who was the dead man in the cemetery? And why was he murdered at the grave of Elisa Gomes? It might be a coincidence, of course, but Inspector Umbelino no more believed in coincidences than he believed in ghosts. So from the registry department he moved on to the department of criminal records, where he asked to be given all the papers relating to the murders of Alphonse Morro and Elisa Gomes. He put the papers in his briefcase and drove to his favorite café, A Brasileira, where he ordered a large pot of coffee and a basket of *pastéis de nata,* those delicious custard tarts.

It was eight o'clock in the evening by the time he finished the coffee and the custard tarts, and by then he had also read the reports on both the murders. He was perplexed. There was something peculiar about the investigation of the murder of Alphonse Morro three years ago. The victim's body had never been found, and Umbelino knew it was difficult to convict someone of murder unless there was a body. This case was clearly an exception to that rule. A Finnish seaman had been sentenced to twenty-five years in jail for killing Morro. The only evidence seemed to be statements taken from witnesses on the quayside, who had sworn that Koskela, the Finnish seaman, had knocked Morro unconscious and then thrown him in the river. All of these witnesses had been interviewed by the same police-man, the officer in charge of the case. His name was Raul Garretta.

Umbelino knew who Chief Inspector Garretta was even though they had never worked in the same district. As far as Umbelino had heard, Garretta was considered to be an excellent detective.

"But this is not the way things should be done," Umbelino muttered to himself as he placed the papers in his briefcase and went home to help his wife get dinner. "This is really not the way. . . ."

∿

The following morning Inspector Umbelino rang Signor Fidardo. João had given him the number.

"I need to have a word with you and Senhora Molina," Umbelino said after introducing himself. "It's about the murder in the cemetery. Could you come to the Estrela police station this afternoon?"

"No, unfortunately we can't," Signor Fidardo answered.

"Why is that?"

"It's quite out of the question. Senhora Molina and I have no intention of going to any police station."

"But why not?" Umbelino asked in a surprised voice.

"Because we are afraid of Chief Inspector Garretta," Signor Fidardo answered. "We're frightened to leave the house."

After this conversation Inspector Umbelino sat in his office chair for some time, trying to think it through. This was the second time Garretta's name had turned up in this investigation. That must signify something, surely? But what?

Umbelino took down one of the Lisbon police yearbooks he had on his bookshelf and leafed through it until he found what he was looking for. After putting the yearbook in his briefcase he left the office and took a tram to Alfama. On the way there he bought a large bag of sugary buns to demonstrate that he wasn't dangerous.

Signor Fidardo was reluctant to allow Umbelino in at first. Only after the inspector had assured him he was unarmed did Signor Fidardo open the door. A short while later they were sitting round Ana's kitchen table drinking coffee. Umbelino produced the police yearbook from

512

his briefcase and went through it until he found a group photograph of the personnel in the criminal investigations department of the district in which Garretta was chief inspector.

"Do you recognize anyone in this photograph?" he asked.

Ana immediately caught sight of Garretta in the back row.

"That one," she said. "That's the one who was here the night before last. He threatened us with a revolver."

Signor Fidardo nodded in agreement.

Inspector Umbelino scratched his head.

"It sounds very strange. Why in the name of all that is sacred would an officer in the Lisbon police be threatening you?"

"He was looking for Alphonse Morro," Signor Fidardo answered.

Inspector Umbelino looked doubtful.

"Alphonse Morro," he said. "I heard that name yesterday too. The caretaker mentioned it. He had quite a story to tell, and I still can't decide whether to believe it or not. You wouldn't happen to have a gorilla here, would you? A gorilla by the name of Sally Jones?"

Ana and Signor Fidardo exchanged glances. Then Ana

stood up and drew aside the curtains in front of the bed alcove. Umbelino went over and looked in, and there I was, sound asleep under a blanket.

"Tell me about her," Umbelino said after they had returned to their seats. "And start right at the beginning."

The inspector left our house on Rua de São Tomé five hours later. He had been thrown off-balance by everything Ana and Signor Fidardo had to tell him. It all seemed so improbable. But Umbelino had been a detective long enough to know when he was being told the truth and when he was being lied to. And he knew that this was the truth.

When he left Alfama, Inspector Umbelino went straight to São José Hospital to talk to Dr. Rosa Domingues. She shuddered when he showed her the photograph of Chief Inspector Garretta.

"That's him," she said. "That's the policeman who wanted to take away my patient."

"What was the patient's name?"

"Alphonse Morro," Dr. Domingues answered. "That's what he told me, anyway."

CHAPTER 72
Uncle Alves

The following morning Inspector Umbelino arrived early at his office in the Estrela police station. Having made inquiries, he now knew that Alphonse Morro only had one close relation who was still alive: an uncle by the name of Alves Morro, who ran a funeral business in Bairro Alto.

Umbelino contacted Uncle Alves by telephone and arranged to meet him at the city mortuary.

Most people think of a mortuary as somewhere unpleasant, but Alves Morro was an exception. He did not seem in the least affected by the big, cold rooms where the smell of death lingered however much the tiles were scrubbed. But then, he did work in the business, as Umbelino could have guessed from his appearance alone: Alves Morro had a look that was gloomier than death itself.

Umbelino lifted the sheet that covered the murdered man brought in from Prazeres Cemetery, and Alves Morro glanced at the thin chalk-white face that was revealed; then he said with a slight snort, "Yes, that's my nephew Alphonse."

"Are you sure?" Umbelino asked.

Alves Morro gave him a look of irritation. "Of course I'm sure. Alphonse grew up with my wife and me."

Umbelino's eyebrows shot up. "He must have been like a son to you, then?"

"Naturally," Alves Morro said without any sign of really meaning it.

Umbelino scratched his cheek in thought.

"This man died just a few nights ago," he said. "How can he be your nephew? Alphonse Morro was murdered three years ago, wasn't he?"

Alves Morro looked at the inspector, his face devoid of expression.

516

"This man is Alphonse," he said. "He obviously didn't die three years ago, then."

Clearly not was the thought that was running through Umbelino's mind. He nodded slowly.

"I assume, Senhor Morro, that you will want to make the funeral arrangements yourself?"

Alves Morro shuffled in embarrassment.

"Who'll be paying?" he asked.

The question threw Umbelino off-balance.

"You . . . do . . . er . . . have a funeral business, don't you? And . . . er . . . being his uncle?"

"Inspector, I've already done quite enough for that boy! It will have to be a pauper's funeral—unless someone is willing to pay me to provide something better, that is."

~

Meeting Alves Morro had been a great success for the investigation, since it meant the victim had been identified beyond doubt. For all that, however, Inspector Umbelino was depressed when he left the mortuary: Uncle Alves was far from a pleasant acquaintance.

There was something else that was upsetting the inspector. He now had a theory as to who had shot Alphonse Morro, and in normal circumstances this would have given him some satisfaction. But this time things were more complicated, in that his suspect was a policeman. And a chief inspector into the bargain. Accusing a colleague of murder was a very serious matter.

What was he to do? To get some sound advice, he arranged to meet his wife, Rita, at their favorite restaurant, and while they were eating lamb meatballs in tomato sauce he told her the situation. When he'd finished, she put her hand on his and said, "There is only one thing to do, my dear, and that's the right thing. But you knew that yourself, didn't you?"

Inspector Umbelino nodded as he took a large mouthful of the plum pie and whipped cream he'd ordered for his pudding.

"If I'm wrong I'll find myself back patrolling the streets as a constable."

"You aren't usually wrong, Fernão," Rita said.

Then, with a pointed look at the plum pie, she said, "Apart from which, a bit of patrolling wouldn't do you any harm, would it?"

"In which case I've got nothing to lose." Umbelino smiled.

"Nothing at all, my dear, nothing at all."

～

That same afternoon Umbelino went to see his boss, Superintendent Servioz, to tell him his suspicions about Garretta.

Servioz was both disconcerted and angry. Here was one of his inspectors accusing a fellow policeman of being a murderer! It was scandalous! Had Umbelino lost his mind?

But Umbelino had stuck to his guns and insisted, so Superintendent Servioz reluctantly promised to bring the matter to the attention of the head of the district in which Garretta worked. It would, of course, have to be done discreetly, and if Umbelino thought he would be given a chance to interview Garretta himself, he could forget it.

"We need to sort out this painful misunderstanding, preferably without you losing your job, Umbelino!" Servioz said sternly, and brought their meeting to a close.

Inspector Umbelino was late for work the following morning. He had lain awake worrying about the case until the small hours with the result that he had overslept. Superintendent Servioz was annoyed, but he had some interesting news for Umbelino: "Chief Inspector Garretta seems to have disappeared," he said. "His boss hasn't seen him for three days. A patrol was sent to his apartment on Rua do Norte this morning. No one answered the door, however hard they knocked."

Umbelino suggested to Superintendent Servioz that they should break the lock and search Garretta's apartment, but the superintendent wouldn't agree to it.

"Let's show some moderation," he said. "Raul Garretta

is an experienced detective officer, and we can't just treat him as a villain! There can be no question of searching his house, Umbelino, unless you can explain to me *why* Chief Inspector Garretta would be involved in this murder. Show me his motive!"

"It was Garretta who made sure that the Finnish sailor Koskela was sent to prison for a murder he didn't commit," Umbelino said. "Perhaps Garretta was afraid he'd be in serious trouble when it was proved that Morro wasn't dead after all. That's why he got rid of him."

"That doesn't hold up," Servioz said dismissively. "No one has submitted a complaint about the police investigation that led to the guilty verdict. The verdict of the court was unanimous. And it would be unlikely that Garretta would be blamed just because proof has emerged that Morro didn't drown that night three years ago."

Inspector Umbelino nodded reluctantly. The superintendent was right.

"Then there must be some other motive," he said.

"Or some other murderer," Servioz said, ending their discussion.

~

Inspector Umbelino spent the rest of the day mulling things over. He stuck to his belief that it was Garretta who had shot and killed Morro in Prazeres Cemetery. It seemed very likely that the murder had something to do with Morro's disappearance three years before. But that trail simply led to further questions. Why had Morro fled the country and convinced everyone he was dead? What really happened on the quayside the night Alphonse Morro ended up in the river? Had Garretta really arranged things so that Henry Koskela, who was innocent, was framed for the murder? Or had the chief inspector just been doing his job as Superintendent Servioz believed? That remained a possibility, but in that case why had Garretta been so desperate to find Morro on the night of the murder in the cemetery?

There had to be some other link between Raul Garretta and Alphonse Morro; Inspector Umbelino felt certain of that. But how was he to discover what that link was, given that Morro was dead and Garretta had vanished?

Inspector Umbelino read through all the papers relevant to the investigation once more, but he was no wiser at the end of it. He was about to pack up for the night and go home to Rita and make cabbage soup and forcemeat-balls when there was a knock on the office door. It was a constable with a message from the technical section at the Baixa police station: Umbelino was to go there at once.

The constable gave Umbelino a lift to Baixa, where a

forensic technician was waiting for him. She was looking pleased with herself.

"We've just finished examining the clothes Alphonse Morro was wearing when he died. Look at what we found."

Morro's jacket was lying on the table, and the lining had been removed. Alongside the jacket lay two Portuguese passports.

"The passports were sewn into the shoulder padding," the technician said. "A skillful piece of work—we very nearly missed them."

Umbelina studied the passports. One was made out in the name of Alphonse Morro, the other in the name of someone called Alfredo Simão.

"There is no such person as Alfredo Simão," the technician said. "That's a fake passport."

Umbelino felt slightly disappointed. He'd been hoping for something better. The fact that Morro had two passports, one of them a fake, was hardly a sensation. It did not progress the case at all.

"You didn't find anything else?" Umbelino asked.

The technician gave a self-congratulatory smile and nodded.

"Indeed we did. I'll show you."

She pulled out a big metal drawer, in which there was a pair of shoes. The technician picked up the left shoe, took out the insole and invited Umbelino to take a look in the shoe. There was a square hollow, about a quarter of an inch deep.

"A little secret compartment or whatever we want to call it," the technician said. "And this is what we found hidden in it. It's a letter, I think."

She passed Umbelino a thin wad of folded papers. He handled it carefully—it was brown rice paper, so thin as to be virtually transparent. Each of the sheets was filled with text written in very small letters, the lines close together.

Umbelino put on his reading glasses and read the first few lines of the first sheet. He knew at once that the case would soon be solved.

Late that evening, sitting in his favorite armchair at home, Umbelino worked his way through the long letter with the help of a magnifying glass and an extra reading lamp. The letter had been written by Alphonse Morro and after reading it Fernão Umbelino felt very sad.

But he was also pleased. Now he had the answers to all of his questions.

~

The following day Umbelino showed the letter to Superintendent Servioz. Servioz read it with growing dismay, and as soon as he had finished it he gave Umbelino clearance to search Garretta's apartment on Rua do Norte.

Under a loose floorboard in Garretta's bedroom Umbelino found five boxes of bullets of the same make and caliber as the one that had killed Morro. He also found a pair of shoes with patterns on the soles that matched those left by the murderer in the cemetery.

The apartment also showed signs that Garretta had left in a hurry and had no plans to return soon. He'd emptied his bank account and taken all the money with him. He'd also taken his passport, but no one knew where he'd gone.

Superintendent Servioz decided that Chief Inspector Garretta was a suspect in the case of the murder of Alphonse Morro and that a description should be circulated.

CHAPTER 73
Red Sails in the Morning

I woke and was immediately aware that something was different. I couldn't go back to sleep. My body refused to do so because it was suffering from hunger pains.

Ana made me milky porridge, and I ate one helping after another. The sounds and images in my head faded gradually, though they did not disappear. And they still haven't. I see and hear them even now, whenever I think of Alphonse Morro.

After eating six helpings of porridge I expected to feel sleepy again, but I didn't. My mind was full of questions. For a start, was that twilight out there, or was it dawn? What was the time? How long had I been asleep?

Ana must have realized what I was thinking because she said, "You've been asleep for nearly five days. We were worried about you, but Dr. Domingues has been to see you several times and she said there was nothing strange about you sleeping so much. Not in view of all the terrible things you've been through."

Then she added, with a touch of concern in her voice, "You do remember Dr. Domingues, don't you?"

I nodded.

Ana smiled and stroked my bristly head.

"Everything is going to be fine," she said. "And it's lucky you woke up when you did. We are expecting a visit."

Ana cleared away the porridge things and laid out coffee cups and plates. A little while later I heard heavy footsteps and the murmur of voices coming up the stairs. One of the voices was Signor Fidardo, and he was the one who opened the door.

"Wonderful! You're awake!" he said happily when he saw me sitting on the sofa. "Perfect timing!"

Signor Fidardo was followed by a huge man carrying his jacket over his arm. His waistcoat was tight across his belly and his trousers were rather too short. His head seemed to be resting heavily on a bed of double chins. He had untidy red hair, and his eyes were a brilliant blue. He was carrying an old-fashioned black leather briefcase in his hand.

Climbing the stairs seemed to have taken it out of the big man. He leaned on the doorpost, wiped the sweat from his brow and loosened his tie before saying hello to Ana and being introduced to me:

"Evening, Sally Jones!" he said in a light and gentle voice. "I've heard a lot about you in the past few days, and I'm pleased that you've woken from your trance, so I can meet you properly at last. My name is Fernão, Fernão Umbelino, and I'm a detective."

The word *detective* made me glance nervously at Ana, but she just smiled calmly and said, "Inspector Umbelino is investigating the murder of Alphonse Morro. You don't need to be afraid of him."

"Crooks are the only ones who need to be afraid of me!" the inspector said with a chuckle as he sat down heavily on one of the Windsor chairs at the table.

Ana served coffee and rolls, along with some kirsch. I drank milk. As we ate and drank, Inspector Umbelino told us about his inquiries. He stuck to the most important points—there would be time for details later.

I was still hazy after my long sleep, but what the inspector had to tell us cleared the fog from my mind. My whole body began to tingle and I found it hard to sit still.

"It has now been established," Umbelino said, "that the man who died in Prazeres Cemetery five days ago was Alphonse Morro. I had a meeting yesterday with my boss, Superintendent Servioz, and he went straight to the Minister of Justice to explain the situation. The minister summoned me to his office early yesterday afternoon. He gave me a signed warrant and told me to go immediately to the central prison at Campolide."

Inspector Umbelino took a mouthful of coffee, looking at me earnestly over the rim of the cup. He went on: "When I arrived at the prison in Campolide I handed the warrant to the prison governor, and he took me to Henry Koskela's cell. Koskela wasn't expecting me, of course, so he was absolutely stunned. I had to explain my visit five times before he understood. And then I had to swear I was telling the truth the same number of times again before he believed me."

The inspector paused once more. He was smiling now.

"Henry Koskela has been cleared of all suspicion of the murder of Alphonse Morro. He will be set free tomorrow."

～

I did not sleep a wink that night, which is not really very strange. I felt as though I had already slept enough for several weeks to come.

Instead, once Ana was asleep, I slipped out through the window, climbed across the roofs and found a concealed position behind a chimney two or three buildings away. It was the exact spot where I had sat through a long, hard night three years before. The night was black—as it had been then—and the lights of the city sparkled—as they had then. In spite of that, I hardly recognized myself: the outlook then had been threatening and terrifying, whereas now I was sitting in the darkness and I felt utterly safe. All those thousands of points of sparkling light were my friends.

But I didn't do much thinking. I merely sat there looking out over Lisbon until the light of the streetlamps began to go pale in the brightness of dawn. The glow of the sky in the east painted the sails of the boats in the harbor red. A storm was brewing. A red sky at dawn means hard weather is on its way. *Red sails in the morning—sailor take warning* was a rhyme the Chief had taught me. And in no more than a few hours I would be seeing him again.

CHAPTER 74
Iron Gates

Inspector Umbelino rang just before eight o'clock to tell us the Chief would be released on the stroke of twelve. Umbelino himself was already on the way out to Campolide because he had a number of urgent matters to talk to the Chief about, which arose from the letter found in Morro's shoe. The inspector did not want to say more than that on the telephone, but he promised there was nothing that need worry us.

The storm moved in over the city during the morning. Strong winds swept through the streets and the rain drummed angrily on the tiled roofs of Alfama. Ana, Signor Fidardo and I caught the eleven o'clock train to Campolide. Ana and Signor Fidardo were very nervous. I could easily understand that, as I was nervous too.

In my pocket I had two cigars for the Chief. Signor Fidardo had helped me choose a good brand in Widow Pereira's shop. I reckoned the Chief must have finished the box of cigars I sent him the year before, and he would almost certainly be dying for a smoke by the time he came out.

Ana had been to the florist's and bought a large bouquet to give to the Chief. Wrapped in tissue paper, it was very beautiful, but on the train she began to regret it.

"Flowers might seem a bit strange," she said. "Usually it's men who give flowers to women, not the other way round. And we don't even know one another."

She passed the bouquet to Signor Fidardo.

"You give it to him instead."

Signor Fidardo waved it away.

"Me? Not me! How would that look? You're the one who bought the flowers, so you'll have to be the one to hand them to him!"

They argued for a while, and then the same thought

seemed to strike both of them at the same time. They looked at one another and then they looked at me.

Which is why I found myself standing outside the prison an hour later with a large bouquet of lilies and tulips in my hand. I felt stupid. It must be unheard of for a ship's engineer to give her captain flowers, mustn't it?

It was lucky that both Ana and Signor Fidardo had taken umbrellas with them. The rain was pouring down on the bare sandy square outside the prison walls. The electrified barbed wire that ran along the top of the wall hummed and sparked. Ragged clouds chased across the sky.

Not a soul was to be seen, and the black iron gates in the wall were shut. I had a dreadful feeling that we were waiting in vain, that the whole thing was a misunderstanding or even a cruel joke.

But then, through the drumming of the rain, we heard a click. A small door, a segment of the great double gates, opened.

First came Inspector Umbelino, his raincoat straining over his belly.

Behind him walked the Chief.

He was wearing the same clothes as when I'd seen him last, three years earlier, though they were looser now. In one hand he was carrying the black instrument case that contained his accordion.

532

For a few moments the Chief stood with his face turned up to the pouring rain. Then he walked toward us. He looked at me first, then at Ana and finally at Signor Fidardo. No one could think of anything to say. It looked as if the Chief was crying, but it was probably just the raindrops running down his cheeks.

Signor Fidardo cleared his throat and said, "It's nice to meet you, Senhor Koskela. Welcome to freedom."

The Chief put down the instrument case, took two steps forward and hugged Signor Fidardo. Then he took Ana in his arms and hugged her until she looked as if she couldn't breathe. After that he hugged me to his breast and I hugged him. We hugged tight and long. The bouquet was squashed to pulp.

~

Inspector Umbelino had a car. Ana sat in the front passenger seat, and Signor Fidardo, the Chief and I squeezed in the back. We were all still having trouble finding anything to say. The Chief had scarcely uttered a word.

The inspector seemed to be the only one who wasn't in the least bothered. As he drove his car over the potholed streets of Campolide, he whistled happily.

Until white steam began pouring out from under the hood!

"Why's it doing that?" Ana and Signor Fidardo said simultaneously.

"No idea," Inspector Umbelino said, pulling up to the pavement.

The Chief stepped out into the rain, and I hurried after him. We lifted the hood.

It wasn't hard to find the problem. The coolant was leaking out through a crack in the cylinder block.

"I think we'll have to leave the car here," the Chief said.

I nodded. It certainly looked like that.

The Chief thought for a moment. Then he looked down the street.

"Didn't we just drive past a scrapyard?"

We had. The Chief and I looked at one another—I knew what he was thinking.

"Worth a try, do you think?" he said.

I nodded eagerly.

The scrapyard was only a block away. Its owner was sitting on a balcony outside his small hut. He was smoking and watching the rain. He brightened up when the Chief explained why we were there, and within a few minutes he had collected everything we needed: a piece of sheet metal, a gasket, some small machine screws, a brace and bit and a screw tap. The Chief paid him a small sum for the materials and promised to bring the tools back quickly.

The inspector, Ana and Signor Fidardo stayed in the car while the Chief and I worked on the engine in the rain. Within half an hour we had sealed the leak, temporarily at least. While I was returning the tools, the Chief filled the radiator with water and told Inspector Umbelino to start the engine. It was as smooth as clockwork, and our seals held up.

"You must have planned this!" the Chief said with a big, happy smile when we had taken our places in the backseat again. "My life in freedom could hardly have had a more enjoyable start!"

CHAPTER 75
The Great Scandal

The Chief moved in with us at the house on Rua de
São Tomé. During those first days he spent most of
the time sitting in Ana's kitchen talking to Ana and Signor
Fidardo. There was so much to discuss. The kettle would
splutter away on the stove, and there was a smell of coffee,
bread and cigar smoke. I would be sitting on the sofa with
my legs drawn up wishing that the four of us could be there
together forever.

The Chief had changed. Not greatly, but enough for me to notice immediately. He now had an ugly scar on one cheek, and his nose was slightly crooked. His hair was gray at the temples, and he moved in a different manner—always watchful in some way. Sudden noises made him jump, and he never turned his back on anyone if he could avoid it. I don't think it was something he was conscious of.

When Ana asked him whether prison life had been hard, his answer was evasive.

"Yes, I suppose ... but the evenings were good. Mostly I would be left in peace in my cell and could practice the accordion. I've never been given a better present. And when you came and sang, Ana, well, words can't describe the joy it gave."

I hadn't been in the least worried about the Chief getting on well with Ana and Signor Fidardo. Nor need I have worried. They seemed to like one another right from the start. When the Chief became restless with all the sitting and talking, Signor Fidardo offered him a job in the instrument workshop.

"I'd love to take the job as long as I can do it properly and not get in your way," the Chief said. "But I don't want to be paid, and I'll pay for my board and lodging. The prison governor gave me some money when he released me, so I'm not completely broke. And I already owe you and Ana more than I can ever repay."

~

There were three of us in the workshop now. Signor Fidardo began making a violin he'd been promising one of his customers for ages, while the Chief and I dealt with repairs. The Chief was a quick learner, and he already knew quite a lot about the mechanism of accordions: to pass the time in prison he had dismantled and rebuilt his accordion several times.

As we sat together working, the Chief and I, I could see he had changed in more ways than I'd noticed at first. When we were on the *Hudson Queen,* he had always made a lot of noise when he was working. He used to talk to himself about this and that, whistle, hum a tune or think aloud about whatever problems he had to deal with. Now, however, he was silent for the most part. Before he went to prison I had usually been able to guess what he was thinking, even when he said nothing. It was impossible now.

One day when the Chief and I had been sitting working in complete silence for almost an hour, he suddenly noticed me looking at him. He gave me a weary and rather sorrowful little smile. "Don't let it worry you," he said. "Three years is a long time. It'll take a while for me to find my way back."

At the end of the working day the Chief would go for long walks, usually with me but sometimes alone or with Ana. His walks would crisscross the city, but they always ended up down at the harbor. He would look at the ships and talk to seagoing men about the state of the trade. When there was a west wind he would sometimes stand for long periods with his eyes closed and his nose turned seaward. Once he said to himself, "Wonder if she's still there?"

I knew it was the *Hudson Queen* he was thinking about.

~

Fridays and Saturdays we went to the Tamarind and listened to Ana. Tears came to the Chief's eyes every time. One evening, since he already knew most of the songs she sang, Ana suggested he bring his accordion with him.

"Not likely!" the Chief said with a little laugh. "It would be like pouring paraffin over cream, that would!"

Ana asked him several times, but the Chief wouldn't budge. He had no wish to perform. At home, on the other hand, he loved to take out the accordion and play it while Ana sang and Signor Fidardo played the guitar. Those were such good times.

When the Chief played, an expression I had never seen before came over his face. He did not look like himself at all, I thought. His head would lean to one side, and his eyebrows wrinkled as though he was in pain. His eyes were looking into the far distance, at something no one else could see.

At moments like that, I wondered whether he would ever really be happy again.

And if that was so, I knew I should never ever really be happy again.

～

A great deal happened in Lisbon in the month following the Chief regaining his freedom. The newspapers wrote almost daily about the Great Scandal. A conspiracy had been uncovered. Powerful men and women at the top levels of society had been planning a coup to overthrow the republic. According to some reports, King Manuel, the exiled monarch, had been ready to return from England and take back power in Portugal.

The coup had failed, but without being discovered. Now, however, it had all come to light. Many people had been arrested, and the police were hunting many more. A warrant was out for the arrest of Chief Inspector Garretta for murder and treason. Bishop de Sousa had fled the country and was under the pope's protection in the Vatican in Rome.

Of course, the Chief and I knew that all of these revelations also had something to do with us and with Alphonse

Morro. But exactly *what* and *how* we didn't understand until Inspector Umbelino showed us the letter.

~

Early one midweek evening Umbelino rang and asked if he could invite himself for a cup of coffee later. He would provide the syrupy cinnamon buns from the Graça baker's shop, and he wanted to meet all four of us together.

It was almost ten o'clock by the time Umbelino knocked on the door. The table was laid and the coffee ready in Ana's kitchen. First we ate and talked about this and that. We were all curious to know what had brought the inspector here so late in the day, and eventually he took an envelope from his pocket and laid it on the table.

"This envelope contains the letter Alphonse Morro had hidden in his left shoe," he said. "Unfortunately my superiors will not allow me to show it to you, it being evidence in a case of murder. But I'm not going to let that put me off. You four, of all people, have a right to read what Morro wrote."

The five of us sat in silence looking at the envelope. Inspector Umbelino took a look at the clock and stood up.

"Gracious, is it that time? I should be off home. I'll be back early tomorrow morning to pick up the letter I accidentally left here. Good night to you all, and thanks for the coffee."

After Inspector Umbelino had left, Signor Fidardo turned to the Chief and said, "You start. . . ."

The Chief shook his head.

"Thanks," he said, "but I'm such a slow reader that you'll all be asleep before I finish. Perhaps Ana will read it to us instead?"

Ana nodded. She reached for the envelope, opened it and unfolded the flimsy sheets. Then she began reading them to us.

CHAPTER 76
Letter from a Dead Man

I am writing this in the Greek port of Piraeus, where I've rented a room while waiting for a ship to take me to Lisbon.

I'm ill. My fever and my cough are getting worse from one day to the next. If I don't survive the journey, these lines will have to speak for me. This is my confession, my witness statement and the sorry story of my life.

My full name is Alphonse Eugene Morro, and I was born in the village of Torrão twenty-nine years ago. My mother died the night I was born. My father was an eel fisherman and drowned when I was ten years old. I was sent to my uncle Alves and his wife, Odíla, in Lisbon. They were my closest relations, so they had no choice but to take me.

Uncle Alves was a mortician, and I had to work in his business after school and on the weekend. I would sweep the floors and change the flowers in the reception room. Once Uncle Alves thought I was old enough, I had to help him prepare the bodies for burial. My clothes always stank of death and formalin.

After leaving school I took an evening course in bookkeeping and accounts. In order to pay my way I continued working in the funeral business, so I was studying at night and preparing bodies during the day.

When I had any free time I used to go to a café close to the church of São Roque. That's where I first saw Elisa Gomes— she was a waitress there. I fell in love with her long before I had the courage to ask her what her name was.

I learned the hours she worked and which tables she served, and in that way I could spend part of every day near her. As time passed we began exchanging a few words when she brought me my coffee, and after several months I was brave enough to ask whether I could invite her to join me for an ice cream at the botanical gardens the following Sunday.

She agreed. It was the happiest moment of my life.

Elisa lived in a room at the Dominican Sisters' home for orphaned young women. She was the only member of her family to survive the ravages of the epidemic of Spanish flu a few years earlier.

Elisa and I became one another's family. We met as often as we could and took long walks in the parks of Belém. Or we would take a train to Cascais and have coffee at a beach café.

We began to dream of a future together and of a home of our own.

When I finished my education I took a job as clerk at a company selling marine insurance. Elisa found work as a housemaid with the banker José Carvalho and his family. We

scraped and pinched to save enough to get married and rent a place of our own, and after a year we decided on a date for our wedding. It was to be in June.

On the fourteenth of May, Elisa tried on her wedding dress. She was murdered the following day.

It was a letter bomb intended for José Carvalho, but he survived. Elisa was the one who took in the post, and the bomb exploded in her hands. The police were certain that anarchists were behind the crime, but they never succeeded in arresting anyone.

I spent the money I had saved for our wedding on a gravestone for Elisa instead. After the funeral I sat by her grave for three weeks. The insurance company fired me for not turning up to work, and without any wages I couldn't pay Uncle Alves for my board and lodging. He wanted me to work for him instead of paying, but I couldn't face preparing bodies anymore. So Uncle Alves threw me out.

I had nowhere to go and simply wandered the city. Eventually the police picked me up as a vagrant, and I landed first in jail and then in the workhouse. No one stays in the workhouse for long. If you don't die of disease, you will die of starvation. I reckoned my end was near, and as far as I was concerned that was just as well.

My salvation was a priest who visited the workhouse from

time to time. His name was Father Felipe, and thanks to him I was given work in a soup kitchen run by the congregation of the church of Santo António. I was paid in kind—food and a bed in the church lodging house.

I did wonder why Father Felipe had chosen to help me of all the poor devils in the workhouse. My guess was that I'd been lucky.

But that wasn't it, as I learned later.

Father Felipe became my friend. Sometimes we used to walk together up the hill to the Castelo de São Jorge to look at the view and talk. Most of the time we talked about my grief. I thought I had nothing to live for now that Elisa was dead.

Father Felipe said I was wrong. Life had given me a new task. I could honor Elisa's memory by fighting the evil that had taken her from me.

It sounded like a comforting thought.

Our conversations began to center more and more on politics and religion. Father Felipe said that the anarchists who had murdered Elisa were the tools of the devil. They were godless and fueled by hatred, and the same was true of the Republicans who had been ruling the country since the revolution of 1910 and forced King Manuel to flee the country. Father Felipe explained to me that the Republicans were enemies of the church and persecutors of the priesthood.

He used to say that we had to fight to bring our king back, otherwise darkness would fall over Portugal for all time. I became more and more convinced that Father Felipe was right, and for Elisa's sake I wanted to join the good people and be part of their struggle.

The first job they gave me was handing out leaflets to spread the message. I would go to a small café in Bairro Alto every evening to pick up a bag of leaflets and a list of the streets where I should distribute them. The text of the leaflets dealt with the same issues Father Felipe talked to me about. They were signed with the initials MB.

MB stood for the Monarchist Brotherhood.

Quite a few of us were involved in distributing leaflets, but I never came to know any of the others. Not even their names. The Monarchist Brotherhood was a proscribed and very secretive organization. The orders I received were quite clear: if there was any sign of the police, I should hide. If they saw me, I should run. If they caught me, I should say nothing. If they beat me up, I should still say nothing. Silence unto death if necessary.

The danger made my task seem important. For the first time since Elisa's death, I felt fully alive.

Night after night I distributed leaflets. The police almost caught me many times, but luck was on my side and I escaped. My luck ran out one hot August night. I was pursued into a cul-de-sac, arrested and taken to the Chiado district police station.

Five policemen interrogated me for four hours without getting a word out of me. At the end of it an officer by the name of Garretta came in and said that they might as well let me go.

Now that I was known to the police, Father Felipe was not prepared to let me continue handing out leaflets. I was desperate, but Father Felipe put his hand on my shoulder and said, "You have the right fire in your belly, Alphonse. It's time you were given new and more important tasks."

A month later I was given a job as clerk in the Lisbon harbor office. It was a good job, which paid well enough for me to be able to move out of the lodging house and rent a small apartment of my own. Father Felipe used his contacts to organize both the job and the apartment for me.

"The Brotherhood needs a reliable man in the harbor office," he explained. "The harbor is strategically important. Whoever controls the harbor controls the city."

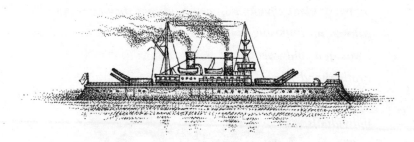

So I became a spy. I met Father Felipe once a week and gave him lists of the vessels entering or leaving the harbor. These were lists I copied secretly at work. The big naval gunboats always used to inform us in advance when they needed anchorages out in the roadstead, and I was in a position to pass on that information to Father Felipe.

Father Felipe was pleased with me, but I noticed he was becoming more and more stressed every time we met. I suspected something significant was going to happen soon.

~

Father Felipe arrived unexpectedly at my place late one evening and told me to go with him.

"Our ruling council is meeting at midnight," he said, "and you have been invited to the meeting."

We must have spent three quarters of an hour walking this way and that round the city while Father Felipe made sure we weren't being followed. Eventually we passed through the gates of an imposing mansion in Chiado. I was so nervous I was in a cold sweat. The ruling council of the Monarchist Brotherhood was, of course, a secret body, but according to rumor all of its members were powerful and well-connected individuals.

The mansion belonged to Maria Monserro, baroness of Castedo. She met us at the door and showed us the way to one of the many rooms in the mansion. Here there was an enormous mahogany table round which sat thirty or so *stern-looking men: aristocrats, company directors, generals, priests and senior policemen. I recognized many of them from pictures in the newspapers, but the only one I had met before was Chief Inspector Garretta, the man who had helped me when I was arrested for distributing leaflets.*

The meeting lasted two hours. The atmosphere was profoundly serious yet also excited and expectant. The time had come; the decisive moment was approaching. The monarchist uprising was to start in exactly ten days. The conspirators in the army and the navy were ready, as were the police and the men of the church.

There was one remaining problem. To ensure the success of the coup, the Brotherhood needed to be able to arm its supporters in Central Lisbon very quickly. A large supply of weapons had recently been smuggled in from Spain: this had been organized by Rodrigo de Sousa, the assistant bishop of Lisbon, who had friends close to the Spanish royal house.

Bishop de Sousa was present at the meeting and promised that he would personally make sure the weapons reached Lisbon in time. The only thing he needed help with was bringing the weapons into the city itself. The Republican Guard was watching all the roads in and out of Lisbon, which meant that the most sensible thing to do was to ship the weapons in down the river.

"So as not to arouse suspicion the weapons will be packed in wooden crates from a tileworks," the bishop said. "But we can't be too careful. It's important to find a ship with a crew that won't ask unnecessary questions."

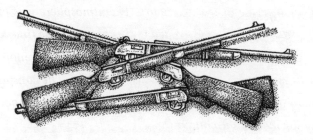

"Your Lordship," Father Felipe said to the bishop, at the same time putting a hand on my shoulder, "this is Alphonse Morro. He is one of our most devoted members. He works in the harbor office and he, if anyone, will be able to select the right ship to transport the cargo."

Everyone round the table looked at me. The stern looks they gave me were so superior and demanding that my knees were knocking under the table.

"Well, Senhor Morro?" Bishop de Sousa said. "Do you know of a suitable vessel?"

My mind went a complete blank for a few seconds. Then I suddenly remembered a small tramp streamer that would be perfect for the job.

"Yes, Your Lordship," I said, and was surprised at how steady my voice was in spite of the situation. "I think I do."

"Excellent!" the bishop said. "Father Felipe has spoken highly of you, and since I trust him, I trust you too. You'll be given the details tomorrow, and then you can go ahead and charter the vessel."

When the meeting was over I felt proud and happy at the trust that had been placed in me. But the happiness did not last very long. Once I was back in my apartment that night, I was seized by profound anxiety. I suddenly recognized the seriousness of what I had become involved in. Armed revolt! There would be battles in the streets. Blood would flow.

Deep in my heart I heard a voice asking whether this was really what Elisa would have wanted. I did not listen to the voice. I couldn't—I was now too far in to pull out.

~

The following day I set about carrying out my part of the plan. The ship I had in mind was the Hudson Queen, a small tramp steamer moored at the quayside below the Alfama district. The ship's skipper was called Koskela, and he came from Finland. The only other crew member was a large gorilla with the reputation of being a skilled engineer. As far as I knew, neither the Finn nor the gorilla was likely to ask unnecessary questions. And since the Hudson Queen

554

had not had a cargo for over a month, Captain Koskela was likely to be in urgent need of money.

I found him at the inn called O Pelicano the next evening. He and his gorilla engineer were having bowls of soup. It wasn't a pleasant meeting. Koskela seemed to be a nice man who didn't deserve to be tricked into a dangerous piece of work. His gorilla watched me in a way that was more human than animal. I had an uncomfortable feeling she could see how frightened and lost I was.

Koskela took the job, and the following morning he and the gorilla departed for Agiere, the isolated little spot where they were to pick up the weapons. They arrived there as expected and met Bishop de Sousa and his men. But then everything went wrong. For some reason, no sooner had the weapons been loaded than trouble broke out on board, and the Hudson Queen ran aground and sank in the river.

Without the weapons it was impossible for the uprising to begin as planned. After a crisis meeting, the ruling council of the Brotherhood made a last-minute decision to cancel everything.

I learned this from Chief Inspector Garretta, who came to my place at four in the morning and claimed that the fiasco was my fault. If he had his way he would shoot me on the spot, he said, but the council had decided I should be given one more chance.

"You have to kill the skipper, the man whose actions led to

our weapons ending up at the bottom of the river. If he starts to talk, there is a risk our enemies will work out what was being planned."

He gave me a loaded pistol.

"Kill the skipper the moment he shows his face in Lisbon. You know where to find him. And bear in mind this is your last chance: if the skipper is alive at this time tomorrow, you will die instead."

I wandered round Alfama and the docksides all day, horrified at the thought of what would happen if I met Koskela. And horrified at what would happen if I didn't meet him. I was trapped, and there was no escape route.

I tried several times to make contact with Father Felipe to seek his advice about the appalling dilemma I was in, but he wasn't to be found.

Late in the evening I came across Koskela and his gorilla in O Pelicano. I don't have words to describe the emotions I was feeling as I waited for them outside. They set off toward the harbor and I followed them.

I caught up with them down on the quayside and drew my pistol, but I couldn't bring myself to shoot Koskela. Deep down inside I'd known that all along. As we stood there face to face, I was ashamed to the very marrow of my bones. The pistol felt like hot lead in my hands, and in the end I put it back in my pocket and began to run away.

We were almost at Comércio Square when Koskela caught up with me. He grabbed me by the collar just as I stumbled over something, probably a mooring rope. A moment later he lost his grip and I fell headlong into the river.

What follows is more important than anything else in this letter: Koskela neither threw nor pushed me over the edge of the quay. I fell. I was the one threatening his life—not vice versa.

By the time I got my head above the surface, I was already thirty yards from the place where I fell in. The current was very strong that night. I am not a good swimmer, and I would undoubtedly have drowned if I hadn't caught hold of one of the piles supporting a projecting pier. By then I must have been a good quarter of a mile downstream.

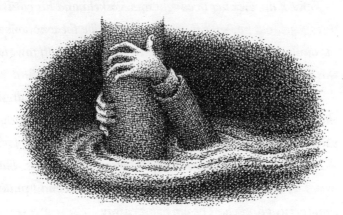

I don't have a very clear memory of what happened next. Somehow or other I pulled myself ashore and started walking. By the time I reached my apartment it was just after three o'clock in the morning. I grabbed some dry clothes, my passport and some savings I had hidden in a drawer in the kitchen and then hurried to Rossio Station, where I took the first morning train to Oporto. My only thought was to get away from Lisbon.

I only stayed in Oporto for a week. At first I had no idea what I was going to do, but after a few days a plan began to take shape in my head.

I had a little luck at last and found a man who sold false passports. Using the name Alfredo Simão, I took a ship to Genoa in Italy and a different ship from there to the Portuguese colony of Goa in India. The journey took a month.

News of my own death caught up with me in Goa. I read a three-week-old newspaper, which reported that a seaman by the name of Henry Koskela had drowned me in the Tagus. He was now under arrest and awaiting trial, accused of murder.

I realized immediately that Koskela did not stand a chance. Garretta would falsify evidence and threaten witnesses to ensure that Koskela was found guilty. I also knew that there were both prosecuting attorneys and judges who were members of the Monarchist Brotherhood. They would simply crush Koskela. The only possible way to save him from a very long prison sentence was to return to Lisbon. I decided to return at once: I could not allow an innocent man's life to be destroyed because of me.

But I postponed my journey home. Not once. Not twice. I put it off time after time for three whole years.

Every evening I would say to myself that I would do it tomorrow. Tomorrow I shall book a ticket to Lisbon. Then I would lie sleepless for the whole night—sleepless because I was afraid Chief Inspector Garretta would appear in my dreams. When dawn broke, I would think: Not today. Tomorrow. I'll book the ticket tomorrow.

Weeks passed and turned into months. I found work in Goa with a company called Albuquerque Trading. They dealt in spices. I did my job and kept to myself. I didn't want to have friends. Why should I want friends? After all, I would soon be going back to Lisbon. That is what I fooled myself into thinking, anyway.

The months became years, and I became more and more unhappy but lacked the strength to do anything about it. On several occasions I sent money to Prazeres Cemetery for the upkeep of Elisa's grave. That was the only thing that gave my life any meaning.

I lived in permanent terror that someone would discover who I really was, and I took it into my head that people in Goa were talking about me. When an opportunity arose to apply for a transfer to the company's branch office in Cochin, I took it and became the manager there. None of the employees were Portuguese—I was actually the only Portuguese citizen resident in Cochin—so I thought no one would find me.

My security did not last long. I had contracted malaria during my time in Goa, but in Cochin my health grew steadily worse and I found it harder and harder to do my job. In the end the boss of the head office of Albuquerque Trading back in Goa fired me and sent a replacement.

I was forced to move out of the company apartment in Fort Cochin and move into cheap lodgings in Jew Town in Mattancherry. The family I rented my room from became my first and only friends in India. They cared for me as if I was a member of their family. It still pains me when I remember how I left them so unexpectedly and without giving them an explanation. One night I just went down to the harbor and paid for a berth on a merchant ship sailing for Piraeus in Greece at daybreak that day.

The voyage took six weeks, with several stops on the way. We arrived here in Piraeus a month ago, by which stage I was more dead than alive. Thanks to the ship's captain I received medical treatment in the Portuguese seamen's mission here, and as soon as I was allowed to leave my sickbed I reserved a berth on a ship sailing to Lisbon. It departs in eight days.

Anyone reading this letter will almost certainly be wondering what made me finally decide to return home. I hesitate to tell the true story, because you will probably conclude
that I have gone out of my mind. But I must take that risk;
otherwise this confession will be less than complete.

I received a message in Cochin. It was written on a single
sheet of paper nailed up on one of the wharves at the harbor.
The message was a short text that my beloved Elisa had written on a miniature of herself she'd had painted. The portrait
was a present to me, and I always carried it in a locket round
my neck until I lost it when I fell into the river at Comércio
Square.

I believe someone must have found the locket and sent the
text to me as a message that only I would understand. I have
my suspicions as to who that might be, but I'll keep them to
myself.

Darkness has fallen in Piraeus now, and from my window

I can see the moon rising over the Aegean Sea. It has taken all my strength to get this down on paper, but it's done. I waited too long before I set off home, and it seems uncertain now whether my strength will last. But it doesn't really matter whether I arrive in Lisbon alive or dead. My body, my passport and this letter should be sufficient to secure the release of Koskela.

If I should manage to reach Lisbon alive, I have only one wish, and that is to pay one last visit to Elisa's grave.

Piraeus, 27 March

Alphonse
Morro

CHAPTER 77
A Funeral Feast

The sky was veiled by thin light clouds from horizon to horizon on the day Alphonse Morro was buried. The still air was filled with the sweet scent of the bougainvillea that was flowering in the gardens and parks of Lisbon.

João had arranged for Alphonse to have his grave alongside that of Elisa. The Chief had made the coffin, and Signor Fidardo carved a beautiful cross from larch wood.

There were seven of us at the funeral. Apart from the

priest there were the Chief and me, Ana and Signor Fidardo, João and Inspector Umbelino. Dr. Domingues had wanted to be there, but she was on duty at the hospital that morning. Ana sang a song about love and was accompanied by Signor Fidardo and the Chief. No one cried, though both João and Inspector Umbelino had very shiny eyes.

We all went back to O Pelicano after the funeral. The place was actually closed, but Senhor Baptista and Senhora Maria wanted to invite us to a funeral feast. The atmosphere was solemn and low-key at first, but the voices round our table grew louder and more cheerful in time with the bottles of beer and small glasses of aguardiente Senhor Baptista brought to the table. When Senhora Maria began cooking spareribs, Inspector Umbelino telephoned his wife, Rita, and told her to forget the potatoes at home and come to O Pelicano instead. One of the guitarists from the Tamarind happened to be passing along the street, but as soon as he heard laughter from the closed bar he came in to see what was going on. In no time at all, the other two guitarists had joined him, bringing their wives and children and a whole gang of musicians from Alfama and Mouraria.

Word of the party spread rapidly round the district, and by the time Rosa Domingues arrived that evening when her shift at the hospital was over, O Pelicano was so full that many people had to sit up on the windowsills with their legs hanging outside. I helped Senhor Baptista by carrying crates of beer up from the cellar. He himself was serving behind the bar, at the same time as singing along at the top of his voice to the band that had formed for the night.

At midnight, tables and chairs were cleared to one side and the dancing started.

Some time in the small hours a pair of patrolling police constables arrived to break up the party because someone had complained about the noise. The first thing they saw when they managed to squeeze in through the door was Inspector Umbelino swishing past in an enthusiastic fox-trot with Dr. Domingues. The constables quickly backed out the way they had come.

I was beginning to feel tired, but I didn't want to go home. Instead I climbed on top of the stack of tables heaped in the corner and sat there looking down on my friends in the crowd below. João was standing behind the bar frightening the local youngsters with ghost stories. Signor Fidardo was dancing with Rita Umbelino—he scarcely seemed to be moving but was actually gliding round the floor in a tight embrace with the senhora. The Chief was playing his accordion in the band, his fingers still hitting the right buttons and keys even though his eyes were slightly crossed from all the beer he'd drunk. Ana was dancing with Inspector Umbelino, and Dr. Domingues was bandaging up a sailor who had dislocated his thumb arm-wrestling with Senhor Baptista.

The party was still going on when the sun rose. The band played an emotional last waltz for the last couple on the floor. I was sitting in the window with Signor Fidardo, and we watched as Ana and the Chief danced cheek to cheek. They looked wonderful together.

Signor Fidardo obviously thought the same thing. He looked at me and asked, "Do you think he could bring himself to stay ashore?"

I thought for a little while and then slowly shook my head.

"I thought that," Signor Fidardo sighed. "What a pity!"

~

A week after the funeral party at O Pelicano, Ana was due to travel to Paris to sing at the Théâtre des Champs-Élysées. Her record had been a major success in France.

After much hemming and hawing Signor Fidardo had decided to go with her. He had a long-standing invitation to visit the most prominent collector of musical instruments in France, who happened to live in Paris.

Signor Fidardo hadn't been traveling for many years and had such a bout of travel fever that it took him two whole days to pack his small suitcase. The Chief and I were given strict instructions as to what we could and could not do in the workshop while he was away. Signor Fidardo could not conceal his anxiety that we might go rummaging among his things.

"What I'd most like would be for you two to take a holiday as well" was what he eventually said. "You have certainly earned it."

Early in the morning a cab came to take Ana and Signor Fidardo to Rossio Station. The Chief and I went out to the street to wave them goodbye and wish them a safe journey. When they had gone, the Chief said to me, "We ought to go somewhere too. What would you say to a little trip up to Agiere?"

I thought that was a wonderful idea.

CHAPTER 78
The Last Meal On Board

The following morning we caught an early river steamer from Cais do Sodré to Constância. We arrived there in the evening and found a simple lodging house for the night.

We were woken at sunrise by the noise of horses' hooves and wagon wheels on the cobbled street outside. It was market day in Constância. A couple of hours later the streets were packed with people. Farmers had their carts lined up in rows on the square and were selling vegetables, fish, wine, tools and household equipment from the backs of them.

The Chief bought us a bag of provisions—bread, cheese, dried fish and fruit. He also took the opportunity to get into conversation with the sellers, and quite soon he had made the acquaintance of a wine grower who lived half a dozen miles from Agiere and would give us a lift with him part of the way. In exchange we would help him sell the jugs of wine he had on his cart.

It became obvious that very few people at the market had seen a live gorilla before. Many of them were happy to buy a jug of wine just to get a closer look at me, so in little more than half an hour the cart was empty and we could be on our way.

We bumped along a rough sandy road for two hours and were dropped off at a bend where the road forked. The farmer continued in one direction, and the Chief and I started walking in the other. The road was dusty and the sun was scorching, but the scenery all round us was densely wooded and beautiful.

The track followed the line of the River Zêzere, some-times at a distance, sometimes close to the water. There were birds with slim beaks and long legs wading on the shallow sandbanks at the sides of the canyon.

After no more than a couple of hours of walking we arrived. Looking down from a hill we could see the *Hudson Queen* lying where we had left her. Our steps suddenly became lighter and faster.

The track led down to the derelict building by the riverside. A piece of the gable end had collapsed since we were last there, but otherwise it looked just the same. We walked out on the crumbling quay. An osprey rose from the funnel of the *Hudson Queen* when it caught sight of us.

We stood for a long time looking at the wreck sticking up out of the slow-moving water. Looters had been there: all the blocks and hawsers in the rigging were missing and the brass on the funnel was gone, as was the radio mast from the roof of the wheelhouse.

"But she's still there, anyway, and that's always something," the Chief said.

~

A little way along the riverbank we found an ancient wooden rowing boat among the bushes. It hadn't been in the water for ages and was obviously leaky—the Chief had no difficulty sliding the blade of his knife right up to its handle between the planks.

We launched the boat and packed the cracks as well as we could with the pine needles and dross from a deserted anthill. It's an old trick. You push the dross into all the gaps and cracks, and once it gets wet the dross expands and caulks the boat.

I rowed and the Chief bailed. We made it quickly to the wheelhouse of the *Hudson Queen* and climbed up on its roof. Since the level of the river was lower than it had been three years before, more of the ship was above the surface. In the bright sunlight we could see down to the riverbed without difficulty. The hull was sitting gently on the sand, and eddies in the current thirty yards upstream showed where we had run into trouble—there was probably a rock or a large boulder back there.

We must have sat there in silence for something like an hour, both of us pondering how we could salvage our ship. In the end, the Chief gave a deep sigh and said, "There's no way of doing it without a good-sized crane on a large pontoon. And we could never get that sort of gear up here. Especially when we don't have any money."

He was right. The *Hudson Queen* would have to stay where she was. It felt as if this was the second funeral in a very short time. We had come here to bid farewell to our ship. There was nothing else to be done.

With another deep sigh the Chief untied our bag of food.

"Last meal on board," he said, and laid things out on the wheelhouse roof.

We stayed awhile longer after we had finished eating. We were finding it hard to tear ourselves away. The Chief was lying on his back, squinting up at the sun and taking a swig now and again from a jug of wine he had been given by the farmer.

Suddenly he sat up and peered over my shoulder. Was someone coming? I turned round to see what he was looking at. There was nothing there apart from the small waterfall just upstream.

I gave the Chief a questioning look. His eyes were still on the waterfall, but his gaze had become empty.

"Dynamite," he said to himself. "Dynamite might do it. . . ."

For a moment I wondered whether the Chief's mind was rambling.

But I suddenly understood what he meant.

We both stared at the waterfall. The Chief took a big swig from the jug and then asked, "Do you think it would work?"

I shrugged. Perhaps, perhaps not.

"But well worth trying in any case?" the Chief said.

I nodded.

We rowed upstream as far as possible and pulled the rowing boat ashore between some rocks. The bank was steep, and there were large granite blocks all jumbled together with crooked pines that were clinging tight to the thin soil. We climbed up high enough to view the river above the waterfall. It was broad and straight and seemed to widen out into a lake farther upstream.

"Couldn't be better," the Chief said, and a gleam came into his eyes.

I agreed with him. It really did look as if things couldn't be better.

~

A little while later we were back in the rowing boat and heading south for Constância. I was doing the bailing now and the Chief was rowing with long, powerful strokes. And he was thinking aloud. Every so often he would interrupt himself and hum a tune that had come into his head. Then he would continue talking about how we should approach the salvage work and what we needed to buy in Constância.

"Dynamite and a fuse, those are the most important things. Matches too, of course, mustn't forget them. We have tools already, in the ship . . . but we can't get at them, can we? We can, though, can't we?"

I nodded.

"And we'll need some sheet steel," the Chief said. "And rivets—or do we have rivets on board?"

I nodded again.

"Good! But if we come across rivets in Constância we'll buy them, just to be on the safe side. And red lead. And we'll need rags. And coal. And something to build a fire in. Lordy, lordy, lordy! This is going to be fun!"

The Chief is back to being his old self, I thought, and I suddenly felt overwhelmed by happiness.

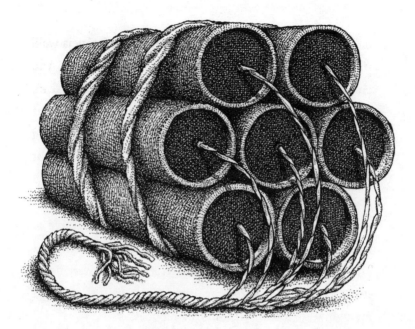

CHAPTER 79
Dynamite!

We arrived in Constância in the middle of the night and fell asleep under the stars on a meadow by the riverside. The sun was already high in the sky when we woke, and we hurried into the town to buy what we needed. That was when we heard the church bells ringing. We had forgotten it was Sunday and none of the shops would be open until the following morning.

We spent the rest of the day walking up and down the

narrow streets of Constância, looking at the boats on the river and polishing our plans. We came up with several essentials that were missing from our shopping list, and we found a bigger and better rowing boat. It had a wide, flat bottom and two pairs of oars—and a for-sale sign hanging on the prow. The price was reasonable, so the Chief bought it without further ado.

The next morning we were waiting at the door when the Constância ironmonger opened his shop. A couple of hours later we had all our purchases on board the new boat and had begun the long row back to Agiere. We were heavily laden, had the current against us and, as if that wasn't enough, were towing the old rowing boat.

By the time we reached Agiere a silver moon had brightened our journey for the last few hours.

As soon as the new day dawned we began carrying dynamite up the steep, stony riverbank north of the waterfall. The river valley was still blanketed in a thick morning mist, but it promised to be a fine day. We concentrated hard on our work, but we didn't rush. You have to be careful with dynamite.

Our biggest problem was to decide where to place the dynamite. It was vital that the great boulders landed in the right place when we set off the rockfall. If we failed, there would not be a second chance. The Chief climbed up and down the slope trying to assess what would be the result if we placed the dynamite there, or there, or there. It wasn't an easy task. There was no guarantee whatever we did.

For breakfast we ate the bread, cheese and sausage we had brought from Constância. The Chief had also bought a kettle so we could brew coffee with the clear river water. After our coffee the Chief lit one of the cigars I had given him.

"It'll bring us luck!" he said.

All the preparations were done. We climbed up to the charge of dynamite and unrolled a couple of yards of fuse. The Chief lit it with his cigar and we ran up the slope and took cover behind two stout pine trees.

What a bang!

The pressure wave made me lose my grip on the tree and I almost followed the rockfall down into the river. When I got back on my feet I saw the Chief waving his arms and jumping up and down behind his tree. He looked as if he'd gone completely crazy. His cap had blown off, his hair was standing on end, his eyes were wide and staring and he looked as if he was choking with laughter. Not that I could hear him—my ears were still ringing from the explosion!

When I looked down at the waterfall, it was immediately obvious that we had succeeded. Pebbles, shattered rocks and enormous boulders had formed an embankment across the top of the waterfall. We had dammed the river. Not a drop could get through!

The water level below the falls should now have begun to drop, and when it had dropped sufficiently, the *Hudson Queen* would be lying on dry land.

~

Once we had got our breath back we rowed out to the *Hudson Queen*. The water level had already gone down four inches.

One hour later we could walk dry-shod on the port side of the deck. We rowed back to the riverbank and climbed up above the rockfall. We could see that the water on the other side of the dam had scarcely risen at all. The river was much wider up there, which was to our advantage.

Everything was going exactly according to plan.

By noon the bed of the river round the *Hudson Queen* was dry. We set up a hand-operated pump to empty out the last of the water from the ship. Here and there we came across floundering fish, which we caught in a bucket and carried over to a large pool that had formed where the deepest part of the river had been.

The hole in the hull was down low on the port side. We had to dig out a hollow in the sand to be able to inspect it properly from the outside. We were lucky: none of the framework had been seriously damaged.

The hole measured about two feet across, and the metal plate above it had been pushed in, which is why she had sunk so quickly.

It was a race against time now. The river above the dam we had created was rising all the time, albeit slowly. We had to repair the hole in the hull before water began running over the top of the embankment.

If we failed, the *Hudson Queen* would refill with water. But if we succeeded, she would float!

~

We worked all day and night without a break. First of all, we hammered out the metal plate that had buckled when we ran aground. Then we measured up the new plate to cover the hole and drilled fifty holes in the hull and in the new plate. That alone took us six hours.

To make sure that the mend would be both watertight and rust-free, we put the rags soaked in red lead between the plate and the hull before we bolted them together. As darkness fell we lit a coal fire and began heating the rivets. By the light of four paraffin lanterns we then replaced the bolts with red-hot rivets, the Chief pounding the tail of the rivets while I held them firm on the inside.

When the sun rose we still had ten rivets to go. The water above the dam had risen and was no more than six inches below the lip. The pressure was building up by the minute, and water was already finding its way through in places, spurting out in thin, strong sprays on the downstream side.

We had just hammered in the last rivet when the dam began to go. I was down on the keelson of the *Hudson Queen* and unaware of what was happening until the Chief yelled down from the deck, "It's going! It's going!"

I barely had time to get up the ladder and out on deck before the rubble dam gave way in the middle and a torrent of water came rushing toward us. The *Hudson Queen* shuddered as the wave hit her stern. For a few seconds we had the sensation that we were traveling backward at a very high speed, but then she began to ease herself off the riverbed.

There was a bucking motion as first the stern and then the bow came up. She bumped and nudged the sandy bottom several times before the strength of the current carried her out into deeper water.

The *Hudson Queen* was afloat!

⁓

Half a minute later we had left Agiere behind us, the Chief was at the wheel and I was sitting on the chart table with my feet dangling down. The *Hudson Queen* was drifting silently downstream past sandbanks and the lush riverside greenery. The only sounds were birdsong and the quiet murmur of the river.

The Chief fished a second cigar out of his breast pocket. When he had lit it, he began humming a song I had heard many times before. But it was a long time since I'd heard it last.

Farewell, you cruel maiden,
Farewell, goodbye, I say,
For I'm weary now of waiting,
So I'm off to sea again.

My ship is weighing anchor
And we're sailing for Marseille,
My love evoked no answer
So I'm off to sea again.

AUTUMN EVENING

Night is falling quickly outside my cabin window, and the last of the daylight is slipping away beyond the western horizon. I have lit an oil lamp so that I can carry on writing awhile longer. Autumn has come to Lisbon, and you can feel it even though the air is still warm.

Almost half a year has gone by since the Chief and I salvaged the *Hudson Queen* on the River Zêzere. We floated her downstream from Agiere to Constância, and from there a river steamer towed us down to Lisbon.

Since our arrival she's been moored at the quayside below the Alfama district and is likely to be there for some time to come. She won't be going anywhere without a boiler, not under her own steam, anyway.

The boiler was destroyed by a series of explosions when the *Hudson Queen* ran aground. And almost everything else on board was wrecked during the three years she was stuck on the bed of the Zêzere. It will take endless hours of work and masses of money before we get her shipshape and seaworthy again.

But we shall do it!

She will be better than ever!

The Chief and I are absolutely determined about that.

We take every job we can get in order to make the money to do it, and we spend all our free time working on the *Hudson Queen*. We scrape and chip off rust and repaint. We work with wood and we weld. We stripped down the engine: that took us more than a month, and I won't even guess how long it will take to put it back together.

I sometimes feel depressed and overwhelmed when I think how much has to be repaired and replaced before we are finished, but the Chief never seems to become dispirited. Never so that it shows, anyway.

"This is what I dreamed about every day and every night I was in prison," he says. "To be free and to have work to do! How could I possibly complain now?"

I do know, however, that in his heart of hearts even the Chief sometimes feels it's all a bit hopeless. On one occasion when he was sitting counting the little money we had managed to save, I took out the maharaja's turban. There is no doubt it's worth a fortune, and with that money we would be able to put the *Hudson Queen* in order in a matter of months.

The Chief understood what I was thinking. He shook his head and said, "That turban was a friendship gift from the maharaja to you. You must never part with it!"

I had guessed the Chief would say something like that, but I was glad to hear it anyway. The turban is a very fine memory to have.

And the renovation of the *Hudson Queen* is making progress, even though we are short of money. Five weeks ago Signor Fidardo helped us get hold of a cheap load of good timber, and we have used it to make new fittings for the cabin. We finished it last night, and we are going to give it an official opening tonight.

As I write this I can hear the Chief singing while he putters about in the galley. He is cooking a fish stew, I think. And I have laid the table very nicely in our new cabin, with real napkins and wax candles. Ana and Signor Fidardo are coming to dinner, so it will be a pleasant evening.

It's been a little while since we saw Ana, because she has been on tour in Spain. Normally we meet quite often. I call into the house on Rua de São Tomé several times a week, and when I do Signor Fidardo goes over to the bakery and brings back something nice. I take the opportunity to sharpen his knives and chisels for him, and sometimes he has accordion repair work for me. My workbench is still there by the window.

All four of us usually have Sunday dinner at Ana's place. The Chief and Signor Fidardo bring their musical instruments, and after the meal Ana sings to us. It's still the high point of the week for me.

Recently, however, I've been feeling a little sad when I sit there with my legs tucked up on Ana's sofa and listen to my friends. I know why. The renovation of the *Hudson Queen* will take a long time, but it won't last forever. Sooner or later she will be seaworthy again, and then it will be time for us to cast off and leave Lisbon. There is part of me that longs for that day, but another part of me hopes it will never come. I don't ever want to have to say goodbye to Ana and Signor Fidardo.

~

I can hear footsteps up on deck. Our guests have arrived! So this will have to be the last thing I write on my Underwood No. 5. It's time to bring my story to a close anyway. I've done what I set out to do, which was to tell the truth about the murder of Alphonse Morro. It has taken me three months. And three hundred sheets of paper and four typewriter ribbons. The writing has not made my nightmares disappear completely, but they are less frequent now. And that's enough to be going on with.

Before I go to bed tonight I shall clean, oil and polish my Underwood No. 5 and then I am going to put it at the bottom of my seaman's chest. And that is where it can stay.

But who knows? There may come a time when I have reason to take it out again.

ABOUT THE AUTHOR

JAKOB WEGELIUS is a Swedish writer and illus-
trator who lives and works in the small village of
Mörtfors. In Sweden, he was awarded the August
Prize for Best Children's Book and the Nordic
Council Children and Young People's Literature
Prize for *The Murderer's Ape.* It is also an Inter-
national Youth Library White Raven selection.
Visit Jakob at jakobwegelius.com.

ABOUT THE TRANSLATOR

PETER GRAVES is a translator from the Scandinavian languages, known in particular for his translations of novels by August Strindberg and Selma
Lagerlöf. He has received many Swedish Academy
prizes for his translations.

PUSHKIN CHILDREN'S BOOKS

We created Pushkin Children's Books to share tales from different languages and cultures with younger readers, and to open the door to the wide, colourful worlds these stories offer.

From picture books and adventure stories to fairy tales and classics, and from fifty-year-old bestsellers to current huge successes abroad, the books on the Pushkin Children's list reflect the very best stories from around the world, for our most discerning readers of all: children.

THE RED ABBEY CHRONICLES: MARESI

MARIA TURTSCHANINOFF

'Stands out for its startling originality, and for the frightening
plausibility of the dangerous world it creates'
Telegraph

THE LETTER FOR THE KING

TONKE DRAGT

'*The Letter for the King* will get pulses racing... Pushkin
Press deserves every praise for publishing this beautifully
translated, well-presented and captivating book'
The Times

THE SECRETS OF THE WILD WOOD

TONKE DRAGT

'Offers intrigue, action and escapism'
Sunday Times

THE PARENT TRAP · THE FLYING CLASSROOM · DOT AND ANTON

ERICH KÄSTNER

Illustrated by Walter Trier

'The bold line drawings by Walter Trier are the work of
genius... As for the stories, if you're a fan of *Emil and the
Detectives*, then you'll find these just as spirited'
Spectator

FROM THE MIXED-UP FILES OF MRS. BASIL E. FRANKWEILER

E. L. KONIGSBURG

'Delightful... I love this book... a beautifully written
adventure, with endearing characters and full of dry
wit, imagination and inspirational confidence'
Daily Mail

THE WILDWITCH SERIES

LENE KAABERBØL

1 · *Wildfire*
2 · *Oblivion*
3 · *Life Stealer*
4 · *Bloodling*

'Classic fantasy adventure... Young readers will be delighted to
hear that there are more adventures to come for Clara'
Lovereading

MEET AT THE ARK AT EIGHT!

ULRICH HUB

Illustrated by Jörg Mühle

'Of all the books about a penguin in a suitcase pretending to be God
asking for a cheesecake, this one is absolutely, definitely my favourite'
Independent

THE SNOW QUEEN

HANS CHRISTIAN ANDERSEN

Illustrated by Lucie Arnoux

'A lovely edition [of a] timeless story'
The Lady

IN THEIR SHOES: FAIRY TALES AND FOLKTALES

Illustrated by Lucie Arnoux

'An eclectic, shoe-themed collection... arrestingly illustrated by Lucie Arnoux'
Sunday Times

THE CAT WHO CAME IN OFF THE ROOF

ANNIE M.G. SCHMIDT

'Guaranteed to make anyone 7-plus to 107 who likes to
curl up with a book and a cat purr with pleasure'
The Times

LAFCADIO: THE LION WHO SHOT BACK

SHEL SILVERSTEIN

'A story which is really funny, yet also teaches us a great
deal about what we want, what we think we want and what
we are no longer certain about once we have it'
Irish Times

THE PILOT AND THE LITTLE PRINCE

PETER SÍS

'With its extraordinary, sophisticated illustrations, its
poetry and the historical detail of the text, this book
will reward readers of any age over eight'
Sunday Times

THE STORY OF THE BLUE PLANET

ANDRI SNÆR MAGNASON

Illustrated by Áslaug Jónsdóttir

'A Seussian mix of wonder, wit and gravitas'
The New York Times

THE WITCH IN THE BROOM CUPBOARD AND OTHER TALES

PIERRE GRIPARI

Illustrated by Fernando Puig Rosado

'Wonderful... funny, tender and daft'
David Almond

THE WHALE THAT FELL IN LOVE WITH A SUBMARINE

AKIYUKI NOSAKA

Illustrated by Mika Provata-Carlone

'Remarkable stories... They are dark but so beautiful, so profound;
subtle and elegant. It is a book that will last all your life'
Irish Times

SHOLA AND THE LIONS

BERNARDO ATXAGA

Illustrated by Mikel Valverde

'Gently ironic stories... totally charming'
Independent

THE POINTLESS LEOPARD: WHAT GOOD ARE KIDS ANYWAY?

COLAS GUTMAN

Illustrated by Delphine Perret

'Lively, idiomatic and always entertaining... a decidedly offbeat little book'
Robert Dunbar, *Irish Times*

POCKETY: THE TORTOISE WHO LIVED AS SHE PLEASED

FLORENCE SEYVOS

Illustrated by Claude Ponti

'A treasure – a real find – and one of the most enjoyable children's books I've
read in a while... This is a tortoise that deserves to win every literary race'
Observer

SAVE THE STORY

GULLIVER · ANTIGONE · CAPTAIN NEMO · DON JUAN
GILGAMESH · THE BETROTHED · THE NOSE
CYRANO DE BERGERAC · KING LEAR · CRIME AND PUNISHMENT

'An amazing new series from Pushkin Press in which literary, adult authors
retell classics (with terrific illustrations) for a younger generation'
Daily Telegraph

THE OKSA POLLOCK SERIES

ANNE PLICHOTA AND CENDRINE WOLF

1 · *The Last Hope*
2 · *The Forest of Lost Souls*
3 · *The Heart of Two Worlds*
4 · *Tainted Bonds*

'A feisty heroine, lots of sparky tricks and evil opponents could
fill a gap left by the end of the Harry Potter series'
Daily Mail

The trip from Alexandria to Bombay with
SS *SONG OF LIMERICK*
and
the trip from Bombay to Cochin with
HMS RANA
including
the trip from Bombay to Karachi with
SS *MALABAR STAR*

BLACK
SEA

CASPIA

MEDITERRANEAN
SEA

Euphrates

Tigris

Baghda

Alexandria

A   R   A

Nile

A   F   R   I   C   A

B

RED
SEA

THE SINKING OF THE SS MINSK

GULF OF